Stefan's soft laugh was unpleasant, his breath warm on her mouth. "Do your new lovers take orders?" He hadn't moved and the weight of his body was solid and resistant.

"Does your fiancée?" she snapped, ignoring the fact that she was powerless against him, too angry at his seizure, rude purpose and insinuation to consider her precarious position.

His head rose abruptly and his eyes in the moonlight gleamed like fire. "Yes, as a matter of fact," he said very softly, his mouth curled in derision. "Your turn."

"Then so do my lovers." She wouldn't give him the satisfaction of knowing she'd refused all the men because they hadn't measured up to him.

His eyes narrowed at her confident tone, a cold fury overwhelming him. "I've heard," he said in a taut, low whisper, "you're much in demand."

He was feeling uncivilized and savagely angry. He was, in fact, very near to losing control, so Lisaveta's answering words were exactly wrong.

"You taught me well," she said, her voice snide and too sweet and taunting.

"...Susan Johnson will thrill you to the core."
—*Affaire de Coeur*

GOLDEN
PARADISE

SUSAN JOHNSON

MIRA®

ISBN 1-55166-854-8

GOLDEN PARADISE

Visit us at www.mirabooks.com

Printed in U.S.A.

To Hafiz...
whose work endured during his own times
of turmoil and through the ensuing centuries
because he spoke great truths and small,
rose above narrow views, believed in a natural
freedom of spirit and, perhaps better than most,
understood the mysteries and passions of love.

With his most famous verse, I dedicate this story.

Oh Turkish maid of Shiraz! in thy hand
If thou'lt take my heart, for the mole on thy cheek
I would barter Bokhara and Samarkand.

Stefan in his own way
was willing to barter as much....

Prologue

Karakilisa, Turkey
July 1877

The medieval fortress at Karakilisa, home to each powerful Khan of the region since the time of the Crusades, commanded the only natural elevation for miles. But over the centuries more civilized owners had refined its functional design, and within its rough walls an elegant white marble palace stood.

And inside that graceful palace, in a high-ceilinged, shaded room built to mitigate the intense summer heat, Lisaveta Lazaroff was packing—or, more aptly, directing the three serving maids in that task. In Javad Khan's palace no guest ever lifted a finger.

"This," she said, and "that," pointing at a single change of chemise and drawers. "And just one blouse, no petticoats." She was taking no more than the bare essentials, traveling light with only the contents of two saddlebags to see her through to Aleksandropol on the Russian border.

Could she afford the weight? she wondered, holding her favorite copy of Hafiz in her hand. No, she decided in the next heartbeat, she couldn't. But once the war was over she'd come back for everything she had to leave behind.

"You won't change your mind?"

Lisaveta turned sharply at the sound of the male voice. Then, seeing her father's old friend Javad Khan, she relaxed visibly. "No. Although it's no reflection on your hospitality," she added with a smile. Javad Khan's hospitality was in fact lavish, but his nephew Faizi Pasha had stopped to billet his troops for two days and had decided Lisaveta would make a fine addition to his harem.

"My apologies for Faizi," Javad said, advancing into the large room, which overlooked a fountained courtyard lush with blooming roses. "His father was Turkish."

This latter statement might seem oblique, but Lisaveta understood all the unspoken and disparaging nuances. Javad Khan, overlord of western Azerbaijan, was wealthy, cultured and Persian. He viewed the Turks as parvenu, perversely orthodox barbarians.

"I can protect you from Faizi," he said. "You needn't leave."

"Thank you," Lisaveta replied, choosing her words carefully. "But I don't wish to be the cause of enmity in your family." She also didn't wish to take the chance that Faizi and his troops might win this particular battle.

Javad shrugged. Family genocide was a cultural reality in his society, where power was often gained at the expense of numerous and bloody rivalries. "My tribesmen are more than a match for Faizi's troops." And as a man with a harem of his own, he couldn't be expected to understand Lisaveta's horror when faced with the prospect of being locked away in a harem herself.

"I don't want any bloodshed over my presence." She smiled again to soften her refusal. "It's best if I leave. Once the war is over I'll return to continue my research in your library. I'm so grateful you gave me the chance." Javad Khan's collection of Hafiz, Persia's greatest poet, was the most extensive in the world, the most lavishly illustrated…and the most private. Only she and her father had ever been allowed access.

"Your father and I were good friends," Javad Khan said simply. "And I've known you, my dear, since you were a babe in arms. My home is your home." His deep voice was without inflection, but she knew that he was quietly offering her the full extent of his hospitality, including the formidable weight of his warrior tribes' military prowess.

"I know." Lisaveta's expression acknowledged the honor bestowed on her by his offer. "And if I weren't compelled by feelings more powerful than rational, I'd stay." Her golden eyes held his. "I hope you understand. With the Russian army garrisoned in Aleksandropol only a hundred miles away, I'd feel safer...." She didn't know how exactly to explain she wasn't willing to trust her life completely to his protection, that the risks of riding through the war zone seemed less daunting than Faizi Pasha's plans for her future.

Maybe that was it. If she left for Russia, she would be in control of her own life, however perilous her journey. In the grip of Faizi Pasha, should that terrible eventuality come to pass, his harem door would clang shut, the world would be locked out, and she'd be a prisoner until she died. She wasn't gambling one risk against the other; her flight was the result of prudently weighing alternatives. As a first-class rider she knew she could reach Aleksandropol in less than a day, and once there she could expect the aid of her countrymen.

Javad was silent for a moment, the serving girls standing at attention as they had since he'd walked through the doorway. For just a brief moment, Lisaveta, Countess Lazaroff, Princess Kuzan if she chose to use her mother's title, felt incongruously as if she'd fallen into a vignette from *The Thousand and One Nights*. Could she assert her authority against Javad Khan, who ruled in the fashion of a medieval prince, *if* he chose to disagree with her wishes? She would be defying a man familiar with life-and-death mastery over his people. And even as sophisticated as he was, the position of women in his milieu was subservient.

Raised by an indulgent father, educated beyond the standards of most men, granted not only the normal freedom of her wealth and position but the additional prerogatives her scholarship allowed, Lisaveta had lived a life distinguished for its independence.

She would rather die than be trapped in a harem.

"I would have had to leave within the month anyway, to

attend the Tsar's ceremony in Saint Petersburg honoring Father's work,'' she said prosaically. ''And the siege of Kars has been lifted, Faizi said. Now should be an excellent time to travel, since there's a lull in hostilities between Turkey and Russia. It's only ten hours,'' she added in defense of her position.

''The area is still alive with troops.''

''I'll travel at night.''

''The irregular cavalry raids at night. It's in their blood.''

''Javad,'' Lisaveta said very softly, ''I wish to leave, for maybe incomprehensible reasons—but I *cannot* stay.''

Javad Khan was very tall, and the straight fall of his silk robes accentuated his height. He gazed down at her for a long moment. ''Then you'll need an escort,'' he said into the quiet of the room. ''And my best horses.'' He smiled. ''And Allah's prayers.''

Lisaveta grinned back, relieved and strangely elated. There was pleasure in taking action. ''Thank you,'' she said.

His dark eyes beneath his white brows were amused. She'd always been a headstrong young girl, but maybe that was a portion of her charm. ''You'll need some peasant clothes,'' he continued, his own grin matching hers. ''If you look like that—'' he indicated her gaily flowered summer frock and dainty blue slippers ''—you'll be captured two miles down the road…for someone else's harem.''

One

Russia, Transcaucasia

Hell would have been an improvement.

There was not a tree in sight, not a blade of grass, just a relentlessly barren plateau too close to the sun and too high for rain.

Prince Stefan Bariatinsky was hot.

He was beyond hot. He was bone weary, sweating hot, exhausted hot.

And he'd been swearing under his breath for the last half mile.

"Are you going to make it?" Haci, his lieutenant, asked.

"Hell, no. I want a big funeral." Stefan smiled, mitigating the harsh severity of his face, which was swarthy by birth and further bronzed by years of soldiering for the Tsar. Although he had his tunic unbuttoned so that it hung open, his heavily muscled chest was sleek with sweat beneath the silver-trimmed uniform, and his leather riding breeches felt slippery against his skin. "With Gypsy girls to dance over my bier," he added with a facetious lift of his black brows.

Not that Stefan had ever restricted himself to Gypsy girls. He was in fact, next to the Tsar, the most fêted man in the Empire, adored by a great variety of women, and not just for his rank and wealth.

He was the most fearless officer in the Empire.

And handsome as sin.

Too handsome, men said, watching their wives' eyes dwell on him.

Too handsome, jealous young ladies said, watching him flirt with a rival.

Too handsome, like his father, older wags remarked, remembering the scandalous ways of the elder Prince.

But impetuously charming, they all agreed.

"It's not much farther," Haci pointed out, for forty of the fifty miles from Kars to Aleksandropol were now behind them. "And in a few days you'll be at the lodge, with Choura dancing on your—well—wherever," he finished with a grin.

Stefan's Gypsy lover was waiting for him at his mountain retreat and she was capable of taking one's mind off any mundane problems. "That thought," Stefan returned, his mouth quirked in a smile, "might just keep me alive until Aleksandropol."

"You only have to last ten miles."

"Don't say 'only.' Right now it seems the end of the earth." Stefan shifted slightly in his saddle, flexing his broad shoulders in an attempt to ease the discomfort of aching muscles and fatigue. It was a hundred and two degrees, and he was so covered with dust that the sweat trickling down his body was leaving paths. His formerly white Chevalier Gardes uniform was now an indistinguishable color that would have been a court martial offense on the parade ground. But he and his personal bodyguard of Kurdish irregulars were riding north toward Tiflis, capitol city of Georgia, for a badly needed furlough after the three-month siege of Kars. Their first night's stop in Aleksandropol would at least afford him the luxury of a bath, food and a woman—in that exact order, his libido tempered by personal demands for comfort first.

The war in the east had ground to a standstill in the blazing heat of July, both Russians and Turks content with maintaining an attitude of mutual surveillance. Both sides in this war— begun by the Tsar in April to save the Christian minorities in the Ottoman Empire from further massacres—were now bringing up reinforcements before resuming the campaign.

Meanwhile the Russian siege of Kars, Turkey's great fortress on its eastern border, had been abandoned and the Russian troops were retiring toward Aleksandropol for some desperately needed rest.

As the Tsar's youngest and best general, Stefan knew the Russians had begun the campaign with too few men, and after Tergukasoff's defeat at Zevin they couldn't afford another disaster. It was vital the troops were allowed some rest before hostilities were resumed.

When the war had begun in April, Kars in Eastern Turkey had been one of three main positions of the Turkish line on their border with Georgian Russia. Russian troops had taken one fortress and garrisoned it, but Kars had cost thousands of lives in vain assaults. The Chiefs of Staff couldn't agree on strategy. Coordination was a nightmare, since whenever reinforcements should have been called up or an assault planned, competing generals fought for control. Stefan's cavalry corps was the only unit to have continued success but at the cost, often, of more men than he could afford to lose...to staff blunders. And even his successes were viewed at times with jealousy.

Stefan had studied military history along with the more recent campaigns and had devised his own tactics to defeat the impregnability of earthworks defended by magazine rifles. To his men he was both a leader and a friend. "Come," he would say, not "Go," and he always explained the situation to them and told them what to do. His men knew he wouldn't ask them to do anything he couldn't do himself. He was viewed as unorthodox in his tactics and to many on the staff as a potential danger with his victories mounting.

But Stefan was weary of the bickering and rivalry among the general staff when he knew that cooperation was needed to win this war—cooperation and more men, sufficient supplies and improved armaments. Much to the displeasure of some of those in the High Command, Stefan had equipped his own men with captured Winchester rifles, when most of the Russian army was still equipped with antiquated Krenek rifles.

He sighed at the inequities and the pettinesses that were costing them thousands of lives. He needed this furlough to forget for a few weeks the awfulness of war and to recharge himself for the coming offensive.

The Turks, too, spy reports indicated, were licking their wounds.

After three months, very little progress had been made. Russia had won some battles. The Turkish army had dug in and built formidable entrenchments and had won some battles by rebuffing Russian advances.

But now Russia was stalled on their march west toward the Dardanelles. And Kars, the most modern fortification in the Turkish eastern border, had held fast against Russian attack.

For Turkey, this was a Holy War for Allah.

For Russia, a crusade to save oppressed Christians in the Ottoman Empire.

The gods for whom all the thousands of soldiers were dying hadn't deigned to give any signs.

Unless the blazing sun was their way of calling a temporary truce.

"Bazhis," Haci muttered suddenly and sharply.

Stefan turned in surprise, because they were now very near Aleksandropol and the marauding Turkish bands generally kept their distance from the cities. But when he followed the sweep of Haci's arm he saw them through the shimmering waves of heat. Fewer than his troop of thirty, he decided, quickly counting. Good. His next thought was accompanied by a twinge of unmilitary annoyance. Damn, there went his imminent prospect of a bath.

Despite his personal wishes, Stefan applied spurs to his black charger. With Haci at his side, they set off in pursuit, followed by his colorful bodyguard, each man the best young warrior of his tribe. All were sons of Sheikhs, their different tribal affiliations evident in the variety of their dress: the red-and-white turban of the Barzani; the green sash of the Soyid; the Herki's crimson and the Zibari's blue flowing robe; each man's horse trappings and brilliant garments streaming behind as they galloped across the plains.

Drawing his rifle from the cantle scabbard behind him as the distance between his men and the Bazhis diminished, Stefan sighted on one of the fleeing bandits. As he'd suspected, the marauders had realized they were outnumbered and were in retreat. None of the Turkish irregular cavalry chose to stand and fight unless they had vastly superior numbers; the native warriors preferred hit-and-run raids.

At the first barrage of fire from the Winchesters favored by Stefan's men, a Bazhi near the rear of the fleeing band flung away a black-clad woman he'd been carrying. With his horse falling behind under the double load, survival outweighed pleasure. The body sailed through the air, the covering shawl slipped away, and long rippling tresses of chestnut-colored hair flared out behind the catapulting form in a beautifully symmetrical fan. Stefan winced instinctively as the woman's body bounced twice before sprawling motionless on the sun-baked plain.

Hauling back on his reins, he tersely apologized to his mount for the sharp cut of the bit. As Cleo came to a rearing, plunging halt, his troop swept past him in pursuit of the Bazhis. Women weren't a commodity as valuable as other types of plunder to Kurdish warriors, and as the best mounted of the native tribes, Stefan's men obviously felt confident they could overtake their prey. Leaving them to their pursuit, Stefan slid off his skittish prancing mare to attend to the woman himself.

Bending over the small still form a moment later, Stefan decided she was merely unconscious rather than dead. Her breathing was faintly visible in a slight rise and fall of dusty drapery...although, jettisoned at a full-out gallop, as she had been, she could be severely injured. She was dressed in the conventional layers of clothing native women affected, the yards of enveloping black chador, the veiling dresses, vest and pantaloons. Reaching beneath the black and tentlike chador, he found her wrist and felt for a pulse...a pulse he discovered a moment later beating in a strong regular rhythm. Perhaps all the layers of clothing and flowing yards of material had cushioned her fall.

Carefully lifting the shawl concealing her face, he scrutinized her briefly through the masking dirt and gray clay dust indigenous to the region. A superficial survey suggested she wasn't very old, probably quite young, since this rugged land aged one prematurely. Her hair, as he had noticed earlier, was considerably lighter than the customary native color. Perhaps she was Kurdish with that shade of hair, or maybe she had antecedents nearer Tiflis, he abstractly thought in a thoroughly useless reflection, as if it mattered what her parentage was.

"Damn," he softly swore in the next breath, impatient, bone tired and inherently selfish. Whatever she was or whoever, she meant problems and delay. But in the next instant, more humane feelings superseded his first moody reaction. Sliding his hands beneath her shoulders and knees, he lifted her slight weight into his arms.

Standing under the blazing sun, he glanced at the empty horizon, swept an observing eye over the flat, arid landscape looking for signs of his men. Nothing stirred except the glimmering flux of the heat waves. Knowing the traditional enmity between his own Kurds and the Turkish Bazhis, and with the possibility of plunder inspiring his troopers, he realized their hot pursuit might reach the walls of Aleksandropol. Which left him to deal with this problem alone. *Merde,* he thought disgruntledly, the last thing he needed right now was a dirty, halfdead native girl who might require medical attention—not exactly a reality in this wasteland—and restoration to her family, if they existed in this war-torn country.

What he needed was restoration himself to the silken comforts of civilization, he reflected grouchily, minus the burden of this female. He shook the girl slightly, optimistically hoping she'd wake and say, "Thank you for rescuing me. My family lives conveniently near and I'll walk home." Instead she continued breathing in limp unconsciousness while sweat ran down his face and back and chest and ultimately into his black kidskin boots.

Deuce take it, what the hell to do with her other than stand here melting? He *could* leave her with the caravan of Armenian refugees they'd passed on the road some time ago. But that, unfortunately, would require retracing his journey. Not a pleasant option in the scorching heat.

Since Aleksandropol was *his* destination for today's travel, she would have to be content with that, as well, he thought, refusing to backtrack when the ultimate comforts of Tiflis and his Gypsy lover, Choura, beckoned. His decision made, he walked the few paces to where Cleo stood. Placing the girl in front of the saddle, he mounted behind her and resumed his journey north.

A slight cooling breeze seemed to spring up as if in affirmation of his decision, and for the first time since sighting the Bazhis, he smiled. His smile altered the moody features of his face, softened his strong jaw and well-defined cheekbones, modified the scowl drawing his heavy brows together, even touched his dark flinty eyes with a brief flash of levity. Lifting his arm, he raked his fingers through the ruffled black silk of his hair, raised the damp curls resting on the silver-encrusted collar of his uniform and felt the blessed coolness on his neck.

A few miles more, he thought with relief. And then a bath.

The same breeze refreshing Stefan drifted over Lisaveta's face as she lay in the crook of his arms. Her eyes fluttered open. Immediately in her line of vision was a bronzed, austere male face, dirt streaked, unshaven. With a terrified start she wondered if she'd been recaptured by the Bazhis. But as her panic-stricken gaze moved downward, she saw the silver insignia of regiment and rank on his uniform collar and shoulder and the frenzied beating of her heart subsided fractionally. He was clearly in the Russian army, but his looks suggested he could be a native warrior. Was he wearing a trophy of war? Without moving, she allowed her gaze to slide downward. He wore a ring on his right hand, a large unfaceted emerald, and that hand was resting on a thigh encased in filthy white leather breeches. Thank God! The natives didn't wear jewelry and would never wear tight-fitting breeches for riding. He was Russian! She was saved!

Her heartbeat slowed to normal and a strange lethargy overcame her, as though all signals to her brain had received the
message of her salvation. She lay for a few moments more
without speaking, feeling utterly safe, feeling as if she were
waking from a sleep, her gaze fixed on the man who held her.
The officer's face, framed by the brilliant light, was streaked
with sweat, and his dark eyes of a distinctive Tartar cast were
narrowed against the hot glitter of the sun. He had a surprisingly young face, she thought, for the general's rank on his
shoulder, a classic aquiline face with an etched handsomeness
enhanced somehow by the dark stubble of beard shading his
jaw. He had a compelling masculine severity of face and form,
a mythological pagan quality of animal strength and grace despite the dirt and sweat. He also looked surprisingly familiar.

And then she found herself staring into midnight-black eyes,
saved from absolute opacity only by curious golden flecks near
the pupils.

His gaze was both benign and dismissive, but his deep voice
when he spoke was courteous. "How do you feel?" he asked
in the local dialect.

Her lashes lifted completely so the tawny gold of her eyes
was visible to Stefan for the first time. His reaction was immediate, instinctive: Kuzan eyes. His friend Nikki Kuzan had
eyes like that, slightly oriental, tilted marginally like hers and
of the same unusual shade. And then he remembered she was
a native girl three thousand miles from Saint Petersburg. She
could hardly be related to a Russian prince simply through a
coincidence of eye color.

"I feel marvelously alive, thanks to you," she answered in
French.

"Ah," he murmured in surprise. "You speak French."
French was the language of the Russian aristocracy, but she
hardly qualified. Was she a teacher of some kind?

"And several other languages as well, all of which I'm appreciative in," she informed him in a voice unshaken and calm.
"The caravan I was traveling with was attacked and I was
abducted," she continued in a firm declarative way. "If you
hadn't come to my rescue, there's no doubt I would have been

those bandits' victim. I'm deeply in your debt and will surely reward you at my first opportunity.''

She spoke so assertively it startled him for a moment, as did the style of her speech. Obviously she wasn't a native. He glanced at her again with a less desultory curiosity. Maybe she was the wife of a merchant or some minor official; her dress was too modest for any higher position. Stefan's tastes, although catholic in rank or status, were inclined toward lush females with silken skin and feminine ways, so his scrutiny of her was brief. She didn't pique his interest in any of these areas. Furthermore, he took mild offense at her offer of a reward. He was Prince Bariatinsky on his paternal side, the only noble family directly related to the Tsars, while his mother's family, the Orbeliani, had been the wealthiest and most powerful dynasty in Georgia since the third century. He took issue at being offered a reward like some bourgeois shopkeeper when he justifiably considered his act no more than simple chivalry. She would do well, he peevishly thought, to learn the accepted way of the world. In his milieu, men gave and women took, not the other way around.

"No reward is necessary," he replied in a mildly repressive tone. "Think nothing of it."

"But I'd feel so much better if I could show my appreciation."

And under ordinary circumstances when Stefan heard those words from a woman, his reaction was predictable.

But this woman was too plain and unattractive, so for the first time in his life he rejected that invitational phrase. Inherently polite, he declined with courtesy. "To know you're unharmed, *madame*, is reward enough," he said.

"*Mademoiselle*," she casually corrected.

"I'm sorry. Was your family—" He didn't precisely know how to ask if her family had been killed in the attack.

"Oh, I was traveling alone," Lisaveta said, interpreting his hesitancy.

After a life significant for a wide and varied profligacy, Stefan considered himself beyond shock, but he found himself momentarily confounded. Young unmarried women didn't normally travel alone, although he realized the war had raised havoc. "How is it," he inquired, both curious and mildly astonished, "you were traveling alone in this war?" He was not a martinet for protocol, but he did not consider a war zone exactly the safest place for a single young female.

"I didn't *begin* my journey alone," Lisaveta explained. "Javad Khan sent an escort with me...."

Stefan immediately recognized the name. Javad was a power to be reckoned with in western Azerbaijan. Was she one of his harem being sent home on a visit? No, he decided, glancing at her peasant clothing. Javad's houris would never be so poorly dressed, nor would he send them out in this no-man's-land. And, he thought next with masculine bias, Javad Khan's taste in women was much superior to this female in his arms.

"But we were so close to Aleksandropol when we met the caravan," Lisaveta went on, oblivious to Stefan's assessment, "that I insisted Javad's men return to Turkish territory. I was on Russian soil now and traveling in sufficient company for safety. Who would have thought Bazhis were in the vicinity, so few miles from Aleksandropol?" She looked up at him then with a translucent gaze reminiscent of an artless child.

A simple woman, he thought, so naive in the ways of the world. And dressed like a peasant, yet sent out under escort by Javad Khan himself. Nothing quite connected.

"Do you live in Karakilisa?" he inquired, thinking perhaps she was a special member of Javad's household staff—a favored housekeeper or cook or harem servant.

"No, I was only visiting Javad, studying his Hafiz manuscripts, when the war broke out," she answered plainly, just as she'd answered all his questions. "He'd granted me permission to use his private archives and I was planning on staying several months more to take advantage of the opportunity, feeling that in that time the campaigns would have moved west anyway, but then...well...circumstances required I leave precipitously."

Now any one of her disclosures would have been enough to startle him, but in the entirety the result was stupefying. First, women were rarely scholars—particularly of Persian erotica.

Second, women weren't allowed any freedom of scope in Karakilisa. It was a provincial Turkish city and Muslim law strictly prevailed. Women lived in harems or under rigid restrictions. They didn't have free rein in a Khan's library. Actually, very few of them were literate.

"Did you say—Hafiz?" he carefully inquired, persuaded on further reflection that he must have misunderstood *entirely*.

"Yes. Do you know his work?" she asked blandly, as if he'd casually questioned the competence of her dressmaker.

He found his eyes drawn to her again when she reaffirmed her unusual activities at Karakilisa. Definitely unsightly, dirty and overweight. No, his first assessment had been correct. How odd. She and Hafiz. It made no sense. He wondered whether he'd been out under the hot sun too long. But she seemed to be waiting for his answer so he replied, "I know of him, of course. I've several of his works in my library, but frankly—" He stopped before he overstepped good manners.

She smiled and her teeth shone surprisingly white against the smudged grayness of her face. "I realize it's unusual," she said, answering his unspoken thought in what he was discovering was her habitually direct style, "but it happens to be my current area of study. And if you shouldn't mind, I'd very much like to see the copies you have."

No delicate wallflower here, he thought, not quite sure if he was offended or not at her forwardness. Both breeding and rank had made the Prince firmly a product of his age, an age that viewed women as pretty, gay, delightful amusements but looked askance at women who dared to be assertive.

"The fact is," she continued amiably as though she openly discussed Persian erotica with any stranger she met, "I'm Count Lazaroff's daughter, Lisaveta Felixovna." She pronounced her father's name with obvious pride, conscious it would be instantly recognized. And of course it was. The recluse count had been, before his untimely death three years ago, the premier Russian scholar of Persian manuscripts.

There, Stefan thought. An explanation for the plain dowdy woman and her unorthodox studies. It helped ease his sense of uncomfortable rapport. Women fell into distinct categories for him: female relatives he treated with kindness and friendship; beautiful women he treated as potential lovers with flirtatious charm; the rest generally received only polite civility on the rare occasions he noticed them. As for female scholars, he'd never met one.

"So you're following in your father's footsteps. Commendable, I'm sure," he said politely. "And you're welcome, of course, to make use of my library," he added in deference to good manners. "I still don't completely understand, though," he went on, inexplicably intrigued by the sheer bravado of this strange woman, "why you left the safety of Karakilisa to venture into the midst of the war?"

"I simply had to leave," she answered in that same clear, affirmative tone he now decided was what displeased him. It made her sound like a man. "Although my host graciously overlooked my nationality when I was detained by the hostilities, and I continued to work, his nephew Faizi Pasha, a colonel in the Turkish army, visited unexpectedly one day. On meeting me, he decided to add me to his harem. Naturally, I was opposed to the idea." Her voice was filled with cool disdain, as if she were saying, "I had to refuse my dancing master's proposal of marriage."

Stefan wondered what in the world the Pasha had seen in her that appealed to him, although the Turks did appreciate what he considered excess female flesh. "I understand your problem," he courteously replied, thinking soon he would be free of this decisive managing woman who grated on his nerves.

"So there was nothing else to do. I *had* to leave."

Again. That authoritarian certainty.

"And the combined forces of the Russian and Turkish armies be damned," Stefan found himself saying with only a mildly disguised sarcasm.

Lisaveta looked at him briefly, her gold eyes reflective. "I didn't care to consider a future locked in a cage," she said quietly, "no matter how gilded the bars."

Stefan immediately regretted his lapse in manners. "Forgive me." She had sounded very human for a moment and he reminded himself she had come through great danger. "And you escaped one peril only to face others."

"None so dangerous in my mind as Faizi Pasha's advances. There's a certain finality about harems…like a prison door shutting for life." Her voice held a winsome quality, and had he known her background of independent living, he would have realized how important freedom was to her. "And my host, Javad Khan, saw that I was well escorted with a dozen Afshar guides. When they left me with the caravan so near Aleksandropol—at my insistence, I might add—I assumed the rest of the journey would be uneventful."

The sheer naïveté in the word *uneventful* renewed Stefan's exasperation. With difficulty he refrained from remarking that only a stupid female would term crossing through the battleground of two armies "uneventful," even with a hundred guides.

"And if I hadn't given my horse to an enceinte woman, I probably could have escaped and arrived in Aleksandropol completely unharmed," Lisaveta added with the self-assurance Stefan found so annoying.

"Good marksmanship," the Prince said evenly, his irritation evident in the hard line of his jaw, "is a given with the native tribes. And the Winchester .44 round will outrun a horse, guaranteed. Your horse might have saved you and it might not have."

Lisaveta's temper was as quick to ignite as the Prince's, but since he'd saved her life, she felt she owed him a certain degree of politeness despite his rebuking tone. She would have liked to point out that her usefulness to a Bazhi was alive and not dead, but smiling instead, as reared to politeness as the Prince, she said with good grace, "You're right, of course." She had learned long ago that men preferred being right, and in circumstances where arguing was counterproductive, she always allowed them that privilege. He was, after all, transporting her to safety.

Stefan's ill humor was somewhat mollified by her ready acquiescence, so he refrained from saying thank-you and having the last word on the subject. Countess Lazaroff's next statement, however, destroyed his short-lived complacency.

"I'll need some money," she said, "when we reach Aleksandropol. If you could lend me a few hundred roubles I could find lodgings tonight. After a long day of this abominable heat, I'd seriously consider selling my soul for a bath." Unfamiliar with any of the nuances of feminine wiles, educated to establish effectively, then deal with a problem, and perhaps at base just as indulged and spoiled as the Prince, she was unaware her simple request would not be viewed as simple at all.

Stefan's resentment returned full force at her damnable tone. He also knew that with thirty-thousand troops bivouacked in Aleksandropol, the only way anyone would find a room was by rank, title and large sums of money. She *was* a woman, though, despite his own lack of interest in her rotund person. No doubt she could find accommodations on her own for a price other than gold. But she was also Count Lazaroff's daughter; he couldn't simply abandon her to the army's train with the other refugees as he would have were she a peasant. He supposed, he thought with a silent sigh, he was obliged to act the gentleman. "Allow me, Countess," he said, only because he'd been taught to protect the weaker sex, "to find you accommodations tonight."

"How thoughtful," Lisaveta replied, as if she hadn't recognized the coercion prompting him, as if she didn't know how hazardous her position would be, alone in an army camp.

"My pleasure, *mademoiselle*," he murmured. They could have been at a court soiree for all their superficial politesse.

"I so appreciate your help." Lisaveta almost choked on the words, for Prince Bariatinsky was the epitome of all she despised in the aristocracy. Too rich, too handsome, too spoiled by both his fame and infamy. She'd recognized him shortly after she regained consciousness, realizing then why he'd seemed familiar to her at first sight. Engravings of the Prince in uniform were prevalent throughout Russia; women collected them to pine over.

At twenty-two he had been the conqueror of the Citadel of Tubruz, at twenty-five the savior and avenging angel of the survivors of the massacre at Mirum. His victories in Asia had subdued at last the Khanates of Khiva and Kokand. In fact, the youngest general ever gazetted in the history of the Russian army was a universal hero. He was the famous and fearless Prince Stefan, always dressed in his white Chevalier Gardes uniform and mounted on his black Orloff steed, challenging death and the enemy at the head of his cavalry.

He was also famous—or notorious—for his love life.

And she suspected the women fondly collecting his likeness were more interested in his amorous exploits than his military ones.

"My pleasure," he tightly replied, wishing for his part that he were with his Gypsy lover, Choura, in the cool altitudes of his mountain lodge, miles away from the scorching heat and Countess Lazaroff. He had no tolerance for bluestocking women and less for unbecoming nonconformist females with a propensity for emphatic declarative statements. She was entirely lacking in the feminine graces and attributes that attracted him to women. In fact, she was damned annoying.

Both seemed mildly irritated at the course of their conversation, and the remainder of the ride into Aleksandropol passed in a peevish silence.

Two

As they approached Aleksandropol, the Russian army's base of operations eighteen miles from the Turkish border, Stefan said in a voice brusque with fatigue, "Until we reach our lodging, I expect you to obey my orders. The city's jammed with veterans of the siege." He didn't say they'd been without women for weeks. Instead he added, "Soldiers at war can't be expected to act like gentlemen." He hoped she wouldn't argue, because he wasn't in the mood to deal with any more of her idiosyncrasies.

Surveying the ranks of lounging soldiers at the city gate, all appearing remarkably large and burly, their eyes trained on her in a disconcerting way, Lisaveta judiciously replied, "Yes, sir."

Stefan glanced down at her swiftly, for her quiet tone and manner were extremely unlike her previous confidence.

"Are we safe from that mob?" she asked, uncertainty prominent in her voice. She was seeing lust with brutal clarity, and it took enormous control to keep her voice from shaking. Stefan was only one man, she thought. Could even his rank protect her from what she saw in the soldiers' eyes? It was the same look she'd seen in Faizi's eyes, although his had been a more leisured inspection. Under the circumstances she felt sure none of these men were interested in leisurely concerns.

Before Stefan could answer he was recognized and a series of cheers erupted, traveling down the ranks of men in a spontaneous cry of welcome. Gruff voices called to him as commander and comrade as they passed through the medieval gate and entered the narrow cobbled streets of the city. Stefan acknowledged the noisy clamor, responding to his men with casual waves and a smile, with personal comments to one and then another, recognizing a remarkable number of men by name. It was obvious he was a hero to them, adored and revered and loved.

But beneath camaraderie and facetious banter, Lisaveta was still aware of the soldiers' eyes dwelling on her as they passed, as hungry wolves would survey a tender lamb. Unconsciously she moved closer to the large man behind her.

After a dozen turns and a winding uphill climb, the crowds of soldiers thinned, the shouting died away, and they reached a small villa the Prince must have known of, for he made no inquiries on the way. Riding through a gateway into a paved courtyard walled round with a low wrought-iron railing, Stefan said, "Wait here," and slid to the ground, his hands steadying Lisaveta on the saddle. Handing her his Colt revolver, he added, "Shoot anyone who comes too close."

"Shoot?" Lisaveta said, not reaching for the extended weapon.

He looked at her for a moment, not wishing to alarm her unduly. But even nondescript as she was, women were in such rare supply she should have a firearm for protection. "A precaution only, *mademoiselle*," he said, "until I return."

"Should I come in with you?" Brave under normal circumstances, she knew she was seriously outnumbered with thousands of troops in Aleksandropol.

"I'll only be a moment," Stefan replied, knowing he'd have to oust the villa's current occupants. He outranked them, but sometimes more than a polite request was required. Additionally, he couldn't be certain the men wouldn't be "entertaining" themselves with some of the available women, a situation that could prove embarrassing for his passenger. Placing the Colt in her hand, he wrapped her fingers around the grip and asked, "Can you shoot?"

Lisaveta nodded, mute and touched with apprehension.

He gave her a smile, the first she'd seen since meeting him, and she understood immediately a portion of his allure. His dark eyes lost their severity, his perfect teeth flashed white, his sculpted mouth reminded her powerfully of classic Greek archetypes come to life. She felt bathed in a sudden shimmering happiness.

"Good," he said, and was gone, taking the entrance stairs three at a time.

Despite the heat, the surrounding air seemed to cool momentarily at his exit. Good heavens, she thought, shaking away the unusual sensation. Was she so gullible, so unsophisticated, that a simple smile from the illustrious Prince Bariatinsky changed the temperature of the sun?

No doubt he was familiar with the power of his smile. No doubt he was familiar with women responding to that smile. Well, that might be, but he was also overbearing and imperious, and while she was grateful for his rescue, she disliked his style of womanizing man.

The next moment she chastised herself for not showing proper gratitude for her rescue. Without him, she'd be dead now or wishing for death. Certainly, it was the height of ingratitude to be pettishly caviling over his lady loves and amorous leisure activities. She was truly grateful. Period. His style of life was incidental. And she summoned a smile to her face in indication of her sincerity.

He didn't seem to notice when he returned a short time later.

"We're set," he said gruffly, and lifted her down.

He was enormously tall, she thought, a wayward perception that she immediately suppressed as totally irrelevant. As if it mattered what he looked like.

"Would you like to *keep* the pistol?"

Had he repeated the question? She wasn't sure, but his dark glance was mildly perplexed.

"No...no...not at all...here," she answered, stammering in a rare unease. You'd think she'd never seen a man in skin-tight leather cavalry breeches, half-nude above the waist, his chest sleek with sweat, his muscles...

She felt the revolver being taken from her grasp and her gaze fell from the prominent definition of his pectorals to his hand, only inches from hers. His fingers were long and slender and very tanned, shades darker than her own. He didn't speak as he replaced the weapon in its holster on his saddle, and while she was debating some appropriate casual remark to cover her unease, he turned back to her, put out his arm like a gentleman at a ball or a promenade and said, "This way, *mademoiselle*."

"Was the villa vacant?" Lisaveta inquired as they ascended the short bank of stairs. She'd seen no one exit.

"A few officers only, *mademoiselle*, who were more than happy to oblige you."

"Have they gone?"

"I believe so," Stefan replied with equanimity, not about to detail the true nature of his confiscation. A small amount of force had been required in addition to the threat of his rank, and the artillery colonel had been swearing as he'd departed through the back door. The transport officers had been willing to negotiate, offering Stefan several hours of their female companions' time, but Stefan fancied cleaner women and had declined. The Countess Lazaroff, he thought, would appreciate sleeping without the raucous sounds of an all-night party. And he, too, would prefer quiet tonight. Choura was only a few days away; he could wait. After three months, he could wait a few days more.

As they passed through the walled courtyard, its fountain miraculously still playing despite the disruptions of war, and crossed the elegantly tiled pavement, Stefan said, "I've commissioned a bathtub for you, and supper. I hope you'll find the accommodations comfortable. In the morning I'll see you have an escort with one of the guarded convoys traveling to Tiflis."

While his statements were courteous, the tenor of his voice implied he was released from any further responsibility by these acts. "The villa is guarded," he added in afterthought to the dust-covered woman in black. "Sleep well." And with a minimal bow he left Lisaveta at the base of the staircase, waving a servant over to escort her to the second-floor rooms.

"Thank you," Lisaveta ironically said to the back of his head as he walked away. "You're too kind." A sudden re-

sentment, disturbing in its novelty, overwhelmed her. Why did
it matter that he dismissed her as insignificant? Why did she
care what he thought of her? She should be above the triviality
of female coquetry.

When her mother had died, her father had returned to his
country estates and never entered the world of society again.
Lisaveta had been raised in a quiet country existence, but she
still remembered her early years in Saint Petersburg before her
mother's death. She had fond memories of her beautiful
mother, a Princess of the Kuzan family, and recalled their pink
marble palace filled with people for parties and teas, recitals
and balls. Each evening before Maman and Papa left for one
of their parties or entertained their own guests, they would
come to the nursery to tuck her into bed, and Maman had
always been gorgeous in magnificent gowns and splendid jewels. When she'd hug Lisaveta good-night, she'd smell of
blooming roses and smile her radiant smile and sometimes slip
her tiara on Lisaveta's curly hair and call her "my baby princess." It wasn't often she thought of those long-ago years in
Saint Petersburg or of Maman's hugs and kisses or of the very
different life her father had once led. She and her father had
lived away from the capital so long she'd forgotten the frivolity
of the aristocratic world existed. And she'd considered herself
insensitive to its amusements and glamour.

But somehow Prince Bariatinsky gave rise to a provoking
sense of inadequacy. And it annoyed her. She never felt in-
adequate. It was his dismissive gaze and tone and attitude—as
though she weren't worth noticing. An incipient spirit of challenge stirred in her at his bland negation of her womanhood,
an unprecedented feeling, not focused enough to even fully
acknowledge, only a tiny flutter of long-suppressed femininity.

And while she despised the Prince for all his arrogant in-
souciant notoriety, she couldn't deny his sinful, obvious beauty.
She'd been too close to the perfect modeled planes of his face,
too near the splendid magnificence of his heavily lashed eyes,
and she was aware despite herself that his tall lean body possessed an unusual charismatic power and virility. She wasn't

the first woman to note these vividly masculine characteristics, she thought, following the servant upstairs. Only the latest.

After arranging quarters for Cleo and his troopers, who would presumably appear once the Bazhis were dispatched, Stefan returned to the villa, took the stairs to his rooms in a run, stripped off his filthy uniform with efficient speed and was in his waiting bath in record time. Submerging himself briefly to rinse the dust from his face and hair, he came up out of the water dripping and degrees cooler, reached for his brandy flask, which he'd set conveniently near, slid back down so he was leaning comfortably against the painted porcelain headrest and sighed his first exhalation of satisfaction in three long months.

Tipping the gold flask engraved with good wishes from Tsar Alexander, he let the amber liquid spill into his mouth, and after his first slow swallow, he smiled into the quiet shaded room. Contentment came from such simple pleasures, he philosophically noted.

In the course of the next hour he emptied the brandy flask while the water cooled, and when he was sufficiently relaxed, the numbing fatigue of the past weeks alleviated not only by the liquor but by the soothing water, he bathed.

When his food arrived sometime later, Stefan was lounging on the bed in one of the silk robes left behind by the villa's owner when his home was requisitioned by the Russian army. The fabric was a cinnamon brocade shot through with a heavy underweaving of aquamarine, and the robe accented the oriental cast of Stefan's features, emphasizing the slight obliqueness of his eyes and the elegant dark wings of his brows. The long-skirted luxurious silk was juxtaposed with his harsh masculinity, the contrast both dramatic and sensual, as if a warrior knight were transposed briefly into a worldly courtier. He'd rolled up the trapunto-trimmed sleeves, an incongruous touch in such a stately robe, as incongruous as his galvanic power contained in the delicate silk.

His dinner was excellent and he ate it with a haste his majordomo would have disapproved of, but the comforts of civilization had been sadly lacking the past few months, the food

at Kars deplorable, and he intended to relish his first real meal
without concern for etiquette. And while he ate and later
lounged again on his bed, finishing the bottle of fine wine the
servant had brought with his meal, Stefan was regaled through
the plastered walls with a tuneful array of songs in the Countess's soft contralto.

She was a most unusual female, Stefan decided, more indulgent in his assessment once the bottom of the bottle of wine
was reached. After all the treachery and danger of the past few
days she seemed in cheerfully good humor. Most remarkable.
He couldn't think of a woman he knew who would have re-
bounded from the fearful perils she'd experienced with such
buoyant resiliency. Her voice, too, had a delicate feminine
charm in song. A shame she was an antidote to look at.

An exemplary officer, Stefan dressed shortly after eating and
went to see that his men were satisfactorily bivouacked. His
guards were flushed with success, much richer for their pursuit
of the Bazhis and celebrating their good fortune with the native
arrack, a potent liquor known for its fiery taste. Several stone-
ware bottles were passed around and shared as the chase was
described in detail, so it was past midnight before Stefan bade
his bodyguards good-night and returned to the villa.

Although the sounds of revelry in the town continued, the
courtyard and villa's interior were hushed and quiet. Despite
the hour the heat of the day had scarcely diminished, and the
area around the small fountain, open to the stars, seemed hung
with a dense dark curtain of torrid vapor. Stefan could almost
feel himself move through successive layers of sultry air.

He'd stripped off his loose native shirt on his way up the
stairs and kicked off his low boots just inside the door to his
room. Tossing the shirt on a chair, he shoved the door shut
with one bare foot and padded across the soft Antolian carpet
to his bed. Unbelting the coarse woven pants he wore, he let
them drop to the floor, then he fell pleasantly inebriated onto
the cool linen sheets of his bed. The first night away from Kars,
he thought contentedly, the pillow beneath his head a luxury
he'd not felt for weeks. The first night he could sleep without
one ear tuned to the pickets' song, the first night he didn't have

to catch himself dozing as he rode patrol. The first night in months he might have had the opportunity to bed a woman. Unfortunately, in a town accommodating thirty thousand troops, one's choices in vice were limited to a less delicate type of female, and he'd decided to sleep alone.

As he drifted off, his thoughts wandered to the very imminent delights awaiting him in Tiflis. Only two more days, he mused, wondering if Choura would still be waiting at his lodge in the hills north of the city or whether her hot Gypsy blood had tired of the enforced leisure and she'd found some new young buck's back to bloody. The memories of Choura's particular brand of lovemaking evoked a surge of pure lust through his senses. He'd found her savage wildness, the uncivilized violence of her passion, an exhilarating change from the delicate refined sighs of the young matrons in the aristocratic circles he frequented. He fell asleep reminiscing about Choura, recalling the perfect length of her slender legs and how she liked to bite and how much he enjoyed her biting, how she danced for him until she was damp with sweat and lust and how the sleek beauty of her body felt beneath his. He fell asleep with a distinct smile on his lips.

It was no more than twenty minutes when he woke to an unearthly scream, the kind of scream he'd heard at night on patrol, the horrifying scream of Russian prisoners being tortured by the Turks. For a moment he thought he was back at Kars. But his palms rested on sheets. He was in a bed. His mind scrambled desperately to climb up from the depths of slumber, his senses perhaps slightly impaired by the liquor he'd drunk. But his years of military service were manifest in his swift response, and he was halfway out of the bed, reaching for his robe, when he distinguished the source of the piercing cries.

The Countess.

In one blurred motion he rose from the bed, grabbed his robe and dashed out into the hall, shrugging into the garment as he strode the few steps to Countess Lazaroff's room. Assuming she'd locked her door, he heaved his weight against the solid wood. The door gave way too readily and crashed explosively against the wall, leaving the plaster in shattered fragments. Catching himself against the jamb, he grunted in disgust. The witless woman hadn't even locked her door.

Some of the guards had been celebrating tonight, as well; it was possible someone had slipped into the villa or perhaps through the window. He scanned the room carefully as he stood in the doorway, alert to danger, ready to spring on an intruder. Moonlight poured in the latticed window, illuminating the room with elegant decorative shapes, and he surveyed each portion of the room in swift perusal.

No one. The furniture was all in place; the latticed shutters were still secured from the inside. The Countess's screams had now subsided into great gulping whimpers that punctuated the hushed silvery stillness like tiny muted starbursts in space.

Once he assured himself there was no danger from assassins or brutal soldiers intent on rape, his dark eyes followed the sound of her soft whimpers. When his gaze finally halted on Countess Lazaroff, he stood transfixed, framed in the shadowed doorway, his head just brushing the arched plaster of the lintel, his wide silk-clad shoulders dwarfing the width of the entry, his dark eyes incredulous.

No dirt on the lady any longer. No muddy face and tangled hair. No features lost beneath layers of grime. No disguising volumes of crow-black material, petticoats and shawls and babushkas.

No indeed, he breathed, dumbfounded, and wondered briefly if he was in the wrong room.

Every muscle, nerve and pulsing vein in his body instantly responded to the vision of flawless female beauty barely concealed by a portion of sheet. The Countess, lush and opulent, huddled fearfully against the simply carved headboard of the bed, one slender hand clutching a small drape of sheet to her throat, the fabric serving more as a foil than a shield for her form. Both her tantalizing breasts were exposed, as was the alluring curve of her waist and hips and thighs. His eyes drifted lower and a numbing chill ran down his spine.

He felt the same way before an attack...alert, adrenaline pumping.

Felt the same way coursing with his borzois...exhilarated, loving the hunt.

The pause was infinitesimal as he assessed his exquisite quarry with the flushed covetous gaze of trophy-room acquisitiveness.

She was dazzling, breathtaking, her heavy chestnut hair gleaming in the shimmering moonlight. Her skin was profoundly white, as though she'd spent her life in dim dark archives, he thought. And he wondered in the next thundering beat of his heart whether she'd hidden away her virginity, too, from the masculine predators of the world. Would she be as precious as the Hafiz manuscripts, as sensuously refined as the medieval erotica she studied?

He had never conceived of a woman so totally made for love—not only splendidly beautiful but extravagantly formed, like some male artist's conception of a perfect houri. And, if she was a scholar of Hafiz, tantalizingly schooled in all the erotic variations of love.

Without taking his eyes from the Countess, he reached out and eased the door slowly forward, took one step into the room and quietly pushed it shut behind him, the sound of the key turning in the lock a minute metallic reverberation in the close humid silence.

She was no longer whimpering but her breathing was still agitated, like that of a child who has cried too long. As he approached her, her eyes lifted to his, muted golden and sultry, he thought, like the heated night. Too practiced to miscue, he read the lady's acquiescence before she was aware of it herself. Too skilled to rush a lady, he slowly walked toward her, quietly sat beside her on the bed and softly said, "It was a dream."

She nodded, unable to speak with his powerful body so close, and she watched motionless as he put out a hand and touched her throat, slid his fingers in a soft caress across the small distance to where her hand clutched the sheet and, gently loosening her grip, watched the sheet fall away.

"The Bazhis can't hurt you now," he murmured, still holding her hand. Raising it slowly to his lips, he touched each of her fingers in sequence to his mouth before lowering her hand to the bed.

His eyes were like black fire, intense and beautiful with none of the heedless inattention she'd seen in them before. And she understood in a flashing moment his extraordinary appeal to women. He was promising her something she inexplicably wanted, and she felt strange quivering, warm tremors from the tips of her fingers through her arms and body into the very center of her being. They were not strange and fearful sensations, but strangely comforting ones—like a cozy fire on a cool mountain night that relaxes and warms at the same time. But she felt something more too, a dizzy, feverish wanting, an elusive wanting that brought a blush to her cheeks. It was the first time a man had kissed her fingers…had kissed her…and in her own, self-absorbed way she thought it quite pleasant. More than pleasant—magical.

"Was your dream terrible?" Stefan softly asked, the way a trusted friend would say, "Tell me your troubles." He put his large hand over hers.

"There were dozens of them," she whispered, shuddering abruptly at the memory. "I wouldn't have survived, would I?"

You wouldn't have wanted to, he thought, but said instead very low, his hand stroking hers gently, his voice soothing, "Hush, it's over…it was only a dream." The Bazhis' reputation regarding atrocities toward women was common knowledge. As unpaid irregulars in the Turkish army they depended on plunder in lieu of pay and were, accordingly, almost impossible to control. They traveled rapidly and they traveled light. Once a female captive had been used to satisfy their needs, she was always killed in a particularly brutal manner. It was understandable the Countess should be shaken by nightmares.

Her eyes were still wide with recollection. "I'm truly grateful for your rescue," she whispered, her eyes glistening with emotion. "And I'm sorry about today," she softly added. "I know I irritated you."

"I should apologize for my rudeness," Stefan said, his own glance tender, his hand lifting to brush aside a tendril of curl that had fallen over her forehead. "If it's any excuse, I'd just come off three months of campaigning and was damn tired. I'm sorry."

"I should apologize to you for all the extra work my rescue entailed."

Stefan grinned with a sudden boyish charm he rarely exposed. "I think we've covered all the social courtesies. You're sorry. I'm sorry. We've both apologized. I'd prefer," he said, his voice taking on a low husky quality, "to consider our meeting a delightful bit of luck. And I intend to reward my Kurd shaman for his mystical intervention." He was only halfteasing. She had been literally thrown into his path and he was enough of a mystic not to disclaim the metaphysical possibilities. "Are you badly bruised?" he asked suddenly, remembering the violence of her fall. No marks were obvious in the moonlight as his dark glance took in the purity of her form.

"My head…is a bit tender…near my right ear."

I'll be careful, he thought.

"And…well—" she shyly smiled "—my bottom is… slightly bruised."

That, too, he mused, I'll treat with care.

"I…should put my clothes on," Lisaveta said into the small silence, unabashed by her nudity but an innocent in seduction. She didn't realize Stefan had other plans. She didn't realize the game was just beginning.

"Did the servants bring you new clothes?" he asked.

"No."

"Wait till morning then, and we'll find a dressmaker. I'll have Haci dredge one up."

"I'm not as unorthodox as you," she said, understanding then the simple chronology of his sentence.

"I think, dear heart," he murmured, touching the soft fullness of her bottom lip with the lightest brush of fingertips, "you're more unorthodox than I."

"Your reputation—"

"Kiss me," he whispered.

She swayed toward him as though his words were the earth's magnetic poles, her mouth and eyes and soft silken body like an offering. "I shouldn't," she breathed, as if the words could stop the melting suggestion of her body.

"I know."

And the two words he spoke were like a promise she must keep. He could tell immediately, so tentative was the touch of her lips on his, that she'd never kissed a man before. But after three months of war Stefan felt as though some benevolent spirit had taken pity on him, giving him a pale unspoiled woman to make love to, as though she were a gift of innocence and purity after the endless weeks of bloody war. He felt no guilt that she was there for him. She was, after all, curiously self-reliant and surely not entirely chaste as a scholar of Hafiz. But at base he simply did what he did best.

And he began by kissing her back.

Lisaveta's first thought, melodramatic and alien to any pre-conceived notions she had of herself, was, He's *attracted* to me. As a woman. A sense of wonder, magnificent in both its novelty and splendor, flared through her body, and she felt the warming flush like a personal sunrise of the soul. There was no denying the reason Prince Bariatinsky's engravings were collected by sighing women throughout the Empire. His head lifted briefly from their kiss and he smiled at her, his face starkly handsome, his dark eyes tender somehow despite their savage blackness. He was, she decided, wicked, sweet unreason, like a fallen angel dressed in sensuous beauty.

"I like your kisses," she murmured. "They warm me everywhere and make me tingle...."

He touched the small straight perfection of her nose with the briefest of kisses, raised his head and, his smile crinkling the corners of his eyes, said, "Thank you." Her ingenuous directness was enchanting now rather than offensive, the sweetly naive empiricism with which she viewed new experiences tantalizing. He would look forward to each artless reaction as the night progressed.

"Kiss me some more." She said it like a child in a candy store—with unreserved demand and delight. Unguiltily, too, as though she deserved it.

"Your servant, *mademoiselle*," Stefan murmured agreeably.

Numerous women in his past would have been shocked at his placid acquiescence. Prince Bariatinsky, one of the most decorated, celebrated men in the Empire, had never been any woman's servant. Skilled and generous at providing pleasure, certainly, but submissive—never.

"You must tell me, sweet Lise," he whispered with teasing huskiness, bending his dark ruffled head, his breath warm on the aching crest of her nipple, "do you like this more?" And he touched the very tip with a tender suckling kiss that abruptly deepened, then bit with tiny caresses so that she felt a searing flame race downward like molten fire to sanctify each pleasure center in her body.

Her sighing breathy moan was an affirmative response.

He moved later to slowly caress her other breast and then trailed lingering kisses up her throat and across the velvet smoothness of her cheek. He nibbled at her earlobes and whispered the amorous love words that he knew roused women more swiftly than torrid kisses. He knew all the play words, the scented, heated, facile words, and she responded as he knew she would, her small hands reaching out to slide up the cinnamon silk of his robe. They glided with her own inherent coquettish languor under the open neckline and over the solid muscled strength of his shoulders.

"You *must* make love to me," she whispered, and pulled him close.

"I must?" There was the minutest pause. They were only inches apart, her golden dark-lashed eyes riveting in their boldness. "And if I won't?" he very softly said, although a white-hot excitement was already rousing him, an impatient fever more pungent than blood lust, more provocative than Hafiz's poetry and gilded interiors.

"I'll give you pleasure," she said very simply, in the rich womanly contralto he'd heard earlier in the evening. Her palms were slipping down over the firmly defined musculature of his chest, and he inhaled sharply as her small hands drifted lower. "I will, you know," she murmured, her voice as sensuous as a Sultan's favorite, trained from the cradle. It was as if she must tantalize him to pique his jaded interest.

He smiled then. Despite her innocence and lack of experience, he knew she would. "I know," he whispered. As a jeweled gift gives pleasure, he thought, as enchantment might be held in one's hands. "It's been three months," he said. "You *will* give me pleasure."

"It's been twenty-two years," she softly said, "and I don't want to wait." Her smile was pure unadulterated sunshine.

He laughed, looking down at her as she half reclined against the pillows, her hands under his robe, resting on his chest, her beautiful face lifted to him, her golden eyes so bright they seemed to glisten with life.

"What if I make you wait?" he teased. He knew how to pace himself.

"You can't," she playfully pouted.

"You're only a Countess." He touched her pouty lip. "I outrank you." The amusement in his eyes spilled over into his grin.

"I'm a Princess, too. My mother was Princess Kuzan. You may have heard of the Kuzans." Her voice was coquettish but touched with an aristocratic pride he recognized. "We own a great deal of Russia. I'm your equal," she breathed, reaching for the tie of his robe, "in rank and fortune."

It stopped him momentarily—not only the fact she was a Kuzan, but the manner in which she uttered the words. She meant it. An equal. It was a novel thought.

"I'll order you," she softly said, releasing the loose knot of his robe, sweeping aside the dark brocade to reveal his hard, masculine, roused body, and he was reminded that the Kuzans were known for their audacity.

He reached out to touch the turgid hardness of her peaked nipples, lifted them slightly until he saw her inhale deeply and briefly close her eyes. "Shall we see," he said, very, very softly, "how equal we are?" And with a shrug he dropped the robe from his shoulders and followed her down on the bed, covering her soft willing body with his.

She felt his weight for a moment before he propped himself on his arms, and she experienced an electrifying defenselessness, thrilling in its effect. He could do with her what he liked.

He was larger and stronger; he could lift her effortlessly like a child into his arms. But in his own way he was defenseless in his need for her, a power she possessed, a power she realized for the first exciting time in her life. It was like standing on a lighted threshold before a vista of perfect paradise. They *were* equals whether he knew it or not.

Her large golden eyes, framed with the lace of silken lashes, looked directly up into his and she said very quietly without entreaty or decree, her heated body throbbing with desire through every nerve and cell and racing pulse beat, "I must have you or I'll die."

And he gave her what she wanted because it was what he wanted, too. She was unlike other women he knew, so different he had no comparison. To please himself he had to please her, too. He was poised on the perimeters of unfamiliar emotional territory and perhaps he did it for her after all. It wasn't a time to debate or presciently attempt to see the future. He wanted her desperately and she him.

He gently touched the heated dampness between her thighs, his arousal quivering in his own need for her. Feeling her readiness and the surprising strength of her hands pulling him close, he said, "Hold on tight," a heartbeat before he thrust into her waiting body and buried himself in her honeyed sweetness.

She didn't cry out. She sighed, a great, melting, bewitching sigh, and he thought she must be a nymph sent from heaven or Olympus or Allah to welcome him back from the war. She reached up to kiss him and he smothered her waiting mouth with a restless kiss, feeling as though heaven had opened, as though his heart were beating outside his body. Then he began to move gently within her so she could feel the enchantment, too.

"My toes are curling," she blissfully murmured against his throat.

"I'm glad," he whispered, and bending his head, he nibbled at her mouth, pressing upward into her until she felt him fill her deep and hard and so intensely that she cried out in ecstasy.

"Am I dying?" she breathed a long moment later when the sound of her voice had faded into the night.

"No, darling, it's the very best of living, trust me," he murmured into the curls near her ear, and the rhythm of his lower body, slow and smooth and carefully choreographed to suit her, to please her, brought the entire focus of the world to the flame-hot center of her body. It *was* living, she thought, breathless, her pulse beating in her ears, her skin so hot she felt as though they were back on the plain of Kars. It was bliss and an open door into paradise. Was this love, too, she wondered, this torrid, melting lust? Did you love a man like this, skilled and perfect and so beautiful?

She hoped not, she thought in the small pocket of logic that remained in her dissolving brain. She hoped not because she'd get lost in the crowd.

It wouldn't be much longer, Stefan decided, short moments later, watching her eyes and the flush on her face and throat, aware of her small hands fiercely pulling him close so she could feel him longer and deeper and more intensely. She was the most flagrantly sensual woman he knew, untouched by convention, more heated in her intemperate response than his Gypsy lover. Maybe it was the Kuzan blood. Sensuality ran unbridled through the family. She was a glowing, extravagant woman and she was about to climax.

He met and joined her passion with his in a driving, insistent wildness that kept her agonized, dying with pleasure for long practised moments until she trembled with small gasping sobs in his arms and he poured, shuddering, into her. Then they lay, sheened with sweat, their heartbeats shaking the bed.

In the course of the summer night they dallied like the lovers in Hafiz, and he taught her what pleasure was. She would say into the moonlit room, breathless with passion, "You know that *too*?"

"And *that*?" She lay gilded with moonlight and pampered indulgence.

"And *that*?"

Finally he laughed and said, "I'll have to show you the Renaissance printmakers and the Japanese, sweet child. Hafiz is only one in a galaxy."

Her smile was new when she looked up at him lying above

her, and it was touched with a delightful sangfroid in addition to her habitual imperturbability.

"How nice," she said.

Three

In the morning the Prince decided against an immediate return to Tiflis. Instead he sent his troopers ahead and pursued idyllic leisured activities with the Countess for several additional days. And when they finally chose to travel north, the Countess's wardrobe having been hastily restored by Aleksandropol's only French dressmaker still in residence, the two-day journey stretched into a number of more delightfully lazy days.

Prince Bariatinsky's household, of course, had been on the alert for his appearance since his men had arrived days before, so when the Prince and Countess drew up to the grand marble staircase of his palace overlooking Tiflis, his entire staff was at attention in the drive while two women—one elderly, the other young—stood on the first broad landing waiting their arrival.

His aunt lived with him, so her appearance was expected, but the younger woman Stefan recognized with a start. What was *Nadejda* doing two thousand miles from Saint Petersburg? He absorbed the shock with no visible change in his expression and bestowed casual greetings on the servants as he helped Lisaveta dismount. After introducing her to his majordomo, who greeted her with a proper bow and a friendly smile, Stefan escorted Lisaveta up the rank of white marble stairs to the broad balustraded landing where the two women waited.

Lisaveta assumed the small, trim, grey-haired woman was Stefan's aunt. He'd assured her Militza would be pleased to have her as a guest before she resumed her journey home to her estate near Rostov. But he hadn't mentioned anyone else. And while Stefan's aunt was smiling, the pretty blonde at her side was not. Was the scowling young lady a niece constrained from her own amusements to wait here and greet her uncle? Or simply some family friend, sulky by nature? She would soon find out since Stefan was about to introduce her.

With his hand lightly holding her elbow, Stefan moved with Lisaveta the short distance across the polished marble landing to where the two ladies stood. "Countess Lazaroff," he said, his voice touched with his usual nonchalance, "I'd like you to meet my Aunt Militza and my—" He hesitated the smallest instant.

"Fiancée," the fair-haired woman interjected firmly, her smile tight.

"Princess Nadejda Taneiev," he said, as though he hadn't spent the last eight days in bed with Lisaveta, "may I present the Countess Lisaveta Lazaroff."

"You wouldn't be Felix's daughter?" Militza asked, ignoring Nadejda's anger and Lisaveta's embarrassment, her casual inquiry similar in tone to her nephew's when introducing his newest paramour to his fiancée.

"Yes," Lisaveta and Stefan answered simultaneously, she in nervous response, he because he found himself strangely concerned his aunt like her.

"I knew your father years ago. He was a delightful dancer."

Lisaveta couldn't help but smile, even though her temper was beginning to rise at Stefan's deceit or omission or whatever word best described his failure to mention he was engaged. Not that she was some naive adolescent who expected an offer of marriage after their intimacy—after all she had wanted him as much, if not more. But she expected a certain degree of honesty. She didn't realize *that* showed her naïveté. Honesty was hardly an essential in matters of amour; play words were more useful, love words, pretty turns of phrase universally applied.

"I didn't know he danced well," she replied, admiring Stefan's aunt's warm smile. So her father's accomplishments weren't confined to scholarly pursuits; this new image was pleasant. "I never saw him dance," she added.

"He was a favorite of all the ladies before your mama decided she wanted him. Did you meet Stefan at Maribelle?" Lisaveta's mother had once owned an estate by that name near Aleksandropol.

"Actually, no. Maman sold it before she died. I met Stefan on the plain between Kars and Aleksandropol." Lisaveta paused, not knowing where or how to begin.

"She was abducted by the Bazhis," Stefan interjected. "We had given chase—"

"And you rescued her," Nadejda said in a malevolent tone.

At Nadejda's vitriolic sarcasm, Stefan's gaze swung from his aunt to his fiancée.

Despite her own fury at Stefan's oversight in informing her of his fiancée, Lisaveta was still deeply grateful to him. Whatever her reservations concerning his character, he *had* rescued her. "He saved my life," she said calmly.

"And you naturally rewarded him."

"Nadejda," Stefan said. The single word was an order to silence.

"Why don't we go up to the house for tea?" Militza interjected, shamelessly pleased Stefan had reprimanded his fiancée. She'd been forced to endure the girl's uncharitable company for Nadejda had unexpectedly arrived in Tiflis with her parents on a visit to the Viceroy.

Felix Lazaroff's daughter was very beautiful, Militza thought, although not to Stefan's usual taste in women, which gravitated toward glamorous blondes. This girl was refined and delicate, her features touched with the ingenue, although her height was a shade above the average. Stefan usually preferred small women. How interesting, she speculated. As interesting as his cryptic note mentioning he might bring home a guest. Haci had defined the word *guest* for her, but more interesting yet was the fact Stefan invited the Countess to his home. A staggering first.

Months ago she'd watched with constrained silence as Stefan coldly selected a fiancée, appalled at his final choice. Nadejda was absolutely without endearing qualities. She was certainly striking, if one favored cool, fair-haired beauties from wealthy, powerfully connected families. But Stefan could have had anyone. When she'd said as much to him rather wrathfully when he'd come back to Tiflis engaged, he'd only shrugged and said, not in explanation but in simple statement, "I only had a week furlough."

Lisaveta was desperately trying to formulate a suitable reply to Militza's suggestion of tea, for she wanted nothing less than to have to socialize with Stefan's malicious fiancée, when Stefan interposed. "Perhaps we could wash up first," he said, stalling for time, thinking hell and damnation, what bloody bad luck. Nadejda should have been in Saint Petersburg, two thousand miles away. "The roads are awash with dust this time of year," he added.

Thank you, Lisaveta thought gratefully, but then Stefan was adroit at lying, wasn't he, she decided, his "surprise" fiancée glaring at her. All she wanted to do was get away from this uncomfortable situation, find a coach traveling north very soon and leave Stefan Bariatinsky to the mercy of his fiancée.

Since they had dallied on the outskirts of Tiflis the previous night, reluctant to bring their passionate holiday to an end, neither Stefan nor Lisaveta was in fact at all begrimed by travel. Stefan's white Chevalier Gardes uniform was pristine while Lisaveta's simple white piqué summer gown was bandbox fresh.

Ignoring the graphic evidence before her eyes, Aunt Militza said with a practiced courtesy, "Of course, you *must* rinse off the dust of your journey. We'll see you on the terrace in half an hour." This latter statement was delivered in a tone very like Stefan's when issuing orders to his men, Lisaveta thought, having witnessed the departure of his troop from Aleksandropol.

And surprisingly Stefan deferred with a nod of acknowledgement. There was an authority higher than his, Lisaveta realized, or at least in some circumstances there was. Or at least for trivialities like teatime there was.

"Come, Nadejda," Militza declared firmly, "you can help me with tea."

Nadejda hesitated briefly, her eyes moving dismissively over Lisaveta to rest on Stefan. She was weighing the risks of refusing when her violet shaded eyes met forcibly with Stefan's dark gaze.

"We'll be along directly," he said, without modulation, and it was that precise lack of inflection perhaps, the utter quiet of his tone, that decided her. After all, Stefan Bariatinsky was the catch not only of this season but of ten seasons past, as well, and she had been raised to be a practical woman.

For a moment after the two women departed, the only sound was the whisper of the wind through the gigantic cypress trees lining the ornate staircase. Grafted from those planted by Catherine the Great during her triumphant tour through the Crimea nearly a century before, they dwarfed even the magnificent villa on the crest of the hill.

"Why didn't you tell me?" Lisaveta said, speaking first, her voice a low, intense, restrained resonance.

She was tanned, Stefan thought, gazing down at her. The crisp white piqué must heighten the color of her sun-kissed skin. He hadn't noticed before. And the slight breeze was blowing tendrils of her chestnut hair across her bare shoulders. Silk on silk, he mused.

"Why?" she repeated, refocusing his attention from more pleasant thoughts.

"I didn't think it mattered," he simply said, which was the truth. His fiancée was quite separate from his love life.

"Didn't *matter*?" Lisaveta's golden eyes were stormy.

He wanted to say the information was extraneous to their relationship but he wasn't that crudely impolite. Instead he said, "The opportunity didn't arise."

"In *eight* days?"

He sighed then, a faint, almost negligible sigh encompassing a vast experience with irate women and unanswerable questions. "I'm sorry," he apologized.

She looked at him with scorn and anger and incredulity. After eight days of unremitting passion, after eight days of laughter and conversation, after nights when neither had slept because their need for each other was too intense, that was all.... "You're *sorry*? For what? That I found out?"

He was primarily sorry Nadejda was in Tiflis, but that too would have been unprincipled to admit, so he opted for a less callous reply. "I should have told you. I'm sorry."

"Yes, you should have."

"Would it have mattered?" he asked then very quietly, touching her arm lightly in an intimate, familiar caress.

His low voice and the gentle intimacy of his fingertips on her skin sent a shiver of warm response coursing through her body. "Don't touch me," Lisaveta said in a tone meant to be harshly emphatic but hushed instead and much too soft.

"She doesn't matter." Stefan's voice too was hushed, and he moved a step nearer.

"She should."

He only shrugged, the convoluted reasons for his choice of fiancée beyond brief or rational explanation. "Don't be angry." His voice was husky, his dark eyes much too close now, just as his powerful body was. Lisaveta moved a step back.

"They might be watching."

"We're only talking."

"I'm not as blasé as you."

"I'll teach you." He smiled then and added in a hushed undertone, "And you can teach me more of Hafiz."

She tried to keep from smiling, she tried to remind herself he was an unprincipled libertine and much too beautiful for his own good. She reminded herself his reputation was legendary, she shouldn't respond to his warm suggestive smile. But he winked at her, his lush, dark lashes falling and rising in a lazy indolent gesture. "We're only on poem nineteen."

All the heated nights and days of lovemaking came pouring back into her memory...with his teasing smile like now, and his teasing hands and lips and expertise. She couldn't resist smiling back. "Scoundrel."

"Never," he said. "A moralist's term, and I didn't hear you complain before."

"I hadn't met your fiancée before."

"My palace has two hundred and eighteen rooms."

"You're much too pragmatic."

"A soldier's training. Forgive me, *dushka*…and forgive her intrusion. I'm truly sorry." He brushed his finger gently along the curve of her shoulder. "I hope she won't upset you. I'd like you to stay and visit." His voice was as warmly coaxing as his smile. "You'll like Militza. She's outspoken but delightful, and I've a month's leave."

This was the first he'd mentioned her staying or the length of his furlough. Perhaps he'd assumed she'd stay, perhaps women always stayed as long as he wished. After the paradise of the past eight days, she understood why that might happen. However, she too was pragmatic and much too sensible to allow herself to become simply another of the parade of women passing through Prince Stefan Bariatinsky's life. "Thank you, but no. I must return home to my estate as soon as possible."

"Stay a few days."

She shook her head.

He gazed at her, his expression unreadable. "You won't?"

"I can't."

"Why?"

"I've things to do."

"Even though I risked my life to save you from the Turks?" She smiled. "Does that work often?"

He grinned. "Every time."

"Except one."

"Truly?"

She nodded. "Truly."

"You'll stay until tomorrow, won't you?" His voice was as courteous as a young boy's, his dark eyes innocently polite. "Aunt Militza will be inconsolate if she doesn't have a first-person account of your adventures, and she *is* a friend of your father's," he added with gentle emphasis.

Lisaveta hesitated, weighing logic against her charged feelings, the apparent sincerity of Stefan's request against the history of his past. "Just tonight?" she inquired, gauging the extent of her risk.

"That's it."

"*If* I don't have to be more than civil to your scowling fiancée."

"Agreed," Stefan quickly said, intent on having Lisaveta stay on any terms. Tonight he'd change her mind. He was confident.

The view was superb from the terrace, the sun pleasantly shaded by a rose trellis, the wind negligible, a samovar of great beauty the centerpiece of a magnificently arrayed tea table, when Lisaveta joined the party of three some twenty minutes later.

Teatime turned out to be interesting.

It was also enlightening.

Stefan, it seemed, had known Nadejda only three days before he proposed.

Lisaveta had never met a true society miss.

Aunt Militza had met one too many and intended doing her best to see that Nadejda didn't enter her family permanently, though she was wise enough to keep her plans to herself.

"Were you raped, my dear?" Aunt Militza pleasantly inquired after the weather and state of the roads and progress of the war had been exhausted as topics of conversation. She offered Lisaveta a plate of pastel-frosted petits fours as though she were asking a perfectly mundane question. At the stunned look on Lisaveta's face, Aunt Militza pointedly added, "I mean by the Bazhis, of course."

Stefan choked as unobtrusively as possible on his mouthful of pâté and glared at his aunt. Nadejda hardly needed any prompting to anger. She'd already been rude to Lisaveta a dozen times. Swallowing quickly, he said, "Rest easy, Auntie, our troop arrived in time."

"How fortuitous," Militza replied, smiling as if the sun had finally broken through after a month of torrential storms. "Isn't that fortuitous?" she repeated, turning toward Nadejda, her smile intact.

"Stefan is known for his good fortune," Nadejda retorted, her lips pursed, her eyes cold enough to chill the equator.

But her words were the truth. He was, in fact, looked upon

by superstitious people as leading a charmed life. Many of the soldiers in the Tsar's army touched Stefan for luck, viewing him as a pagan deity of sorts. He'd never been wounded, never harmed in all the years of leading his troops into battle, although he was always conspicuously in the lead of his cavalry, dressed not in battlefield uniform but in the striking white dress uniform of the Chevalier Gardes. His men would follow him anywhere, and on more than one occasion his bold charges had changed the course of battle.

"As is our entire family," Stefan's aunt cheerfully declared. "Although Lisaveta must have a guardian angel, too, traveling alone in a war zone. Why ever were you out there?"

Lisaveta explained in some detail why she'd been in Kara-kilisa and why she'd left so precipitously.

"A harem?" Aunt Militza said, obviously fascinated. "How exciting."

"Only from a distance," Lisaveta plainly replied, "I assure you."

"How disgusting," Nadejda said, her inflection managing to include Lisaveta in her assessment.

"And Hafiz?" Stefan's aunt went on as though Nadejda hadn't spoken. "He's one of my favorite poets. You must see Stefan's collection."

"*I* haven't seen it, Stefan," Nadejda pouted. "Why haven't you shown it to *me*?"

"You wouldn't like it, Nadejda," Militza said bluntly. Turning back to Lisaveta, she asked, "Don't you think Hafiz compares favorably with Ovid?"

"I think, Stefan, that if you have a collection you favor, I should know of it," Nadejda declared peevishly, arresting the consumption of her sixth frosted cake to state her annoyance. "At Madame Lebsky's Academy I won a first prize for poetry. Madame Lebsky said she'd never heard a better iambic pentameter."

Stefan was briefly at a loss since conversations about his collection of erotica were not usual in mixed company at tea. He frowned at his aunt over his fiancée's blond head. Nadejda, momentarily distracted by the recalled beauty of her verse, was inwardly focused, her eyes half-closed in contemplation.

Stefan's aunt only smiled at him warmly as though she were beyond reproach.

"Darling," Nadejda said, her resentment forgotten with the memory of her cleverness in poetry, "would you like to hear my prize-winning poem?"

There was only one suitable answer, he knew, and he gave it.

They were instantly regaled with breathy drama and coy smiles to a rhyming description of a lake at sunset. Nadejda's metaphors were sugary, her similes strangely food focused. Long moments of heavy-handed rhyme later, Stefan worried he'd ever be able to enjoy a sunset again without visualizing caramel syrup dripping over the horizon.

Polite applause followed the poem's conclusion, however, a pleased preening smile graced Nadejda's flawless face, and an insidious sinking feeling settled in Stefan's stomach. He'd only squired his fiancée to receptions and balls the week he was on leave in Saint Petersburg, and their conversations had been interrupted and minimal in such circumstances. Was she truly so vacuous?

"Thank you, Nadejda," Militza said dismissively, although her tone was scrupulously cordial. "Stefan, why don't you take Nadejda for a stroll so that Lisaveta and I won't bother you with our discussion of Ovid."

Militza's suggestions were always delivered as well-mannered commands, but Stefan balked this time, his temper and patience on edge in his unaccustomed role of chivalrous fiancé to a woman who wrote such dreadful pedestrian poetry. "The Countess Lazaroff and I have some business to discuss, I'm afraid," he said. "She requires some bank drafts for her journey home. If you'll excuse us until dinner." He rose abruptly in no frame of mind to be further thwarted by his aunt or any female.

He needn't have concerned himself with his aunt's response. She was delighted to let her nephew go off with his new lover on whatever flimsy pretext he chose, and her smile was beatific when she gazed up at him towering above her. "By all means, Stefan, the Countess must be assured of her financial resources after having been left destitute on the steppes. Should we put dinner off until ten?"

Stefan's emphatic "Yes" and Lisaveta's "No" clashed starkly.

"My financial affairs won't be difficult to arrange," Lisaveta explained with a calm she was far from feeling. "I'm sure a banker in Tiflis will accommodate my needs. And if my name isn't recognized, either Papa's or cousin Nikki's will be sufficient." Lisaveta refused to fall into any of Stefan's plans. If he couldn't abide his fiancée's company, she wasn't going to be a convenient alternative, and if he thought he could snap his fingers and have her follow him, he had a lesson to learn. "Thank you, Stefan," she said with serene sweetness, "but your concern is unnecessary," and she reached for her teacup.

His arm shot out across his aunt's chair, his fingers closing around Lisaveta's wrist with her fingers just short of her teacup. "No reason, *mademoiselle*, to involve Nikki when my banker is amenable. And you forget," he said, his voice softly emphatic as he pulled her to her feet, took the lace napkin from her hand and placed it on the table, "your father's papers, which Haci saved from the Bazhis, need your attention."

She imagined he *would* prefer not involving Nikki, and as far as papers... He was thoroughly without scruple. There were no papers. For a moment Lisaveta considered exposing him before his rancorous fiancée. It would serve him right. She would simply deny the fictitious papers in embarrassing detail, but on second thought, he was offering her escape along with his own, and it didn't make much sense to suffer here over tea when freedom beckoned.

"I'm sure it won't take more than a few hours to sort them all and make certain nothing important is missing," he said, smiling, conscious she was acquiescing. "Should we say dinner at ten?" He waited, confident and assured, his intense dark eyes offering her...pleasure.

She waited perhaps five seconds before replying, because his assurance annoyed her. "Thank you," she finally said. "I'd like to see Papa's reports, but we needn't put off dinner." She turned to Aunt Militza. "Eight will be fine."

Aunt Militza conceded equal points to the two protagonists. How interesting the Countess would be for Stefan. He was familiar only with acquiescence and command. Countess Lazaroff apparently was, as well. "Eight it is," she said. "Now run along. I'm sure Nadejda and I would be bored to tears with reports."

As Stefan and Lisaveta left the terrace Nadejda was saying, "Stefan must show me his collection for it will be mine, too, very soon, and poetry is such a love."

"You are completely unscrupulous," Lisaveta said irritably, trying to shake his hand from her wrist. Stefan had guided her across the terrace and through the glass doors into the palace with what appeared a polite courtesy, but his grip was steel hard and he wouldn't be dislodged. "Let go of me!" Lisaveta snapped, struggling to wrench free. "You're unprincipled...selfish...you're—"

"—attracted as hell to you," he finished with that smile of his that she'd learned in the past week was capable of melting the polar ice cap. His fingers still firmly circled her wrist as his long stride took them rapidly through the drawing room adjoining the terrace.

"Don't try and dazzle me with that damn smile," she pettishly rebuffed, already feeling an answering heat through her senses.

"Temper, darling, the servants are watching." His smile was benign.

"I'm *not* your darling," she repudiated, "and knowing you, I'm sure the servants have seen considerably more than a woman arguing with you." Bristling with outrage at her body's eager, complacent response, vexed at *his* complacent response to a fiancée in the house, indignant he could so cavalierly ignore all but his own selfish interests, she continued huffily, "Knowing you, they could probably write their own manual on amorous technique simply from walking in on you, since you have no sense of propriety—*Stefan*, where are you taking me, tell me this second or I'll cause a scene, I swear, better yet, let me go and I'll forget any of this happened, I'll see you at dinner. Why don't you,'' she breathlessly went on as she was pulled down the hallway at a pace she had to run to accommodate, ''spend the remainder of the afternoon showing Nadejda your Hafiz collection.''

He laughed then. He didn't slow his progress, but clearly he was amused. ''Do you think she'd like it?'' His grin was wicked.

''I think you might have trouble getting her to the altar if you did.''

''It's a thought,'' he softly said.

''You don't know her, do you?''

He was opening the door to his study, his favorite haven in his two-hundred-and-eighteen-room palace, a comfortable room filled with mementos precious to him. ''I only saw her for a week, six months ago. She writes, and I answer occasionally.''

Lisaveta wasn't a complete recluse from the aristocratic world she'd been born into. She understood most marriages were arranged for a variety of reasons having nothing to do with love, but Stefan had so much to offer a woman it seemed a shame he'd chosen such a bride. Even the manner of his choosing had been unusually prosaic. ''When will you be married?''

''Sometime next year, I suppose.'' He could have been telling his valet which boots he preferred for all the feeling in his voice. ''It's not a first priority, believe me. I may be dead by then if the Turks break through at Kars. Come sit down and talk to me,'' he said in a different tone, a quiet reflective nuance underlying his calm directive.

''I don't want to.'' She stood straight and tall, free now from his grasp.

He hesitated a moment before dropping into a down-cushioned chair upholstered in a tapestry incorporating his princely arms. Looking up at her he said very softly, ''I wish you would.''

Lisaveta sighed. His harsh features were tranquil, his powerful body relaxed against the burgundy silk, his dark eyes intent on her. Alone in his inner sanctum, surrounded by his personal mementos—photos of the Tsar; framed portraits of his parents, himself; precious jeweled icons and cabinets of medals; dress swords and weaponry—he was charismatic, the warrior in repose, the savior of Russia in private, the most sought-after man in Europe, and he was asking her to sit and talk.

Perhaps she had too many principles when he had none, perhaps she would later rue her choices, perhaps she should simply say yes to his invitation—and perhaps if his fiancée were not down the hall she might. But Lisaveta resisted being classed with all the other women to whom he'd extended similar casual invitations. She would make her own choices. Not he.

"I can never thank you enough for saving my life," she said, beginning to pace slowly before him as though her movement added authority to her resistance.

A promising start, he thought, and relaxed further.

"And certainly I'll remember forever the pleasure of the past week."

The feeling was mutual, he reflected. The days with Lisaveta had been not only passionate beyond his usual lust but different in character because they spoke to each other, their conversation an easy exchange of ideas and feelings. He'd never talked with a woman like the Countess Lazaroff. She seemed very like a friend, but much better, he decided a moment later, because she was a lush and sensual woman, as well.

"You are quite frankly—" Lisaveta stopped and gazed at Stefan levelly "—much better than any erotic fantasy I could have imagined." She was beautifully straightforward, and more than her compliment he admired her candor. "However—" and she began pacing again "—I'm not inclined to continue our pleasant relationship under your fiancée's nose. I know this isn't a concern for you but it is for me. Let's just say—it was nice." She stopped before him again. "But let's be sensible."

He'd listened politely, neither moving nor interrupting while she expressed her feelings, only watching her silently as she moved across the thick Kuba carpet, his dark eyes drifting occasionally to her slippered feet crushing the luxurious pile. Hand loomed near his mountain home, the navy-and-russet carpet reminded him powerfully of childhood summers, of his favorite retreat...and of his wish to take Lisaveta there. "I don't want to be sensible," he said, unmoving still.

"And *I'm* not interested in what you want." Lisaveta stood utterly motionless, as though her explanation had clarified both her mind and her restlessness.

Stefan's voice was almost hushed when he answered. "Are you interested in what *you* want?"

She didn't pretend to misunderstand either his tone or his words. "Are you talking about sex? Why don't you just say it? Do you want to know if I want you?"

He shook his head, his first movement since he'd dropped into the chair, and even that response was minimal.

Her brows rose in brief surprise. "You don't?"

"I already know that. I was wondering if *you* were willing to acknowledge it."

His casual arrogance annoyed her. Prince Stefan Bariatinsky was much too confident. "I'm not afraid to acknowledge it. Surely after our leisurely trip north you're aware of my interest in your...assets."

He smiled faintly at her choice of words.

"I'm not, however, interested in the current triangle, which includes your fiancée."

"I had no idea Nadejda would be here." His voice was low and matter-of-fact. It wasn't an apology, only a statement.

Lisaveta grimaced. "But she is. And angry and resentful. With reason. I don't blame her."

"We could leave."

"No we couldn't," she protested. "No, I don't *want* to. No, I'm not open to other options to satisfy your salacious urges. No! Don't touch me!" she impassionedly finished as Stefan rose with a startling swiftness.

He stood very quietly for a moment as though her words had rebuffed him, and then he reached up to unbutton the collar hooks of his uniform tunic. The silver braided collar loosened and he pulled it away slightly from his tanned neck. "I won't if you don't want me to," he softly said, his hand dropping to his side.

"Good. I don't." She should have moved away then. It would have imparted more credulity to her declaration. But she didn't, and he took note of that omission.

"Do you know how much death and carnage I've seen in the past three months?" She didn't answer, and he continued, only his voice conveying his restlessness. "The Turks can skin a man alive," he quietly said. "It takes hours the way they do it. The screams are unearthly. You never forget them." He drew in a deep breath before continuing, and his voice dropped even further in volume. "They echo in your mind and make you break out in a cold sweat. They keep you awake at night, they make you pray to God you're never captured alive. They make you vow to die fighting. And you wonder at your courage, at your will to go on to another month of war, or two or six months, when you hardly sleep anymore, when you're afraid to shut your eyes because it could mean your death or, worse, your capture. When you haven't been clean in weeks and the food is grim or at best adequate. When you hear every day of another friend who's died. Thousands of Russian troops have died in assaulting Kars, and the only reason I'm on leave now is that replacements have to be brought up." His gaze surveyed the luxury of his surroundings as if to reassure himself he was safe from the black demons of the war and then came back to her.

"You helped me forget last week," he declared very simply.

"You did for me, as well," Lisaveta replied.

"We helped each other then." He smiled his achingly beautiful smile. "And you reminded me there's goodness and laughter and love in the world."

"I know, Stefan," Lisaveta breathed, her voice almost inaudible, the quiet of the room surrounding them like silken solace. "I know what you're feeling. Life and living mean so much more to me now for having almost died. But I won't…" she quietly added. "Please…" Her eyes were the color of warm sunsets and not pleading so much as patient. "Just thank you…I mean it truly. Thank you for everything."

She knew her feelings were becoming too involved with Russia's most exalted hero. He was so much more than his grand and valorous public image. She was drawn to his wit and intelligence as well as attracted to his harsh beauty, while his gentleness and expertise as a lover were pure perfection. She could never stay, so she must leave before her feelings were so deeply committed he would be forever in her heart. Her chin lifted a scant distance and her voice took on a new determination. "I'm going upstairs to rest before dinner and I intend to leave in the morning."

"You're sure?"

"I am."

He smiled. "And nothing I can say will change your mind?"

"Stefan," Lisaveta said, returning his smile, feeling more confident with her decision made, "you can have any woman in the Empire. You don't need me." Turning to go, she couldn't resist the obvious pointed barb. "Besides, Nadejda's here to entertain you."

It was not a pleasant thought. "Bitch," he whispered, the word ambiguously caressing.

Lisaveta grinned. "I couldn't resist. Forgive me." But her apology was lighthearted and unapologetic. "Until dinner, *mon chou*," she buoyantly said, feeling new strength in the rightness of her choice, and blowing him a smiling kiss, she left.

"Until tonight, *mon chou*," Stefan softly breathed. He'd make love to her then and convince her to stay, the best soldier in the Tsar's army vowed. And he'd never lost a campaign in his life.

Four

Nadejda wore lavender crepe de chine with diamonds in her hair at dinner, and were it not for her disagreeable tongue she would have been the picture of radiant beauty. She had, however, since being seated, complained of the heat, taken issue with the servants' casual behavior and condemned the country style of food numerous times. Her patience curtailed by yet another remark about its quaintness, Aunt Militza coolly said to her, "Stefan has a Georgian palate and refuses to have a French chef."

"We have *always* had a French chef," Nadejda replied, as though her wishes were primary, as though she were already running the household. Her mama had assured her she would have total control since men preferred detachment from household functions.

"Perhaps you should think of adding a Georgian chef, as well," Militza retorted, trying to keep the annoyance out of her voice. Her family had been royalty for a thousand years before the Taneievs had been elevated to princely status.

"Surely Stefan enjoys French cuisine, don't you, my dear." Nadejda turned to Stefan with her winning smile, the smile she felt had successfully gained Stefan's attention in Saint Petersburg six months ago.

Stefan, dressed comfortably in the embroidered silk shirt and loose trousers native to his mother's land, was sprawled back in his chair, his wineglass in hand. His expression had remained unreadable while Nadejda had complained, Militza had seethed and the two women had discussed him as if he weren't present. While he appreciated Militza's advocacy for his taste in food, he could only see the disagreement escalating, and Nadejda's opinion on food or anything else was really rather incidental to him. He'd chosen her for a bride because her family was well connected at court, not for personal reasons. After the irregularity of his own childhood and his father's disgrace and loss of the Viceroyalty of the Caucasus, Stefan didn't care if Nadejda Taneiev liked African chefs, as long as the stability of the Taneiev family was intact. He was marrying that dependable stability, the court attachments, the conservative background. But he disliked the cattiness of Nadejda's tone and her grasping possessiveness as much as the thought of continuing disagreements over dinner when all he wanted to do was relax and drink his favorite wine from his own vineyard.

"I eat anything," he said blandly. "Militza, you know that. Nadejda can keep her French chef by all means. When you've campaigned as long as I, you learn to eat anything." He was the perfect host, pleasant, affable, ready to step in and smooth over controversy. "Georgi, more wine for the ladies." His majordomo, who stood beside Stefan's chair, signaled for a footman.

"Oh, no," Nadejda refused, waving away the servant. "Mama says a lady never has more than two glasses." Her lavender eyes, cool as her disdain, cast a scornful glance at Aunt Militza, who'd been keeping up with Stefan's consumption over dinner.

"Your mother was from the north," Militza curtly said, her brows drawn together in nettled pique, "where all they drink is tea to keep warm. Leave the bottle," she added to the young footman filling her glass.

Stefan couldn't help but smile at Militza's snappish answer to Nadejda's prudery. It could be a battlefield of a dinner, he thought, managing to hide his grin behind his uplifted wineglass. When he raised his eyes a moment later as the glass touched his lips, his gaze met Lisaveta's, and immediately memories returned of the bottle of wine they'd shared one morning in an enormous wooden tub set out on a flower-bedecked terrace. The sun had been warm, and they warmer still, hot with need and tumultuous passion, and the wine, chilled in a nearby mountain stream, was ambrosia to senses already attuned to pleasure. They had made love endlessly and then much later laughed with silliness and frivolous intimacy, as if they were the only two people in the world. Tonight, he thought, he'd touch her again and kiss her and make her laugh and give to her the enormous pleasure she'd given him.

Lisaveta dropped her eyes first before his dark gaze, more concerned with appearances than he. Stefan never cared about comportment; in that he was his father's son. Only his betrothal to Princess Taneiev was an aberration in personality. No one on either branch of his family had ever been practical. There had been no need with their wealth and status, but then, none before him had seen their father die in slow degrees, consumed by drugs, none had seen their father die a broken man living in exile at the spas of Europe. So Stefan was going to be practical in the one facet that had been his father's downfall. He would have a wife beyond reproach; he would have children with a legal patrimony from birth.

"Do you like my wines?" he asked Lisaveta. "They say some of the Georgian sun is captured in each bottle." He spoke to her as though no one else existed at the table.

"It does warm one's senses," she replied, her smile enchanting. After several glasses of wine Lisaveta found herself relaxed and without rancor. In fact, after listening to Nadejda over dinner, she'd actually begun feeling sorry for Stefan. The young woman was devoid of amusement or charm, fastidious only of her position and the refined affectations of society. How dreary for Stefan, who loved to laugh.

"It reminds me," Lisaveta went on, holding her glass up to the light, its golden contents rich and sunshiny, "of a special wine from Tzinondali Papa and I once had. Papa called it Angelglow because one's blood turned warm."

"Those," Stefan said, smiling back, "are my vineyards."

"*My* papa prefers French wines," Nadejda interjected. "He says only French wines are of superior quality and fit for the palate of a gentleman.'' She spoke to the table at large as though she were delivering news of importance. "The Emperor, you know, only drinks French champagne.''

Stefan knew better—Tsar Alexander had a fondness for his vintages and they'd shared many bottles together over the years—but Nadejda's insipidity wasn't his concern. "I'm sure you're right," he said in a detached way, more interested at the moment in the beautiful flush on Countess Lazaroff's cheeks. Had her smile been as suggestive as her remark or was he imagining her response? His eyes took in her azure gown and the way Militza's pearls at her neck and ears set off her sun-kissed skin to perfection. Considering the haste required of the dressmaker in Aleksandropol, she'd done exceptionally well, and his glance drifted down to the provocative splendor of Lisaveta's breasts displayed so enticingly by the low-cut décolletage. Even her skin exuded warmth; it glowed like his wine with fragrant allure, and he could almost smell its heated perfume.

Shifting slightly in his chair to accommodate his arousal, he glanced at the clock. Nine-thirty—four more courses to go. A brief half hour, he hoped, in conversation in the drawing room, and then everyone could retire. He was impatient and restless. Lisaveta was near enough to reach over and touch, but he couldn't. Because this stranger who was his fiancée had decided to spend several days in residence while her family visited the Viceroy in Tiflis.

Militza had to ask him twice whether Archduke Michael had returned to Saint Petersburg, and when she did finally gain his attention, his answer was brief. He didn't participate further in the conversation, and after all the discussion of his taste in food, he hardly ate, as though he were host by requirement but detached from the actual proceedings. Georgi, on an informal footing with his employer, coaxed him to try the sturgeon, which Stefan did to please him, but he wouldn't be cajoled to taste anything more until the sorbet—a lemon ice, Georgi reminded him, he'd favored since childhood.

He seemed very different here tonight, Lisaveta thought, a prince in his palace, familiar with deference, accustomed to being waited on, intent on his own interests, polite to his aunt with a genuine warmth but no more than civil to his fiancée, although he had every intention of spending the rest of his life with her. None of the casual intimacy she'd seen last week remained in his character; none of the animated banter or amused laughter she'd come to know was apparent. Not even a critical comment materialized to make him seem more human. And when Stefan rose directly after the lemon ice, she wasn't surprised.

"Forgive me, ladies," he said, excusing himself, "but I promised Haci some time after dinner. Thank you all for a pleasant evening," he added, then bowed politely and left the table.

As the door closed behind him, Militza said, "He was bored."

"Stefan isn't one for conversation," Nadejda retorted, as if she were the expert on Prince Stefan Bariatinsky after a week's acquaintance.

Poor child, Lisaveta thought, remembering their heated conversations on subjects as esoteric as Kurdish shaman mythology or as trivial as the state of dressmaking in Aleksandropol. She'd found Stefan a charming conversationalist, but if today was any indication of his attachment to Nadejda, he'd treat his wife abominably. She felt a sudden sympathy for the Princess Taneiev.

"If you don't mind," Nadejda declared, addressing Militza in a tone that suggested she didn't care if she minded or not, "I'd like to take charge of the dinner for my parents tomorrow night. Papa will *not* eat this—" her pouty lips curled upward in reproof "—native fare. I'll have a chef brought over from the Viceroy's palace."

Lisaveta's sympathy instantly evaporated at Nadejda's insufferable tone and priggish demand. Stefan might not deal with his future wife affectionately, she reflected, but his wishes in turn weren't of the slightest interest to her. Their bargain for a marriage of convenience apparently was equally made. Princess Taneiev didn't love Stefan, it was obvious. She didn't look at him with affection or longing. She seemed immune to his sensuality—a startling revelation to Lisaveta, who found his attraction so powerful it outweighed all perceptible logic. But Nadejda was very young and perhaps simply unawakened. Or more likely, as her prudish comments on a variety of subjects denoted, she was very much attached to her mother's primly artificial views on life. She would probably find the concept of love too emotional. Mama no doubt would have a homily to that effect.

A shame when Stefan was so very easy to love.

A shame, she thought with a flashing spontaneity of feeling, when she could love him so very much.

"Bring over the entire staff if you wish, my dear," Aunt Militza replied, her voice suspiciously warm. "Stefan won't mind at all," she added with an innocence that was entirely out of character.

"Very good," Nadejda replied in a tone one would use to a servant. "And if you have other plans, I'm sure we won't need you in attendance tomorrow night." It was a blatantly rude dismissal. Nadejda was extremely self-centered, a personality trait humored by her parents, who had allowed her whims in every instance save those that might interfere with theirs. She had been pampered, spoiled in a small-girl way and schooled in the normal studies considered proper for refined young ladies, which meant that she was, in effect, uneducated. Her world was luxurious but narrow, and she considered her wishes preeminent because no one had to date disabused her of that notion. Stefan had a tendency, it seemed, to be abrupt and caustic, if today was any indication, she decided, but Mama had warned her of men's moodiness and told her it was best to ignore or simply smile it away and then later...do as you wished. She thought Mama's advice quite sensible, and certainly everyone agreed her smile was radiant. She used it on Militza.

"I did have plans for bridge," Militza said, her meekness so unusual anyone with half a brain would have been instantly alert.

"Well, that's settled then," Nadejda said, pleased Stefan's aunt was eliminated from her family party. She had tried to like her but found Militza had very little conversation; she couldn't talk about fashion or the latest gossip from Saint Petersburg. She read, it seemed, and helped train Stefan's polo ponies and actually oversaw the farms and vineyards on Stefan's estates. Nadejda found her odd, and thought Mama and Papa would prefer an intimate evening alone with Stefan.

"If there's anything you need…" Militza offered.

"No, thank you, I'm sure the Viceroy's staff is adequate, and since tomorrow will be an enormously busy day," Nadejda said, rising, "I'll retire early. Have the carriage brought round at nine and I'll drive to the Viceroy's to gather the necessary servants." She could have been addressing her housekeeper. But then Nadejda viewed herself as a superior young woman from a superior family, and while the Orbelianis might be wealthy, they were, after all, not Russians but Georgians. She found it very satisfying that Stefan on his father's side was related to the Tsar.

"Pleasant dreams, my dear," Militza responded, her expression wreathed in smiles. "I'll see to the carriage." When Nadejda swept from the room in a froth of lavender crepe, Militza leaned back in her chair, motioned to have her wineglass refilled, took it from Georgi with a complacent sigh and said, "Thank you, Georgi, we won't be needing you any longer. Tell the staff to retire. All this will wait until morning." She indicated the table with a small gesture.

Leaving the bottle within reach, Georgi stood for a moment at her side. He was a middle-aged man with the dark coloring of the region and a pleasant manner. "The Prince seemed—" He searched for the word, obviously used to discussing Stefan with Militza.

"Bored, Georgi, there's no polite way to say it. Princess Taneiev is dismally boring and deplorably stupid. He's going to hate himself a week after the wedding."

Too courteous to denigrate a female, Georgi mentioned instead, "The Prince won't want to see the Viceroy's staff, Princess. Why did you allow her license?"

"Because he'll be furious, Georgi, that's why." Militza's dark eyes, very much like Stefan's, gleamed with glee.

Georgi beamed, an instant coconspirator. "Ah...of course, and our staff is dismissed then for the day."

"We wouldn't want you 'natives' to get in the way of those frogs from the Viceroy's, Georgi. Everyone has the day off." Sheer unmitigated cheer resounded in Militza's voice.

His bow was sweepingly dramatic, indicative of his own agreement to Militza's plan. "Thank you, Your Excellency." Turning to Lisaveta he inquired politely, "Would you care for more wine, Countess, before I leave, or perhaps a sweet?"

"No, thank you," Lisaveta replied, intrigued by the extent servant and mistress felt they could interfere in Stefan's life, "although Stefan's wines are exceptional."

"We think so," Georgi returned. His family had been personal servants to the Orbelianis centuries before Georgia was annexed to the Russian Empire. The vineyards, he felt, were as much a part of his family as Stefan's. In fact, his brother was head vintner for Stefan.

"A shame Nadejda's family drink only French wines," Militza said very softly.

Directing his attention back to his mistress, Georgi said in an equally soft voice, "She won't do."

"Exactly."

"If you need anything, Excellency, the staff is at your disposal." His tone was moderate, but aware of the warrior code so prevalent in this area of the country, Lisaveta wondered precisely what "anything" implied.

"We'll begin by clearing the palace," Militza briskly said. "Please have everyone out by morning. Stefan should appreciate that interference from his fiancée."

"Excellent idea, Princess." Georgi reminded her, grinning from ear to ear.

"I know," Militza winked. "Have a pleasant holiday."

"Won't he be angry with you?" Lisaveta asked as soon as Georgi left. She was unfamiliar with palace intrigue, her own tranquil life with her father insufficient education for the subtleties of manipulating people. As an only child with her father alone for company, Lisaveta was unaccustomed to the machinations of society. "What if Stefan discovers what you've done?"

"I expect he will first thing in the morning. Actually I'm counting on it, but then I'm only accommodating his fiancée," Militza replied, her sweet tone one of unalloyed delight. "The one," she reminded Lisaveta, "he picked out in three days because she best met his requirements for *stability*."

"I see," Lisaveta said when she didn't see at all, when she envisioned instead a tangle of complications and disorder. "You can't mean stability," she added, as the word registered. "Not for Stefan. He lives his life on the brink."

"As did his father before him." Militza expelled a small sigh. "Which is the basic problem." She looked into the golden liquid in her wineglass for a brief moment before her gaze came up and she went on, "You must know of Stefan's father's lengthy liaison with Princess Davidow and the scandal."

"Only vaguely," Lisaveta answered. "Father was reclusive after Maman died. His studies absorbed him increasingly—to fill the void of Maman's loss, I suppose. As I grew older, they occupied me, as well." It was natural she'd adopted her father's field of study since she'd always traveled with him. "The only scandal I'm fully aware of," Lisaveta added, smiling a small rueful smile, "is Stefan's reputation for amorous intrigue."

Militza shrugged. "A young man's normal interest," she said. "His father's scandal, though, is going to ruin Stefan's life." She looked at Lisaveta across the remnants of dinner. "He hasn't said anything to you of his family?"

"Nothing except you wouldn't mind me as a guest. As you saw earlier today," she went on, her fingers tracing the pattern of the tablecloth in a nervous gesture, "he hadn't even mentioned he had a fiancée."

"He didn't expect her to be here, although that's no excuse, only an explanation…and in a way, perhaps that omission is typical of Stefan. Because of his background, he rarely confronts emotion directly."

"Do you think so?" Lisaveta's question was contemplative

more than inquiring, for in many ways Stefan was an intensely
emotional man.

"In terms of his family, at least," Militza said, and Lisaveta
had to agree. In those terms he'd been extremely reticent.

"There was a love affair, wasn't there," Lisaveta said, trying
to recall the exact circumstances, "between Field Marshal Bariatinsky and—"

"My sister." Militza's words seemed suspended for a moment in the quiet of the room.

"Stefan's mother?"

"Yes. They shocked society by living together openly all
the years of the Field Marshal's Viceroyalty of the Caucasus,
although my sister, Damia, was married to another man. When
Stefan was born, our parents adopted him to ensure the conti-
nuity of the Orbeliani line and fortune. I had no children, there
was only Damia and myself, and if Damia's husband wished
to, he might have laid claim to the child. Indeed, he would not
allow a divorce, vowing to fight a divorce action to his last
rouble. The potential for complications, as you can see, was
enormous." Her explanation was rapid and direct, as though
the words had been said a thousand times before.

"I knew of the Field Marshal, as every schoolchild does, but
not—" Lisaveta hesitated, searching for a polite phrase
"—of…the entire background." How extreme were the con-
trasts in their childhoods, she thought. Stefan's life had been
led in the glare of publicity from birth while hers had been
almost a country hermitage.

"You knew, then, that Stefan's father was forced to resign
the Viceroyalty. Damia's husband, after opposing divorce for
years, suddenly instituted proceedings, naming the Field Marshal as corespondent. After twenty-five years of valorous service to the Tsar, his career was over.'

Militza must have been a young and elegant lady then, Lisaveta thought, as diminutive and darkly beautiful as a Persian
miniature. "How devastating for him…for everyone," Lisaveta said, and how wretched, she thought, for a young boy
trying to understand.

Militza sighed again, recalling the heartache and sorrow.

"The Field Marshal and Damia were married in Brussels after the divorce, but I'm afraid the example of what overpowering love can do to a proud man had a profound effect on Stefan. At the time his father was relieved of his viceregal post, Alex was at the zenith of his career, and while the Tsar still sought his advice, for they had been companions since childhood, his hands were tied. As Viceroy, Alex embodied the Emperor and as such couldn't be corespondent in a divorce proceeding. He had no choice but to step down. He was forty-five."

"How old was Stefan?"

"Ten."

She had been six when her mother died in a riding accident, and that loss had tempered her entire life. "How much did Stefan know...of...the events?" she inquired, trying to imagine him as a young child, coping.

"He seemed to grow up overnight."

And in those hushed words her question was answered. "How sudden was the change?" Lisaveta inquired, her own voice oddly muffled, and at Militza's expression she answered herself. "It was sudden. They lived abroad, didn't they...."

"At first they retired to Alex's estate in Kursk, but he was restless, still raging with life. He couldn't stand the confining tranquillity of country living. He was a conqueror with nothing to conquer and he needed distractions." Militza had always felt the wreckage of such an illustrious career could not have been the happiest foundation for a marriage, and the procession of half-lived days—then years—at Plombières, Ems, Baden-Baden, the capital cities of Europe, had to have been touched with regret along with the ennui. "They left Russia," she explained, "after just two months at Kursk, taking only two servants and Damia's jewels. From that point on the family's aimless wanderings from spa to spa in Europe began destroying Alex. Stefan watched his father turn to morphine, saw his health worsen until he died at Ems when Stefan was fifteen. Damia committed suicide two weeks later. I sometimes think," Militza said, recalling the vivacious dark beauty of her sister, "Stefan blamed his mother for the loss of his father...or blamed love. He made up his mind then never to lose his soul to a woman, a principle he's adhered to for over a decade now."

"And yet he's marrying."

"For an heir. Both the Bariatinsky and Orbeliani fortunes require one, and I must confess my insistence may have had something to do with his decision. His style of soldiering does leave one holding one's breath."

"He never spoke of...this," Lisaveta softly said. "How sad it must have been to lose both your parents so young." How terrible it must have been for Stefan, she thought, to see his father die so uselessly.

"And yet in many ways he was very lucky to have parents who loved him so," Militza declared. "He was doted on from the cradle. Alex had led a life much like Stefan's has been the last many years, known for its searching the limits of sensation in love and war. When he fell in love with my sister, Damia, many thought it inexplicable. But—" Militza half closed her eyes for a moment, against that memory and her own "—love is...mystifying, is it not?" She sat more upright abruptly, as if relinquishing hold on all the memories from her past. "Stefan was Alex and Damia's only child. He was the center of their world—which may both explain and condemn him to his present path."

"I don't understand how he can be so ruthless about his own marriage after seeing and experiencing such love. Surely the circumstances..."

"Stefan was deeply scarred by the manner of his father's death. Alex had been Russia's greatest hero for a quarter of a century, yet he died in exile." She leaned her head against the chair back and briefly shut her eyes. How often had she wondered what might have been if Alex's enemies hadn't persuaded Davidow... "You can see," she said, opening her eyes, "Stefan's childhood was...unusual."

"It certainly explains, in some ways, his choice of a wife. Nadejda and her parents appear on good terms with the current Viceroy. How does Stefan feel about the man occupying the position once held by his father?"

"There is deep-seated animosity. Melikoff is the son of the

man who replaced his father. He holds a post Stefan might have inherited.''

"Does Stefan *know* Nadejda's parents are visiting the Viceroy?''

"I didn't tell him, but he found out," his aunt said, blunt as a hammer blow, "from the servants.''

"You wouldn't have told him?" Lisaveta's words were blurted in astonishment. She had been reared to honor simple truth.

"I wanted him to find out from his fiancée. She has such an irritating way about her.''

"He may not find her irritating.''

Militza treated Lisaveta to a candid stare. Her eyes were dark with kohl in the fashion of the Caucasus, and brilliant with derision. "He hardly notices her.''

It was unkind, but Militza's words consoled her; had Stefan adored Nadejda she would have been...what? Unhappy? Dejected? Jealous? Taking a serious grip on the reality of the situation, Lisaveta reminded herself that her feelings were incidental to the facts. Stefan was engaged; Nadejda was his fiancée. Whether she or Militza envisioned problems in the marriage was irrelevant. But a niggling voice wasn't so easily acceptant of rational argument, and she found herself saying, "Have you tried to talk to him about...well...his feelings for Nadejda?''

And she knew that one thoroughly unrealistic part of her longed for Militza's answer to match her own ideal.

Was it the wine? She'd always considered herself immune to fairy tales. But then Stefan had opened a new world to her in the days past, a world in which poetry took corporeal form and creative fancy was dream and fantasy and extravagant, breath-held actuality all in the same moment. Maybe she'd begun to believe in fairy tales after all.

"I've talked to him a hundred times," Militza said, arranging the used silver on her dessert plate as if their balanced placement might somehow carry over into Stefan's life. "I've tried every imaginable argument," she went on, exasperation and remorse equally audible in her voice, "in the months since his engagement took place. I've tried reasoning with him—about the merits of at least a mild affection as basis for marriage. I've suggested he consider spending some time with his fiancée before he makes a final decision. I've pointed out to him the negative aspects of his future in-laws in terms of their humanity—or lack of it. He listens without argument, but he's obstinately determined in his course.

"He says love is dangerous.

"He says most of his friends have married for dynastic reasons…most of society, for that matter.

"He says the kind of love he wants is readily available…and he doesn't have to marry it.

"He says his marriage is a pragmatic step—a career decision." Militza sighed again, wishing she could transfer wholesale to her nephew all she knew of the beauty and fullness of love, and then promptly apologized for her pessimism. "You must think me addled to first tell Stefan to marry and then complain of the style of his choice, but I want more for him than what he chose," she said in a quiet voice. "I want more for him than a career decision. And, frankly, I'm at my wit's end. Do you know how close he is to marrying that…that—"

"Beautiful prig?"

"You're too kind." Militza's snort of disgust at the vacuous young Nadejda flared her fine nostrils. "I'd use harsher words, beginning with empty-headed and stupid."

"She's very young." Lisaveta felt obliged to try to maintain a certain impartiality.

"That's no excuse. You're not much older but your brain functions."

"My education was—" Lisaveta paused, considering the numerous inadequacies of her nonfeminine instruction "—a man's education, I'm afraid. While I've always appreciated the variety of my schooling, much of a female nature was neglected. Nadejda, no doubt, has superior skills in those areas." Beginning when she was seven, her father had drawn up a liberal educational schedule for his only child. It had been balanced: languages, eight ultimately; poetry, of course; mathematics, engineering, literature, experimental agriculture and carpentry—to give her a practical bent. But he'd overlooked the feminine refinements.

"You needn't be so gracious." That kind of intrinsic compassion reminded Militza of Lisaveta's father. He'd been an outrageously benevolent man. "Nadejda does not possess superior skills, save those of arrogance."

"You must admit she experiences no discomfort in arranging an entire viceroyal staff. I couldn't say the same for myself. There are times, particularly now that I've seen Stefan in situ as 'Prince,' that I feel Papa and I led a very unsophisticated life."

"That was Felix's fault," Militza asserted. "He should have had you brought out in Saint Petersburg." Although, she mused, perhaps Lisaveta's attraction to Stefan was that precise lack of feminine accomplishments, the kind he'd seen used to inveigle and entrap, the kind he'd learned to evade with such practiced finesse.

"Papa was always too busy on a new project to take the time. I've never been to a ball, not a real one," Lisaveta said. "The parties in the country were informal gatherings."

"You do dance?" Militza mildly interrogated, considering a new tack in her offense against Nadejda. The Countess was the only woman Stefan had ever brought home; even his note referring to her possible visit had held within its spare language a sense of happiness. Perhaps the beautiful Countess could open Stefan's eyes to the deficiencies in his fiancée. Perhaps the lovely Countess could prevail where reason and logic had failed.

"Yes, Papa hired a dance master from Paris to teach me." Lisaveta smiled at the memory of her father taking time each afternoon to watch her at her lessons. "Now that I've learned Papa was such a fine dancer, his interest in that single modish skill doesn't seem so odd."

"Marvelous!"

Militza's response was so forcefully expressed that Lisaveta's brows rose in surprise.

"Stefan likes women who dance well," Militza said in answer to Lisaveta's startled reaction.

"From his reputation," Lisaveta levelly said, "he apparently likes women for a variety of reasons."

"You'd understand that better than I." Militza's smile was warm.

Lisaveta blushed…from her décolletage, past her pearls and up her throat to her cheeks.

"You needn't be bashful." Militza's gaze was direct but cordial. "There's nothing nicer in the world than love and lovers."

"Now I *am* embarrassed." The rose flush on her face turned more vivid, and Lisaveta's expression was one of artless misbehavior.

"Nonsense," Stefan's aunt retorted, her voice genial. "You're perfect for Stefan and he's obviously enamored, since he brought you home. He's never done that before." How sweet her innocence, Militza thought, and how rare; Stefan must be enchanted by such chaste virtue.

"I shan't be staying." Lisaveta spoke as David might have to Goliath, with resolution starching an inherent uncertainty.

"Why not?" Militza was genuinely shocked. After Stefan's extraordinary invitation into his home, she didn't think a woman alive would refuse his hospitality.

"I have responsibilities at home." In exactly that manner an angel might refuse the devil's temptation.

"I suppose it's Nadejda," Militza said bluntly, realizing she wasn't dealing with the usual style of aristocratic paramour Stefan favored, who would have found Nadejda no more than a minor inconvenience.

"As a matter of fact, yes," Lisaveta answered as bluntly, omitting mention of a variety of other reasons impelling her departure, reasons less clearly enunciated, less intelligible. Reasons having to do with desire and temptation and a man who could raise the temperature of the Arctic with a smile.

"I do wish you'd reconsider staying," Militza said, dismissing Nadejda's presence in much the same way her nephew had. "Dinner tomorrow should be interesting."

Interesting, Lisaveta thought, was a mild word for the collision of forces about to take place. "You're attending?" she asked, wondering if she'd misunderstood.

"I have a feeling," Militza said with soft sarcasm, "my bridge party will be canceled at the last minute. Nadejda," she went on, her voice dangerously smooth, "doesn't realize who she's up against with Stefan."

"If my own feelings weren't enough to spur my departure, certainly the prospect of dinner tomorrow night with Nadejda's parents, would be sufficient incentive," Lisaveta said, amusement prominent in her pale eyes. "I wish you luck, with Mama and Papa in attendance."

"It's going to be dreadful, isn't it," Militza said, her voice sunny with expectation. "And none of Stefan's staff available."

"And only French cuisine," Lisaveta added, pronouncing the word with Nadejda's precision.

"And gentlemen's wines…from France." Militza was patently jovial. "I can't induce you to stay?"

Lisaveta laughed. "Never. The thought of Nadejda's mama and papa terrifies me completely."

"A shame. Of course, you must do what you think best, but between the two of us," Militza said archly, "I'm sure we could open Stefan's eyes to the multiple inadequacies dear Nadejda possesses. It would surely be an act of the greatest charity."

"Charity?" Lisaveta murmured, smiling slightly.

"Our Christian duty, my dear." Stefan's aunt was happily smug.

"Seen from that perspective, I wish I could help. I've never actually been involved in an act of Christian charity. Papa, you see, wasn't of a religious bent." She was teasing, but then so was Militza.

"Pshaw, my darling Countess, your sweet kindness to Stefan was definitely charitable."

The teasing light in Lisaveta's eyes was instantly replaced by something more grave. The splendor of Stefan's affection required no charitable impulses to enjoy. He offered paradise as a gift…and laughter and pleasure. "You mistake my reasons for staying with Stefan the past week," Lisaveta quietly said.

"No, my dear, I don't," Aunt Militza replied, her own tone serious, as well. She'd seen much of the world, had been married twice and enjoyed her share of lovers in her youth. She understood Stefan's attraction to women.

"Then you know why I must leave. It's a matter of pride."

"I understand," Militza said, herself a product of a regal line dominated by Queens. "But Stefan will be disappointed."

"Not for long, I'm sure."

Stefan's aunt stared for a moment at the golden liquid in her wineglass, debating how honest to be with the young woman so new to Stefan's life. And then she decided Lisaveta was not only intelligent but perceptive in terms of human nature. "I suppose you're right," she ambiguously answered, choosing at the last second something less than blunt honesty. To date, no woman had interested Stefan for more than a month, and that was the unflattering truth.

Militza's reply was no more than Lisaveta had expected, and while she knew she was right about leaving, her decision didn't allay the sense of loss she was feeling, as though some golden idyll had come to an end—an absolute, unequivocal end. But leave she must, or eventually bear the humiliation of Stefan making that decision for her. "I think I'll try to depart early tomorrow before the bustle of Nadejda's replacement staff overwhelms the household."

"Before Nadejda rises, you mean."

Lisaveta nodded. She had no wish for further conversation with Stefan's future bride.

Sympathetic to Lisaveta's feelings, Militza said, "I'll order a carriage for you then at, say, seven?" She looked to Lisaveta for confirmation.

"Thank you. The sooner I leave, the more comfortable I'll feel."

"Stefan doesn't want you to go, does he?"

"No."

Aunt Militza's active brain saw fascinating possibilities all converging tomorrow—an angry frustrated Stefan would be a perfect ingredient at Nadejda's family party. "You're sensible to leave, I suppose." She spoke softly, as if thinking aloud, as if gauging the next step in her campaign against Nadejda.

"That's what I told him."

"And?"

"He said he wasn't interested in being sensible."

"He isn't...never has been. You'll be the first, you know." Stefan's aunt spoke abruptly, the cryptic words offering endless possibilities of meaning to Lisaveta.

"The first?" Lisaveta asked, curious how any woman could be first in anything with Stefan's libertine reputation.

"The first woman to walk away from him."

Lisaveta was initially flabbergasted and then angered. Apparently Russia's favorite Prince had been extremely overindulged. "In that case, I'm sure the experience will do his character good."

"Perhaps." One thing was certain, Militza thought, he was going to be furious, and she'd seen him furious on more than one occasion. Prince Stefan Alexandrovitch Orbeliani-Bariatinsky had a vile temper. "Do you ever get to Saint Petersburg, my dear?" Militza asked in lieu of her more lurid reflections. "I would enjoy your company if you ever should."

"As a matter of fact, I'm invited next month to a special award ceremony commemorating my father's literary work for the Tsar. It'll be my first trip to the capital. And thanks to Stefan," Lisaveta graciously added, "I'm alive to attend it."

"Well, then, we may meet again. If all goes well tomorrow night," Militza briskly said, "I may be free to travel north. By all means call on me."

With genuine feeling, the two ladies promised to see each other should circumstances allow. On that warm note Lisaveta bid good-night, since she would have to rise early in order to be ready to depart in the morning.

When Lisaveta entered her room a few moments later, she closed the door and stood with her back against it, her eyes shut, her head resting on Stefan's carved coat of arms embellishing the elaborate portal. She relaxed, visibly, a great sigh lifting her breasts in lush mounded splendor above the low neckline of her gown. Militza's pearls resting on the rise of her breasts caught the light with the movement and glistened in iridescent luster.

An appreciative audience of one lounging on a chair near the dressing alcove reminded himself to buy her pearls like Militza's. "Nadejda *can* be wearing, can't she," Stefan drawled, and delighted in Lisaveta's sharply drawn breath. Surely she had the most beautiful breasts he'd ever seen.

Her eyes were suddenly open. And glaring. "How did you get in?" she snapped, irritated by his casual drawl, offended by his satirical remark about his fiancée, particularly annoyed at his assumption he could enter her bedroom at will.

He looked at her from under half-lowered lashes, as if gauging the sincerity of her question. It must be rhetorical certainly, but he answered because she seemed to be waiting for a reply. "I own this palace, darling," he softly said.

"You do *not*, however, own me."

She said the words so heatedly it excited him, the thought that perhaps he could.... Were she not a Russian noblewoman, were she perhaps one of the native women in the various outlands of the Empire, he could very well own her.

"You jump to conclusions, sweetheart," he said with a wicked smile, "although the possibility interests me."

"A pity, then, you don't have enough money."

He was enjoying her anger. He was simply and unconditionally enjoying the sight and sound of her after waiting to touch her for all the tedious afternoon and evening. "Tell me your price, *dushka*," he said in a low, husky voice, baiting her for the pleasure of the game. "I think my credit is good with the Tsar."

She stood very straight, her palms pressed against the carved wood panels, her golden eyes brilliant and wrathful. "I'm sorry to disappoint your acquisitive nature, Prince Bariatinsky," she said, slowly, so each word fell into the silence between them like a tiny drop of rage, "but I'm priceless."

Amen to that, he thought, taking in the full impact of her beauty. Beyond the conventional attributes of her classic features and opulent form, she was radiantly alive, as though a fire glowed inside her, a flame of passion and wit and, more important yet, a warm capacity for giving. She was unique in his experience with women who invariably asked for things, however subtle the asking. And he wanted to feel that heated display very soon and mitigate his hunger for her; he wanted beyond reason to possess the indomitable Countess Lazaroff, not just for tonight but for as long as he desired.

"You must leave," Lisaveta said, interrupting his introspection. Prince Bariatinsky was not used to introspection. He preferred action, a principle any of his troopers would acknowledge. In fact his intrinsic impulse to action was probably his greatest asset and the reason the Tsar's army had been so successful the past decade.

Rising from his chair, he decided it was time to close the distance between him and the fascinating Countess.

Five

"I'll scream," she said as he began to move toward her.

"Perhaps you didn't know," he replied, continuing his forward progress, his mouth curved in a warm smile, "my wing is separate from—" he paused, deliberating briefly on his choice of words "—the others." He was very close now so she had to look up to see his face. "I arranged to have you in…my wing." His dark eyes held hers. "Scream if you like," he softly said, "but I've no intention of hurting you." His hand came up to touch her and she moved away from the door. Stefan took a moment before following her to turn the key in the lock and slide it into his pocket.

"If I were you, I should think it humiliating to find restraint necessary." From the relative safety of the center of the room, Lisaveta sharply upbraided him.

"I'm a lazy man," Stefan murmured, immune to her provocation, testing the door latch to see it was locked, "and not inclined to chase you…anywhere." Teasing mockery underlay the moderation of his tone.

"What do you call this?" Lisaveta heatedly retorted as he advanced on her again and she retreated.

He grinned. "Foreplay?"

"I thought you were more subtle," she hissed.

"And I thought you more attuned to your feelings."

"I told you how I felt this afternoon."

"You told me only that you won't continue our friendship because of my fiancée."

"That's precisely how I feel."

"No, you *feel* the way I do…you feel the Angelglow," he murmured. "You feel deprived after a week of indulging your senses. You feel your skin against the silk of your chemise and petticoats. And," he finished in a husky whisper, "I can help you."

Stefan's words triggered the floodgates of sensation. He was advancing closer and she found her will to retreat diminishing. "How can it matter," he softly asked, "if we make love again?"

"It matters to me," Lisaveta said, low and breathless, but he was very near now, and all she could think of beyond her declaration of principle was how excruciatingly *fine* he had felt deep inside her, how perfectly he knew the chronology of her arousal, how hard and strong his powerful body felt beneath her hands, how his mouth felt touching hers…the way it would…now—

"No!" She found the will somewhere to resist.

For a flashing moment she saw his anger before she slid away under his arm.

He silently watched her run to the door and try the latch, watched her bang her fists loudly against the solid mahogany door and swiftly turn to face him a moment later, her cheeks flushed with her effort. "You can't force me," she said, her voice intense with emotion.

"I'd never force you, sweetheart." He dropped into a chair, held his hands out, palms open in surrender, and with genuine sincerity said, "I told you I wouldn't hurt you."

"Open the door then."

"I *didn't* say I'd open the door."

"Are we splitting hairs?" she angrily retorted.

"Are we?" he calmly responded. "To deny yourself what you want purely on principle seems like Jesuit dialectics. We shouldn't be engaging in polemics when we both agree we want each other."

"We don't agree on that."

"Do you remember Deva, when the night air was so sultry on the balcony your skin slipped against mine when I slid you down my body? Tell me you don't want to enjoy that pleasure again. Tell me you don't want to experience the sensations you felt that morning when I fed you strawberries for breakfast, *first*." His voice was hushed because she hadn't wanted to wait but he'd insisted.

Lisaveta knew she'd never be able to eat strawberries again without remembering the heated crying need she'd felt that morning. Nor forget how beautiful Stefan had looked, his dark hair wet from the bath, his bronzed skin damply sleek in the brilliant morning sunlight, his enormous power and strength overwhelming the small cottage room, enhancing his potent virility, and she'd wanted him so badly she'd ached. As she did now.

He hadn't moved in his casual sprawl, his arms resting on the chair exactly where they'd dropped after his yielding gesture. "Tell me," he said very softly, looking darkly handsome and splendid, his silk shirt open at the neck, the fine linen of his trousers accentuating the slimness of his hips and the corded muscles in his legs, "tell me you don't want me and I'll leave."

Lisaveta's cheeks were still flushed, but no longer from her exertions banging on the door. The color pinking her cheeks came from within, from the heat pulsing deep inside her, the heat of desire she'd tried valiantly to deny or suppress or pretend didn't matter as much as principle and pride.

"Tell me," he said again, his low voice like a velvet caress in the stark silence of the room.

She should say, "Go," she thought, gazing at him, but a fresh rush of desire inundated her senses at the sight of him. He was aroused, it was obvious, and a melting heat responded at that knowledge. Lisaveta shivered as she stood in the balmy night air of Tiflis in July.

"Are you cold?" he inquired, knowing she was not. He rose to his feet in a slow graceful movement.

"No," she whispered, as if her answer would hold him at bay.

"I didn't think so," he murmured. His gaze traveled to her bed and then back again in leisure invitation. "I know everything you like," he said with a soft emphasis on "everything," as though he were offering her carte blanche in pleasure.

And after endless hours making love in the week past, she knew he was capable of tumult and tenderness, playful savagery and the most delicate enchantment. Was he addictive, as well?

Lisaveta was so naively new to all the sensuous sensations that she wondered briefly if indeed it were possible. How else did one explain this hot, ungovernable, incautious urge, this unfathomable insistent pulsing through her blood and brain and sensitized nerves—that she must have him again or die?

"*Are* you addictive?" Her query was hushed, a question not only of reason but of feeling.

He was startled for a transient pulse beat as he quietly waited for her, because curiously the same speculation had come to his mind. Unlike this naive child, he wasn't a tyro in amorous games. He wanted her with an unfamiliar and disquieting urgency. Heedless of protocol, of his fiancée, of Nadejda's conservative parents, he intended keeping Countess Lazaroff until the very last minute of his leave. If that wasn't addiction, it was something very similar. So he smiled and said, "Yes," and in the next breath added, "Does that help?"

Stefan's smile was relaxed now, his thoughts on less taxing issues than the possibility of falling under a woman's spell. He'd shaken away his disquietude with his facetious reply and he was charming predator once again. His most practiced role.

"I'm serious, Stefan. It unnerves me."

"Don't be serious, darling. Please." He moved swiftly toward her, recognizing the most potent of her resistance was past. "War is serious, dying is serious. Making love is unmitigated pleasure…and joy." His voice was perhaps more intense than he wished, but Kars was too recent in his thoughts, the stench and horror not removed yet from his memory.

"When do you go back?" She'd seen the flicker of distress in his eyes.

"Twenty-one days, six hours, give or take a few minutes.

Haci will come for me." His words were carefully devoid of emotion…too carefully controlled.

"Up against that," Lisaveta quietly said, putting out her hand, "I am being foolish."

How trivial her selfish motives of jealousy and resentment seemed when Stefan had only a short leave before going back to the brutality of war. How childish it seemed to say, "I won't love you," when she wanted to, with all her heart. How unimportant the issue of Nadejda's presence when he was here and wanting her with the same passion flaring through her senses.

He could die, she realized suddenly, when he returned to the war. What would she have then? The warmth of this memory tonight or the empty virtue of having refused him? Her fingers lightly touched his in affirmation and welcome.

As his hand closed over hers, he gazed down at her, thinking how fresh and young and untouched by the wretchedness of the world she looked. He wondered for the briefest moment whether she might be some apparition of his imagination.

But she smiled up at him, reminding him of her luscious corporeality.

"No, not foolish," he said in a quiet tone, then shrugged, because he knew she was only responding as any young woman of sensibility would. Nadejda's presence was a damnable obstacle. Taking both her hands in his, he pulled her close. "I'm just being selfish. Forgive me, *dushka*, but I am. And if it's any sop to your conscience or morality, I won't *let* you go tonight."

"In all honesty, I doubt I could have left you, Stefan," Lisaveta whispered. "But in the morning I must."

"I'll change your mind." He laughed then, buoyant as a young boy, plans already racing through his mind. "I'll show you my mountain retreat. You'll love it. It's secluded and high above the sultry heat. The pines reach clear to the sky. There's a stream running through the courtyard and—"

She kissed him then with tears in her eyes, because she couldn't stay and be drawn closer each day to a man she already was too much in love with. But she would love him tonight and stay with him one last time, as though she wouldn't relinquish paradise without that final lingering look back.

He intended to woo her with all the skill he'd acquired since first making love to his governess at thirteen. In the intervening years since Mademoiselle Dovrieu had come to instruct him in French art and literature and quickly lured him into her bed, he'd become accomplished at pleasing women. Perhaps Ursulina had much to do with his admirable competence. She'd taught him very young the valuable lesson of generosity. Sexual pleasure wasn't taking but giving, she'd benevolently declared. She'd proceeded in the ensuing two years, while he learned France's contributions to painting, architecture, drama and literature, to show him in a variety of ways the inescapable truth to that statement.

So he intended to give his darling Countess whatever she wished, however she wished, as often as she wished, and by the time morning came she'd have changed her mind about leaving.

He kissed her tears away first, with light brushing kisses, holding her gently in his arms and sighing in soft restraint when she reached up again to claim his mouth with hers. He was intensely aroused and had been from the moment she'd walked into the bedroom, but he only held her close, tasting the sweetness of her lips, gently stroking her back, waiting until she made the first tentative overture for more than kisses. He wouldn't rush her or force the pace; he wanted only to answer her need. Although, he thought with a confidence schooled by hundreds of satisfied women in his past, there were moments ahead when a sensuous form of aggression would be satisfying. But not yet.

Lisaveta was standing on tiptoe in order to reach Stefan's mouth, her arms raised high to twine around his neck. Stretched taut against the solid strength of his body, his arousal hard and explicit against her stomach, she felt like a human offering to some pagan god. He could have her, they both knew; she was clinging to him as though a worshiper at the altar of his sexuality, not indifferent or detached but alive with yearning. Stefan was right when he'd pressed her short moments ago to

admit her need. She wanted him, she realized without pride.
Her blood was pulsing through her veins in her readiness, her
senses urgent in their submission. With a twinge of illogic and
female conditioning, she wondered why he was content with
kisses alone.

She moved her hips then with the merest of teasing pressure,
and was pleased to feel Stefan's arousal swell in response. He
was not, perhaps, content only with kisses. "You missed me
today," she murmured, her smile the tempting one of Eve.

Looking down at her flushed and beautiful face, Stefan answered with his own captivating smile, "You noticed."

Beneath the casual restraint of his remark ran his habitual
arrogance. "Mmm," Lisaveta replied, her soft voice coyly
thoughtful and teasing, "I think so...."

"And reversed your decision on celibacy."

He *was* arrogant, she realized, about his physical attributes
and prowess, although justifiably so. "I don't necessarily believe in celibacy," she sweetly said, intent on moderating his
arrogance, "but I do believe in a *variety* of experiences." She
was baiting him, her soft emphasis intentional.

"Really," Stefan quietly replied, compelling himself to suppress his sudden flare of anger. "In that case," he murmured,
his eyes darkly seductive in a way Lisaveta didn't recognize
because she'd never seen him celibate for an entire day, "I'll
contrive not to bore you with redundance."

"Thank you," she said, her own surge of resentment impelled by his obviously nonredundant expertise. "This will be
different tonight, then, won't it," Lisaveta breathed, "like a
farewell performance." It angered her that she still meltingly
wanted him, it angered her that she could no more walk away
from him than she could stop breathing.

"Let's just call it mutual...intoxication," Stefan whispered.
And not a farewell at all, he thought, but rather the beginning
of—no caution was necessary in his silent contemplation; he
could frankly call it what it was—a carnal adventure.

They were both, despite their anger and resentment, profoundly aroused, and as Stefan was deciding he wouldn't wait
after all for Lisaveta's overtures, she reached her arms up and

snaked them around his shoulders. Then, so quickly he didn't have time to protect himself, she stretched upward and sank her teeth into his bottom lip.

"So you don't forget me," she said as he stood rigidly silent, his lip bloody, his impulse to strike out curbed with only the most forceful restraint. Her arms were still on his shoulders, his loose at his sides, until suddenly, in an offensive response intrinsic to his nature and profession, his hands slid around her to the base of her spine, splayed out and crushed her to him so tightly she could feel the blood pulsing in his erection.

"You won't forget, either, darling," he said with a lazy drawl, "I promise." Lifting her into his arms in a flurry of silken skirts, he carried her over to the bed and dropped her onto the green brocade coverlet. "Do you want music?" he asked, not looking at her, pulling his shirt over his head, treating undressing and atmosphere as equally commonplace.

When Lisaveta gazed at him in astonishment from the crush of azure silk in which she lay, he added, glancing at her briefly as he tossed his shirt aside, "I could have the musicians come up." He paused a moment unfastening the first of his trouser buttons and grinned. "For the farewell performance."

"No!" she quickly retorted, realizing he was serious, realizing he probably wouldn't be embarrassed making love before an entire massed orchestra, aware his musicians were likely more familiar with this room than she was. "No music, please," she appended, wanting to make herself perfectly clear, suddenly struck with the awareness that—with or without music—Stefan Bariatinsky made her heart and quivering senses sing, made life a sweet melody of pleasure.

He shrugged, as though lack of music might be a stumbling block to his enjoyment but he'd defer to her wishes. His deepening smile was redolent with courtesy and charm. "Whatever you wish," he softly said, kicking off his boots while she watched, fascinated by his extraordinary beauty and its effect on her. And when he stripped off his trousers and underclothes with an ease that spoke of repetition, her breath caught for a moment in her throat.

He was massive—muscled, powerful, spectacularly aroused.

Lisaveta shivered in anticipation. Despite all logical arguments to the contrary, he was a temptation she couldn't resist, a prize she coveted, a pleasure she must have...and she found herself reaching to undo the jeweled buttons on her gown.

"Let me do that," Stefan softly said, moving toward her, seating himself beside her, brushing her hands aside without waiting for her answer.

"I hate you, you know," Lisaveta whispered, the dampness between her thighs a contradiction to her words, her hand lifting to glide over Stefan's sharply defined pectorals, the dark hair on his chest rough to her touch, the feel of him beneath her hand the antithesis of hate.

"It doesn't matter," he answered, not about to argue the illogic of her declaration, his slender fingers deftly sliding her glittering buttons free. It doesn't matter what you call it, he thought—for her desire was evident and obvious, her face and neck and throat pinked with excitement, her hips moving languidly as if anticipating his entry—as long as you feel it. A moment later when his hand slid under her opened bodice and beneath the silk of her chemise, stroking the pliant softness of her breast, her eyes closed and she moaned softly. He smiled. Her hate, he reflected, as his other hand crumpled the blue silk of her skirt upward over her legs, had a tantalizing focus.

She had only to look at him, she contemplated, mortified and indefensible against his presence, to feel herself open in welcome, and when he touched her, her skin took on a heated glow. Tonight was all she dared stay, the terminus and final allowance of her submission to Stefan's dominating passion. Tonight, she told herself, even as she reached for him, just one last time tonight and then she'd walk away from this overwhelming compulsion.

She was wet before he touched her there, she was hot and damp and slick as cream when he slid his fingers in to rouse her and test her need and give her pleasure. She uttered a small cry, swallowed partly in her throat when his fingers reached the quivering limits and stroked, a trembling ecstasy shuddering through her senses. Before he could even undress her she climaxed, as if the long and celibate day had been frustrating and wearing on her restraint, as well.

He kissed her open mouth then, drawing in her small panting breaths, taking pleasure in her need for him, thinking with an unhurried tranquillity that he liked the feel of her silk gown next to his skin.

"And now it's my turn, greedy child," he murmured into the sweetness of her mouth. Drawing her into his arms, he rose with her to a comfortable position against the painted headboard, gilded with Venetian exuberance, rosy-skinned putti and garlanded borders. Without speaking and with a pertinent haste indicating his own ardent libido, Stefan lifted Lisaveta and balanced her above his rigid arousal. She helped him then because he needed one hand to draw up her ruffled skirt and petticoat, the practical design of her lacy drawers no impediment, and she guided him until they were in perfect conjunction. It was his turn to groan softly, his dark lashes drifting downward as she closed around him, and it seemed, he thought for a moment, sliding slowly upward as though paradise had taken corporeal form, as though physical and spiritual experience coalesced into one beautiful woman seated astride him. He understood in a single explosive revelation, strangely rose-hued and glowing, why so many religions had over the millenia worshiped female deities.

This intense pleasure searing his mind and body was centered on her hot female body, on the perfect melting fit of her around him, on the slippery gliding invasion, on his possession of her. Suddenly he was desperately rampant, like a volcano about to explode.

He resisted the impulse as long as he could because he understood the gratification in delay, but Lisaveta's voluptuous breasts were brushing his chest as she moved on him, her soft bottom enticing against his thighs, her kisses wet and warm and delicious, and even repressing his need, he knew it would soon be over.

The long hours of wanting her were taking their toll, her scent alone bewitching, and she languidly eased herself back down each time with exquisite slowness. She remembered what he liked, she was deliberately pleasing him. She didn't hate him, he knew, nor he her. A scant pulse beat later, his hands closed harshly on her waist, forcing her down as he thrust upward, and when she cried out he poured into her as though he hadn't climaxed in a hundred years.

He didn't move afterward for long minutes, incapable of action or even thought. Only feeling held reign, and he clasped Lisaveta in his arms while paradise receded in slow degrees.

She kissed him first then, in the quiet of the enormous room where he'd placed her for exactly this purpose, and wondered how she could still want him so, knowing that.

He kissed her back without profound contemplation of the unanswerable questions; he kissed her back because she gave him unique pleasure and an odd inexplicable happiness and he liked the feel of her breasts against his chest.

He undressed her much later when their bodies had cooled— or more appropriately, mildly cooled, since their passion was undiminished, only temporarily assuaged—and had her wash herself so he could watch.

"If you don't mind," he said.

"If you'll let me wash you next," she softly replied.

"And if I say no," he answered, his voice playful, for she could do what she wished with his blessings.

"Then," she said, with arched brows and a temptress's smile, "I suppose I'll have to tie you up first."

Her statement had predictable effect on his arousal and his own smile was wolfish. "In that case I'll decidedly say no."

As it turned out, neither was patient enough for prolonged games, too ravenous for each other. The remainder of the night passed in simple tender passion, more amorous than erotic, more precious in its closeness than its lust. Lisaveta knew each moment brought her nearer to losing him; Stefan wasn't interested in exploits but in holding her near, and the rapture of their lovemaking was conspicuous for its need and naked disclosure of their feelings.

Very late, when they lay exhausted in each other's arms, Lisaveta whispered, "Stepka," the sound of his name a sigh of sated pleasure.

He stiffened for a moment. No one but his father had ever called him by the diminutive Stepka, and he hesitated briefly, equivocal responses racing through his mind.

Then Lisaveta smiled up at him as she lay on his chest, her chin propped on her hands, and he decided he liked the sound of the name when she said it. The tension drained from his muscles, and although Lisaveta didn't realize it, she'd set the first wedge in some very long-standing defenses erected years ago by a young adolescent determined never to succumb to love.

"My sweet Lise," he murmured, and kissing his fingertip, he gently brushed it across her luscious bottom lip. "I adore you."

Her smile was winsome, her eyes bright suddenly with tears. "The feeling, Stepka, darling," she whispered, "is mutual."

The room was still in shadow when he felt her pull away. "Where're you going?" Although drowsy and half-asleep, he automatically tightened his arm around her.

"To ring for chocolate." She knew it was Stefan's habitual start to the day.

"Now?" His eyes were closed, his murmured question husky with sleep.

"For later."

"Ring later, sleep now," he muttered, and tugged her closer.

They'd been up most of the night, and if Lisaveta hadn't been taut with nerves over her departure, she would have been sleeping, too. She lay quiescent in his arms for what seemed ages, waiting for his breathing to deepen, and long minutes later when he rolled over, she slipped from his embrace.

She stood by the bed, nude in the cool morning light, the summer air smelling of damp lilies from the garden below, watching him out of caution but also out of her own poignant need. She wouldn't see him again and she wanted a last look before she walked away from the most perfect and beautiful days of her life.

Her gaze traveled lovingly down the great length of his body and then up again with lingering slowness as if she could etch on her memory forever the sight of him. He'd rolled over so his face was resting on his pillow, and she visually traced the perfection of his classic features, in profile now, like Alexander's head on a Macedonian coin. Since Alexander had conquered Persia centuries earlier, perhaps the classic genes were truly incorporated. There was much of his mother's elegant Persian heritage, too, in the refined detail of his severely modeled features, in the beauty of his long-lashed eyes and the delicate curve of his mouth. In height and stature, in musculature and strength, he must favor his father however, she thought. Field Marshal Bariatinsky was reputed to have equaled his ancestor Orlov in size.

She looked for a moment more at his slender hands, the great corded muscles running down either side of his spine, the softness of his curls lying like black silk on his neck and the sleek broad expanse of his bronzed body, as if tying the parcel of her memories together.

"Goodbye, Stepka," she murmured so softly the words never touched the air, and then silently moved away from the bed to the adjoining dressing room. Her clothes were all gone from the wardrobe, packed by silent hands in the night...only one traveling gown was left hanging in the armoire. She smiled, hoping whoever had quietly seen to the disposition of her luggage hadn't been disturbed by the noises from the adjacent bedroom.

She liked the choice of traveling dress, she decided. The soft pink linen was perfect for a summer day. Lifting the jacket from the hanger, she noticed the note tucked into her pocket. "Please keep the pearls as a remembrance of our meeting. They do your beauty justice." And Militza had signed her name in a spidery Arabic penmanship. Lisaveta reached up to touch the earrings still in her ears and smiled, reminded of how Stefan had told her he liked her dressed only in her earrings.

How generous Militza was, she reflected...like her nephew, who had given her love and laughter and enchantment she would always treasure. But she would leave the necklace; it was too precious...and—lying as it was on the bedside table—too close to Stefan. She dared not return to the room.

"Thank you, Militza," she murmured, tucking the note back

into the pocket, knowing the pearl drop earrings would remind her always of Tiflis and a night of love and passion. And remind her, too, of a man who had taken hold of her heart.

She dressed after that with a calculated briskness, forcing her thoughts on her journey ahead, refusing to become maudlin over a situation that had always had a foreseeable end. Leaving by the servants' entry into a back hallway, she found her way to the wide empty second-floor corridor, walked the length of the east wing to its juncture with the massive curving central staircase and, moving down the polished marble steps, reached the main entrance. Opening the door herself in the servantless palace, she saw her carriage, as arranged, waiting for her.

With a small bow the coachman explained a valise of roubles had been placed inside the carriage for her, and he and the two outriders were at her disposal.

She was comfortably seated with the friendly informality typical of Stefan's staff, the carriage door was closed, and at the crack of a whip the horses broke into a gentle trot.

The morning sun was a perfect summer maize.

The air was tepid and calm.

Stefan's white marble palace, crowning the heights above Tiflis, began diminishing in size.

It was over.

When Stefan woke two hours later, he lazily rolled on his back and with a casual sweep of his arm reached out for Lisaveta. Only the smoothness of silk sheets, the great expanse of empty bed, met his hand, and he swore even before he fully opened his eyes.

Damn her! Instantly alert, he snapped his head around but knew without looking she was gone. Furious, he shouted for his valet and lunged out of bed. Reaching for his trousers, he thought it odd when Ellico didn't appear. He shouted again. As he swiftly dressed, he cautioned himself to deal with his feelings less emotionally, although for a man who operated a good deal on instinct, curbing his emotions required more control than he was currently feeling. Perhaps, he suggested to himself, trying mightily to gain a calm perspective at the same time he was cursing buttons that failed to button rapidly enough, Lisaveta was in the dressing room or on the balcony. Perhaps, he thought, pulling on his boots with a small grunt of exertion, she rose early and was breakfasting with Militza.

Like hell, his dominant passion noted as he grabbed his shirt and strode to the bank of French windows facing east. Pushing the gauze curtains aside, he scanned the small balcony adjoining the bedroom because he was going to take five seconds to be reasonable.

She wasn't there....

His nostrils were flared in anger as he crossed the large bed-chamber to the dressing room door, and shoving it open with the palm of his hand, he stood in the doorway and swore.

"Damn her!"

He could scratch the possibility of her breakfasting with Militza.

He could reject other possibilities of her presence in other areas of his palace, as well. From the looks of the armoire, stripped clean of her gowns, his darling lover had flown the coop.

"Ellico!" he roared, turning to retrace his steps, recrossing the Shirvan rug in almost a run. He was out the door into the hallway before he considered how curious it was that his voice wasn't heeded. In the next moment, discarding speculation on his servants' inefficiency, he refocused on the important over-riding issue of Lisaveta's escape. His choice of word in regard to her leaving was symptomatic of his military background or perhaps more aptly of his proprietary feelings.

Striding down the corridor, he shrugged into his shirt while his mind raced over all the possibilities of her destination. Or more importantly, when she had left; her destination was, in his current frame of mind, not likely to be reached. Tucking in his shirttails with a minimum effort, he covered the distance down the carpeted passage with haste, distracted from the un-usual quiet by more prominent considerations. When, *exactly*, had she left? Had she traveled by carriage...or horse? She had luggage, of course; she'd have gone by coach. Good. He could overtake her more easily.

The Orbeliani family motto was, I Am God's Spoiled Child, and Stefan had been operating too many years under that maxim to deny himself anything. He wanted Lise, so he would have her. Regardless. And that word encompassed a myriad of disastrous possibilities he chose to ignore.

At the stables he paced restlessly while Cleo was being saddled, intent on taking off in pursuit, agitated at every moment lost, knowing each minute placed Lisaveta farther out of reach. She'd be traveling to Vladikavkaz where the railway line ended. The military road was the only one out of the Caucasus. At least he didn't have to deal with numerous possibilities. Glancing up at the sun he disgruntledly thought, Damn, it was late.

"When did Countess Lazaroff leave?" he asked tersely.

"Orders were to have the first carriage ready at seven." A minimum staff had been left at the stables to service the carriages for Lisaveta and Nadejda.

Stefan's dark brows rose. "First carriage?"

"Princess Taneiev leaves at nine."

"She's leaving?" The pleasure in Stefan's voice was noticeable.

"Only to the Viceroy's palace, Your Excellency." The young groom's tone was sympathetic. Servants always knew all the gossip, and the relationship between Stefan and his fiancée was common knowledge.

If Lisaveta had left at seven he'd need Haci and some of his troopers, Stefan decided, Nadejda dismissed from his mind much as he'd dismissed her from his life. Lise had nearly two hours' head start and Cleo couldn't overtake her alone. He'd need fresh horses.

"Find Haci—I'll finish that," he said briskly, taking the bridle from the groom. "Where the hell *is* everyone?" he asked next, finally consciously noticing the dearth of servants. Normally the stable yard was bustling with activity in the morning, since Stefan kept a string of racers and polo ponies that had to be exercised. He had a stable crew of fifty.

"Princess Taneiev is bringing in French servants, Your Ex-

cellency, from the Viceroy's palace. For her parents' dinner
tonight. The staff is off for the day."

"The staff is *what*?" Stefan's voice was a low resonant
growl.

"Off, sir." The boy's eyes were innocent.

"Everyone?"

"Yes, sir."

"On *whose* orders?" There was a distinct rumble of leashed
fury beneath his soft tone.

"I don't know, sir." Georgi had made it plain Princess Orbeliani was to be protected.

"Well, who told you?"

"Georgi, Your Excellency."

"Get him!"

"He's gone, sir."

"Hell." Stefan jerked the bridle buckle in irritation and almost got bitten for his temper, since Cleo's equine personality
was far from placid. "Sorry," he quickly apologized to his
horse. "Damn women," he went on as though his mount understood, and perhaps she did, because she nuzzled Stefan's
shirtfront as if in sympathy. "Get Haci, then, dammit. I don't
fancy *he* was dismissed." A mild sarcasm underlay his gruff
tone. "And where do you keep my rifle and revolver?" The
weapon mounts on his saddle were empty.

"In the tack room, sir…in the gun cabinet."

"Thank you—hurry—don't be alarmed," Stefan added, al-
tering his menacing rumble. "I'm not angry with you." He
could see the young man's apprehension had mounted at his
own increasing irritation. "But bloody hurry," he softly em-
phasized.

Already his thoughts were moving forward to assess the various points where Lisaveta would have to stop to change
horses. In that respect he had a distinct advantage. He and his
troopers could travel almost twice as fast as a coach. Twice as
fast, for certain, he corrected himself, with the state of the military road to Vladikavkaz. He did the simple arithmetic in his
head, traced the backtracking in his mind and gauged their
estimated arrival at his mountain lodge. By four o'clock at the

latest. How nice. He could show Lise the magnificent mountain sunset.

And he smiled for the first time since waking, a man once more in control.

Six

Fifteen minutes later—ten minutes too late for General Prince Orbeliani-Bariatinsky, who had sat mounted, snapping orders, since Haci and his men had arrived on the run—the troop of mounted men galloped out of the stable yard. Sweeping around the west wing of the palace, kicking the carefully raked gravel drive into shambles, they found themselves on a collision course with the carriage waiting for Nadejda. She was late and only now strolling down the bank of marble stairs, her parasol up against the mild morning sun.

Upon sighting Stefan, she stopped poised on the first landing and delicately waved her white gloved hand.

Oh, hell! Stefan thought. Damnation! They could have swerved around, avoiding both the carriage and his tedious fiancée, but, influenced by years of good manners, he hauled Cleo to a sudden skidding halt, his troopers followed suit in a chaotic rearing stop behind him.

Delicately fanning away the cloud of dust rising from milling horses, Nadejda smiled in greeting, as though she and Stefan were meeting on a promenade. "Good morning, Stefan. Isn't it a delightful day?"

Hell, no, Stefan thought, banal phrases, in his current mood, only further ignition to his anger. Nadejda made an incongruous picture on his palace steps. He'd never thought of her as actually *living* in his home. A fiancée seemed apart somehow—a name one referred to in conversation, a distant future, as in someday-ay-ay-ay, bride. His only memories of her were as his beautiful companion at balls and parties in Saint Petersburg. But she would be actually physically installed in his home. The second small fissure in his staid and practical image of matrimony appeared. Nadejda at table last evening had been the first appalling crack.

Cleo, recognizing perhaps Stefan's impatience, was sidling nervously, dancing in staccato prancing agitation at the base of the stairs.

"Give my regards to your parents," Stefan said with civility if not good humor, but he couldn't bring himself to extend his greeting to their host, the Viceroy. Although he and Prince Melikoff often met in public since both were prominent figures in the Caucasus, Stefan's enmity toward the usurper of his father's post was undiminished. Melikoff was essentially a courtier, neither a soldier nor a diplomat, and he treated the native tribes with the arrogant disdain of that clique. With his own heritage from his mother's family closely linked to the native tribes, Stefan not only resented Melikoff's parochial vision but took personal affront at his ethnic slurs.

Nadejda stood twirling her parasol in what seemed to Stefan an irritating affectation and Cleo was about to take a nip out of someone if he didn't get moving soon. "Darling," Nadejda replied, her lashes lowered and raised in some ridiculous flirtatious parody, "you can offer your regards to Mama and Papa yourself. I'm on my way now to fetch them."

Luckily Stefan couldn't see his troopers' expressions behind him for they were exchanging amused glances after having just been hauled away from their breakfast in order to accompany their Prince on a scorching chase after his escaped lover. Being Muslim, they saw no ethical problems in having more than one woman; they were allowed four wives. None of them, however, quite understood what their Prince had seen in the blond woman with the lavender eyes and too-sweet voice. He normally had better taste in women. Having served him as bodyguard for years, they were in a position to know his tastes.

"I'm sorry to have to miss your mama and papa, but orders came in this morning and I must leave." Stefan's voice was mild, but his grip on Cleo's reins was straining the muscles in his right arm.

"Nonsense, Melikoff can rescind any orders. I'll simply tell—"

"No." His voice interrupted, restrained and taut. "Melikoff gives no orders to me."

"Don't be silly, Stefan, he's the Tsar's representative for the entire Caucasus." She spoke as though she were informing him of one of life's basic facts.

"I take orders directly from the Tsar, not Melikoff."

She made the mistake of stamping her foot. It was exactly the wrong thing to do in the current circumstances, although with Stefan's personality, perhaps it would always be objectionable. "You *can't* go," she unmistakably said.

Stefan's eyes widened momentarily, Cleo felt the stab of the bit in her mouth, and then Stefan said very softly, "I must."

"You'll be back for dinner certainly." The parasol had stopped its languid twirling and her pouty lips were pursed.

"I'm afraid not." Each word was clipped.

"I'm bringing over Melikoff's staff," she angrily declared, "to serve."

"I'm sure Aunt Militza will appreciate it," he curtly replied, angered beyond words at her presumption. No one replaced his staff; they were like family, new generations replacing the old and serving the Bariatinskys or Orbelianis through the centuries. "Move this carriage," he snapped to the coachman. "Immediately!" It was a gesture of authority only, for his men could ride by in smaller formation, but it pleased him to exercise his power in her presence. Bitch, who did she think she was? was his first spontaneous thought. His second thought, more rational and hence more disconcerting, was that once they were married, she *would* be ordering his household.

"Good day, *mademoiselle*," he said grimly, and swinging Cleo around, he rode past the carriage. His men followed him in good order, smiles on their faces, looking forward to the chase. It was a perfect morning for a ride; they always preferred a hunt to simple riding.

As they swept down the drive, the sprawling city lay before

them, nestled in its cradle of hills...a series of villages, citadels and bazaars swarming up and down the cliffs and conical hills, divided by the gorge of the river Koura. Stefan maintained what he considered a restrained pace through the steep streets of the Nari-Kala, the Persian citadel with its Armenian quarter. He led his troops across the bridge to the center of town, where the Russian or Europeanized buildings had been constructed fifty years ago, and holding Cleo in with effort, he continued past the theater, the Nobles Club, the public gardens, administrative buildings and shops selling all the luxuries of Europe. As his troops ascended into Avlabar, the Georgian town with its fortress and the church built by Vakhtang Gourgastan, the founder of Tiflis, Stefan began counting the streets as they passed, his jaw clenched tight, his breathing controlled. The last dwellings of the Gypsy quarter straggled away finally into dusty wastes, and letting out a whoosh of breath, he relaxed his grip on the reins and gave Cleo her head.

Sensing his restive mood she tossed her head, caracoled a dozen paces as if to say, I understand, and then, stretching out in a racing drive, flew down the road.

The fast-moving troop gained on Lisaveta slowly. Each post stop on the Georgian Military Road delayed her, while Stefan's own horses were ridden in relays without stopping. Each trooper led a string of mountain ponies ready to be swung onto at a gallop, an effortless action for men considered the best riders in the world.

Stefan was silent, riding full-out, all his energies concentrated on arresting Lisaveta's flight. She was more determined than he expected but not, he brusquely reflected, likely to outrun him, Nadejda's interference notwithstanding. And thoughts of Nadejda, Melikoff, her parents, her damnable affectations, all added fuel to his already heated temper. Haci made the mistake of mentioning once that riding the horses to death wouldn't accomplish their mission, but his warning, however gentle, gained only a flinty look from Stefan, and he too fell silent.

Lisaveta traveled at a leisurely pace through the rich Georgian lowlands, then as the road began to ascend, the carriage wound upward slowly through sombre defiles, past forts and ruined castles, the snow-covered mountains all around on the far horizon. She was in no particular hurry, mildly fatigued from her sleepless night and perhaps at base reluctant to be leaving.

She had to depart, she knew, but that fact didn't obliterate her disinclination. How nice it would have been to stay if she could have quashed all sense of pride, if she could have reconciled herself to the recreational position Stefan required.

He needed surcease from the war, a sensual holiday to mitigate the impact of twelve weeks of campaigning. She was opportune and convenient. Perhaps there were women willing to be only a convenience for Stefan.

She found she could not.

She'd also found Nadejda a deplorable obstacle. Or perhaps the extent of Stefan's casual resolution to marry Nadejda was the more potent stumbling block.

There was a small voice inside her brain saying to all her logical assessments, *You'd be so much better,* and she smiled at the sheer bravado of such audacity.

Better for what? Better in which way? Better than the hard and practical reasons Stefan had for marrying Princess Taneiev?

Hardly.

But better able, she admitted with a small sigh of regret, to love him.

From that disastrous thought she was determined to distance herself, and distance herself as well from the physical allure of Prince Bariatinsky.

The driver was singing at the top of his voice. Gazing out the window, she smiled. It was a glorious place they were driving through, reddish cliffs hung with ivy and crowned with deep green pines, far above them the gilded fringe of snows and far below the river thundering out from a black misty gorge to become a silvery thread glittering in the sun. She should be grateful—for the beautiful day…for her memories.

* * *

Stefan was swinging onto his fifth mount since Tiflis, dropping into place without checking the horse's galloping stride; he rode bareback as easily as on his padded saddle and had the calluses to prove it. Even as he strung out the long braided lead, allowing the riderless ponies to drop back, he glanced at the sun swiftly and then at the road descending into the valley below. The Georgian highway, which had been hacked through the mountains in a titanic five-year struggle, clung to the rock face of the mountains, descending and mounting through valley after valley, through gorges and defiles, each as familiar as his own landscaped acres.

She couldn't be too far ahead now since they'd been on the road for almost three hours. His blue lacquered coach was distinctive and Lisaveta noticed as well for her beauty; each post stop knew exactly when the carriage and lovely lady had passed. She was, according to the ostlers at Tskhinval—the last fort before the Krestovaia Pass—no more than fifteen minutes ahead.

Stefan nudged his Orloff mare into more speed, and Haci, waving the men behind them forward, whipped his own mount to close the distance between himself and Stefan.

Ten minutes later they caught sight of a vivid flash of royal blue disappearing over the crest of a rise and Stefan smiled, a wolfish smile not entirely without malice. He was hot and tired, dusty after three hours on the road and in the mood to blame someone other than himself for this morning pursuit. Sliding his Winchester from his saddle mount, he fired six rapid shots into the air and then slowed his horse to a canter. His driver and outriders would recognize the signal.

The chase was won.

"Why are we stopping?" Lisaveta asked the mounted man outside the carriage window, apprehensive after hearing the rifle fire to find the coach coming to a standstill in the middle of the road. Bandits were still prevalent in the mountains, and if they were being attacked, surely they shouldn't be stopping.

"Were those shots?" she added, hoping the way a child might for a reassuring answer.

"The Prince, *mademoiselle*," he said, resting both hands on his saddle pommel and smiling. He had begun the trip addressing her with the rigid protocol required by many nobles, but she had resisted being called "Your Illustriousness" and he had deferred to her wishes.

"Are you sure?"

"Yes, *mademoiselle*."

"But we're over four hours out of Tiflis."

"Almost five, *mademoiselle*," he corrected.

"Why would 'the Prince'—" she duplicated his pronunciation "—be riding north?"

"I couldn't say, *mademoiselle*," the young man politely replied, although he had a pretty fair notion why, having lived in Stefan's household all his life.

"Need we wait?"

She could have been asking him, "Is there a God?" so startled was his expression. But, of course, she understood as well as the astonished young outrider why Stefan was on the road to Vladikavkaz.

And she didn't think he was bringing a proposal of marriage.

In the next moment she chastised herself for unrealistic presumption as well as for demanding justice. She had with eyes wide open and entire free will entered into her relationship with Stefan, and now suddenly she was requiring decorum. It was unjust to him and to her sense of freedom. His pursuit, however, was also unjust to her sense of freedom, and she hoped he'd be reasonable to deal with.

Maybe he was simply coming after her to say goodbye.

As the sound of hoofbeats neared, the outrider moved away from the carriage, and swirling dust drifted by her window, mingling with men's voices raised in greeting, the jingle of harness, horses' neighing in recognition of stablemates. She heard Stefan's voice, too, in the melee of sound, and moments later the carriage door swung open.

He filled the small portal, wearing his clothes from the previous night, his face sweat-streaked and moody, his hair in damp curls, his lip still slightly swollen where she'd bitten him. The sun was at midpoint and hot even at the mountain altitudes.

"Come," he said curtly, and put out his gloved hand.

No proposal of marriage, that terse command, nor a poetical declaration of goodbye. Not that she'd expected either. But then she'd also not expected the cold chill order. He could be a man of persuasive charm.

"No," she replied, for a tangle of reasons she'd already spent hours dwelling on.

Wiping his forehead with the back of his gloved hand, he said, "Don't push me, Lise. We've been riding our ass off for almost three hours."

"Is that *my* fault?" Her mild sarcasm took issue with his egoistic viewpoint. She was hardly to blame for his willful urges; she'd certainly not asked him to follow her.

"Who the hell else's?" he growled, immune to her reasoning, tuned in to his own sense of inconvenience.

"I told you I was leaving," she said, her declaration inflected with emphasis. "It couldn't have come as such a surprise." The scent of his sweat struck her as a breeze blew in from the open door and it was overlaid with the cologne he favored, a special blend distilled in the bazaar from local flora. She was reminded instantly as the fragrance struck her nostrils of other times they'd been heated—by a riding of another sort. She wondered then how useful her words would be, or how irrelevant against a man of Stefan's determination.

His answering sigh was audible only to her, and his voice dropped in volume. "I'd love to stand out here in the middle of the mountains under a hot sun," he said very softly, "after two hours' sleep in clothes I haven't changed since yesterday, and argue the fine points with you, Countess, *if* I was in the mood for an argument—which I'm not."

Her question was answered, but not without invoking her own willful disposition. "And that means?" Lisaveta slowly said, a flare of resentment responding to his princely peremptoriness and sulky dark glance—to his notion she could be ordered about like a minion.

"It means the discussion is over. You'll need a horse for the rest of the journey, so kindly give me your hand and I'll help you alight."

"And if I don't wish to journey with you?" she said, narrow-eyed and combative. For all her life she'd had charge of her actions, trained from early childhood to be responsible for her own decisions. She didn't take kindly to orders, princely or otherwise. She was too privileged herself, too wealthy, too educated to fall into a subservient role.

Stefan glanced around briefly. His men were lounging on their ponies, but even the most objective observer wouldn't doubt their capacity for action. "Really, darling, save yourself the embarrassment of being taken bodily from this carriage."

"Are you abducting me against my will?" Her shoulders had straightened in defiance.

"Hell, no. I'm taking you on a more scenic route home, and don't start all that 'against my will' dialogue because we settled that last night. I'm only here to accommodate your…" His smile was libertine and assured and he considered saying "lust" but gentlemanly decided against it. Women normally preferred a more romantic term for their carnal urges. "Wishes," he very softly finished.

"My wishes are to continue north in this carriage."

"And you will…eventually."

"When will that be?" she inquired, each word chill with icicles.

He seemed to be silently calculating. "Twenty days, sixteen hours, give or take a few minutes. It depends on Haci."

"Damn you." He intended to keep her his entire leave.

"My feelings exactly," he grimly said. "Now if you don't mind…" He reached for her.

She inched backward into the corner of the seat. "What if I resist?"

His eyes shut briefly. "Hell, Lise, you'd think I was going to stake you out on a mountaintop as prey for the eagles. You'll *like* my mountain lodge, believe me."

"It's the coercion I take issue with."

"Would you like a princely invitation? I thought I did that last night." And he had, with grace and courtesy and delight in his descriptions of his mountaintop aerie.

She had no choice, short of being dragged kicking and

screaming from the carriage. She was outnumbered, weapon-less and quite alone against Stefan and his men. But she could at least protest. "I want to categorically express my dissent," she said, her voice unsteady with frustration, "to this—this—"

"Holiday? Fine. Great. Accepted. Can we go now?" He placed one foot onto the metal step, tipping the carriage with his weight. "Ready?" he said with a smile.

"You're incorrigible and shameless and completely over-bearing," Lisaveta fumed, staring at him with bold contempt.

"Masha keeps telling me that. Does it matter when you com-mand a large portion of the Tsar's army?" His grin was teas-ing, self-assured and provoking.

"You *can't* keep me captive," she intemperately said. Then she took another look at Stefan's purposeful stance and ex-pression, noted the number of his mountain men and changed both her inflection and phrasing. "Will you really keep me captive?" she asked, struck suddenly by her absolute vulner-ability.

"I'd prefer you as my guest." His voice was gallant once again and amiable. She was more beautiful than he remembered and he'd missed her terribly already in the few short hours she was gone. "I can promise you—" his words dropped to a husky whisper and he thought of the delight she brought him "—a pleasant holiday."

"I won't go of my own free will," Lisaveta stubbornly in-sisted against the overwhelming odds facing her, against his whispered promise and her own indiscreet volition, resisting to the last, because with Nadejda in the wings and the hundreds of other women in his past and future, why should she docilely become one of them?

His sigh was a well-bred exhalation of tolerance. "I didn't think you would," he said, reaching in, grasping her hand and pulling her forward as if she were weightless. "Close your eyes and think of the Empire," he cheerfully teased, lifting her out of the carriage and swinging her into his arms in a swish of silk petticoats and crisp pink linen. "You're absolved of all moral blame. Guaranteed. With my reputation I'll gladly take the role of abductor."

"You don't care what people think, do you?" Her face was very close to his as he held her in his arms, and she didn't know if the blazing sun or Stefan's closeness was the cause of the heat racing through her senses.

He thought for a moment of the fishbowl of scandal he'd grown up in and of all the scandals since. "Not really," he casually replied, not looking at her, striding purposefully toward Cleo.

"Do you care what people think of me?" she quietly asked.

He stopped for a moment as he was about to lift her onto the red padded, quilted leather saddle, his expression suddenly solemn. "My servants and troopers are trustworthy. Nothing will be said."

"And Nadejda?"

He considered briefly how he could protect her against that moral outrage. "Masha will help," he declared, understanding that stronger measures might be required in countering Taneiev perturbation. "She has great influence in society. And Alexander will champion you should you need more powerful protectors." He spoke of the Tsar in intimate personal terms, pledging her the full extent of his privileged status and position. His dark eyes were grave and very near as he held her in his arms. "Would you like that in writing?"

I'd like a license of sole possession, she inexplicably thought, so you'd be mine alone for always and ever. But then every woman he'd ever known, no doubt, reacted similarly. He was rare and beautiful and much too attractive in a million ways. He was going to be—was already—all-consuming and disastrous to her peace of mind. But since she couldn't conceivably have what she wanted, and he wouldn't welcome the true nature of her possessive impulse, she discarded utterance of her irrelevant whimsy and said instead, "You can't absolve a person's reputation by fiat."

"Yes, darling, you can." Swinging her up onto Cleo, he followed, then settled her across his lap. "If it's the Tsar's fiat," he said matter-of-factly. "Kiss me," he whispered, smiling down at her, his plans on track once again.

"Not with everyone looking." Lisaveta was shy yet and inexperienced in the ways of brazen and public courtship.

While Stefan preferred privacy for his amorous dalliance, it wasn't a requirement. "Then I'll kiss you," he said. And he did.

They rode for half a day over treacherous, almost impassable trails, climbing all the time, pausing occasionally on a rocky promontory to rest the horses, dismounting once to water the mountain ponies at an icy rushing stream. Portions of the trail were no more than a yard across and Lisaveta clung to Stefan through these passages, her eyes shut against the terrifying sight of the valley, distant and small a half mile below, then a mile below. Immune to the terrors shaking Lisaveta's nerves, Stefan was relaxed, joking with his men, exchanging stories and reminiscences in their native Kurdish, brushing Lisaveta's hair occasionally with a light kiss, smiling at her, soothing her when she shivered in his arms.

Late in the afternoon when the air had cooled considerably with the high mountain altitudes and the sun had begun its journey toward the horizon, the party reached a pine grove dappled with shadow, scented with pungent fragrance. Riding through the limpid, iridescent-shot sunlight and cool dimness, they came after some time upon a whitewashed lodge roofed in green glazed tile. The building was without systematic plan, all asymmetrical and sprawling with mullioned windows and decorative porches, vine-covered trellises and assorted bays that had the look of being added on by whim. It was perched picturesquely on a sloping escarpment that fell away beyond the lodge into the openness of the sky, its center portion graced by a landscaped courtyard through which a mountain stream, bordered by a carpet of flowers, ran.

It had the charming look of a fairy tale.

Out of its apricot-painted, vine-covered doorway a dark-haired young girl came running, cast, it seemed, for a part in the fairy tale. Her slender form, clad exotically in brilliant, luxurious Gypsy attire, was lithe as a nymph; her bare arms and legs and feet were the lush olive of her Romany heritage;

her wildly curling tresses streaming out behind her shone like black silk.

"Stash, Stash, you're home!" she cried, her great dark eyes gleaming with delight, her arms thrown open wide in welcome.

Lisaveta stiffened in Stefan's arms the same instant he saw Choura's expression alter as she became aware of Lisaveta. Oh Lord, he thought, I forgot. "Don't move," he murmured to Lisaveta, cognizant of Choura's temper and her skill with a knife. In a rapid staccato delivery he spoke to Haci next. The dialect was unfamiliar to Lisaveta, but his intent was clear. His voice was gruff and exasperated. As Haci swiftly urged his horse forward to intercept Choura's forward dash, Lisaveta surveyed Stefan's impassive face. As Haci scooped the Gypsy girl up in one arm and rode out of the courtyard, out of sight behind an enormous stand of rhododendrons, Choura's screams echoing above the rustle of the wind in the pines, Lisaveta noted Stefan's air of apparent detachment. No more than an inconvenience—immediately dispatched.

"Will he drown her?" Lisaveta maliciously inquired. This was the common method of disposal for members of the Sultan's seraglio. "Or will I simply be added to your harem?"

Stefan was tired and hungry; he'd been riding for more than six hours after a night with little sleep and his fatigue was achingly real. He was not presently inclined, especially after finding Choura still vividly in residence, to politely accept sarcasm from the woman causing him all his discomfort. "I was saving your skin," he bluntly said, "protecting you from Choura's knife."

"I can protect myself, thank you," Lisaveta replied, haughty and incensed; Stefan had not only left a fiancée behind but had a woman in reserve here, as well.

"Not unless you move real fast," he sardonically murmured. "She could carve you up in under thirty seconds."

"Do women fight over you often?" Her barely contained fury was evident in her voice. It was enough to know her own feelings were disastrously involved—against her will and better judgment—but to see Stefan's women conveniently available wherever he lived, and to hear him plainly suggest they might fight a rival for his affection, was galling.

"No," he quietly said, his own self-control additionally provoking in face of her outrage. "Now if you'll excuse me briefly."

"And if I won't?" Her objection was anger only and having the last snappish word—or perhaps most of all, wishing she had the power he did to bend the world to his will.

He looked down at her for a long moment, his expression benign, as if an angry child were thwarting him. "Nakun will see you to my study," he said, neither answering her question nor acknowledging her challenge. "Please make yourself comfortable." With the merest nod he signaled one of his men.

"I don't *want* to make myself comfortable, Stefan." She tried to control her voice as he did, so she wouldn't sound so adolescent. "I want to go home. I refuse to be your...captive," she finished in sputtering frustration. "And if you think for a minute," she added, trying to squirm out of his steely grasp, "that I'm going to quietly submit to your goddamn—" her voice was rising now because he was beginning to smile "—suzerainty like some docile Gypsy girl—"

He laughed. *Docile* was the last word he would have chosen to describe Choura.

His laugh only further ignited Lisaveta's indignation. "I suppose a man who kept five Persian houris for his exclusive enjoyment at Kokand," she snapped, "finds this all amusing. But *I* refuse to be your entertainment!"

Good God, he thought, how far had that story traveled. But he only said in a calm tone, "You needn't get agitated. Accept my apologies for Choura. She was...er...an oversight. I'll straighten everything out and be back shortly."

"An *oversight*?" Her voice was almost a whisper. "Like a forgotten package, you mean?" Her golden eyes were the color of the sky before a thunderstorm. "Or an inconvenience?"

"Lord, Lise, relax. There's an explanation. I'll straighten things out."

"Haven't you been listening to *anything* I said?" Lisaveta cried. "I don't want everything straightened out, I don't want you to continue talking to me in that serenely undisturbed tone as though you were taking confession, and I *do not wish to be here*!'' Each word was punctuated with a blow to his chest.

Stefan's troopers regarded Lisaveta's vehemence with varying degrees of amusement. They all viewed women as diversions to a warrior's life, and from appearances their Prince was going to be highly diverted when he took the Countess to bed.

At the moment, however, Stefan knew he had to deal with Choura first, and arguing with Lisaveta wasn't accomplishing any useful purpose. ''Do I have to have you tied up?'' he inquired in the placid tone that grated so on Lisaveta's nerves.

Her eyes opened wide in aghast speculation. He wouldn't, *would* he? She realized he was closely related to these Kurdish troopers with their wild and barbaric looks. He lived at times in their way under a warrior code, but did he actually mean ''tied up'' when he said it in that quiet tone? And if he did— the small unpleasant thought surfaced—for what purpose? ''Tied up?'' she blurted out, her breath unconsciously in abeyance, anticipating his answer.

''Will you accompany Nakun into the house or do you have to be restrained?'' He could have been asking her if she preferred a lemon ice or champagne during a set change at a ball, for all the emotion in his voice.

Lisaveta glanced for a swift moment at the swarthy native tribesman dressed in black turban, tunic and full-cut trousers, standing patiently in his soft Asiatic boots at Stefan's side, waiting further orders. She rapidly took in the array of his weaponry: crossed bandoliers; saber belt and pistol holster; the shined and oiled new Winchester taken as booty from a dead Turk slung across his back; the matching set of silver-engraved daggers tucked into his belt. With the pragmatic deduction of an intelligent woman she murmured, ''You needn't tie me.''

''Splendid,'' Stefan cheerfully said, as though no one had been discussing bodily restraint, as if the topic of conversation were banal and unthreatening, as if the word *splendid* fitted this horrendous situation at all.

''I'll 'splendid' you,'' Lisaveta hissed, as Stefan lowered her into Nakun's arms, ''just as soon as I get the chance.''

Stefan's smile was wolfish. "In that case, I won't keep you waiting long." He touched her cheek with a caressing fingertip. "Darling…" But his voice when he spoke to Nakun the next moment was coolly commanding. "Lock the door," he said, "in my study, when you leave."

SEVEN

Seven

The elaborate clock in the study depicting tides and changing constellations was exquisite, but its hands moved annoyingly slowly. At frequent intervals, Lisaveta would interrupt her angry pacing to check its progress and find no more than a minute had passed since she'd last looked. She'd already admired the magnificent view from the expanse of windows lining one wall, noted the craggy mountain landscape and snowcapped peaks in all their awesome splendor, stood transfixed while an eagle swooped in sweeping arabesques across the emptiness of space between her mountain and those distant ones and understood with absolute certainty she could never find her way down the craggy peaks and survive. Unlike the free-flying eagle, she was Stefan's captive.

After that sobering observation she'd sat down abruptly, her eyes unfocused on the panoramic grandeur of blue sky and rugged mountaintops, her mind attempting to deal with the finality of her position. When no ready answer materialized in the chaos of her mind, when no escape seemed possible from this mountain aerie, she'd resumed her pacing again, her rapid strides as agitated as her thoughts.

Despite Stefan's imposing palace and polished manners, he was, beneath his civilized veneer, as much a native warrior as his men. He looked the same: hawklike, swarthy, bristling with weapons. She recalled her first sight of him, when she'd thought she'd been captured by another savage tribesman. Only his Chevalier Gardes uniform had distinguished him from his cohorts that day near Kars. And while she'd learned much of the subtlety and nuance of his charismatic personality in their days together, his tribesmen, too, might be as complex and charming.

She was disturbed and perplexed.

She was indecisive about her unsubtle and profound attraction to Stefan.

She was a bit fearful, too, so far removed from the world on this remote mountaintop.

But she was—beneath and beyond and above the confusion of her feelings—primarily angry.

That fact was startlingly clear when Stefan walked into the room twenty minutes later.

A rose jade figurine of a Tang emperor's celebrated concubine, a special favorite of Stefan's for the cutwork in her trailing gown, narrowly missed his head as he ducked out of the way. The jade depiction of Li Shi Mia thrown at him was followed rapidly by his inkwell, several of his malachite paperweights, and before he could bob and weave across the distance separating them and wrench a silver wine ewer from Lisaveta's grasp, he'd lost the crystal container to his Cellini inkwell and two of his animal-shaped paperweights.

He wondered if perhaps Choura's anger had been easier to deal with. She'd been pacified by a handsome gift of roubles, a promise to send her two racers from his stables and a soothing combination of lies and compliments. When she was smiling once again, he'd had to carefully decline her offer to join a ménage à trois in his bed. "Perhaps some other time," he'd said politely.

And with that promise, her money and two prime horses, she was content. She would be escorted by some of his men to the nearest village, from which she'd find her own way home. Her smile when she'd left had been satisfied and her parting remark perhaps more prophetic than he wished.

"She won't be as easily bought off, Stash, my beauty," she'd said, wrapped in an emerald green shawl to match the jewels in her ears. She blew him a kiss and smiled. "I wish you luck."

He could use a little now, he thought, tightly holding both Lisaveta's hands and trying to sidestep her kicking feet. "Damn you, Stefan, I won't be treated like this," she panted, out of breath from her struggles. "I'm...not...some...Gypsy girl...you can buy...for a few roubles...and spirit away to your...mountain lodge."

"Fifty thousand," he said, moving slightly to one side to avoid her slippered foot.

"Fifty thousand!" she exclaimed, ceasing her combat for a moment to digest the enormity of Choura's price. "Are you mad? The Emir of Erzurum never paid over twenty thousand for the very best Circassian women."

Taking advantage of her momentary pause, he quickly said, "I did it for you. She's gone."

"Why?" It was a small explosive exhalation of sound as spontaneous as her astonishment.

He didn't know, so he couldn't answer, but a response was required to her question so he evasively said, "I forgot she was here. I've been gone for three months." He shrugged then the way he often did when she pressed him to gauge his feelings, and added one of those platitudinous lies that often served as satisfactory conclusion to an evasion. "She was probably ready to go anyway. Choura dislikes solitude."

"And yet," Lisaveta murmured, "she waited here for three months?" Jealousy underlay her remark, overwhelmed her like a gale at ten thousand feet in these mountains, for she knew very well why a woman who disliked solitude would wait three months for Stefan. He was worth a three-month wait—or a three-year wait.

"She probably couldn't find her way back down," he lied, treading warily, infinitely pleased she was talking to him again instead of screaming at him or throwing his treasured pieces of sculpture at his head.

"She probably didn't want to," Lisaveta quietly said, her golden eyes holding his in a steady gaze.

"*I* didn't want her here," he said, his simple statement a

bald declaration of his feelings, his eyes unflinching. "I sent her away for you. I left Nadejda entertaining her parents at my palace tonight for you. Is that enough?" He released her hands, gazed at her for a moment as though looking for the answer himself, then walked away to the windows.

Bracing his hands on the molding above his head, he stared out on the majestic landscape that had always served as solace for him, the stark rugged mountains that had been sanctuary for him at times he needed peace.

But today his thoughts were in turmoil, his emotions disturbed, his fiancée left behind without concern for the consequences, Choura dismissed more callously than he liked. For Lisaveta.

"So," he said, turning back, his own feelings resentful now, "is it enough? Tell me." There was demand in his voice, an unconscious authority.

Standing in the center of his masculine study, Lisaveta heard the new chill in his voice, saw the beginning of a scowl draw his brows together and awkwardly felt on the defensive. "You should have let me go," she said, adding when he didn't move or respond, "It would have been better for both of us."

"I didn't want to."

"God's spoiled child," she softly declared, for the Orbeliani motto was familiar throughout the Empire for its arrogance.

Stefan raised one brow fractionally. That precept had been his family's guiding principle for centuries; he could no more ignore the privileged culture in which he'd been reared than she hers. In many ways she was as unorthodox as he, and he said exactly that without rancor or censure.

For a short silence Lisaveta seemed to consider his statement. Her life, of course, had been more male than female in education, in the freedom and independence encouraged by her father, in her choice of scholarly discipline. She was, she supposed, not precisely conventional, and their meeting that first night at Aleksandropol... She smiled. "We both perhaps have taken what we wanted," she answered.

She was without guile, he thought, one of her numerous charms.

"I *did* fancy you that very first night, didn't I?" she said.

His smile was as angelic as a young choirboy's. "I detected a slight interest."

"So I can't be assessing blame exclusively."

"If you wish to be perfectly honest, no," he said, "but I dislike the word *blame* for anything that's passed between us. I prefer happiness...or joy—"

"Or paradise on earth."

He grinned. "A good approximation."

"I should thank you, then, for sending her away."

He moved toward her, his smile intact, his hands open in peace. "If you like," he said.

"And thank you for spending fifty thousand roubles because of me."

"Plus two racers from my stud," he added, close enough now to touch her outstretched hands.

"I should feel flattered."

"I certainly hope so," he murmured, taking her small hands in his.

"And how many days do we have?"

"Twenty."

Her smile diminished slightly. "I might have to leave sooner for Papa's ceremony in Saint Petersburg. I've a personal invitation from the Tsar. I should stop at my home in Rostov first. My cousin Nikki's expecting me...." Her voice trailed away because the observance honoring her father's work translating Hafiz had seemed until this moment of great importance.

Stefan wasn't going to touch that...not after reaching harmony once again, not this minute when he held her hands in his and their holiday in the mountains was just beginning. "Fine," he said, his own smile lush with warming passion, knowing he had days ahead to change her mind or adjust her travel timetable. "Whatever you want."

Drawing her close, he stood for a small space of time with her body touching his, savoring the first tentative prelude to pleasure, feeling at peace, at home...alone with the woman who'd come to preoccupy his mind and senses, isolated on his mountaintop with the woman he wanted to spend the next twenty days making love to.

"I'm sorry about the abduction," he said softly, his hand reaching up to take the first hairpin from her hair, "but I didn't want to lose you."

Lisaveta touched the bridge of his nose, tracing down its arrow-straight length as if she marked him for herself, as if that small gesture were possession. How nice it would be, she thought, if it were possible to gain possession so easily, if one could simply say, "I want you too, for always. For the pleasure you give me and for your smiles, for the laughter we share, for the enchantment of being in your arms." But she was sensible enough to say instead, her voice teasing and hushed, "I'll make you do penance for the abduction."

His hand stopped just short of his desk, where he'd been placing the pins from her hair, and arrested in motion, he looked at her from under his dark brows and smiled. "How nice," he said.

"You needn't sound so pleased," Lisaveta murmured, mocking irony in her tone.

"Darling," Stefan whispered, taking her into his arms and drawing the length of her body against his so she felt the extent of his arousal, "your whims are my command."

A flare of excitement raced through Lisaveta. Although she knew as well as he that his amorous words were playful, a rush of gratified power spiked through her. She did indeed command him. "Are they really?" she said, moving her hips enticingly, testing the measure of her advantage.

"Right now, *dushka*," Stefan whispered, taking her face between the palms of his large hands, "for want of you I'd sell my soul."

And jettison your fiancée? she wondered, the wretched consideration coming from nowhere to spoil the moment. Perhaps if she'd asked right then he would have said yes to please her and please himself. But she didn't ask, because she wanted him too much and was afraid of his answer. A man in Stefan's position didn't marry for passion; Militza had made his intentions plain.

"My price isn't that high," she said, her arms wrapped around his waist, a curious contentment invading her mind. He was here with her; because of enormous effort he was here with her; his fiancée was alone at his palace and there was satisfaction in that. She wouldn't be more greedy. "I don't want your soul, although I think I should be worth at least as much as Choura."

While her tone was teasing, Stefan gazed at Lisaveta with a slightly altered expression. Was she like all the others after all? he wondered. Although he'd never begrudged gifts to his lovers, he'd found Lise's generosity of spirit unique. Was she perhaps only more subtle in her demands? His voice when he spoke was quiet and restrained. "Of course, darling, you're worth much more. What would you like?"

"You'll think me foolish," she prefaced, blushing at what she was about to say.

"Never, sweetheart," he replied, admiring the innocent color on her cheeks, knowing he would give her whatever she wanted regardless of her request. He was not an ungenerous man. Her large tawny eyes were looking directly into his despite her blushing hesitancy, and he thought again how her frankness appealed to him.

"I want you to love only me, to forget all those other women," she blurted out, a desperate and unfathomable urge impelling her, inexplicable and beyond her control. She hurried on when she saw the startled look in his eyes. "I mean now...for these days we have together." When he didn't answer, she added softly, "The fiction will do, Stefan, and don't ask me why, but it's important to me." Had she been asked to define her feelings she would have been at loss to explain. She loved him, she thought with a cymbal-crashing revelation, neither annotated nor detailed but explosive and deafening inside her head. And she wanted her love returned.

For a woman who was not only a scholar but an expert in a man's field, for a woman who'd decided to ride across the battleground of Kurdistan in the midst of war, for a woman who'd traveled up his harrowing mountain trails with a minimum of vapors or complaint, she looked suddenly as vulnerable and artless as a young maid. She didn't want extravagant gifts or large sums of money; she wasn't intent on binding him in a female way he'd learned at a very young age to avoid. She wanted only his love.

And for the only time in his extremely varied experience with women, his heart was touched, not simply by the naïveté of her request but by her utter candor. "Gladly," he replied, his emotions evident in his voice, "with intemperate feeling and pleasure."

When her face lighted up at his response, her joy and happiness immediately apparent, a warmth of unprecedented feeling washed over him. Gently lifting her face to his, he said very, very softly, "I plight you my love on this mountaintop," pledging surety to her and with that pledge, unknown to Lisaveta, offering his love for the first time in his life.

He lifted her in his arms then, as though his patience had a finite limit, and carried her out of his study and up the small curved staircase. The polished wooden railing resembled a sinuous grapevine, curling upward as it would in nature, minutely detailed with beautifully carved tendrils, leaves and fruit; the treads were covered in lush grass-green carpet, silken and luminous. So close to nature were these creations of man she almost expected to gaze up and see stars in the sky.

"Where are the stars?" she playfully murmured.

As if he read her mind, as if they were so completely in harmony he knew what she was thinking, he answered, "In my room."

Past the top of the vine-draped stairs, at the end of a narrow hallway hung with candlelit icons and illuminated paintings reminiscent of glittering jewels, Stefan pushed open double wooden doors, hinged and ornamented with brass serpentine animal forms, and stepped into a room he'd known since childhood.

Toys were stacked on shelves and tabletops; a wooden rocking horse painted dapple gray in primitive craft style with large staring eyes and an unusual smile gazed at them from a window embrasure; a special glass case held massed armies of miniature soldiers. The polished wood floor was covered with fur rugs, as was the plain four-poster bed, although the elaborately embroidered, lace-trimmed white pillow covers were an incongruous sight in this young boy's room.

The dormer windows were curtained in plain blue linen, made less plain by the entwined Bariatinsky-Orbeliani family crests woven in gold thread and picked out with sapphire jewels. While austere in design, Stefan's room spoke eloquently of his family's enormous wealth, from the sable rugs to the cabochon emeralds in his rocking horse's eyes.

And the stars.

When he pointed up with a smile so she'd look, Lisaveta saw a lapis lazuli arched ceiling set with diamond stars.

"You have a fortune in your ceiling," she couldn't help but say. Even though her mother's family was in the exclusive ranks of the Empire's wealthiest and the Lazaroffs were far from paupers, she'd never seen anything like the lavishness of Stefan's households.

"My mama's Persian background," Stefan explained. "The Orbelianis had a different standard of wealth than the rest of the world." He didn't reply with either apology or pretension but simply made a statement of fact. "I wanted to see the stars at night when I went to sleep, I told Mama when I was very young and this lodge was being built."

"Does Choura like your diamond stars?" She couldn't restrain her remark although she'd valiantly suppressed it twice before it came tumbling out. Her jealousy was stridently real and Choura was wildly beautiful by anyone's standards, an untamed dazzling enchantress.

"I haven't brought her here." He'd never brought *any* woman to this room. It was exclusively his in a selfish introverted way. He'd never wanted to share his past or his feelings—all openly visible here in his mementos and childhood toys. He'd preserved the shelter of this room intact against the personal disasters that had decimated his family. His happiest memories of childhood were inventoried and cataloged by each particle and belonging in this room, and until today he'd never wanted to expose those intimacies to anyone.

Lisaveta's gaze was skeptical.

"Her room was on the main floor facing the courtyard," he matter-of-factly said, secure in the truth. "I'll show you if you—"

"No," she said. "No, don't show me." The thought of Stefan and…her…in any room made her feel green-eyed with resentment. "So she never saw this?" It wasn't that she didn't believe him, only that she found it hard to believe.

Stefan set her down carefully in an oversize chair upholstered in royal blue damascene, squatted down in front of her so their eyes were level and said, this man who was known to prize his personal privacy, "Ask me everything and then you'll be content."

"Don't patronize me, Stefan."

"I'll answer honestly." And that, too, was a startling admission from Stefan, who by virtue of necessity in the sheer number of his amorous liaisons considered evasion an essential.

Lisaveta sighed, her expression rueful, her golden eyes innocent as a young girl's. "I'm sorry. Do you think me excessively possessive?"

"I think you've brought me unmitigated joy the week past is what I think." He grinned. "And I'm in no position to be passing judgment on character."

She smiled back, charmed by both his admissions. "True," she unabashedly said, happily accepting both his statements. "Why didn't she see this?" she asked then, because she wanted the detail behind his action, because she wanted the pleasure and luxury of hearing he hadn't cared for Choura as much as he did for her.

"I didn't say she didn't see this. She may have when I was gone. None of the doors are locked."

"Why?"

"Why aren't they locked?" A lifetime of evasion wasn't so easily jettisoned.

Lisaveta gazed at him with mock severity.

"It was my room," he said bluntly. "I didn't care to bring her here."

"Why?"

He shrugged. "I don't know." His reasons were not so easily disentangled from the muddle of his past. It had been a matter of survival, perhaps, for a man who'd seen his world destroyed while very young. His dark eyes held hers for a moment. "Introspection is a new concept for me, *dushka*. I'm sorry," he said, apologizing for the inadequacy of his answer. "It didn't seem right. Is that sufficient?"

"*I'm* sorry," she said, recognizing the effort he'd made in answering, "for being so insistent. It's as though I've no control over my jealousy."

"We're well matched then, sweetheart, because I must keep you by me...regardless..." He left the sentence unfinished, for each knew the difficulties evaded to bring them here together.

His shoulders seemed very wide only inches below her eye level, the breadth of his chest like a solid wall before her. His black eyes beneath his heavy brows were like a force of nature, so vibrant and intense was his glance. He was dynamic power and energy and a magnetic beauty she could no more relinquish than the earth could stop turning on its axis. With a curious finality she said, "And I want you selfishly for myself alone."

His voice was intense and gruff. "We're agreed then." She looked the most perfect woman he'd ever seen, rosy-cheeked, her golden eyes bright with spirit and passion, her slender form dwarfed by the custom-built chair made to suit his own enormous frame. Her traveling suit blended perfectly with the royal blue of the chair as if she'd planned her wardrobe for the eventuality of this moment. The dusty-rose linen, trimmed with white organdy collar and cuffs, buttoned in steel-gray mother-of-pearl, dramatized both her femininity and warmth and he wanted her in his bed with an urgency he'd never experienced before.

"I can't wait any longer," he said, the way a young boy might. "Have I answered everything now?" Anyone knowing Stefan would have been shocked at his grave diffidence. He was not a humble man.

"Have I told you how happy you make me?" Lisaveta replied, astonished at the exhilarating bliss she felt in his presence.

"And I can make you happier," he murmured, his smile

roguish and familiar, his mood restored. Adoring women were a constant in his life. He was back on familiar ground.

"Arrogant man," she whispered.

"But you need me," he whispered back, reaching for the buttons on her jacket.

She stopped his hand. "We need each other." She waited with an arrogance matching his own.

"Yes," he said, engulfing the hand that stayed him but holding it gently in his warm palm. "We do."

They made love right there in the chair because it was most convenient for their unbridled passion. The second time, when their frantic need had diminished slightly so they needn't so selfishly take from each other, they tested the luxury of the sable rug.

Stefan carried her after to his bed and deposited her like the Princess she was on the crested lace-trimmed pillows and white ermine coverlet. Gazing at her lying flushed with pleasure, her rich chestnut hair in silky disarray across his pillows, her golden eyes half-lidded in the drowsy aftermath of lovemaking, dressed only in Militza's pearl earrings, her slender voluptuous body close enough to touch, he said uncharacteristically, his voice a deep low growl, "You're mine." There was nothing logical in his declaration; emotion moved him, not reason.

Her lashes lifted that fraction necessary to afford him a direct remonstrance. "Temporarily," she reminded him, her own independence as stubborn as his, their personalities matched in imperiousness.

"We'll see," he replied, emotionally unwilling to relinquish her, impelled in his present need to brand her as his property. He didn't question the unorthodoxy of these sensations; he only acted on them.

"No, we won't see," she retorted, unwilling to submit when he wouldn't. The man was engaged; they'd both agreed on the limit of their holiday. Unless some facet of his life changed, which was highly unlikely, locked in as he was to the necessity of a court marriage, she wouldn't further indulge him.

"You're not in any position to resist my wishes," he quietly said, his smile the kind that might or might not extend into genuine warmth, "on *my* mountaintop."

"Are we talking more of your archaic notions of captivity?"

"Call them what you will. I'm not concerned with your choice of words."

"I won't be dealt with as an object of your obsessions," she reminded him, gazing boldly up at him as though she weren't lying nude in his bed hours from the nearest hint of civilization.

She saw his struggle to respond congenially to her words and saw, too, the enormous control necessary to bring his wild impulses to heel. "I keep forgetting," he said, moving away from her and striding with a naturalness unconstrained by his nudity to a small liquor cabinet, added no doubt when his boyhood was past, "you want to be equal." He said it benignly, as an overture of peace, unaware of the inherent repudiation in his statement.

His words, however benevolent in spirit, were the same challenge Lisaveta had faced all of her life. They brought her to a sitting position in the middle of his ermine bedcover.

"I don't wish to be argumentative," she said in a voice of suppressed emotion, watching him pour some of the local liquor into a small glass, "but it's not that I wish to be equal, I am."

She'd been raised to be equal, had sufficient wealth to be equal, was educated by a great number of tutors to be more than equal to most men and had consequently never felt inferior as a woman.

"Sorry," Stefan apologized, "of course," and lifting the glass to his mouth, he swallowed the fiery spirits. His apology was the mindless variety one automatically expressed when bumping into someone accidentally or stepping on someone's toes in a crush. "There now," he said, placing the empty glass back on the cabinet, "have I told you lately how I adore your very sweet stiff-backed pride?"

His grin was intimate and effortless and Lisaveta wondered how many times he'd evaded controversy with that grin.

"I'm not seventeen," she quietly retorted, annoyed with his repertoire of avoidance.

"You *look* seventeen, *dushka*, word of honor." He had no intention of arguing over who had more power. While he understood her need to challenge the inequalities, from his male point of view, the world offered her little chance of succeeding. He'd been in positions of supreme power too long to have any delusions about the position of women.

"Do women have to be young to please you?" Sweet malice and condemnation colored her soft tone.

He'd reached the bed as she finished speaking and he inhaled softly as if with restraint before he quietly said, "No, darling, they don't, and I don't want to fight. I do that every day in a much more bloody fashion than you could ever imagine. I want only to love you and hold you and make you smile, and if apologizing for all the inequities to women of the past millenium will help, I offer that apology." He looked down at her, enormous in his towering height and breadth of shoulder, his eyes dark and heated and strangely seductive in the harsh masculinity of his features. "There now, is my blanket apology accepted?" His grin broke dazzling white against the swarthiness of his bronzed skin. "Or do I have to beat you into submission?"

She grinned back and sighed herself, realizing the futility of their stalemated issues. "Incorrigible man. Are you beyond reform?"

Sitting down on the bed then, he pushed her backward with the lightest pressure. "Reform me, darling," he murmured, following her down, lying atop her so she felt only the silk of his muscles and none of his weight. His smile was breathtaking and a breath away. "You've twenty days."

"Somehow," Lisaveta murmured, her mouth so close to his that tiny vibrations of sound passed between them, her eyes matching the teasing in his, "I don't think you're serious."

"I'm serious," he demurred, adjusting her hips a scant inch to accommodate him. "I've never been so serious," he unseriously said.

She hit him.

He responded by playfully nipping her earlobe.

At which point she tried to squirm away in sportive frolic.

Her small struggles amused him and aroused him, and the kiss he took from her was lush and endless and sweetly benevolent.

"I *will* reform you," Lisaveta breathlessly whispered when her mouth was released at last, her declaration only half in jest.

"I look forward to my schooling," Stefan softly replied, sliding her up the mellow ermine so he could settle between her legs. "Tell me, Countess," he murmured a moment later, his chin resting on her thigh, his eyes black and liquid with passion, his hands moving to ready her for his tongue, "when you feel I've made...progress."

All thought of anything beyond insensate pleasure disappeared from her mind as Stefan's tongue slipped into her. He licked and stroked, the taste of her blending with the distinctive flavor of their lovemaking, his own body reacting to the intemperate welcome of hers.

They were a matched pair, he thought, in passion and desire, a combination of personalities so perfectly meshed he could almost feel her urgency in his own body. When she moved to refine the tactile sensations more exquisitely, a flare of excitement raced through him, and when she moaned in luxurious gratification, the muted sound echoed in his own mind.

Then he realized with a start that she was inexplicably moving away from him, a teasing smile of undisguised allure on her face. "I think I'll rest for a while," she purred. She was all feline grace and temptation...and she was lying a full two feet away, her weight resting on both her elbows, her eyes indolent under half-lowered lashes.

"I think you're lying," he said, his voice low and husky. "I think you can't even wait a minute for what you want." He was sprawled opposite her, his bronzed skin dark against the ermine, his heavy brows mildly raised in mocking remonstrance, his smile amused.

"Is this a contest?"

"Not from here it isn't." There was undisputed confidence in his tone.

"Are you always so superior?"

"I prefer...realistic," he answered very softly. "Now don't move and I'll make us both happy."

She moved.

She almost managed to escape the bed.

Almost.

With lightning speed he lunged across the bed, his fingers closing around her ankle just before her foot hit the floor. Rolling over on his back, he scooped her into his arms in a single diving motion, depositing her on his stomach with effortless finesse.

"So you're physically stronger," Lisaveta begrudgingly said, but she was smiling.

"Do I have to apologize for that?" He was playing her game with lighthearted boyishness.

"Actually, it has its advantages." Her voice was a rich contralto, her golden eyes heated.

He laughed out loud and, reaching out, gathered her into his arms and rolled over her so she was pinned beneath him. "Beg me," he said, his smile angelic.

"With your libido," she whispered, her own smile sunshine bright and assured, "I don't have to."

"Maybe I have willpower."

"Not with me you don't."

She was right, but anyone knowing Stefan in the past would have been fascinated at his lack of control and his lack of concern at his lack of control.

"It must be your intelligence," he teased, "attracting me."

"No doubt," she ironically replied.

"And perhaps a touch of your hot-blooded Kuzan lust," he added, his face very close to hers, his dark hair brushing her cheeks, the feel of his body an invitation to pleasure.

"I thought maybe there was something more than my mind," she lazily murmured, "that interested you...." She moved minutely beneath him, her full breasts silken friction against the crisp hair of his chest, her legs sliding comfortably around his. "It's just a wild guess," she added, reaching up to touch his lips with her tongue, "you understand."

"Good guess," he murmured, gliding into her so gently she

could count the exquisite seconds in her mind before she was filled with him, bliss so flooding her senses she felt heaven must be near and if she looked up past the diamond stars she'd see angel toes. And when he was deep inside her, he made it even better. He moved that minute distance more so her breath caught in her throat, white flame racing hotly through her blood. His rhythm was slow when he began moving in her, penetrating and withdrawing with an expertise that he'd learned very young brought women to a pitched and tempestuous climax, to a screaming panting climax. And she answered the deliberate driving motion of his lower body with her own fevered passion.

"I'll beg," she breathed, short of breath and clinging to him sometime later when he'd stopped for the shortest interval to kiss her parted lips. She'd reached the point where she was going to peak without him and she wanted him with her.

"No need, *dushka*," he softly murmured. "I only wanted to kiss you.... There." His smile was indulgent as he slid into her once more. "Is that better?"

She couldn't answer because her mind was exploding with pleasure. She couldn't answer because words were incidental to the awesome rapture singing through her blood and through every quivering shuddering nerve in her body.

He met her passion then with his own, understanding her wishes with an unspoken comprehension that was partly skill and partly intrinsic emotion. They climaxed together, falling over the edge of the world onto soft white ermine.

He opened his eyes first and thought himself the luckiest of men. Twenty days left, he reflected, with the extravagant Countess.

Lisaveta's lashes rose with effort long moments later. She was new to the excessive sensuality of Stefan's companionship, or relatively new, and she didn't have his stamina. "I want to sleep," she murmured.

His smile was unselfish and accommodating. "Sleep, darling, as long as you wish."

He had twenty days left in paradise.

Eight

After Haci and the troop were dismissed the next morning, the days of their holiday continued in delight and…innovation. It was also a time of unalloyed happiness. In some small ways the Prince came to understand the nature of Lisaveta's independence. At least he tried, she indulgently thought. But steeped as he was in the culture of the Caucasus, Oriental in its social and political traditions, he had deep-seated traditions to reconcile.

His mother's family, while Georgian for centuries and thus Christian, were Persian in heritage and suzerains over large Kurdish tribes—nominally Muslim in religion, although their shaman past was still an integral part of life. These native tribes of Central Asian extraction were warrior cultures in which males were supreme, training for war a way of life and women's concerns incidental to their existence. Stefan had grown up in their midst.

His father had been born in Saint Petersburg, but he'd spent his adult life subduing the Caucasus and then ruling it for the Tsar. Field Marshal Bariatinsky had loved the mountain region and its exotic, exuberant, often violent life. The warrior culture spoke to his own soldier's soul.

Conditioned as Stefan was by a society in which harems were the norm, where warfare was the only occupation for a man, where the larger concerns of imperial expansion overrode personal interests, he was making conscious adjustments in his sentiments to accommodate Lisaveta's different perception of the world. He was trying to accommodate her notions of equality, her inexperience outside of the sphere of literary scholarship, and what he considered an idealistic vision.

She noticed his tolerance for her beliefs and his constraint when he couldn't agree. He tried not to argue, although their philosophies were at times starkly opposed. She, too, trod lightly when discussing controversial topics.

For the first time in her life, Lisaveta was experiencing a time spent purely for pleasure. For many years, she'd dealt with solitary scholarship and dusty tomes, with linguistic detail, not with this dizzying, intoxicating delirium of feeling. She was, as it were, on holiday from the circumstances of her life.

For his part, Stefan experienced not so much a break from the amusements of his past as a heightened awareness of what pleasure could be. A pleasure amplified beyond the physical, a pleasure so intense and joyous he woke at night and gently hugged Lisaveta to assure himself his sensations were real. In the days of their mountain retreat he felt again the unconditional happiness of his early childhood before he grew old enough to realize his family wasn't like others: His mother wasn't married to his father but to another man; his grandparents were his legal guardians to protect his legacy from the unknown man his mother had once married; his parents' profound love was mysteriously measured by a society as quick to punish as adore. And his long-held and dearly bought cynicism diminished in direct proportion to his happiness.

They bathed in the flower-bordered pool dammed up above the courtyard, warmed by their love to withstand the brisk temperatures of mountain streams, and rubbed each other dry amid moss-covered stones and verdant ferns, only to fall prey to the sensations provoked. The pool was their garden of Eden, their own green paradise, and they swam in the sunlight and moonlight and made love in the cool slipperiness of the water and on the scented banks of the stream.

"Will I last twenty days?" Stefan gasped one afternoon as he collapsed beside Lisaveta, his passion momentarily spent but his desire for her insatiable.

"At least I know why your reputation is so formidable," she sweetly replied, her own breathing ragged.

Her tone brought his head around and he looked at her from under his hand thrown across his forehead. "Are we being catty?" he replied, his mouth lifted in a grin.

"How do you ever find time to fight the Tsar's battles?" she said in a tone that was definitely feline.

"It's your fault," he bluntly said, although the kiss he gave her mitigated his words.

"Don't blame *me* for your satyric ways. I met you only a fortnight ago while your reputation has been circulating about the Empire for years."

"Much exaggerated, *dushka*," was his negligent reply.

"Oh, really…this is an aberration, then."

"Yes, darling, Lise," Stefan said, exhaling deeply, "you definitely are."

"I don't know," she playfully said, pleased he wasn't so enamored with all his other women, pleased her wanted her more, pleased with a female vanity she hadn't realized she possessed that he couldn't satisfy his desire for her, "if I like being called an aberration."

"Would you prefer seductive witch?" He was up on one elbow now, gazing at her as she lay beside him on the green mossy bank, his dark eyes amused.

She pursed her lips in mock disapproval. "It smacks of evil."

"Well, this pleasure is certainly not that. Do you like—" he traced a light finger down the column of her neck "—delightful nymph?"

She considered for a moment, as if this discussion were one of substance, then with reservation said, "Too poetical, Stefan, darling. I'm an archrealist."

He could have argued with her assessment. The unreality of their holiday together was so far removed from the mundane that he questioned at times whether he'd died and gone to heaven. "Delectable charmer," he pleasantly offered, "or captivating enchantress?"

Her eyes narrowed transiently at the ease with which his descriptions flowed. "Do you have many of these?" she softly inquired.

"Thousands," he teased.

"In that case I'm leaving," she responded with a hotness not altogether feigned. He'd said all these things before to too many women, and green demons of jealousy ate at her reason. Even the beauty of his body, as he lay, nude and virile, irritated those feelings. How many women had seen him so? Relaxed and charming, perfection in face and form.

"Going where?" he mildly inquired, his gaze surveying the mountain peaks surrounding them.

"Away…home…into some other man's arms," she heatedly said, wanting revenge for all his past lovers, in words at least.

"In that case, I'll have to tie you to my bed."

His calmness more than his statement shocked her. "You wouldn't!"

"In a minute," he said, his eyes having lost their amusement at talk of another man.

"I don't believe you," she replied.

"Leave then and test me." He hadn't moved in his lazy sprawl, but a new alertness was evident, as though he were coiled to spring at any suggestion of movement.

"You mean it, don't you?" she softly asked, astonished at how little she knew the man she'd been in constant company with for more than two weeks.

"I'm a possessive man," he replied as quietly as she. He was, but never before with women. He chose to overlook the significance of this discrepancy, knowing only that he wouldn't let her leave. Too many generations of royal blood, both Russian and Persian, flowed through his veins, too many tribesmen owed him obeisance, too many regiments obeyed his commands, to nurture humility. He would take what he wanted and keep it until he no longer wished it.

"I want to be alone," Lisaveta whispered, this new image of Stefan a chill shock to her senses.

"Don't go far" was all he said, as King Darius might have commanded a harem girl centuries ago.

And when she rose from his side and walked away, he watched her, no benevolence visible in his eyes.

Lisaveta sat on a window seat in a small parlor on the far side of the lodge, away from Stefan and Stefan's room. Wrapped in a soft mohair robe, her knees drawn up to her chin in a contemplative pose, she was trying to come to terms with the fact that she loved a man who was anathema to many of her most fervent beliefs.

How was it possible, she thought, her fingers smoothing in an unconscious gesture of indecision over the soft white wool of her robe.

She'd always assumed one fell in love with someone who idealized those principles one most cared for oneself, a man who was handsome but also kind and loving and imbued with a certain humanity. Was that all fantasy—the ideal, the perfect Prince Charming melded into her naive image of love? Was this even love she was feeling? Perhaps it was only sensual infatuation for Russia's most lionized hero. Was this overwhelming need to be close to Stefan love or merely obsession from another female hero-worshiper?

She wished she weren't so unpracticed and unfamiliar with the sensation. Since she'd never been in love she had no guidelines or experience to draw on. And Stefan never spoke of love. He spoke of adoration and enchantment, of need and desire, but never love.

That omission, she realized, was the dilemma in her own uncertainty. If his declarations were of love, would she even be questioning her feelings? She wouldn't, she sadly thought. She would be joyously oblivious to this unhappy speculation.

So how did she deal with her emotions in the absence of any reciprocal declarations from Stefan? The one she'd wrung from him to love only her for their holiday time had been carefully worded—although in truth, those days ago, her demand had been as inchoate as his answer was glib.

Can you love a man who not only sees a woman in an inherently subservient role but is quite literally deluged with submissive women willing to love him on any terms?

Her answer, she sorrowfully realized, was yes.

Can you love a man who not only is engaged to be married but is callous and selfish enough to leave his fiancée in pursuit of his own pleasure?

That answer too, after a minimum of introspection, was also yes.

Can you love a man who plans to leave you when his furlough is over with nothing more than a goodbye?

She touched the texture of the native rug covering the window seat, as though an answer lay beneath its rich and glowing color like a jinni in a bottle. It had been woven, Stefan had said, in Haci's village, and its colors were the favorite deep scarlet of the local tribes, contrasted with decorative detail in the expensive indigo carried overland from the East. Her pale hand lay on the stylized flame motifs, their crimson tones like blood, juxtaposing the fluffy white mohair of her robe and the rug's dramatic geometric designs, a stark contrast in color and tactile image, a contrast, too, of metaphoric innocence and the austere symbols of Stefan's tribal world. She didn't have the hard resilience of Stefan no matter how much she favored independence; she would never understand completely the primitive savagery of his background. She was a scholar, and he was a man of action.

Who unfortunately saw women as only adjuncts to his life— minimal adjuncts.

She sighed dramatically because she was alone and the sensation was comforting, and then she sighed again because there was satisfaction in her silliness. She smiled a little after that, thinking she was indeed being melodramatic beyond all sensible proportions. It wasn't as though she'd been deceived about Stefan's intentions from the very beginning. He'd been careful to promise nothing.

Now she wanted to blame him for her own vast affection when he wanted neither love nor blame. He only wanted the pleasure of her company.

Papa had once said years ago, on a rare occasion when he

spoke of Maman that he treasured the time they had together
as a gift from God and he had Maman always in his memory.
Maybe she should deal as appreciatively with her time on Stefan's mountain. Maybe life didn't always transpire exactly according to one's wishes. Maybe she was as selfish as she ac-
cused Stefan of being for wanting him to change his life for
her.

Stefan, on the other hand, didn't question his feelings of
happiness. Lisaveta was superb, she was beautiful and passionate, she entertained him with her charm and intelligence, she
was grace and elegance and also girlish innocence in scintil-
lating variations he found forever exciting. She wasn't a
woman with a predictable personality and manner—the kind
he always grew bored with. He'd experienced no sense of jaded
ennui with Lisaveta and they'd been in continual company for
more than two weeks. If he'd contemplated the novelty of *that*
circumstance, perhaps their feelings would have been more in
accord. Prince Stefan Bariatinsky, however, prided himself on
his hedonist principles, and contemplation of any kind was
nonessential.

He thought instead in practical terms. The Countess was unhappy and pouting or pouting and angry or any combination
thereof, all of which could probably be satisfactorily relieved
by a handsome gift or two or ten. Since his mountain lodge
was often used for his amorous entertainments, *and* since females were prone to emotional outbursts and tears, he kept a
ready supply of restorative baubles on hand.

So he rose from his languorous repose near the pool shortly
after Lisaveta entered the house and, after dressing, went to his
study, where his safe was housed. Pulling out a large chamois
bag from it, he proceeded unceremoniously to dump its contents on his desktop. The jewels and jewelry and small carved
animals in semiprecious stones fell out in a tumble of color,
fractured light and glitter.

Spreading them out with one abrupt motion of his palm, he
searched the disarray for items that would appeal to Lisaveta.
Her hair was a rich chestnut but not so dark that dramatic

jewels were appropriate, and her temperament was so naive and
green-grass new at times that he automatically thought of
pearls. Drawing out a three-strand necklace clasped with a pale
rose of South Seas coral, he set it aside. The gold diamonds
caught his eye next as though they were nudging his thought
process. Of course, he realized with sudden delight, the rare
pale yellow diamonds from India were a perfect match for her
eyes. He lifted the drop earrings from the scattered jumble of
rainbow hues.

They had once belonged to Marie Antoinette, the jeweler
had boasted. After the revolution they had found their way into
Catherine the Great's collection along with many other émigré
treasures. They brought one luck, the jeweler had added, at
which point Stefan had skeptically raised a brow, since Marie
Antoinette's life had not been crowned with success. "The earrings, Your Excellency, were her maidservant's means of escape from Versailles so they were lucky, you see—they bought
her life."

Stefan smiled now at his recollection of the jeweler's wide-
eyed recitation of the little maid's miraculous escape from the
guillotine, and holding the oddly pear-shaped diamonds up to
the light, he thought how perfect the pale jewels would look
against Lisaveta's golden skin. Her skin glowed as though it
were touched by the soft paint of sunset or kissed by a warm
morning sun. It made one want to touch it to see if it was as
warm as it looked. And he remembered in the next flashing
moment how she felt beneath him, how she *did* feel warm,
with the sensual heat of welcome and passion.

He set the earrings beside the pearl necklace and then
plucked out two tiny jade turtles, because Lisaveta had admired
a small water turtle yesterday at the pool. She'd mentioned that
that particular color was rare where she lived and had blushed
when he'd complimented her on the rarity of *her* beauty.

He wanted more, though, than the usual gift of jewelry; he
wanted something to make her smile again. Something special.
It came to him a moment later as he sat at his desk mentally
eliminating all the habitual gifts he gave to his lovers—the

female gifts of furs or perfume or gowns.

Hafiz.

He found her five minutes later after searching the upstairs first. When he entered the room she turned her head but didn't speak.

"Don't be unhappy," he said immediately. "I'll be *very* good from now on." He smiled then like a contrite young boy.

He looked very much unlike a small boy, though, in the loose leather breeches worn by the mountain warriors and an embroidered shirt in the same gunmetal gray. His feet were bare, his shirt open at the neck, and all he lacked was a gold earring to take on the full-fledged appearance of a brigand. His deeply bronzed skin and overlong hair did nothing to dispel the image of bandit, and when he pulled out the handful of jewels from his pocket, offered them to her on his open palm and said, "My apologies, *mademoiselle*," she thought for a moment she'd been transported to another time.

But it was not another time really, but actually that Stefan Bariatinsky lived a very similar life to that of his Kurdish body-guards. "Did you pay for those?" she asked in a voice that gave him to understand that his apology was not instantly accepted.

"In a manner of speaking," he replied, responding to the doubt in her voice. Her question, of course, implied he had not.

"Meaning?" she coolly inquired, thinking him the most beautiful man she'd ever seen and trying without success to remain angry with him.

"Meaning—" he grinned widely "—of course, moppet." He decided he also adored her for her sweet pouty bottom lip, which reminded him strongly of a spoiled little girl. "I paid for them," he assured her, "or my business agent paid for them, or someone else on my sizable staff in Saint Petersburg brought a smile to Lazant and Sons establishment, I'm sure of it. Now take them."

When she wouldn't, he dropped them into her lap. "The canary diamonds were Catherine the Great's," he said, his grin undiminished. "She was, I hear, pouty like you."

"Which I'm sure your ancestor Orlov was able to mitigate with his…" She let the insinuating pause lengthen.

"Charm?" Stefan offered.

"Is that what you call it?"

"A euphemism of course."

"Blood must run true." It was not a compliment.

"I understand the Kuzans are reputed to be hot-blooded," he replied softly. "Although there are, no doubt, exceptions on the family tree," he added with a mocking irony that implied she was not one of them.

"Is this an argument over passion?"

His expression matched his brigand garb, as did his suggestive predatory tone. "I certainly hope so." But he saw immediately that he'd gone too far in his teasing, and with a self-assurance devoid of the insecurities of lesser men, he became instantly conciliatory. His wolfish expression altered into contrition and he said with genuine regret, "I don't want to argue. I don't want you unhappy." His voice, his intonation, his entire manner were without jest. "Tell me what to do."

Everything she wanted to say was melodramatic and infantile. So instead of saying, "Leave your fiancée for me," as she longed to do, she compromised with a statement that told at least half the truth. "Don't be an autocrat with me."

"My word on it," he quietly said. "And?" he prompted her, because he could tell there was more from both her hesitancy and mood.

"There's no 'and,'" she lied.

"But there is. Tell me." He was intent on pleasing her.

She looked down at the necklace and earrings, objects of beauty and luxury so casually given, fingered the two small jade turtles nestled in the white mohair of her robe and sighed, her gaze on the exquisite ornaments. "I don't want to argue anymore, and if I tell you we will. Besides…"

He coaxed her when she didn't continue. "Besides…"

"Nothing, really, darling," and she smiled for the first time since he'd come into the room. Nodding at the book he held in his hand, she changed the conversation from the futile controversy over their differing beliefs. "What's that?"

"Your friend Hafiz." Understanding her tactic, he obliged her.

"He's here? I thought he was at your palace in Tiflis." She was so immersed in the fabric of the poet's life and work that she spoke of him as a living being.

Stefan smiled. "He's both places."

"Let me see." Her voice was excited, her face animated with delight, and he knew he'd selected the right gift.

She moved the jewelry from her lap when he handed her the small leather-bound book and he thought how rare that gesture was in his experience. No other woman he knew would have casually set aside a fortune in jewelry as though she were putting away an empty tea glass.

When she carefully opened the rare volume to the frontispiece to check its provenance, her face lighted up. "A Baghdad Rotan edition! Where did you ever find it? There's only two outside the Ottoman Empire." She looked up at him quickly. "And this is one of them."

"The other's in Paris."

"They were both in Paris."

"Were," he said quietly.

Her gaze lingered on him for a moment more, as she was reminded of both his enormous wealth and power. How much had it cost him to prize this loose from its former owner? And then the vital opportunity for research overcame her speculation. "May I take notes from it?"

Her eyes were the color of brilliant sunshine. "You may have it," he said.

"I couldn't," she exclaimed. "It's nearly priceless. The ones in Turkey are never displayed. Even the ones I was studying in Karakilisa were only available to me because of my father's long friendship with the Khan."

"If you don't take it," Stefan genially said, "*I* shall pout."

For a moment she considered both his levity and seriousness. "You mean it."

"You have never seen anyone pout as brutally as I."

Her smile was pure sunshine. "You really mean it." He

could have been giving her her complete heart's desire for the joy in her voice.

"I mean it, *dushka*...truly."

"In that case I accept," she readily agreed, "because you've been a monster and I deserve it, but mostly because I've lusted after this book for an eternity."

"You don't like the jewelry."

"Oh, yes, Stefan, it's wonderful! I didn't mean to be ungrateful. It's very beautiful and I'll think of you every time I wear it. But, darling, *darling*, you can't know how much this book means to me."

He found himself strangely jealous on two counts. First, because she had casually mentioned she would remember him with the jewelry as if he were a summer fling at one of the spas, as if she'd think of him later only when clasping the pearls around her neck or slipping Catherine's canary earbobs in her ears. He could visualize her in a year or so, saying to some man she'd married as she put on the yellow diamond earrings, "What was his name again...?" And second, he took mild issue with the adoration in her voice over the book. He envied the damn book!

"Thank you, thank you, thank you," Lisaveta cried happily. Carefully placing the book on the windowsill, she threw herself at Stefan, wrapping her arms around his neck.

I've thirty more books by Hafiz, he thought smugly, savoring the feel and scent and excitement of this remarkable young woman who'd been thrown into his path on the Plain of Kars. He was looking forward to offering her the remainder of his gift. "You're very welcome, moppet," he murmured, his arms folded around her, her head resting against his chest. "And we're not going to fight again, I promise."

"It's my fault, too," she said softly, clinging to his strong shoulders, knowing she never felt happier than in his arms. "I should overlook your autocratic ways. They're cultural...that's all."

"I'll be better."

"And I'll be more understanding."

His voice had a smile in it. "I see only blue skies ahead."

"Without a cloud," she sweetly added.

He laughed. "How long will all this harmony last?"

"Till the end of time or your first surly remark," Lisaveta dulcetly said, "whichever comes first."

"Or yours."

"It won't be mine."

"Is this a contest?"

"Depends on the wager."

"Say…loser bathes the winner for a week."

"You're on, *mon général*."

It was a wager that could have only winners.

Nine

Now, while all this teasing bantering was taking place on the mountain rim of the world, Nadejda was saying to her mother, "Must we have the graceless woman over for tea? She has no manners at all."

"Yes, we must. She's his only aunt, and it's fortunate for you, my dear, that Papa and I talked some sense into you when we did or you might have done something foolish."

"I don't know how you can be so lenient, Mama. He ignored you and Papa, as well," Nadejda said, her face fretful with annoyance. She was still abed though it was past noon, the bedclothes scattered with crumbs from her breakfast tray.

"Darling, these things happen. Stefan was called back to the front." Although Princess Irina Taneiev was as swift to take offense as her daughter, her added years of experience cautioned her to prudence. One never, she'd reminded both her daughter and husband the day of Stefan's abrupt departure, risked losing a fortune such as Stefan's over something as foolish as temper.

"Well, he could have sent *me* a note, too. You'd think I'd have more importance than his old aunt."

"His *only* aunt, darling, which is the point. She has no children. Think of it for a moment, Nadejda. Where will all her fortune go? Remember, she's outlived two wealthy husbands in addition to being an Orbeliani with her own personal assets."

Nadejda brightened visibly. She'd been raised to consider her beauty a negotiable item and she understood the value of money. "Why, to Stefan and me of course."

"Exactly. And that's why we'll continue to entertain Stefan's aunt until your papa's business is finished here in Tiflis." Nadejda had moved into the Viceroy's palace with her parents after Stefan left, but her mother had seen to their continuing relationship with Militza. Although once Vladimir and the Viceroy had completed the details of their arrangement to supply artillery to the army, Irina had no intention of spending an additional minute in this sleepy provincial capital.

"In that case, I'll be polite to the old bitch. Is Stefan really her only heir?" Nadejda asked the question as if verification were required for the nasty task ahead.

Her mother nodded significantly.

"Oh, very well," her daughter distastefully agreed.

So when Militza came for tea, Nadejda was as civil as her mother's promptings could make her. Spoiled from a young age, however, she found it difficult to instill any warmth in an endeavor she found tiresome. Had Stefan seen her outside the ballrooms and formal dinners of their brief courtship, he would have noticed her very narrow focus of attention—herself. But in the short days of their acquaintance he'd only played the courting male. Nadejda was at her very best as the center of attention; she played well to an admiring throng; it was her favorite role—her only role. In it she was without peer.

"Did Stefan give you any indication in his note when he might next have leave?" Princess Irina was saying to Militza, and Nadejda yawned without any attempt at concealment.

"I'm afraid the war is in great flux now," Militza replied, noting Nadejda's discourtesy. She did not mention the real purpose of Stefan's note. Although he had made use of Haci's return to Tiflis to make apologies to Militza for leaving so abruptly, he'd wanted most to see that Masha would open his town house to those of his men who weren't going to their villages on furlough. Haci, for one, was looking forward to the female pleasures available in Tiflis, the capital city of the Caucasus.

"It's such a shame Kars is proving recalcitrant. I do hope it falls soon so all the young men will be back for the season." Irina saw the war as an obstacle to her social activities.

"I'm sure the Tsar's officers agree with you," Militza ironically replied. Another afternoon in company with the vacuous Taneiev women was reinforcing her conviction she must intervene in Stefan's disastrous marriage plans.

"I really don't understand what's taking so long," Irina continued complaining, as if the war were a personal affront to her standards of speed. "Surely the Muslim rabble will capitulate soon. Vladimir says Grand Duke Michael is going down to investigate."

As daughter to a general, sister-in-law to a field marshal, wife to two military men and Stefan's aunt, Militza was well aware of the formidable opponents Russia faced. This war wasn't going to be a question of waiting patiently in dress uniform for the Turkish commanders to signal defeat. She'd heard enough from Stefan in his letters from the front and her own contacts with the Chiefs of Staff to understand the particular brutality of this campaign. "Michael will find his journey eventful" was all she said. Her faith in the Tsar's brother was faint; Michael drank and gambled better than he officered.

"Mama, I won't hear another word on this dreary war," Nadejda snapped, tearing a small piece from her macaroon in testiness. Her fifth macaroon, Militza noted. The girl would approximate her mother's girth someday and Stefan liked slender women. "I'll be glad when we're back in Saint Petersburg where every other word isn't about the silly war," Nadejda finished petulantly.

For a man who'd devoted his life to the army, Stefan apparently hadn't selected a wife inclined to view his profession with sympathy, Militza reflected, although she did have considerable affection for macaroons.

"And I wish Stefan would have taken my advice and had Melikoff rescind his orders back to the front."

Militza abruptly ceased contemplation of Nadejda's capacity for macaroons. Melikoff? Nadejda had suggested Stefan petition *Melikoff*? Militza would have bartered a year of her life to have seen her nephew's expression at that recommendation. There wasn't a man he hated more than Melikoff. When they met in public as they did occasionally in the small world of Tiflis society, Stefan quite literally glared daggers at the man whose family had replaced his as Viceroy of the Caucasus. Only his promise to Alexander II, his Tsar, had kept him from challenging Melikoff to a duel. Alexander wouldn't have the scandal, he'd said, of Stefan killing Melikoff.

"He wouldn't?" Militza casually inquired, watching Nadejda's face for her response.

"He said he only takes orders from the Tsar, which I don't fully understand because Melikoff distinctly told me he was Stefan's superior."

"Perhaps Melikoff neglected to make that clear to Stefan," Militza sardonically replied.

"Well, he should then," Nadejda asserted, tossing her chin up in an affected way that might have been charming in a four-year-old. "And everything would be much nicer. Stefan could come home from that ridiculous war and we could begin making marriage plans."

"If you'd like to write Stefan a note suggesting that, it seems sensible to me," Militza said, her face as bland as her tone. "I could have a groom deliver it to him."

"Mama, the macaroons are gone," Nadejda noted fretfully. Then, as if Stefan's future were secondary to her sweet tooth, she added, "I'll drop him a note on the subject before we leave."

"You're leaving?" Militza could have been on a treaty negotiating team for all her understatement and calm.

"Tomorrow or possibly the next day," Irina interposed. "Poor Nadejda is bored so far from Saint Petersburg, and I confess—" she smiled artificially "—although Tiflis is enchanting, I miss the stimulation of court."

What she meant was that she feared being away too long from the machinations of court politics. Stefan would also appreciate Nadejda's boredom with his native city. Militza dearly hoped Nadejda would include in her note an indication of her feelings on that subject, as well. "My wishes then for a pleasant journey," she said cheerfully. She chose not to mention she'd be following soon. Once Stefan actually returned to Kars, she also intended a trip to Saint Petersburg.

Leaving the Viceroy's palace after tea, Militza felt her years and, in the logical assessment of things, despaired whether she'd be successful in dislodging Nadejda as Stefan's fiancée. Her nephew was stubborn at times in his wishes and he hadn't lightly undertaken his choice of bride. His selection hadn't been whimsical but rather utilitarian, and her hope of discrediting Nadejda was minimized by that judgment. Stefan had made clear to her that the question of liking Nadejda was incidental to the usefulness of her family. Vladimir Taneiev controlled many of the ministers of state, although the army had always remained independent. It was actually Vladimir that Stefan was marrying and the power he wielded in the inner circles of government.

Tsar Alexander spent less and less time in the daily activities of government now that his young mistress and their three children were actually installed in the palace only a floor below his consumptive wife. Rumor had it the Tsarina was determined to hang on to life as long as possible to thwart her young rival. Although ravaged as she was by tuberculosis, she'd already outlived her physicians' estimates by five years.

In Saint Petersburg Militza intended calling on all her old friends to inform them she might be in need of their favors. Even though she wished Stefan to renege on his engagement for his own future happiness, she wasn't unaware of the possible consequences. Prince Vladimir Taneiev was known for his vindictiveness; many political rivals rued the day they'd opposed him. Several were spending their remaining years in Siberia thanks to his implacable vengeance, and while Irina and Nadejda might be foolish and superficial, it would never do to underestimate Vladimir.

However...she felt she had sufficient influence herself to oppose any possible obstacles Vladimir might establish, provided she could convince Stefan to sever his ties to Nadejda. And Stefan's personal relationship with the Tsar was a very strong advantage. To a point.

Through bitter experience they all knew there were circumstances where even the Tsar had bowed to pressure.

On the same July night that Militza sat at her desk composing a list of friends in Saint Petersburg who might be needed should Vladimir turn difficult, and Stefan and Lisaveta were dining alfresco under the dark whispering pines, Choura was the featured entertainment at a bachelor party in Tiflis at Chezevek's Restaurant.

The windows were all thrown open to the heated night air, and Captain Gorsky, the host for the night, was in shirtsleeves in the middle of the floor encouraging Choura with energetic and clapping and smiles. The Caucasian music had a pulsing rhythm of drumbeats interwoven with melodies both plaintive and voluptuous. The sound seemed to tremble in an insistent, fevered undulation, angry at times, hypnotic at intervals, convulsive, monotonous and galvanic. And Choura danced in her own expressive way: languorous and slow, stamping and impetuous, in a stylized version of courtship, of pursuit and retreat and ultimate seduction. She was wild and untamed, her dark eyes flashing, the lamplight flickering and glittering off her necklaces and rings and bracelets as she whirled, her bare feet barely touching the floor, her red silk skirt fluttering like flower petals in the wind. Her black lace blouse barely covered her firm young breasts, and when she smiled in sensual invitation, Captain Gorsky wasn't alone in planning on spending a portion of his wealth on the beautiful Gypsy girl, now that she was back in circulation.

When the musicians fell silent on a flourish of drumbeats, a roar of applause erupted in the room as every man gave vent to his approval.

The party was in celebration of a junior officer's engagement, and all the high-priced courtesans in Tiflis were in attendance. Since Stefan was on cordial terms with many of them, and since Stefan rarely missed occasions of this nature, he was repeatedly asked for.

"He's with his new lover up in the mountains," Choura cheerfully replied to those interested parties, "and he paid me

fifty thousand roubles for my time." She was proud to announce the amount of her new worth. Stefan's payment would
serve notice her prices had gone up. And when the identity of
this newest paramour was demanded, her answer was equally
cheerful. "Countess Lisaveta Lazaroff," she'd announce, a fact
she'd discovered *after* her return to Tiflis, when one of the
Gypsy grooms in Stefan's stables relayed the gossip from the
villa on the hill. "He's taken her captive," she would finish
with obvious relish.

"Captive!" the courtesans whispered with a particular
breathy eagerness memories of Stefan induced.

"Captive!" the officers breathed, their imaginations running
wild.

Had the lady screamed or fought or passionately yielded?

Yes and yes and she didn't know, Choura would answer with
a suggestive smile. But if she hadn't yielded eagerly, certainly
she had yielded.

The scandal was delicious. Leave it to Stefan, everyone said,
to abduct a lady. He'd always been a law unto himself. Like
his father, they said.

She must be extraordinary in bed, the ladies all thought, for
Stefan's transient interest in women was well-known. He'd
never stirred himself to pursue a woman before; an abduction
indicated staggering attention. They were incredulous. What
does she look like? they asked then, intrigued by her unique
success. And the men listened, too, because they wanted to
visualize this unusual woman.

"She's pretty," Choura said blandly, seated on Captain Gorsky's lap like a dark and languorous kitten.

"*More* than pretty for Stefan, I'd say," a woman remarked,
her escort's head nodding in agreement.

Choura shrugged, not inclined to unduly praise her succes-
sor. "I suppose," she said.

"Is she small? He likes small women," a petite blonde re-
clining on a floor cushion noted, her waist hand-span narrow.

"She's tall."

"No!"

"With brown hair."

"Brown hair? She can't." This was not a paragon of conventional beauty; this was not a woman in Stefan's usual style.

"Well, she does," Choura complacently replied. She was now richer than a shopkeeper for her friendship with Stefan, and as a businesswoman who was secure in her own beauty, she was without personal jealousy for her replacement, although she was amused by the difficulties Stefan might encounter. "She was screaming at him, too," she said with a grin. "I mean *screaming*."

She *must* be good in bed, the men all decided, because surely her looks didn't appear remarkable. And screaming at Stefan? Normally he wouldn't have stayed a second in company with a vituperative female. Wherever had he found her?

"She was thrown away by the Bazhis," Choura added as if the men had spoken aloud.

Aha, everyone agreed, male and female. To have survived the Bazhis was superhuman. She was a superwoman, and the men hoped that when Stefan tired of her, as he surely would, the Countess would consider one of them to entertain her. No one contemplated love in their speculation on Stefan and his latest bed partner, but certainly, they decided, carnal passion was the proper phrase—unique, spectacular carnal passion to so fascinate Stefan.

Oblivious to the sundry contemplations of their relationship, Stefan and Lisaveta basked in a contentment rich with passion and amity, their world insular, isolated by choice, their existence narrowed to two people and love.

They didn't worry about scandal and gossip; both were immune to the motives inspiring such concepts. Stefan, of course, was inured after a lifetime in the limelight, and Lisaveta, for exactly opposite reasons, was equally inured. She had lived too long in her own self-contained world, in which respect and personal choices and one's actions were determined without considering what other people thought. And both were intelligent enough to understand that wealth and position made most things possible in the world.

They entertained each other with openness of spirit and joy

through the multitude of days. They slept when they wished and woke without schedule; they teased each other and smiled and made love, of course, in infinite variety. They lay in the sun in the afternoons sometime and swam then to cool off; they rode occasionally and walked the mountain trails and ate the Spartan meals prepared by the servants from the village nearby. Stefan frequently cooked for Lisaveta himself with a competence she should have perhaps expected.

He showed her, too, where the eagles nested on the rim of the escarpment, and they lay flat on their bellies overlooking the valley miles below, watching the adult pair teach their young how to fly.

The blue open sky was above and below them, the wind blowing their hair, the sun warm on their skin, the eaglets endlessly fascinating as they swooped and tumbled and steadied themselves on the cresting wind currents, soaring for lengthening distances.

"I envy them," Stefan said one day, rolling over on his back as he followed the flight of the fledgling, "that freedom. At times like this," he went on in a quiet voice, looking up into the sunlit sky, "I don't want to go back."

"At least not for a thousand years," Lisaveta agreed, her chin propped on her hands, the wind blowing her hair in tossing ringlets.

Some days they read to each other under the pines near the house or lying on the terrace, Stefan reading some of the verses he'd composed and surprising Lisaveta with the rich emotion in his poetry. She'd never glimpsed that intense and introspective side of him. In turn she'd read—or rather recite, because she knew them by heart—her favorite poems of Hafiz in the original Persian. Stefan would answer her in his mother's language, its melody sweet, he said, to his ear.

They never talked of the war or the days ahead; by unspoken agreement they conversed only of topics without contention. In silent understanding they wished to enjoy each other's company as if the days were numbered for eternity.

It was a tremulous balance of happiness—like a shadow or

a dream, ungrounded and bound to dissolve when reality intervened.

Stefan resisted thinking of the passing time or his furlough's end.

Lisaveta pushed aside any feelings beyond their temporary enchantment, existing only in the golden glow of her happiness, refusing to think of tomorrow.

But one morning Haci rode into the courtyard and their underlying fear of time had to be faced. From the bedroom window they watched him dismount and brush the dust from his trousers and wipe the sweat from his upper lip with the back of his hand.

He glanced up to Stefan's bedroom window and saw them and waved.

Their holiday was over.

Their trip down the mountain was quiet, partly because constant alertness was necessary for survival on the rugged trail and conversation was distracting, but primarily their silence was the uncommunicativeness of voiceless feelings. Both Haci and Stefan faced a return to the front; the Turks had had time to reinforce their defenses while the Russians were bringing in new troops. Their increased fortifications would be costly to the Tsar's army, and while one could briefly set aside the savagery of war with a beautiful woman on a mountaintop or in a Tiflis brothel, the return to battle and the imminence of death were prominent in both men's minds. Additionally, Stefan had to struggle with a feeling of loss. It was an unfamiliar melancholy directly related to Lise, a novel and unwelcome sensation he forcibly attempted to suppress.

Lisaveta, more open to her need for Stefan, wondered how she would survive without him. All she could hope for was to keep back her tears until he was gone.

Stefan's carriage was waiting at the military road, the same coach she'd been abducted from long days ago, her luggage all carefully in place as it had been left.

They stood politely on the road while Haci directed the drivers and postilions in unloading Lisaveta's few things from the

pack horse, finding they couldn't conduct the banal social conversation that circumstances required.

For a man of Stefan's experience, the inability was striking.

For Lisaveta, who'd spent most of her life outside society,
the lack of ready chatter was less unusual. But tears still threatened to well up in her eyes, and she was determined not to
embarrass herself with that ultimate naïveté.

They watched the driver tie the last satchel in place, the
silence between them uncomfortable. When the man scrambled
down and everyone took their places on the coach, Stefan
turned back to Lisaveta and finally spoke. "Thank you for everything," he said in a quiet voice that wouldn't carry beyond
their position. "I hope your journey to Saint Petersburg is
pleasant." He was dressed in full uniform and his bearing was
grave, as were his dark eyes.

Lisaveta tried to smile but didn't succeed. How nice it would
be to have more experience in these matters, she thought, so
one could smile convincingly, as if their casual leave-taking
were as mundane as the parting of dance partners at a ball.

"Thank *you*," she replied, her own voice as grave as his,
"for a delightful holiday." There. At least she'd accomplished
the requisite words if not the precise nuance of tone. "And I'm
sure my trip to Saint Petersburg will be uneventful," she added,
pleased she was able to so calmly articulate the words.

"I've sent a message to Alexander," Stefan said, his tone
brisker now, as if he were reiterating instructions to a subaltern,
"since you'll be seeing him at your father's ceremony, and—"

"You needn't have," she interposed. "I'll be staying with
Nikki. I haven't seen him since Papa's funeral, but I'm sure
he'll see—"

"I wanted to," he interrupted, feeling he should do something for her beyond a casual goodbye. She was rare and precious and he felt this need to protect her and perhaps in the
process protect the uncommon memory of their time together.
Entrée to Alexander II would guarantee her success at court.
He could do that for her; Alexander's friendship would also
offer her safety from Nadejda and her family. Stefan had no
illusions of what their response would be should they discover

his leave had been spent with Countess Lazaroff. She would need Alexander II and all of Masha's connections, as well, although Nikki was a formidable opponent. Nevertheless, he'd talk to his aunt when he returned to Tiflis, he decided.

"Well, thank you then," she said with what she hoped was suitable detachment.

He sighed, hearing but not really listening. He longed to take her in his arms and kiss her for a millenium, to take her home with him or to Kars or anywhere he went. But he couldn't. "Goodbye," he said instead, then opened the carriage door and put out his hand to help her in.

"Goodbye, Stefan," Lisaveta said with forced composure, trying not to feel the strength of his hand under hers, thrusting from her mind the memory of Stefan's powerful body.

He smiled briefly and momentarily his eyes shone with his familiar laughter. "Tell Sasha he owes me for the redoubt at Jangelar," he said with a familiarity few men in the Empire could equal.

"If I see him, I will," she replied, thinking it highly unlikely she would be talking to the Tsar so intimately.

"You will," Stefan said, his grin the natural boyish one she loved.

"You seem sure."

"I'm sure" was all he said. *"Bon voyage."* Quickly shutting the door, he signaled the driver on.

The last sight she had of Prince Stefan Bariatinsky was of him gracefully swinging up on Cleo, the mare's prancing impatience stirring up a flurry of dust on the road. He waved his hand as if he knew she was watching, and wheeling his sleek black racer, he set off for Tiflis and the war.

Her tears came then, sliding over the barriers she'd controlled until Stefan was out of sight, wetting her cheeks and her bodice, soaking her handkerchief. All her anguish and heartache finally poured out. She would never see him again, repeated the doleful litany in her mind, never…never. She'd never listen to him laugh at some silliness or feel the warm solidity of him beside her as she slept or be able to touch him when she woke in the morning. But it was more than missing his vivid physical presence. She had fallen in love with him, despite all her attempts to the contrary, a head-over-heels, ungovernable love that inundated her mind and body and spirit. He had become as essential as air to her.

Had, she bitterly thought, was the operative word with Stefan Bariatinsky. And you're breathing still, she cynically reminded herself in the next beat of her pulse. People do not die of love.

But for all her practicality she still indulged her wretchedness on the journey to the railhead; she cried until she couldn't cry anymore, until only great gulping sobs were left. Then, tearless and exhausted, she merely thought of him. She found herself memorizing him against an unknown future, as one would a treasured poem one wishes to keep always, committing to her mind small and cherished details of his perfection: his stark handsomeness, both elegantly Persian and incongruously savage like the warrior tribes he commanded; his power, not only of musculature and height but of disposition; the gentleness she'd so often experienced; and most of all his smile. The most charming smile devised by man. A smile she'd basked in, a smile she'd often brought to his lips, a smile she'd kissed in amused reply. A smile she'd first seen in Aleksandropol.

She shut her eyes and saw him as he'd looked that first night in Aleksandropol, dressed in silk robes and limned by moonlight; she remembered how he'd looked when she'd wakened beside him, drowsy as he often was early in the morning because he woke more slowly than she; and she saw him as she had each day of their holiday, seated nude on the bank of his mountain stream with the sun on his wet hair, content, at peace and at home. He belonged in the mountains, he said.

A shame she didn't, as well.

Stefan made a conscious effort at conversation with Haci on their ride back to Tiflis. He needed distraction from his thoughts; he needed to distance himself mentally as well as physically from a woman who'd become too much a part of his life. It unnerved him, this need he felt, this intense craving to have her riding beside him, talking to him, making him happy. What a strange word, he abruptly thought, one he'd never considered as particularly significant. He'd thought in terms of excitement or action, stimulation or pleasure, never happiness.

Was this what had happened to his father? Had this sudden need for one particular person struck him as suddenly? The thought terrified him for a brief mindless moment, as though he'd lost control.

"Tell me, was Choura in form at Chezevek's Restaurant," he said, turning to Haci, intent on repudiating these indications of misplaced emotion.

"She's bragging about her new price." Haci's smile flashed against his bronzed skin. "She's increased in value, thanks to you."

"She wouldn't have left otherwise, and I wasn't in the mood to haggle. My offer was one I knew she'd take."

"Was the Countess worth it?" Haci asked familiarly. He was the same age as Stefan, and they'd shared more than years of soldiering; they'd grown up together, for Haci's father had been aide to the Field Marshal.

"More, unfortunately." They spoke in the Kurdish dialect, although Haci was as proficient as Stefan in French, and the softly guttural diction lent impact to the plain answer.

"That's a problem," Haci said with a sidelong glance at Stefan.

"I don't *want* it to be a problem, so it *won't* be a problem." Stefan had turned to him, his eyes narrowed against the sun or his own resentment. "And I don't want to talk about it."

"Fair enough," his childhood friend said. "Do you think the Grand Duke Michael will get the Turks to the bargaining table?"

"Do you think the Grand Duke can find his behind with a road map?" Stefan sardonically replied.

"In that case I'd better bring my winter gear."

"I'd recommend it." And Stefan nudged Cleo into a trot.

Stefan stayed with Haci in the seclusion of his town house, sending Militza an invitation for dinner that evening. More restless than usual, he refused Haci's invitation to Chezevek's later, had his valet repack his kit twice, annoyed his chef with his presence in the kitchen for menu changes and was, in short, noticeably high-strung and moody.

Taking notice of his temperament immediately upon arriving, Militza took one glance about the drawing room and said, "She's gone, I take it."

"Yes," Stefan said tersely. "And Nadejda?"

"Safely on her way to the excitement of Saint Petersburg. I have a note for you, by the way."

His head came up immediately and he swung around from the liquor table, where he'd been pouring some wine for his aunt.

"From Nadejda," she explained, alert to his swift response.

"Oh." The single word was blatant disappointment. He resumed pouring.

"Would you like to see it? I brought it along."

"Later. Have you heard the news of the Grand Duke? Haci tells me he's out to end the war speedily." He'd recovered from his miscalculation and the grin he turned on her was sportive.

"She's telling you to listen to Melikoff and not return to the war, and yes, I talked to Michael before he left Tiflis. He's utterly naive about the Turks."

"If she mentions Melikoff, maybe you'd better toss it. Michael is utterly naive about everything, believe me. He's going to blow it, guaranteed, and we're all going to have to get our asses down there in double time to save his." His smile was still cordial, a social smile without sentiment.

"Read it," Militza said. "You'll find it enlightening."

He didn't try to evade her this time, but after handing her a glass of wine and sitting down on the opposite couch, he softly said, "Perhaps I don't want to be enlightened. Perhaps I want to be blissfully ignorant, and perhaps I want to marry Vladimir Taneiev's ministerial influence but I can't, so I'm marrying his daughter."

"She'll make you unhappy."

"I won't be seeing much of her."

"She'll still be the mother of your children."

"I'm counting on it." The words came out stone cold and grim.

"Does that mean so much?"

"To me it does."

"What about love?"

He quirked a brow. "It hasn't been a problem."

"What if you fall in love someday?"

"Masha, darling," he said with light sarcasm, "remember to whom you speak. Being married doesn't preclude being in love. As you recall, I'm a product of such a union."

"What if you want to marry her?"

His eyes took on a flinty cast. "It won't happen to me, Masha. Rest assured. Now, could we change this subject, since we've already exhausted it on numerous occasions in the past? I'm marrying Nadejda whether—" he grinned then, and his tone lightened, as if to mitigate the curtness of his previous declarations "—she knows Melikoff or not."

Militza snorted both at the mention of Melikoff and at Stefan's stubbornness. "He's a pig."

"Yes, but an influential one, you will agree, dear aunt of mine."

"So you persist in your path to—"

"Destruction," Stefan offered cheerfully.

She gazed at him without speaking for a short time. Since he was alone at home with her, he wore black silk, a shirt and loose trousers belted in costly gem-encrusted gold; the slippers on his bare feet were fine kid, black too, and embroidered with ruby beads. He could have been one of his princely Persian ancestors. But unlike them, he wasn't allowed the luxury of a harem. "Boredom," Militza threatened. "You'll be bored in a day."

"Well, then I'll leave." He was lounging and unthreatened by his aunt's bullying.

"Not for long I'd guess, or Papa Vladimir will grow resentful."

"A soldier's life is not his own," Stefan sweetly replied.

"I thought you and the Countess enjoyed each other," Militza interjected, as persistent in her maneuvering as Stefan was in his evasion.

He hesitated the barest fraction of a second before replying, a fact duly noted by his aunt, as was his altered expression. "As a matter of fact, we did. She's a delightful woman."

"I thought so, too. She reminded me of her mother in her youth. The Kuzans were always…unconventional."

Militza's delayed emphasis on the last word sent a rush of sensation through Stefan's body as though he could see Lisaveta again in all her glorious unconventionality. He needed her already, had recalled a dozen times that afternoon how she felt in his arms and how she felt as he slid into her heated interior, how she matched his passion or exceeded it at times so he had to calm her and slow her and bring her whimpering and impetuous to climax.

"Do you think so?" His aunt's words, obviously repeated, roused him finally and he looked at her, perplexed. "Do you think she bears any resemblance to Nikki?" Militza asked, a satisfied look in her eyes. Another nail in the coffin, she jubilantly decided.

"Her eyes, of course. The Kuzan eyes are notorious." And he thought of her golden eyes, flagrantly exotic, unvirtuous, torrid, like her lovemaking.

"She's tall, too," Militza said. "The Kuzans are known for their height."

A moment passed before he responded, preoccupied as he was with memories of the beautiful, heated Countess Lazaroff. "Yes," he said finally in a voice more subdued than he intended, "she is."

"Will you be seeing her again?"

Stefan's "No!" was so swift and harsh that Militza raised her brows in mild astonishment.

"Did you have a spat?" she asked.

"No, we didn't, and if you don't mind," Stefan said in a tone that made it clear he didn't care whether she minded or not, "I'd like to discontinue the discussion of the Countess Lazaroff."

"Of course, darling," Militza replied pleasantly, pleased

with his agitation. "I was curious only. Now what do you see as the first campaign move against the Turks? Haci tells me some larger calibre artillery is scheduled to be brought to Kars."

The remainder of their evening visit was devoted to topics pertaining to the war.

He didn't inquire once about his fiancée or the letter she'd left for him, but Militza was careful to bring it to his attention before she left. "You should read it, Stefan," she admonished, indicating the pastel envelope lying on the lamp table, "in the event it requires an answer."

"My secretary can answer it," he replied, but relenting at his aunt's judgmental glance, added, "oh, very well, I'll read the bloody thing. Satisfied?"

Her contented smile was answer enough.

"Do be careful now, Stefan," she went on to say as she stood to leave, adjusting her shawl against the cool evening air.

"One can't be careful, Masha, and win a war." But his smile was warm; he understood her platitude.

"Well, send me a message occasionally, so I know you're safe." Her words were a ritual of goodbye because both knew he conscientiously sent her letters every other day. Reaching up to touch his cheek tenderly, she softly whispered, "Go with God."

The letter forgotten on the table, he left the next morning before dawn, Haci beside him and his troop following in fault-less formation. They were equipped for a fall campaign, fully aware progress had to be made before the winter set in. They pressed their mounts because news had it the Grand Duke was meddling. If he had his way, a full-scale attack might occur in the next fortnight, whether they were prepared or not.

Ten

When Lisaveta had arrived at Vladikavkaz, she'd been met by the Tsar's envoy and one of the Tsar's railway coaches. With politeness and protocol she'd been escorted into her private car, told by an obsequious aide that her wish was their command and invited to enjoy her journey north.

Astonished at first by her preferential treatment, she inquired whether they had the right person. She was assured they did. The young officer smiled winningly and said, "Please, *mademoiselle*, relax and make yourself comfortable. The Tsar looks forward to meeting you." Pampered by a full staff of servants, she sped northward to the capital.

The next morning over breakfast she asked the Tsar's equerry whether all the guests to the ceremony commemorating her father's work were treated so royally. He hesitated only the minutest moment before replying, "My orders were to escort you, Countess, and beyond that I don't know. I never," he added politely, evading her question nicely, "question the Tsar." He knew of course that a telegram from Prince Bariatinsky had set the Tsar's orders in train; he also knew scholars, even scholars honored by the Tsar, were rarely treated with such pomp. And while not privy to the details of the Prince's telegram, he'd already come to his own conclusions apropos of the Countess Lazaroff's relationship to the Prince. As a man of the world, he understood Bariatinsky's request and, perhaps upon seeing the lady, understood also his possible reasons for ensuring she had private accommodations.

Perhaps the Prince was protecting his paramour from prying eyes or other men's advances; maybe he merely wished her journey to be as luxurious as possible. Certainly, whatever his reasons, the lady was worth the effort. She was breathtakingly beautiful, her fresh blooming youth not only dazzling the eye but stirring the imagination. In her peach-colored summer frock adorned with cream lace flounces at neckline and cuffs, she seemed both lushly opulent and heatedly alive.

At the Countess's request, a message was sent from Moscow to her cousin Prince Nikki Kuzan, informing him of her arrival time. When they detrained at the Station Sud, Nikki and his wife, Alisa, were at the platform to meet them. Amid hugs and kisses, introductions were made, since Nikki had married rather precipitously since her father's funeral and neither woman had met. While Nikki dwarfed the pretty redhead at his side, he deferred to her, his smiles those of a besotted man, and as the two women chatted with the familiarity of old friends, he listened with amusement and courtesy.

"Do you think," he said at last, breaking in during a short pause for breath on his wife's part, "we could rediscover the merits of royal rail travel and the Russian landscape in the comfort of our home?" His grin was appealing. "And let all these vastly bored officers and railway officials leave?"

"Oh, dear," Alisa said, glancing at the ranks of officialdom standing at attention.

Lisaveta flushed in embarrassment at her discourtesy. Unused to royal entourage, she'd simply forgotten they were present, having in the past always traveled in the utmost simplicity. "By all means," she said, and with a directness that Nikki watched with interest and the entourage found delightful, Lisaveta shook hands with and thanked each man.

When they arrived at Nikki's palace on the Neva Quay, Katelina, Alisa's daughter from a previous marriage, two-year-old Alex and the new baby were all waiting with their nannies and descended on their parents with squeals of excitement. Katelina was eight now and poised in an engaging way that would shatter abruptly when Nikki teased her. Alex was a chubby toddler, testing his curiosity and independence with tugs on Lisaveta's skirt and questions of his own. He pronounced his baby brother's name in a charming two-year-old lisp, and Lisaveta thought how warm and loving the small family appeared. The children were allowed at the table for dinner, served unfashionably early to accommodate their bedtimes, and when the last child was tucked into bed, the three adults settled in the drawing room for tea and sherry.

The intervening years since they'd last met were discussed, Nikki and Lisaveta exchanging pertinent details of their lives. Nikki's new family, of course, was a more staggering alteration than Lisaveta's continuing research, and Lisaveta listened with interest to the story of Nikki and Alisa's courtship and marriage. She could see they were happy, and she found herself wishing her relationship with Stefan might have had the same fantasy ending. Stefan was apparently more immune to Cupid's arrows...an unfortunate circumstance when she had found herself so vulnerable.

Eventually, the reason for Lisaveta's visit to Saint Petersburg was spoken of.

"Uncle Felix is much revered by the Tsar," Nikki said, warming the glass of brandy he preferred drinking in his cupped hands. "This ceremony is more than the usual diplomatic dispersal of medals in a palace stateroom. A dinner is planned and a ball with a very select guest list."

Unaware of the reason for Alexander's unusual favors, Lisaveta said, "Papa did have a very special relationship with the Tsar. They corresponded for years, although their letters were mostly analyses of obscure translations or interpretations of particular stanzas. It was a bit," she added with a smile, "like playing chess through the mails."

"And you came to follow in your father's footsteps," Alisa said. "I suppose you've been asked countless times whether you find the field unusual."

Lisaveta nodded. "Hafiz seems very normal to me, raised as I was in the midst of his research. The exotic qualities of the topic elude me. It's rather like a comfortable old sweater."

Nikki smiled. "An uncommon metaphor for Hafiz, I'd warrant, but I understand. Mother's Romany blood may seem exotic to others, but their culture is prosaic and second nature to me. I may see it as interesting but certainly not exotic."

"Exactly," Lisaveta agreed warmly.

"Be warned, though," Nikki cautioned out of concern for his cousin's feelings, "some in society may see your interest in other terms."

"I understand," Lisaveta replied, her smile intact. "Papa was careful to apprise me of those possibilities years ago, and I've all the bland phrases readily available. I deflect the rabidly curious, politely correct the detractors, and I tell the mildly inquisitive that Hafiz was a troubadour of sorts, much like the medieval European ones. He composed love songs. It sounds all very innocent." She was composed, Stefan's pearls at her neck, a sherry in her hand, unintimidated by prurient interpretations of her work.

"Should you need a champion beyond the curiosity seekers, I'm at your disposal," Nikki offered, "and apparently the Tsar is, as well. Note was taken, you can be sure, of your arrival in a royal railcar."

"His special courtesy was very kind.... I was wondering, perhaps, if Stefan had anything to do with it." She spoke moderately without inflection, and her golden eyes were guileless.

"Stefan?" Nikki carefully repeated, knowing only one Stefan that close to the Tsar, conscious as well of *that* Stefan's libertine reputation.

"Bariatinsky," Lisaveta supplied.

The Tsar's overture of hospitality was immediately crystal clear.

"You know Stefan?" Nikki asked casually. He and the Prince had been frequent compatriots in female amusements before his marriage, had in fact been friends from their days in the Corps of Pages.

"I met him by accident on the Plain of Kars," she said, and proceeded to describe her dramatic rescue, their journey to Tiflis and her meeting with Militza and Nadejda. She didn't, however, detail the exact chronology of these events, nor did she mention their two-week holiday in the mountains.

Nikki, though, knew the distance from the Plain of Kars to Tiflis. He also knew Stefan's propensity for beautiful women and knew Stefan had been actively involved in the siege of Kars for several months. Stefan would not let an opportunity like Lisaveta innocently pass, certainly not after being deprived of female companionship for so long.

"Princess Orbeliani is pleasant, is she not?" Alisa mentioned, having met Militza several times at Stefan's over the past few years.

"Utterly charming," Lisaveta declared with warmth. "Her candor is—"

"Much like Stefan's," Nikki finished.

"Yes," Lisaveta answered. "Both are without subterfuge." There had been times in the past few days as she traveled north when she had wished Stefan had been less bluntly frank. She would almost have wished to cling to the unreal hope that they would meet again rather than the reality of their parting. He had said a simple goodbye. And meant it. The sorrow she felt for a moment, knowing she would never see him again, was evident on her face.

"He's back to Kars, then?" Nikki inquired, aware of Stefan's habit of transient affairs. But this time, with a female relative of his involved, he viewed Stefan's amorous amusements with less tolerance. And Lisaveta was obviously despondent.

"As I understand it," Lisaveta replied, recovering from her futile grieving over Stefan with a ready logic she'd always commanded. Mourning his loss wouldn't recall him, and she was in Saint Petersburg for the first time in her life and about to be introduced into society. There was enjoyment in the prospect. "Apparently the Grand Duke is on some fact-finding junket," she added, able to smile again.

"Making trouble no doubt," Nikki snorted. "Will Stefan be coming up to Saint Petersburg soon?"

"I don't know."

And his question of Stefan's interest was answered. "We'll

have to see you're introduced around," he said avuncularly, annoyed despite his own sexual adventuring that Stefan had preyed on his cousin. His sense of outrage surprised him momentarily—it must be a sign of domesticity. He smiled at Alisa. "Alisa will see to your gowns. Won't you, darling?"

"I'd love to." Since she knew many of Nikki's friends and their predilections she, too, had come to her own conclusions about Stefan Bariatinsky and the Countess. Lisaveta was very splendid, her disposition charming; Alisa understood what Stefan had found alluring. There were, however, scores of men less ruthless in amorous dalliance and she meant to see that Lisaveta enjoyed herself in Saint Petersburg. "Did you bring something for the ceremony? For the ball? Do you have a court dress?"

"No...on all counts, I'm afraid. My baggage was all left behind when the caravan was attacked, although it wouldn't have been adequate anyway, and while Stefan had a dressmaker at Aleksandropol repair my wardrobe deficiencies, it was a sketchy arrangement."

Nikki was not pleased to hear Stefan had clothed his cousin; he'd done the same too many times himself for the paramours in his past to misunderstand the nuances of the situation. "How many days do we have," he said in a crisp voice, "before the ceremony?"

Alisa looked sidelong at her husband as he sat beside her on the sofa. He was angry about Stefan. "Two days," she said, and added with a placating softness, "it's plenty of time, dear. Madame Drouet will manage."

Turning to her, he smiled an apology; he knew she was actually suggesting they would manage to repair the hurt caused by Stefan's philandering. "Of course, you're right." Of Lisaveta he asked, "Are you up to a day of standing and being measured and fitted?" It was obvious from his tone that he had taken on her protection in all things.

"To please the Tsar, of course. What do you suggest, Alisa? I'm completely ignorant of fashion, existing as I have so long in the country."

And the conversation turned to deciding on the basic requirements she would need to be entertained by the Tsar and Saint Petersburg society.

The next three weeks were like a young girl's dream come true. The Tsar feted Lisaveta beyond the ceremonial functions surrounding the honors given her father. He invited her to small dinners at the palace, he took her out riding in his carriage, he sent gifts and flowers, he danced with her always at the balls he attended, and he wasn't known to exert himself as a dance partner. He was, in a word, assuring Countess Lazaroff's success in Saint Petersburg society. His deliberate patronship was noted and remarked on, although even without the Tsar's recognition, Lisaveta's beauty would have gained her avid attention.

The whirl of parties, dinners, balls, the deluge of admirers, was heady. Enormous numbers of bouquets and male callers descended on the pink marble Kuzan palace on the Neva Quay, and the Countess Lazaroff became the most sought-after belle in Saint Petersburg. Lisaveta enjoyed her first encounter with Saint Petersburg's gilded set; she danced and flirted and smiled; she met everyone of importance and was treated with the deference and fervor her beauty and the Tsar's favor engendered. She appeared in the Kuzan box at the ballet and opera; she attended musical soirees and afternoon teas; she danced till dawn and slept till afternoon; she indulged herself completely in the aristocratic world of luxury and amusement.

But in the rare moments of respite from the dizzying diversions, she would recall the quiet solitude of the mountains and the man she'd come to love. Against the yardstick of that cherished time, the glitter of Saint Petersburg paled. She'd promised Alisa to stay until Katelina's birthday and she would, but after that she intended returning to her country estate. Once the war was over she'd accept the Khan's invitation to return to her study of his collection in Karakilisa. In the meantime, she could begin collating her voluminous notes and, she reflected with a small sigh, try to forget the man who'd captured her heart.

Lying back against the bed pillows, her gaze on the sunlit

window the maid had opened to the afternoon air, she determinedly shook away the melancholy of Stefan's departure from her life and briskly thought, Now then, was it a poetry reading this afternoon or a piano recital? And dinner tonight was at one of the numerous grand dukes. Should she wear her emerald satin or her fuchsia tulle? Stefan's pearls would compliment either. She wished he could see her wear them.

That afternoon, though, she decided to forego the piano recital and found comfort instead in the Tsar's gift of a manuscript—*The History of the House of Musaffar*—a rare and special monograph she'd seen only once before. For a few hours as she immersed herself in the confusion of the minor dynasties who ruled over Fars and Kirman in the fourteenth century, she was able to forget her own confusion over wanting a man beyond her reach. She was even able for a brief time to diminish the powerful presence of Stefan in her mind.

In the following days, she escaped whenever she could to the quiet of Nikki's library and began working again, taking careful, minute notes from the manuscript, translating the sometimes cavalier chronology of Viziers into a plausible sequence, making duplicate notes for the Tsar's collection. Hafiz had lived in a turbulent time and his delicate love songs must have been created to the clash of arms, the inrush of conquerors and the flight of the defeated. Anarchy had prevailed, and invader after invader forced the city of Shiraz to submit to his rule. If Hafiz had survived such chaos and destruction with his inimitable gift of philosophy and song intact, surely she could overcome the melancholy of an unrequited love.

And she found a measure of solace in her familiar tasks.

Stefan heard the first glowing comments a week after Lisaveta was introduced by the Tsar at her first formal ball; one of his officers returned from leave in Saint Petersburg with the news. The Countess Lazaroff had been christened the Golden Countess for her sublime radiance and glorious eyes, he'd been told. She was, Loris said, the absolute center of every male's attention. She was more than beautiful, he'd gone on ecstatically, as though each word weren't doing disastrous things to

Stefan's detachment; she was witty and gay with the charming cachet of her Hafiz scholarship. The intriguing possibilities in her exquisite looks and exotic background were a tantalizing lure. Men were lined up for a turn on her dance card, favors were offered for a seat beside her at dinner, and the drawing room of the Kuzan palace, where she was staying, was awash with floral tributes and besieging men. Loris went on at some length, driven by his own enthusiasm but also indulgent to Stefan's known partiality for gorgeous women. Rumor had it, he finished at last, two grand dukes had proposed.

The shock of those initial stories had taken several days for Stefan to rationalize satisfactorily. He'd never remotely imagined Lisaveta as society's reigning queen, although certainly her beauty was breathtaking. Rather, he'd thought her uninterested in the superficiality of society. Loris must have been exaggerating, he decided after several more days of contemplation. And for a man who'd forgotten women as easily as he'd seduced them, Stefan found himself uneasy with his feelings regarding Lisaveta. Eventually with the same kind of determination Lisaveta had summoned in regard to *her* memories, Stefan decided Loris's statements were probably primarily rumor and so dismissable. Even if they weren't, he had no further interest in the Countess. She'd afforded him a delightful holiday but he disliked prolonged relationships and it was all over now.

He was able to maintain his objective and habitual savoir faire until Dmitri and Kadar returned three days later from their leaves with stories of the Golden Countess as their foremost topic of conversation. They discoursed endlessly on her abundant attractions: she danced like an angel, and Stefan found himself inexplicably annoyed he'd never danced with her; she could make you laugh effortlessly without the silliness of other women, and Dmitri and Kadar both detailed numerous instances of her humor—to which the officers in the staff tent guffawed aloud; her gowns were lush like her beauty, but then Nikki Kuzan understood feminine fashions and had taken her to his wife's dressmaker. When Dmitri began describing Lisaveta's voluptuous form, Stefan glowered. He almost said,

"You can't touch her," and only caught himself in time. But when they both remarked on the canary diamonds she wore in her ears, so perfectly matching the gold of her eyes, Stefan abruptly said, "I gave her those," as if the four short words acknowledged his territorial prerogatives.

All the officers in the large tent looked at him. They were curious he knew the Countess, of course, also they heard the temper in his voice. Most of them took cogent note of his tone. If Bariatinsky was laying claim to the woman, it wouldn't be wise to step in his way. Although in the past Stefan had never shown enough concern for a woman to exert himself, perhaps the Countess was different. She must indeed be special.

It was Captain Tamada, just returned from the western front, who added the final straw a day later. To a brooding and un-usually moody Stefan, who was playing a silent game of sol-itaire in the officer's mess, he said, "What you need, Stefan, to lighten your mood, is a night with the newest belle in Saint Petersburg. I saw her myself only a week ago, and she puts the delectable Helene to shame. Have you heard of the Golden Countess?"

A moment later, after Stefan had swept his cards on the ground and stalked out, the Captain turned to a fellow officer who was writing a letter home. "What did I say?"

"He knows her," the man answered, and shrugged.

"And doesn't like her?" Tamada inquired.

The letter writer shrugged again. "Damned if I know, but I'll tell you this. I wouldn't mention her name again if he's around."

That night Stefan suddenly decided that since the campaign wasn't scheduled to begin for two more weeks, due to delays in transport of munitions primarily, he'd travel to Saint Peters-burg.

It was an unusual decision, one likely to cause comment, but the Turks, too, had still not conveyed more than light replace-ments to the front. And since the weather had continued to be unseasonably warm, any large movements of troops from re-serves in Erzurum or the Black Sea ports or Istanbul were considered unlikely. It would be suicidal without adequate supplies of water.

Additionally, the Russian engineers were still constructing the new telegraph lines encircling Kars, and their completion was delaying the attack, as well. Unlike Alaja Dagh, where lack of organization had cost the Russians their victory, the assault on Kars was going to be fully coordinated. Until that time, however, Stefan's presence as the general in command of cavalry was really unnecessary. And since he was as prudent a soldier as he was prodigal a man, he had conscientiously delegated those few duties that would have concerned him during the hiatus.

But his unusual decision to leave the front *did* cause considerable comment, as did his given reason: he wished to visit his fiancée. Everyone knew Stefan never mentioned his fiancée, and when her name came up occasionally, he immediately made it plain he wasn't marrying for love.

So bets were taken on the real reason he was traveling so great a distance, and the Countess Lazaroff figured prominently in those wagers. More complicated odds were negotiated on the outcome of his visit; both his temper and odd moodiness were factored in the point spread.

He went alone because he didn't want company in his sullenness; he also went alone for speed.

Haci had protested at first. "The road to Aleksandropol isn't safe," he'd said, his voice cool with reason.

"I'm in a hurry," was Stefan's blunt reply.

"Have I ever slowed you down?" his friend inquired, watching Stefan toss a few basic items in his saddlebag.

Stefan looked up, the dim lantern light in the tent they shared casting dark shadows across his aquiline features. His smile was brief but apologetic. "No offense, Haci. I should have said I want to be alone."

"It's still dangerous."

Stefan had resumed buckling the red leather straps securing the side pouches. "I'll be careful."

"You don't know how to be careful."

"I'm traveling at night…that'll help."

"You're crazy!" Haci went so far as to grab Stefan's arm for attention. "The road's almost impassable since the transports chewed it up. Cleo could break a leg in the dark."

"I wasn't planning on taking the road." With anyone else he would have shaken the restraining arm free. Out of courtesy for their friendship he ignored it, testing all the closures one more time before sliding an extra knife into his belt.

"Is she worth it?" Haci quietly asked, his hand falling away. "Worth your horse and maybe your life?"

Standing upright, Stefan exhaled gently before answering. "I don't know," he said quietly. "I don't know why I'm going, I don't know what I'm going to do when I get there, but—" he slid his saddlebag over his shoulder, took a quick glance around the small tent to see if he'd forgotten anything, still practical despite his tumultuous feelings "—I'm going. I'll be back in two weeks."

"Even traveling fast," Haci persisted, heedful of the tremendous risks even if Stefan chose to overlook them, "you won't have more than two or three days in Saint Petersburg."

"I don't need much time." A flat statement.

"You may want more," Haci reminded him, aware of Stefan's craving for this woman.

"Then I'll bring her back." He was not to be deterred or dissuaded.

"Not here, certainly," Haci swiftly said, alarmed at the extent of Stefan's imprudence.

"No…but closer."

He was determined to have his way.

"And if the lady protests?" Haci softly inquired.

Stefan's expression was one Haci had seen hundreds of times before as Stefan sat astride Cleo waiting for an attack: part exhilaration, part cold calculation, with an intrinsic vital energy glowing from his dark eyes. "I'll see that she doesn't," he said very, very quietly. And then he grinned. "Wish me luck now on my night ride."

Their friendship was unconditional; Haci smiled. "*Bonne chance*, you fool. You'll need it."

Eleven

~~~⚬⚬⚬~~~

He rode across the high plateau under a brilliant orange-colored moon, but he noticed neither its brilliance nor its color, so intent was he on his thoughts. He was reckoning distances and assessing times, gratified he was doing something at last to expedite a resolution to his sharp-set hunger. The string of ponies he led carried him in relays steadily north until he stopped briefly in Tiflis to eat and to pick up a small escort. He left a note for Militza because he didn't wish to wake her at four in the morning. Also, she would have argued with him or questioned him, neither of which he cared to deal with. He had no answers to her arguments; he hardly knew himself what was driving him.

A telegram had been sent ahead to hold the train at Vladi-kavkaz, and when he reached the railhead fifteen hours later, he handed his pony over to a groom, said goodbye to his escort and collapsed in his bed on his private railway car. He'd been without sleep for almost three days.

The train to Moscow had been waiting eight hours for him, so gratuities were handed around by his steward to the officials, who'd been treated only to a swift smile and thank-you from the Prince before he'd boarded. Stefan fell asleep before the train was under way and slept through until the next afternoon, fully dressed except for his wet overcoat, discarded in a heap on the parlor floor, and his boots, mud-caked and stained, which were discoloring the bedroom carpet. Three days' growth of beard darkened his face, his fingers and toes had been numb since noon, when the sleeting rain had begun in the mountains, but the worst was over and he fell asleep with a smile on his face. He'd survived this far.

He woke south of Saratov to eat and wash, and when he opened his eyes the second time, Moscow was only an hour away. From there to Saint Petersburg he paced or sat brooding, his mind preoccupied with disturbing elements of jealousy and need. He resented his obsession with Lisaveta; he resented this flying trip north; he resented the thought of other men courting her. But he resented most his own lack of control. He must see her and have her and keep her for himself alone. The sensation was entirely without reason, without precedent…and unsettling. More than that, it was inimical to a man who prided himself on his detachment.

Dressing for the ball that night, Lisaveta adjusted the bodice of her gown for the third time, for the décolletage was more revealing than she remembered. Turning to Alisa, who had brought in a diamond brooch to gather the green brocade neckline a shade higher, she said, "I don't recall having this problem when I first wore this."

Standing at a slight distance, Alisa surveyed her guest attired in a glamorous ballgown cut simply with juliet neckline, a small cap sleeve and a gatherered bustled train. "Have you felt well lately?" she asked, the faintest reflection evident in her voice.

"Perfectly," Lisaveta replied, tugging at the offending neckline, immune to the subtle rumination infusing Alisa's question. "Perhaps I've put on a little extra weight with all the elaborate dinners lately. I'm really not used to a lavish menu, Papa and I always ate less exravagantly. I suppose some extra weight would account for this bodice no longer fitting." Her full breasts rose provocatively above the plunging décolletage.

"*Are* you putting on weight?" Alisa's question was quiet and speculative. No further word had been mentioned concerning Stefan Bariatinsky, but Nikki was sure a relationship had existed before his cousin reached Saint Petersburg. When Alisa had mildly suggested he was being too cynical, that surely every woman in Stefan's proximity wasn't automatically involved with him, her husband had only said, "*Dushka*, he was at the siege of Kars for months...months without a woman. Need I say more?"

That circumstance wasn't to be ignored, and knowing Stefan's reputation under even benign conditions, she'd had to admit Nikki was probably right. So quickly calculating the number of weeks Lisaveta had been in Saint Petersburg and the approximate date of her rescue by Stefan, Alisa considered that Lisaveta's added weight might have a more consequential base than simply overeating.

"Do you think you might be pregnant?" she asked, her own experience with the early signs of pregnancy contributing to her abrupt question. "I'm sorry," she added as Lisaveta turned pale and swung around from the mirror to face her. "Was I too blunt?"

"No...well, yes, I suppose...in a way," Lisaveta stammered, her golden eyes wide with astonishment. "I mean—I—how could I be...that's to say," she quickly amended, not naive enough to discount her many weeks with Stefan. "I can't be...can I?" Her gaze was blank or internally focused, as though she were contemplating an interior dialogue without proper answers.

"I don't know," Alisa softly replied, moving to her side and guiding her over to a chair. "Could you be?"

Sitting down like one stunned, Lisaveta leaned back against the cabbage rose chintz and inhaled deeply before answering, her mind swiftly counting days and weeks. "I can't be" she repeated, but she was finding that the arithmetic didn't fall conveniently into place.

She wasn't naive about the possibility of a pregnancy; she was, however, totally without experience *with* pregnancy. Having been raised in an unconventional milieu without childhood playmates, girlhood chums and young women's intimacies of conversation, she had no knowledge of the actual bodily changes provoked by pregnancy. She *felt* fine, and while her menses were slightly more than two weeks late at this point, that kind of variation had happened to her before. She couldn't be, she repeated silently.

It was denial pure and simple.

It was an absolute essential in her present state of mind.

"Is it Stefan?" Alisa asked.

Lisaveta straightened her shoulders, and her voice was normal again when she spoke. "I'm sure there's another explanation," she said, bolstering her belief in some other more reasonable interpretation for her gown not fitting. "And in any event, Stefan's engaged to Princess Taneiev." She said it as though that fact excluded the possibility she might be pregnant.

"I'm sorry…you're right."

"Don't be…really. Everything was very civil. He's not to blame in any way."

"He has responsibilities at least," Alisa said, her pansy-colored eyes grave.

"As do I. Ours was a mutual attraction, Alisa, I wasn't seduced. He's not the villain." She smiled then at the odd word for Stefan's extravagant loving. "No, definitely," Lisaveta went on, her tone softly reminiscent, "I've no regrets about what we did."

"Do you love him?"

"Every woman he meets loves him, as do thousands more who adore him through his engravings and heroic deeds." It was an equivocation, but an answer nonetheless.

"An engagement isn't necessarily binding," Alisa quietly offered.

"His is for his own reasons. Thank you for the concern, Alisa, but—" Lisaveta lifted one bare shoulder in a small shrug of practicality "—I'm not some young innocent."

Regardless of Stefan's engagement, his reasons for it and Lisaveta's extravagant courtesy, under the circumstances Alisa felt impelled to suggest, "Stefan should at least know."

"There may not be anything to know. I'm sure there isn't. And think how embarrassing that would be to unnecessarily accuse him." Lisaveta gave a reassuring smile to her hostess. The color had returned to her face and her expression was without anxiety. "Look…I'll wear something else tonight, and after Katelina's birthday next week, I'm planning on returning to my country estate anyway." Lisaveta's voice was moderate; she was dealing with the situation as she normally dealt with issues: logically assessing a problem and then resolving it. At least that was what she believed. "Before I came to Saint Petersburg," she went on, "no one knew me, and I'm sure my leaving will cause little stir. I like my country estate, I'm very much looking forward to my studies again, and I'm not," she finished, her smile appearing again, "likely to miss the frantic schedule of a society belle."

"You're taking this all remarkably calmly." Under the circumstances Alisa was surprised at Lisaveta's tranquillity. She should have been hysterical or angry or sobbing or concerned...or at least open to the suggestion of pregnancy, considering her time with Stefan.

Was it possible, Alisa briefly thought, that Lisaveta knew of some unusual, esoteric method of birth control, discovered in some old manuscript, learned from some ancillary reading to Hafiz, unearthed among the tribes of Kurdistan? Was she unconcerned because no real possibility of pregnancy existed? But as she had known Nikki's cousin for only a few weeks and since Lisaveta had never confided any of the details of her relationship with Stefan, Alisa felt awkward asking such an intimate question.

"If falling into a faint would help, I'd consider it. However—" and Lisaveta smiled ruefully "—it won't change or alter a minute of my past. So...do we pin this offending neckline together with your brooch or substitute the burgundy silk."

She apparently was intent on changing the conversation, Alisa decided. "It *is* looser," she said, debating whether she dared pursue the topic further.

"The burgundy it is."

"How can you be so cheerful?" Alisa inquired. Hesitant or not, she was disturbed by Lisaveta's serenity in the face of a possibly portentous issue.

"How can I not be when I think of Stefan. He's a remarkable man." Lisaveta's smile was self-assured when she stood abruptly in a swish of silk. "And I'm sure you're wrong."

While Lisaveta changed, Alisa excused herself and went to speak to Nikki. As usual, having dressed swiftly, he was patiently waiting for the ladies in his study, his feet up on his desktop, a glass of brandy half-drunk. He looked relaxed, leaning back in his chair, and he smiled in greeting.

"Madame Drouet has outdone herself, darling. You look exquisite." Alisa's pistachio-green damask gown was festooned with garlands of pearls and crystal, her fine shoulders and bosom rising above a low décolletage trimmed with pink silk chrysanthemum petals.

"Thank you, dear," Alisa automatically said, making sure the door was closed behind her. Turning back to her husband, she announced, "I think she's pregnant." She stood stiffly, her back to the door.

"Who's she?" Nikki asked, but his feet had already dropped to the floor and he was sitting upright, his posture belying his casual inquiry.

And he knew the answer to his question before his wife said in a short expulsion of air, "Lisaveta."

"Stefan."

"Of course." Her reply seemed distracted for a moment, her mind in the grip of unresolved pique over Stefan's cavalier treatment of Lisaveta.

"Damn!"

"Thank you," she crisply said. "My sentiments exactly." In her voice was affront for the casual victimization of women in these circumstances. "And she's cheerful," she added, her astonishment evident.

"Are you sure?"

"That she's cheerful?"

Nikki raised one dark brow in contradiction. "That she's pregnant."

"She says no, or probably not or maybe not, all in a calm, deliberate way that unnerves me, but the signs rather disagree. She's not had her menses since she's come to Saint Petersburg and her gowns are getting tight. She's eating too much, she says, like a young naive girl would."

"Which she might be. Oh, God," Nikki groaned, and leaned his head back against the soft green leather of his chair.

"You know Stefan's engaged to Vladimir's daughter." Alisa had moved across the room and sat down now in a chair across the desk from Nikki.

"If you're right about Lisaveta, he'll have to get disengaged," Nikki growled. "She's my cousin."

"Lisaveta says Stefan is intent on his marriage to Nadejda."

"Has the man no scruples?" Nikki's face was darkened by a scowl.

"You should know, darling, since he was so often your companion in—" his wife paused significantly "—adventure."

"Point taken," Nikki replied with a crooked grin, leaning forward to clasp his hands on his desktop. "But I've reformed." His golden eyes were both amused and affectionate as he gazed at his wife.

"Would he, perhaps?" Alisa suggested, aware what profound changes she'd made in her husband's life.

His eyes turned flinty. "If she's pregnant, he will whether he likes it or not," Nikki replied, and no suggestion graced his voice, only peremptory command.

"Can you force Stefan?"

"Damn right I can." Nikki's voice was soft with restrained anger, his eyes half-closed in contemplation of that necessity.

"Would that be prudent...for Lisaveta?" Men responded differently to compulsion, and while Alisa might take issue with Stefan's casual liaisons, she was realistic about the possible results of forcing a man of his temperament.

"The prudence, or lack of it, can be debated *after* they're married. She's my cousin, dammit, and he should have thought of that before he seduced her!" Nikki's assessment didn't have the subtlety or nicety of Alisa's.

"Unfortunately, he's at Kars."

"If necessary, he can be called back for his wedding," Nikki said grimly.

When Nikki suggested as much to Lisaveta as they rode to the Gagarins' ball, his tone courteous instead of grim, she replied, "Don't be ridiculous, Nikki. You needn't play avenging relative for me. I wasn't some simple young girl unaware of my choices. I'm quite content."

"And if there's a child?"

Their golden eyes, identical in color if not mood, met and held steadily for a moment.

"There isn't," Lisaveta said, her gaze dropping away first. Despite her denial, she recognized she'd been intimate with Stefan too often in the past weeks to discount the fact she might be carrying his child. And at the thought, both stupefying and strangely pleasant, she felt a flutter of sensation in the pit of her stomach as if her body were trying to tell her something. "But if there should be," she said, raising her gaze again to confront her cousin, "I'm perfectly capable of rearing a child. My father raised me alone."

"It's not the same." Nikki wasn't concerned with child development but rather with protocol.

"It may be for me," Lisaveta said very quietly, as determined as Nikki to decide the direction of her life. She wouldn't be persuaded to change her mind even though both Nikki and Alisa tried to reason with her.

They brought up all the societal pressures she would be exposed to.

"Not in the country," she answered.

"Sometimes the country is worse—more provincial and conservative."

"Nikki, darling, Papa and I were practically hermits. It's not a problem."

"Well, think of the child in that isolation."

"It might turn out like me, you mean?"

Nikki smiled a rueful smile. "No, I don't mean that."

"Nikki, you of all people to be lecturing me on protocol. You've said all your life that a Kuzan can do anything."

"This is different."

"How?"

"You're my cousin."

She grinned. "And Stefan must pay."

"Damn right." And then he grinned, too. "This is not logical, is it?"

"No, Nikki, I'm afraid not." From the first moment Stefan had walked into her room in Aleksandropol, logic had ceased to function in her mind. She more than anyone understood that.

"Nikki, dear, Lisaveta knows best how she feels," Alisa interposed, touching her husband's arm in a small gesture of restraint.

"The decision, of course, is yours, Lise," he said immediately, his voice congenial. "Forgive our interference." His smile was bland; his words a lie. He had no intention of releasing Stefan from his obligations. "Everything will work out," he added as a polite disclaimer. "I'm sure."

"Or course it will," Lisaveta replied with alacrity, her tone remarkably cheerful. "I'm as much a Kuzan as you, and we make things work out, don't we?"

Nikki's frame seemed larger in the confining space of the carriage, his size overwhelming the narrow dimensions of the interior, but his voice when he spoke was mild. "We *always* make things work out," he said.

Stefan arrived at the palace on the Neva an hour after the Kuzans and Lisaveta had left for the ball. "Prince Gagarin," Nikki's butler said to him, "is celebrating his newest Rembrandt acquisition at his villa on the islands."

"When did they leave, Sergei?" Stefan stood impatiently waiting for the answer.

"At ten, Your Excellency. Would you like me to send them a message?" Stefan was wearing an informal tweed jacket and riding pants; Sergei assumed he wouldn't make an appearance at an evening party in such dress. "I could have brandy brought into the library for you."

"Thank you, no."

"The Prince will be sorry he missed you."

Stefan smiled politely. "I'll be seeing him later. An hour, you said?" He had taken two steps toward the door, and the footman was already opening it when Stefan turned back. "Did the Countess have an escort?"

"No, sir."

Twenty minutes later, Stefan arrived at Prince Gagarin's villa. They had been twenty very long minutes in which he cautioned himself to prudence, warned himself against making a scene, knew without illusion his mere appearance would be scene enough, thought transiently of returning to his own palace for evening clothes, as quickly discarded the notion because he refused to take the time when hours counted on this flying trip, told himself he would simply say, "Good evening, Countess, may I have a moment of your time?" and then they would find someplace quiet to talk. That was of course a euphemism for what he really wanted to do, for what was causing the blood to drum in his ears and pulse through his body, for what had driven him across the length of Russia.

His entrance was as dramatic as he knew it would be; everyone in Saint Petersburg thought him halfway across Russia in Kars, but the drama extended as well to his notoriety, his handsome good looks, his unorthodox attire and tantalizing curiosity. Why had he come? Why hadn't he been announced? Why was he scanning the crowd with interest?

He stood perhaps five seconds in the entrance to the ballroom before the first whispers began, and in five seconds more he was surrounded by well-wishers and admirers, by beautiful women and inquisitive statesmen. He politely evaded them all, offering brief answers to their avid questions or courteous refusals or smiling acknowledgement to the compliments even as he moved forward, his gaze intent on the dance floor. He hadn't seen Lisaveta yet or Nikki and his wife, and he wondered restlessly if they'd changed their plans.

The ballroom was ablaze with light, the crystal chandeliers illuminating the large room as if it were noon, the throng of twirling dancers a blur of colored silk and jewels and ornamented uniforms. His own swelling entourage, its rising buzz of whispered comments, exclamations and cries of recognition, was beginning to contest the orchestra's music, and he'd just reached the border of the dance floor and finally caught sight of Lisaveta dancing with a young lieutenant in the Tsarina's Hussars when the music abruptly ceased.

"Ladies and gentlemen!" the leader of the orchestra cried, his eyes on Stefan, his baton raised, "we have the honor of welcoming the Conqueror of Tubruz, the Savior of Mirum, the fearless General Prince Stefan Bariatinsky!" The orchestra director's hand chopped the air, his baton falling in a swift arabesque, and in a muted fanfare of oboes and bassoons, embellished with a flourish of drumrolls, Stefan was presented to the hundreds of guests.

Oh, hell, he swore under his breath as an aisle to the bandstand opened like the passage through the Red Sea and all eyes were directed his way. Hell and damnation. But there was nothing to do under that numerous gaze but graciously acknowledge his introduction. Striding swiftly through the passageway of smiling and congratulatory guests, he lightly leaped onto the stage and bowed to the assembled guests. Modestly accepting the frenzied applause and cheers, he spoke then as he did to his troops, with informality and cordiality: the war was going well; Russia's soldiers were sure to conquer the Turks; the assault on Kars was certain to be victorious this time. He was humble and charming, he was gracious and smiling, he was a potent spokesman for Russia's sacred duty; the crowd loved him.

Lisaveta's first irrelevant thought when, with fluttering pulse and wide-eyed astonishment, she watched him stride toward the stage was, he's not dressed for the ball. His cavalry twill and tweed was a startling contrast to the jeweled and ornamented throng, and he was overpowering in his size. She'd forgotten in the weeks away from him how tall he was and how the width of his shoulders dwarfed other men...and how his smile dazzled.

Her second, more relevant, observation concerned his reason for appearing dressed like that. Her heart began beating in a small rhythm of hope.

Perhaps he'd come for her, she thought, like a young maiden pining for her absent lover. Perhaps the most popular man in Russia was here in Saint Petersburg for her. How fairy-tale perfect it would be if her love were requited, if he could no more live without her than she could without him, if he'd traveled across the breadth of the Empire to sweep her into his arms.

Stefan's speech when he spoke, though, wasn't of frenzied lovesick longing but was essentially political. His manner was one of ease, as though he stood often in riding clothes before a ballroom, and when he stepped down into the crowd after several rounds of additional applause, he didn't seek her out but was immediately surrounded. Even Lisaveta's dance partner apologetically asked her pardon to withdraw and greet the General. She smiled him off with a wave and then moved to a quiet corner away from the stage, watching Stefan in the midst of the adulatory crowd, complex and confused feelings of desire conflicting with pride tumbling through her mind.

"I won't be staying in Saint Petersburg long, but thank you," Stefan was saying for the twentieth time to an invitation, when his searching gaze fell on Lisaveta again over the heads of the importuning crush pressing round him.

Two men were approaching her as she stood near a console table adorned with an enormous arrangement of fucshia-colored lilies, and her welcoming smile to their mannered bows triggered a surge of resentment. The Golden Countess had used that same smile on him. He'd seen it early in the morning and late at night, in bed and out-of-doors, over the dinner table and across a small cool mountain pool. He'd always thought it was her special smile, used for him alone. But there she was, displaying it for other men.

His temper showed minutely in a faint crispness in his voice, but it was several tedious minutes more before he was able to disengage the last beautiful clinging woman from his arm, make the last gracious refusal to dinner or something more intimate and break away from the mass of people intent on fawning sociability.

The floor was open between them because the orchestra hadn't yet resumed playing, and when Stefan stepped out onto the polished parquet, his progress was noted by every pair of eyes in the room.

He was obviously on some urgent mission, dressed as he was; he wasn't simply passing an idle night two thousand miles

away from the war. And while his fiancée was in attendance
tonight, no one to whom he'd spoken had heard him ask for
her. The style of his engagement, though, was common knowledge, and none of the guests labored under the illusion that he
was here for Nadejda. So they watched, avidly curious and
titillated by the demonstrable impetuousness of his appearance.

The Golden Countess, it was seen as he crossed the midpoint
of the ballroom floor, was apparently the object of his advance.
And it didn't surprise a single soul. Prince Bariatinsky had
always had an eye for the exotic in women, and surely the
Countess was exceptional. Was the rumor true, too, that the
Countess and he were…friends? Did Nadejda's spiteful disregard for the Countess have basis in fact?

It looked very much as though it did.

The buzz of speculation rose in a low humming resonance
like bees over a flower bed as the distance between the General and Countess lessened. People instinctively held their
breaths…waiting.

Reaching Lisaveta in three strides more, Stefan acknowledged the two men at her side with the merest of curt nods
and brusquely said, his voice very low and, Borsoff said later,
hot with temper, "Countess, may I have a moment of your
time?" Without waiting for her answer, he took her hand in a
grip just short of punishing and, leaving the two men open-
mouthed, began stalking toward the terrace doors.

They were the focus of everyone's breath-held scrutiny, but
the three people who might actually have done something were
all missing at that moment. Nikki was in the card room as was
his custom at balls, Alisa had been cornered in the refreshment
room by a young matron intent on describing her last confine-
ment in lurid detail, and Nadejda was petulantly upbraiding a
maid in the powder room for not adjusting her shoulder flounce
properly. So Stefan was allowed to pull Lisaveta from the room
unimpeded.

Stiff-armed, he pushed the terrace door open, dragging her
through without ceremony onto the flagstone terrace overlooking the manicured grounds falling away to the shoreline. The
evening was cool, the breeze off the Baltic harboring the first

faint touches of fall, and Lisaveta shivered at the sudden contrast to the heated ballroom. Walking no more than a few paces from the opened door, a distance just barely outside the range of direct illumination from the lighted entry, Stefan pushed her back against the ivy-covered stucco and, bending down, kissed her.

Twelve

It wasn't a kiss of welcome or greeting or even pleasure; it was distinctly a kiss of possession, as if the harsh pressure of his mouth somehow indelibly acknowledged ownership. Struggling against his strength the moment she realized his intentions, she protested verbally as well as physically to his brutal kiss.

"You're drunk," she remonstrated, turning her mouth away with effort, shoving uselessly against the solid muscle of his chest, her hands small in contrast to his massiveness.

"I haven't had a drink in five days, *dushka*," he replied, his voice a growl, the endearment an epithet in tone, his arms tightening around her. He'd been traveling day and night for five days while she'd been smiling her special smile and offering more no doubt to every fawning man in Saint Petersburg. He knew what she could offer, he knew what her smile prefaced. He had been told she was everyone's darling and jealousy ate at his reason. His lips brushed over her cheek, his lower body pressed into her, and intent on being the next recipient of the Golden Countess's favors, he said, "Relax, darling, this won't take much of your time."

Those were not words of love or the sentiments of a lovesick swain, and while he'd come and taken her away, his intent appeared wholly without feeling. "Take me back inside, Stefan, damn you," Lisaveta whispered hotly. His mouth was millimeters from hers, and her body was pressed against the ivy wall with such force she could feel the buttons of his jacket imprinted into her flesh.

His soft laugh was unpleasant, his breath warm on her mouth. "Do your *new* lovers take orders?" He hadn't moved and the weight of his body was solid and resistant.

"Does your fiancée?" she snapped, ignoring the fact she was powerless against him, too angry at his seizure, rude purpose and insinuation to consider her precarious position.

His head lifted abruptly and his eyes in the moonlight darkness gleamed like fire. "Yes, as a matter of fact," he said very softly, his mouth curled in derision. "Your turn."

"Then so do my lovers." She wouldn't give him the satisfaction of knowing she'd refused all the men because they hadn't measured up to him.

His eyes narrowed at her confident tone, a cold fury overwhelming him. "I've heard," he said in a taut low whisper, "you're much in demand." So all the rumors were true. She'd been entertaining herself with a variety of lovers since she'd arrived in Saint Petersburg. Loris and Dmitri and Kadar and Tamada had all been telling the truth. How many lovers had she had? he hotly thought. He could almost feel his temper as a palpable heat rising in his body—or was it lust…or both? He knew too well how eager and erotic the Countess's style of entertainment was and knew she had the spontaneity and energy to delight a great number of lovers.

He wanted to punish her for her bewitching ways, and then call out and kill each man she'd slept with. In an earlier era he may have done that without a second thought. But one didn't publicly beat women any longer or lock them away in nunneries, and duels were, at least in theory, uncivilized.

He was, however, feeling uncivilized and savagely angry. He was, in fact, very near to losing control, so Lisaveta's answering words were exactly wrong.

"You taught me well," she said, her voice snide and too sweet and taunting.

It wasn't what he cared to hear. He would have preferred all the gossip to have been false; he would have preferred finding her asleep in her bed instead of at a ball, or discovering her quietly studying in some isolated library or embroidering, if women actually did that, or performing any number of other safe, innocuous, acceptable feminine pursuits. He would have preferred anything but her last reply. A strange wildness overcame him, as if he were an adolescent again, totally without restraint.

"Let's see then," he murmured, his chill voice matching the breeze off the Baltic, "if you remember everything I taught you." His hands moved up her back as he finished speaking and came to rest on her shoulder, his fingers sliding under the neckline of her gown in a small gesture of possession.

"Don't you dare." Her own fury and self-determination reverberated through her heated words. Her eyes shone like golden flame.

He stood, his hands lightly cupping her bare shoulders, his touch gentle as though his intentions were benign, as though her fury were irrelevant. "Darling, don't be naive. I attack redoubts bristling with artillery and enemy. Surely—" his fingertips traced the curve of one shoulder, an incongruously delicate juxtaposition to his heated words "—you don't think one small woman can stop me." His voice was very low, unhurried, almost tranquil.

"I'll scream," she challenged. Her hands were still caught against his chest, his body still curtailing her freedom.

"Perhaps later," he replied casually, his palm already sliding up the slender column of her neck. "You always scream," he softly murmured, "at the end." The tip of his finger gently tapped the yellow diamond pendant swinging from her ear. "I'm glad you like the earrings."

"You can't do this, Stefan," she warned. "Someone could walk out any moment." Her voice was more contained than her emotions with Stefan's aroused body pressing into her flesh. "Just release me now and you can go about your business." She tried to keep her tone reasonable and moderate.

"But *you're* my business." His answer was a teasing murmur, his hands drifting down her shoulders once again, stopping to test the resistance of the gold lace ruffle just below the curve of her shoulder.

"You came all the way to Saint Petersburg to see me?" Her query was laced with doubt and a dizzying curiosity and suspicion, too.

"Of course." His reply was so blatantly nonchalant it resisted belief. "And now," he said, the hush of his voice as languorous as his half-lidded eyes, "I'd like to *see* you."

"Stefan, be sensible," Lisaveta pleaded, suddenly realizing he was fully intent on satisfying his passion, here, now, within sight and sound of the ballroom. "Please..."

"I remember," he said with a faint smile, "you always pleaded—" his voice dropped to a whisper "—and were impatient."

His tone and words kindled heated memory and Lisaveta fought against the images evoked. She would not be seduced by him; she wouldn't be dragged from a ballroom with abrupt and staggering discourtesy and then begin to melt because his deep low voice was reminding her of endless hours of shared rapture and, yes, of her impatience and the reasons for it. Taking a breath to steady her tremulous feelings, she forced her mind away from those arousing memories.

"Stefan," she implored, not certain she could curtail his full intent, "at least move away from the vicinity of the door, I beg you."

He didn't pretend not to understand. Her voice and inflection were intense. Glancing briefly at the opened doorway no more than three feet away, he said, "Darling, you've taken on new refinements in Saint Petersburg." His words were sardonic and challenging, as if he wanted further concessions from her. "What will you do if I move?"

She didn't answer for a moment, provoked by his suggestion she had to somehow please him first. "Why must I *do* something to keep you from being pigheaded?"

He shrugged. "I thought we were negotiating for a new venue."

"A new venue?" Although she spoke in a whisper, the violence of her feelings was evident. "Is that what you call rape now?"

His lashes dropped fractionally in ironic reply. "Really,

sweetheart, why all the ruffled outrage? It's not as though my wanting you will harm you in any way.''

"This spectacle—should someone walk out of the ball-room—notwithstanding!'' she fiercely replied.

He sighed as though her stinging response required at least one reasonable party. "Very well,'' he said, not in explanation but in magnanimity, "we'll move.'' And lifting her into his arms, he walked with her across the terrace and down the three wide stairs to the lawn below. "Is this better?'' he inquired politely, as if the location of his assault on her were the only point in question.

Lisaveta lay rigid in his arms, refusing to touch him, and gazed around, her golden eyes incredulous. Stefan was standing at the base of the stone stairs directly in line with the ballroom door, in the middle of a great open expanse of lawn, the moon bright overhead. "No,'' she indignantly retorted, "this is *not* better!'' She bit off the words as if they were poison.

He turned so they faced the villa, kicking the train of her gown out of his way. "You decide then,'' he said with no more emotion than if they were discussing the merits of lavender versus yellow kid gloves as a fashion accessory.

"Why are we doing this?'' Lisaveta breathed, dismay vibrating in every hushed syllable.

Stefan looked down at her for a moment and his face in shadow held a menacing quality. "I know why *I'm* doing this,'' he said, his intention absolutely plain in his simple declaration, "and at the risk of further offending you, I don't really care why you are or aren't. I hope that's not too blunt.''

It was another galaxy beyond blunt. "In that case, my decision is irrelevant,'' Lisaveta quietly said.

He didn't answer because the substance of his reply was clearly understood, and he thought for a moment how powerful jealousy was. He'd never been this rude to a woman before. In fact, he prided himself on his charm with the opposite sex. But then, he'd never been barraged by such overwhelming frustration before, and the force of his emotions was driving him. He felt it unkind to liken this to war, but the simile came prominently to mind. Lisaveta was the redoubt he wanted and he intended to triumph in his assault. She was the eternal enticing female who bewitched him like Circe or Venus, and he coveted her—at Kars, on his ride to the railhead at Vladikavkaz, on his train journey north and now, here, this instant.

Moving a few feet from where he stood, he set Lisaveta on her feet within the shadow of the terrace wall and without speaking slid the lace ruffles off her shoulders, forcing the bodice of her gown downward over the fullness of her breasts until they were exposed, pale white and enticing in the moonlight.

She stood rigid beneath his hands, knowing resistance would be useless, hating him at that moment for his callous indifference but feeling also an unnerving familiarity to the touch of his hands.

Placing his palms with infinite slowness under her breasts, he lifted them high, surveying their mounded beauty. His eyes were calculating as a critic; no soft emotion shone from their blackness. When he considered all the other men who might have admired them thusly, his temper flared. He was angry and tormented, twisted with jealousy, and it showed in his stance and moody expression, in his deplorable aggression and in his words.

"What do they usually say? How lovely, Countess?" Each quiet word was hollow with aversion.

"I don't answer to you," Lisaveta whispered, stung by the rudeness of his remark, trying for a moment to twist free until his fingers squeezed sharply and she instantly stood quiescent.

"I think we've gone over this before. The concept," Stefan softly said, "of physical superiority."

"Stefan, this isn't like you." She hesitated for a moment and then added. "I wish you'd reconsider."

He almost laughed. How quaint and bland a statement after he'd traveled across the expanse of Russia to do exactly this. "I'm afraid I won't," he said.

"I'll resist." Her voice was flat.

"Fine."

He didn't seem concerned and the mildness of his reply was more unnerving than his harsh anger. She knew she couldn't prevail against his strength. "Will entreaties help?" She was appealing, her voice softly earnest, trying any measure to deter him. Any second someone could walk out on the terrace, any moment they could be seen.

He released her breasts and for a moment she thought she'd succeeded in deflecting his purpose, but he didn't even glance at her when he answered, absorbed in lifting the gathered folds of skirt out of his way. "No," he said, struggling momentarily with the lawn petticoat beneath the burgundy silk, "nothing will help." The lightweight charmeuse fabric of her gown and the fine tissue of her petticoat was crushed around her hips in swift efficiency, and without pause, single-minded with jealousy and desire, Stefan slipped his fingers between the opening in her drawers and slid them inside her.

With shame and consternation Lisaveta felt his fingers glide into her moist interior without resistance, his nearness alone rousing her passion despite all rationale; he had only to touch her and she welcomed him, insensible to her anger or logic, as if her body could anticipate the pleasure he offered and willingly, selfishly, turn liquid with wanting. Fighting the staggering impulse to sigh in satisfaction, she stood motionless under his hands, resisting with all her faculties the building waves of bewitching sensation, determined to appear unmoved.

She'd simply remain impassive, she told herself, her eyes already closing against the pulsing between her thighs; she *wouldn't* respond, she'd ignore the flame racing through her blood and heating her skin, bringing a flush to her face and throat and naked breasts. She'd forcibly detach herself from the languid provocation of Stefan's gently stroking fingers, from their acute, intense penetration. She'd *not* allow him the satisfaction of—she caught her breath as his fingers touched her deep inside and uncurbed pleasure pulsed upward.

He smiled at her response and his success and then glanced for a moment at the terrace wall above them. Had he heard voices?

He moved her back a few steps until they were in the deep shadow, partially concealed, should someone walk down the steps, by a lacy pungent juniper, its deep bluish-green black in the moonlight.

"Stefan, you're mad," Lisaveta whispered, her back against the cool stone, her spine rigid because she, too, had heard the voices now.

"Mad for you, Countess," he murmured, intent on unbuttoning his trousers.

Oh, Lord, Lisaveta thought, terrified and aroused and staggered by her own wanton desire. "Wait, Stefan…" She spoke in a hushed undertone. "Wait till they're gone…or we could go…somewhere else. Stefan, please…"

But he was lifting her already as though she hadn't spoken. Holding her with the weight of his arm immobile for a moment and bending his legs, he entered her without preliminaries, his urgency reflective of his driving need. He was unconcerned with her pleasure or displeasure, oblivious to the people above them; he wished only to assuage his turbulent passion and in so doing exorcise his tempestuous fierce craving for her. He held her securely against the granite wall in a rhythm of demand, forcing her entire weight upward with the sheer strength of his compelling hunger, all the jealousy eating away at him, exploding in each forceful stroke, all of his anger at the Countess's favored position as the reigning belle of Saint Petersburg provoking his punishing power. He would, he thought, driving in impatiently, the frustration of their separation and his lengthy journey impelling each upward thrust, rid himself once and for all of his tormenting intoxication.

"Where do you suppose they went?" a woman's voice said, drifting over their heads in the moonlight.

And buried deep inside Lisaveta, Stefan closed his eyes against the drumming ecstasy racing through his senses.

"I'd say they're in his carriage on their way back to his palace. He looked like a man in a hurry." A knowing inflection underlay the masculine voice.

Knowing that, hearing that, feeling the full impact of that haste, Lisaveta wondered how she could be so defenseless against the pleasure Stefan provoked, immune to scandal and the presence of people a scant few feet away.

His mouth closed over hers, teasing, rousing, as if to say, "Ignore them, let me take your mind off them, think only of

seductive feeling…like that and that and that,'' the rhythm of
his lower body a powerful adjunct to his enticing tongue.

Wanting only to sustain the pervading rapture, to feel him
more intensely, all her resistance forgotten with the throbbing
splendor beating through her senses, the couple above them
relegated to oblivion, Lisaveta slid her arms around Stefan's
shoulders and pulled him closer. Her mouth opened to his
sweet demands, her heated body melted around him.

As if she'd spoken, as if she'd said remember, he instantly
wanted more. He wanted more leverage, he wanted to press
deeper, he wanted with feverish impatience to enhance the tantalizing bliss. Lifting her suddenly, he held her with one arm
while he wrapped her legs around his waist, then swiftly, as if
these were the last few moments in eternity, his hands slid
down her back to slip under her bottom. Supporting her entire
weight now, secure in his possession, he slowly penetrated,
focusing with self-indulgent intemperance on burying himself
to the limits of his need.

Lisaveta gasped as extravagant pleasure washed over her.

Stefan held his breath for a moment, absorbing the riveting
luxury of unrestrained sensation.

"Nikki's going to be looking for the Countess soon. Someone went to fetch him from the card room." The female voice
held that cozy chatty ambience of casual gossip.

It was madness to cling to him, Lisaveta thought, hearing
those ominous words, sheer unadulterated lunacy to let herself
thrill to such voluptuous feelings. But she was inundated by a
feverish desire so torrid it was melting away every sensibility
in her body save her own carnal urges.

She'd been celibate too long—it had been three weeks since
the mountains. Was that excuse enough for this madness? She
chose to ignore the fact that no man of her numerous suitors
in that interval had so much as piqued her interest, sexual or
otherwise. And under the circumstances, crude as they were at
this moment, with lust dominant and love unmentioned, it was
wise of her psyche to suppress that thought.

"I'd be interested in Nadejda's reaction. Should we go inside
and watch the fireworks?" The man's voice was infused with

a keen curiosity. "Her scenes are always memorable, and Bariatinsky and the Countess seem to have left."

At that moment, Lisaveta cried out, overcome with a peaking intensity of rapture.

"Did you hear that?" It was the woman's voice.

Stefan's mouth swiftly covered the remnant of Lisaveta's cry, responding automatically, his reaction to danger instinctive, while his body continued uninterrupted its tantalizing and measured rhythm.

"It was the orchestra. See, there it is again." The couple's voices receded as they returned to the ballroom.

Stefan's head came up then and he grinned, his dark glance regarding Lisaveta with amusement. "You'll have to be more quiet, *dushka*," he murmured, "or we'll draw a crowd."

"If not for *your* self-indulgence," she whispered, "the problem wouldn't exist."

"If not for *your* popularity, Countess," Stefan sardonically replied arresting all movement for a moment, "there wouldn't be a problem."

"*I* don't have a problem." Her indignant whisper hung for a moment in the darkness.

"Neither do I," Stefan lazily drawled, and just as she was beginning to think she could defy her pulsing needs and gain control over her feelings once again, Stefan moved inside her, setting every intemperate nerve in her body to tingling.

No! she silently disavowed, feeling the first tremulous flutters begin, Stefan's eyes too observant, too knowing. She shouldn't, she mustn't climax, she must resist behaving like a lascivious trollop under that amused insolent stare.

"No-o-o-o," she whimpered against the injustice of her emotions and her peaking ecstasy.

Lisaveta's gratification triggered Stefan's own release. Their passion matched as it had so often in the past, and he fought against responding so exactly to her unbridled sensuality. She was flamboyantly sexual, resplendent in her voluptuousness, and every man reacted to her as he did.

He tried then to restrain himself, to set himself apart from her legions of lovers. He intended to use her for his own purposes, pragmatic purposes; he wouldn't be tempered by her response, and he controlled his prodigal impulses for a moment more. But Lisaveta reached up then to kiss his mouth in unthinking desire as she peaked, her lips soft and sweet tasting as he remembered, and he groaned into their lush resiliency, felt his shuddering climax begin and knew he couldn't stop himself.

"No…" he softly disclaimed as his white-hot lust poured into her.

"No," they whispered in unison as their bodies met in perfect harmony and the universe stood for a suspended moment in starlit brilliance around them.

Short minutes later, tugging the lace ruffles up over her breasts, he patted them lightly in place, shook out the lace flounce on her shoulders and then slid her petticoat and the burgundy silk of her skirt down over her legs. Without expression, he buttoned his trousers and tucked in his shirt while Lisaveta stood in shock and anger, furious at him…and at herself for responding so intensely. Still without speaking, he straightened the cuffs of his shirt, adjusting them to his jacket sleeves as though it mattered with no one in sight, and then with a quiet, "Thank you, Countess," he walked away.

She watched him stroll down to the shoreline and then disappear into the birches bordering the lawn, wanting to strike out at him in outrage, wanting to follow him with a screaming tirade of wrathful indignation, wanting also, unfortunately—disobedient thought—to cling to his arm and say, "Take me with you."

Her feelings were in untidy anarchy, a complicated muddle of wishful fantasy, lovesick yearning and indiscriminate rage. He was too beautiful and self-assured, too sought after and resistant to love. And it was bitter fate that she should want him anyway.

Still warm, with cheeks flushed and pulse pounding, Lisaveta welcomed the sea breeze. Shutting her eyes briefly, she leaned back against the cool granite, letting the sensations of sated passion subside. She shouldn't have been so physically recep-

tive, she thought uneasily; she should have been less suscep-
tible, shown more control and resisted him. Why couldn't she
coolly deal with Stefan, save herself the humiliation of matching his need with her own, instead of crying out in delight,
clinging to him, wanting him desperately? His motives, though,
were never in question, even if hers were disordered and be-
wildering; his were purely carnal. And while he denied being
drunk tonight, she wondered if perhaps he was. How else did
one explain his shocking behavior?

But perhaps Stefan lived constantly on the brink of scandal;
maybe if she were to ask, Nikki and Alisa would confirm that
seizing women in ballrooms and making love to them where
all the world might observe was ordinary procedure for Prince
Bariatinsky. He did, after all, number Catherine the Great and
Prince Orlov among his ancestors, and both had been monumental egos in an era that subscribed to monumentality as a
credo. And from all Militza had told her of Stefan's father and
mother, they had shown every sign of regarding impulse as a
virtue.

And while she might decry the vice of capricious impulse,
she in fact had reacted just as spontaneously. Her initial refusal
had stemmed from anger. She had wanted him, too, and he
must have been aware of her body's response even as she protested.

It was impossible any longer to deny her need of him. She'd
proved it, demonstrably, tempestuously, and she might as well
confront the truth.

She belonged to the legion of women—ex-lovers, current
lovers and future lovers—who found Stefan irresistible.

Thirteen

~~~~~ ⟡ ~~~~~

Walking through the informal English gardens facing the sea, Stefan found his coachman visiting with the other drivers near the stables and had himself driven to the Yacht Club. Settling into a club chair near the windows, he had a servant bring him a bottle of brandy, watched as the man filled a glass to the point indicated by his finger and then, thanking him with a smile, began drinking. There was no possibility he could sleep tonight, and the liquor might help to mitigate the distasteful sense of affront and self-reproach assailing him.

He shouldn't, of course, have forced himself on Lisaveta.

Yet she had responded like a practiced tart, damn her. How many other men had enjoyed her favors the past few weeks...? The thought of other men touching her maddened and inflamed him, made him resentful, made him covetous.

He hadn't known exactly how he'd proceed once he saw Lisaveta again. He had intended to make love to her and by so doing exorcise his burning need for her, feel nothing but relief and return to Kars, although beneath his pragmatic resolve had been the more realistic possibility that he would, if necessary, bring her back with him.

Since he wanted her still, there was no question now of what to do, only of methodology.

He would simply have to carry her off, he decided, draining his glass and staring into the clear crystalline bottom. As he had before. And once she was settled in the mountain lodge, she'd be happy and content…as she had before. He would see to it.

Other men had wives and established mistresses; the practice, in fact, was prevalent. And while the inclination to install a confirmed mistress had never tempted him before, there was no reason why he shouldn't.

At this time of night the club chairs were deserted. The gaming tables two rooms away were the site of all activity, the brilliant lights and noisy play removed from the quiet of the parlor fronting the sea. He poured himself another drink and looked out the windows for the first time since he'd come into the room. The slips and docks and pier stretched across the flat horizon. Masts of sailing craft and smokestacks of larger yachts were silhouetted against the moonlight. The breeze had dropped off so the banners on the outside deck only flapped occasionally on their standards; the stars were radiant in the sky.

As he gazed at the tranquil scene and vast sparkling sky, his mood seemed to alter. He was less restless now, perhaps the liquor was taking effect, and the chaos of his feelings was sorted out…a decision made. The Golden Countess was about to be taken off the market—whether she liked it or not.

He hadn't been at the Yacht Club long because the brandy bottle was only half-empty when Nikki walked into the lamplit room. He stood for a moment just inside the doorway, surveying the large area punctuated with leather chairs and sofas, writing tables, newspaper and magazine racks and silk-shaded chandeliers. His tawny eyes narrowed momentarily when he caught sight of Stefan lounging in his chair near the window, and with purposeful stride he walked over to him.

"I've been looking for you," he said, not bothering with social amenities. He'd been to Stefan's palace on the Fontanka first, and then to several cafés Stefan favored, before thinking of the Yacht Club, and he was irritated and badly out of temper.

"So you found me," Stefan idly replied, not inclined to be chastised by anyone. He knew why Nikki was here, and glowering like some wrathful deity, but the woman was available to the entire city. Surely *he* needn't bear the brunt of Nikki's censure.

"What did you do to Lisaveta?" Each word was a ground-out challenge.

While cognizant of Nikki's temper, Stefan matched him in his own terse resentment. "Only what, from the sound of it, every other man in Saint Petersburg's doing," he drawled casually, his sardonic expression masking his indignation at her popularity.

"If we hadn't been friends so long, I'd kill you for that remark." Nikki's golden eyes were hostile. "I'll say instead, you're dead wrong."

"Not from what I hear." Stefan hadn't moved from his comfortable pose, the glass of brandy in his hand resting on the chair arm, his eyes only half-open, as if their conversation were of negligible interest to him.

"Your informants are mistaken," Nikki retorted, his voice so soft it was almost a whisper, his stance vengeful, his Saint George medal and ribbon the only splash of color in the severity of the evening dress. "You could have hurt her."

One dark brow lifted in the studied calm of Stefan's expression. "She didn't appear to be in pain. To the contrary—"

"She's pregnant."

It looked for a moment as though Stefan had stopped breathing, but he quickly recovered and carelessly said, "So?"

Nikki's golden eyes flared like brilliant flame, his features took on the menace many men had seen across the dueling field. "So," Nikki murmured softly, "I understand you're the father, she's my cousin, and I'd like to know what you're going to do about it."

"Can you prove it?"

"I can kill you," Nikki breathed, his voice between a growl and a whisper, "and then it won't matter."

"Perhaps not a satisfactory solution for the lady, though," Stefan replied in an equally soft tone. "Do I understand she wishes to marry me?" His inquiry was insolent.

"She claims not to. She also claims she's not pregnant."

Stefan's brows rose. "And yet you're hounding me."

"She's apparently an innocent, although—" and it was Nikki's turn to raise one dark brow "—I'm sure you're more aware of that than we."

Stefan had the grace to acknowledge his responsibility there but took issue with the timing. "If she's not sure," he went on, no longer lounging, his glass put aside, his dark eyes intent on Nikki, "why couldn't it be someone else's. She's been here nearly a month."

"The girl is chaste as country air."

"Remember to whom you speak." Stefan's drawl was remonstrance.

"Present company excepted," Nikki said, his well-considered gaze taking in the altered posture and attitude of his friend.

"Then why is it," Stefan said, his voice intense with jealousy, "I've heard such contrary rumor?"

Nikki smiled for the first time. "Rumor only. She's flirtatious. Everyone wants her. It doesn't necessarily follow they were successful. And they weren't. Don't tell me," he went on, his mouth quirked in irony, "you deserted your cavalry corps for Lise and her gallants."

"The munitions and artillery are bogged down," Stefan muttered. "We're weeks off schedule. How do I know," he demanded, his tone different now, his dark glance keen, "it's untrue about the other men?" He wanted verification. He wanted assurances. He wanted absolutes, this man who'd lived his own life so differently.

"Because she came home with us every night in our coach and Alisa tucked her in and said good-night. Is my word sufficient against your jealousy?"

"Every night?" Stefan wouldn't so easily relinquish the maddening gossip concerning the Golden Countess.

Nikki gazed at Stefan from under his dark brows, the golden Kuzan eyes almost translucent in the lamp glow, his voice when he spoke significant in its utter lack of emphasis. "Every night," he said.

"She's exactly the same," Stefan said very quietly, trying to sort out the confusion and disarray of his thoughts. "I don't know if I believe you.'' How could she respond as she had with him and not fuel the rumors and gossip for the exact same reason?

Nikki shrugged. ''That's your problem, Stefan. I can't obliterate your jealousy.''

Stefan's gaze widened.

''You might as well face it,'' Nikki said with a grin. ''That's a hell of a long trip you just made.''

''Don't remind me,'' Stefan grumbled.

Pulling over a chair facing Stefan, Nikki sank into it and smiled benignly. ''She'll be flattered to know you relinquished duty for her.''

''You misunderstand,'' Stefan protested.

''How long have we known each other, Stefan? Since we were fifteen? Tell me honestly that you're here for other reasons.'' He waited, feeling vastly better than he had when he'd first confronted Stefan.

''I *could* be here to visit my fiancée.''

''Appalling thought,'' Nikki replied, his smile sunny. ''Were you sober when you proposed to Nadejda?'' he asked with masculine bias.

''No.''

''I didn't think so.''

''It wouldn't have changed things, had I been.''

''Because the House of Bariatinsky-Orbeliani needed an heir.''

Stefan sighed. ''Yes, because of that.''

''But, good God, *Nadejda*.'' Nikki's own sigh was weighty with rebuke.

''It didn't matter who it was.'' Stefan swirled the liquor in his glass and then gazed across at Nikki from under his heavy brows. ''I was tired of looking,'' he slowly said. ''Masha had been nagging me for nearly two years,'' he added with a negligent shrug. ''And I only had a week in town.''

''Also, Vladimir has court influence sewed up.''

''Which overshadowed points one through three,'' Stefan sarcastically murmured.

Nikki wasn't unrealistic. Vladimir was powerful. "So Vladimir was the deciding factor."

"With *my* family background," Stefan concluded, images of their years of wandering in Europe and his father's painful decline vividly recalled. "Or was," he added, all his carefully considered plans for a conventional engagement, marriage and family in jeopardy. Nikki would be adamant about marriage, he knew, if Lise was pregnant, and even he was beginning to question the merits of an arrangement he'd deemed extraordinarily suitable only months ago. All because of a beautiful Countess he'd just been brutish to because he was jealous of every man who looked her way. "*Merde* and bloody hell," he swore, realizing he was indeed jealous, "now what?"

"Exactly why I'm here," Nikki cheerfully replied to the gloomy man sunk into the brown leather chair. "First ask her to marry you."

He was offered a slow and searching look. "And what of Nadejda?"

"Engagements are made to be broken." A bland smile accompanied the platitude.

"At the risk of upsetting your plans," Stefan neutrally said, "I should point out the contracts are rather lengthy and signed."

"You can afford to buy her off. You own half of Georgia. And remember to be persuasive when you propose. Lise is curiously independent."

"I'm supposed to beg her to marry me?" For someone who'd only considered marriage a final necessity, the prospect was dumbfounding. "Maybe we should rethink this. She's probably not pregnant. She probably doesn't want to marry me if she is."

This reasoning received a scowl from Nikki, who viewed family honor as quite apart from other of his casually held beliefs regarding male-female relationships.

"She will?" Stefan said, responding to Nikki's scowl. "You don't know if she will," he went on, answering his own question.

"If she's pregnant," Nikki very quietly said, "you're marrying her."

"And if I don't?" Stefan as softly inquired, thin-skinned and touchy when given ultimatums.

Nikki lifted his hands in a gesture of goodwill. "Let's not ruin a pleasant friendship. You care about her or you wouldn't be here causing a scandal at the Gagarins'."

"I *am*," Stefan wryly admitted, "a hell of a long way from Kars."

"Exactly," Nikki said.

"All right. I'll talk to her."

"Do you want to come back with me?"

"Now?" It was evasion pure and simple. Stefan had been a bachelor too long.

"Tomorrow morning," Nikki pointedly said, and rose to leave.

"Tomorrow morning," Stefan agreed, and reached for the brandy bottle.

Why was it, he reflected, the subdued heat of the brandy sliding down his throat, more daunting to contemplate marriage to Lise than to Nadejda? He answered his question without a flicker of delay. Because he *cared* about Lise, cared enormously if he faced the hard facts of his motivating influences in coming north. Unlike Nadejda, if they were to marry, he couldn't ignore her. He couldn't continue in his current style of independent living as he'd planned to do with Nadejda. Until this moment, he thought with a startled sense of discovery, he'd never realized need for a woman could be so confining.

On that morbid note, he refilled his glass, only to reflect on further restrictions should he marry Countess Lazaroff. She could be a demanding woman and insistent; she also had an imperious streak, due no doubt to her Kuzan blood, and she argued with him often and vehemently if she disagreed. He wasn't in the mood that evening to contemplate the more positive side of their relationship. He saw only in this marriage, so different from the kind he'd contemplated with Nadejda, the absolute end to his freedom. The thought prompted him to swallow the contents of his glass, necessitating another refill, a sequence that continued into the wee hours.

Stefan wasn't in the best humor the next morning, touched as he was with a slight headache, nor was the recipient of his call in any better spirits. Lisaveta had spent a sleepless night debating the appalling negatives in her attraction to Stefan. Both were uneasy, also, considering the circumstances of their last meeting.

Why had he come? she wondered when the footman came to fetch her from the library. Surely there was nothing to say after last night. Had she not thought she would appear cowardly to refuse his card, she would have.

He automatically rose to his feet when she entered the drawing room, but slowly, to favor his throbbing temples, and immediately apologized. "Forgive my actions last night at Gagarin's," he quietly said. "I was entirely at fault."

Since Lisaveta's sleepless night had to do with the humiliation of her unrestrained surrender to the irresistible Prince, she wasn't in an absolving mood. "Yes," she said with censure and disapprobation, "you certainly were...but then, you and shameless excess are synonymous."

Stefan opened his mouth to speak, about to remind her of the nail marks she'd left on the back of his neck, but decided against it and said instead, "I'm extremely sorry."

Lisaveta scrutinized him sharply, since his tone was much too contrite for the Prince Bariatinsky she knew. But perhaps he had manners after all, or perhaps a conscience. Regardless, this visit was over. "If you came to apologize, consider it done. Good day, Prince Bariatinsky."

"Wait."

Her hand was on the door latch. "Yes?" she said in stern inquiry, as a teacher might.

She was dressed in a morning gown of cucumber green, plainly cut, and she looked quite different from the seductive beauty of last evening. She looked...scholarly, he decided was the proper word. Even her chestnut hair was braided into a coronet, enhancing her puritanical image, and she wore only

Militza's pearls in her ears for jewelry. Why did he find her chaste and virtuous appearance so sensual? Was it because her unornamented frock was suppressing what he knew lay beneath? Or was it her cool and distant attitude he found challenging? He wished, he decided, to take down her braids and unbutton her high-necked gown; he wished to touch her soft warm flesh and bring her to life.

"You had something more to say?" she prompted as the silence lengthened, but there was demand in her tone rather than geniality.

Restored to his purpose, he said, "Yes...actually I do." He found himself at a loss momentarily on how exactly to begin. How precisely, he wondered, do you politely ask, Are you pregnant, and if so, is it mine, and if so, should we marry, and if I propose, will you accept, and do you really want this or find it as embarrassing and awkward as I? Not to mention the overriding fact he still had a fiancée, who might or might not be easily disposed of, Nikki's nonchalance notwithstanding.

He didn't contemplate asking questions about love, because in the current circumstances it was irrelevant. But the thought of love did enter his mind in a strange and elusive way, because he had faced last night the solid truth of his journey north and he hadn't been able to place the impetus on lust alone. As the brandy in the bottle declined he had had to admit that assuaging his lust could have been accomplished with infinitely less effort in Aleksandropol And he could have saved himself eight days of travel.

"Am I supposed to guess?" Lisaveta coolly asked into the new small silence, not in the right frame of mind to parry verbally with the man who'd entered her life with the abruptness of a meteor, made himself essential to her without even trying with the same casual charm he extended to all women, and then as abruptly took his leave—only to disastrously repeat his performance in an abbreviated version last night. She was bitterly resentful of his charm and her attraction to his careless seduction.

"I talked to Nikki last night," he said in way of gentle introduction.

"And?"

Apparently she wasn't going to make this easy. He took two steps forward so they wouldn't be conversing across so great a distance and, editing the bluntness of Nikki's statements of last evening, said, "He mentioned, or suggested…that is—he's aware we spent some time together before you arrived in Saint Petersburg."

He had gone home from the Yacht Club soon after sunrise and bathed and breakfasted. An early-morning ride had helped marginally to clear his head and he'd come directly to the Kuzan palace afterward, as some men ascend the scaffold briskly in order to speed the inevitable. His hair was still damp from the sea mist that lay over Saint Petersburg in the mornings.

Lisaveta knew he'd been out riding, dressed as he was. And she took issue with the even tenor of his life. Presumably a morning ride was routine in Saint Petersburg. Last night's events might have disrupted her life wretchedly, but his customary practices obviously remained unchanged. Her voice was mildly peevish when she said, "I didn't make a particular secret of my knowing you, although rest assured, Prince Bariatinsky, I didn't make an issue of it, either."

"Stefan," he prompted, and sighed. "Good God, Lise, stop standing there like some avenging angel. Look," he said, moving close enough to take her hand, "come sit down so we can talk."

She resisted for the briefest moment because the simple act of holding his hand was doing disastrous things to her heart rate. And what could they possibly have to discuss? she thought, after last night. She said exactly that the next moment, and his voice was solemn when he replied, "I'm abysmally sorry, *dushka*. I was jealous and that's the honest truth."

She looked up at him, surprised, and he was startled himself at his admission.

"So we should talk," he said, tugging at her hand, and this time, touched by his candor, she followed him. They sat on an Empire sofa, rose-colored like the carpet, with a careful distance between them, both cautious and circumspect, both plagued by a sleepless night…and touchy.

"Since there's no way to lead urbanely into this," Stefan said, feeling more like a young lad than the Commander of the Tsar's Cavalry, "I'll simply say—" he took a short extra breath for courage against the coolness of her eyes "—Nikki told me you're pregnant."

"It doesn't concern you."

He should have been ecstatic with her temperate reply; it had in fact been his own first reaction to Nikki's disclosure. Inexplicably, he wasn't. He was annoyed. "Of course it concerns me," he said, sounding pompously stuffy even to himself.

"Look, Stefan…" It was the first time she'd used his Christian name since she'd walked into that room, and it gave him pleasure, as if somehow he were succeeding against her cool reserve. "Nikki may not have told you…the—" Her hesitation over the word *pregnancy* charmed him. She was in many ways too sweetly naive for the brutality of the world, and a novel sense of protection overcame him. "The…situation," she went on, "may not develop into anything you need concern yourself with."

"*Are* you pregnant?" Suddenly he wanted to know rather than be left out with her equivocation.

"I don't know," she said, a blush pinking her pale cheeks.

"What do you mean," he inquired, his voice hushed, "you don't know? Have you or have you not missed your menses?" he asked bluntly.

The flush on her face deepened, but her voice when she spoke was firm. "I don't answer questions like that." She thought he looked tired, his dark eyes underscored with faint shadows and half-lidded, as if it were an effort to hold them open, and he was here this morning because he'd talked to Nikki last night. Because Nikki had talked to him. About her. And she resented the notion that Prince Bariatinsky was trying, under duress, to distinguish what his minimum responsibilities were.

"Actually," she said decisively, "I don't answer to you at all. As a matter of fact," she added, "I'm quite independent of you. As you no doubt prefer, since I don't recall any discussion of a future when we parted after our holiday at your lodge.''

''Hell, Lise, you're making this difficult.''

''On the contrary, I'll make it very easy. Shall we drop the subject?''

''Maybe I don't care to drop the subject.''

''And maybe I don't care whether you care or not.''

''Dammit, I'm just trying to get to the bottom of this.''

''And then what, Prince Bariatinsky, will you do?''

There was a short silence. ''Nikki says I have to marry you.''

Lisaveta's eyes took on the gelid glint of an arctic winter. ''Is this a marriage proposal?'' she inquired in a sherbet-sweet accent.

''Yes, dammit, it is,'' he growled, exasperated at her evasion, frustrated with her disinterest.

''Well, then, dammit, I refuse your gracious offer,'' she snapped.

''You can't refuse me,'' he snapped back, this man who only hours before had been appalled at the prospect of marriage.

''But I just *have* and that, I think, concludes our conversation. If you'll excuse me, Prince Bariatinsky. Your fiancée, perhaps, would be a more suitable recipient of your charming proposals.'' And she abruptly stood.

As abruptly his hand closed around her wrist and he dragged her back down. ''You'll leave when I tell you to leave.'' He hadn't traveled five swift and fatiguing days across the Empire to be dismissed like some servant.

''You forget, General, you're not dealing with a subaltern,'' Lisaveta wrathfully flared, struggling to free herself from his steely grasp. ''Your orders mean nothing to me.''

''Does this mean something, then?'' he asked, and pulled her roughly into his arms and kissed her, something he'd been wanting to do since she'd first entered the room.

She fought against his strength and his encroaching mouth and tongue, but she was effectively imprisoned in his arms despite her violent efforts. And unlike last night, when only consummation was a priority, Stefan lingered and teased, he tasted the sweetness of her lips as if she were new to him, as though young ladies wearing coronet braids were an untried flavor, as though he'd traveled five days and nights to exchange kisses like a proper gentleman.

She was surprised at first, after the initial shock of his aggression, because she'd expected his anger again and found instead a tenderness and restraint. He only kissed her, dulcetly, delicately, on her mouth, her cheek, her eyes, on the tip and slender fine bridge of her nose. And only when at last, at long last, she began kissing him back, did his mouth slowly drift downward over the silky curve of her jaw onto the warming flesh of her throat.

He carefully released her arms, which he'd been restraining at her sides in measured degrees until she leaned into him of her own accord, and he began breathing again in a normal rhythm.

"I shouldn't let you kiss me," she murmured above his bent head, her hands resting lightly on the solid muscle of his shoulders.

"But you are," he answered, his deep voice a husky low resonance against her throat, his slender dark fingers beginning to slide the small jet buttons at her collar free.

"You're too practiced...I should resist," she whispered, her eyes half-shut against the tremors of pleasure rushing through her senses.

"And you're not practiced at all," he whispered back, raising his head to look at her. "I find it arousing." He smiled then, a small faint smile of gratification. "Although resist if you like, Countess. I'd find that arousing, as well."

"I hate your licentiousness," she quietly said, her tawny eyes accusing in a curiously erotic way. Perhaps it was the feline quality of her slightly oriental eyes or the manner in which she surveyed him from beneath the lacy fringe of her lashes.

"I can tell," he said, brushing his palms over the tips of her hardened nipples visible through the cucumber-colored silk of her gown.

"And I hate your damnable assurance," she added hotly, but her voice was husky with a desire he recognized.

"I, however," he murmured, his hands moving upward to slip two more buttons free, "adore your temper." His fingers slid inside the eight inches of open neckline he'd freed and he slowly stroked the mounded fullness of her breasts. His hands were as warm as she remembered, and gentle and skilled. Lisaveta's eyes briefly shut and she moaned in warming bliss as luxurious sensation flooded through her body.

But a moment later she sharply said, "No," steeling herself against the pleasure he so easily roused, refusing to willingly surrender again, wishing to save herself from the humiliation she'd experienced last night. Her eyes were focused once again and aggressive, her hand coming out to rest on his wrist. "Don't touch me."

His wrist, muscular and strong-boned, dwarfed her small hand. "I want to," he replied, no aggression in his voice, only patience and courtesy.

"You must allow me my prerogatives," she said quietly, and waited.

His wrist moved under her hand and drawing back, he shook her hand free. "Your obedient servant, *mademoiselle*," he said in a parody of good manners, but his voice was tinged with surliness, like a restive boy called to order.

"You're sulking," she declared, her tone suddenly teasing, because he was moody and scowling, his large frame sprawled against the pink feminine sofa like some great dark thundercloud.

"I don't sulk," he said with unmistakable sulkiness.

"You can't always have your own way," she said, thinking how very beautiful he was even when he was scowling.

"But I always have," he replied with neither apology nor ostentation. He smiled then, because she was studying him as though he were an archaeological oddity. "I recommend it."

"What happens when you don't have your way?"

He shrugged rather than answer her, for he wished to avoid further argument. "Why so polemical, *dushka*," he said instead. "There are pleasanter ways to pass the time."

"Making love, you mean."

"Precisely."

"And if I don't wish to?"

"Come, darling," he murmured, "you always wish to."

"I don't right now."

He surveyed her for a moment as she had so recently him, and then said mildly, "If you take your dress off, I'll marry you." His remark was facetious and blasé and remarkably genuine.

"According to Nikki," she reminded him, "you'll marry me whether I take my dress off or not."

"Hmm," he said.

"Yes, exactly." Her smugness was genial, not malicious.

Another short silence and then he said, "How emphatic are you about your prerogatives?" He was smiling now with a buoyant cheer that made him even more appealing, and she was suddenly jealous of all the women who'd seen that particular smile. It was an intimate smile of exceptional grace and charm, like a promise of personal fulfillment.

"About as emphatic as you are about yours."

"Hmm," he said again. Her honesty was always demonstrably plain.

"Is this difficult, this style of courtship in which a woman doesn't fall immediately panting into your arms?" Her golden eyes were amused.

"'Difficult' wouldn't be my choice of word. I'd say time-consuming," he drawled, his grin boyish. "But then I've still a day and a half before I have to go back."

Fleeting surprise showed on her face. "Back?"

"To Kars, of course. You didn't think the war was over?"

"Are you going to win?" she asked in an intemperate rush of words, fearful suddenly she might lose him after all, not to Nadejda or a multitude of other women but to something far worse. It altered her perspective instantaneously and made his presence in Saint Petersburg treasured.

"Of course," he replied with his usual expansive confidence. "I always do."

"The undefeated Prince Bariatinsky," she said softly. He was heralded not only as the youngest commander in the Tsar's army but as the only undefeated general in Russian history.

"At your service, *mademoiselle*..." Out of uniform he looked vulnerable suddenly, not a symbol of the Tsar's Empire or the strength of Russia's army but simply a man, who was smiling at her and teasing her. A man who'd come a great distance and quite plainly wanted her. A man she loved beyond reason or sanity. "You will be careful, won't you?" Lisaveta said gravely, her mood transformed by a stabbing reassertion of fear.

"Darling," Stefan said, his smile intact, untouched by her anxiety, "you survive by *not* being careful. Don't worry about me."

She attempted an answering smile of reassurance but a tiny shiver ran down her spine as if some unseen specter had tapped her on the shoulder.

"Are you finished now?" he asked. She looked at him blankly.

"Talking," he said. "I've only a day and a half." His grin struck away her last vestiges of apprehension.

"Some men subscribe to a touch more gallantry," she mockingly chastised.

"They probably have more time than I," he retorted, unchastised and smiling still.

"Is that my cue to fall willing into your arms?" A coy and teasing response.

"I'd like that." And while his dark eyes were amused, his voice was suddenly serious. "You own my heart, *dushka*," he added very softly, acknowledging at last the feelings he'd fought so long, the feelings that had taken him from Kars. "And I'm helplessly in love."

Tears welled in her eyes and she swallowed once before answering. "Oh, Stepka," Lisaveta whispered, reaching out to touch his hand, "what are we going to do?"

"I'm marrying you," he said simply, as though he'd understood that eventuality always and not only in the last few revealing moments, and then he sighed a little because he could already feel the burden of the past engulf him. All the bitter memories came rushing back, all the whispers ignored and uncertainties felt, the malice and hurt surrounding his parents' grand passion recalled as if it were yesterday. And now he was doing what he'd sworn never to do; he was letting love for a woman compromise his future plans.

Consciously shaking away his reservations, he drew Lisaveta into the curve of his arms, the feel of her warmth next to him mitigating the jarring foreboding. "And you're marrying me," he whispered, her soft braids like silk under his chin. "Do you like the sound of that as much as I?"

"We shouldn't," she murmured, distraught. "I shouldn't. It's asking too much of you." She understood he was relinquishing all his carefully wrought plans, the ones so painstakingly arranged to overcome the shadow of his father's disgrace, the ones he'd considered a logical solution to the pain of his own unorthodox childhood. He was risking, too, his own illustrious career if Prince Taneiev were vengeful. Men had fallen from favor with the Tsar for smaller infractions. And since Alexander was insulated from the world, his information often censored and altered in the political cauldron of court intrigue, there was never any certainty one's case would be presented objectively.

"Nonsense," Stefan said, "everything can be resolved." A striking statement from a man who'd vowed never to love a woman so madly that it affected his life or career.

"You don't have to marry me," Lisaveta quietly declared.

"But I wish to, *dushka*, and besides," he said, drawing away so he could look at her, a faint grin lifting the corners of his mouth, "Nikki will kill me if I don't."

"Vladimir Taneiev might kill you if you do." No levity infused her remark.

"True. However," Stefan briskly went on, "I understand his greed outstrips his ethics. I'll offer him large sums of money."

"Could I help?" she said then. "I could at least do that."

He looked at her in mild astonishment because he'd never had a woman offer to pay his way. "You *were* raised differently," he said in murmured wonder, "but thank you, no. I've plenty." An understatement from the heir to two family fortunes that individually could have run the Empire for a decade. "And now that I've offered you my name, my wealth, my future, do you think you could say yes out of consideration for my feelings?" The laughter in his eyes reminded her of a young boy intent on play.

"Oh, yes," she said then, young-girl breathless with suffocating happiness. "Yes, yes, yes, yes, yes..." she whispered, feeling a joy so profound she trembled. She loved him beyond the normal scope of emotion, she loved him with an incoherent, jubilant elation that stacked pleasure upon pleasure to the rooftop of the world.

She had made her objection, offered him a chance to reconsider his proposal out of decency and a kindly courtesy. He didn't have to marry her because Nikki was insisting or because of the possibility she carried his child. She knew, too, how much his previous plans for marriage were based on the sadnesses in his past.

But when she'd made those required objections and he'd refused them all in his teasing, smiling way, she'd allowed the full measure of her happiness to invade her heart, so she felt now a rosy warm magic, as though she could touch the whole world and make it smile with her. She couldn't have accepted him had he been coerced or reluctant. She was too prideful herself to take a husband who didn't love her immensely. And he did, it was plain. Beyond his teasing and irony, it was clear he loved her so much he'd come across Russia for her and would marry her even in Vladimir Taneiev's shadow.

"I'll make you happy, Stepka," she whispered, her face alight with love, "always."

And he knew with that certainty reserved for those rare and perfect unions, she would. He'd searched for her, blasé and unknowing, too long to doubt it.

He knew it with that blinding flash of mystic revelation.

With a Zoroastrian belief like burning flame.

With a shaman magic—he knew it.

He smiled, thinking of an additional intuitive reason more: she said "Stepka" with the exact inflection that his father had, and in all the world he'd found someone to love again. Or perhaps she had found him, he thought, considering how they'd met.

"And I'll try, little mother," he murmured, "to make you *both* happy."

Her eyes showed a small startled reflex and she said very softly, "It's a very new thought...."

"The way it works, darling," he said, his smile so close she could feel its warmth, "you'll have time to get used to the idea."

He kissed her then, and she him, with a giddy smiling kiss that tasted of love and delight and wonder. They had both found the illusive prize of life, the spilled-over love chalice of everyone's quest, the insupportable marvel of requited, deep and perfect love...and it seeped like blissful sunshine into every corner of their mind.

Their kiss in the normal sequence of events turned in time from sunshine into licking flame, and it was then Stefan gathered Lisaveta into his arms with effortless strength, rose from the sofa with a fluid grace and began walking toward the doors leading into the hallway. As if already mated in mind and spirit, he said, "I'm taking you to my palace," before she could ask her intended question.

Fourteen

But Nikki was waiting in the corridor, seated on a bargello-upholstered Venetian chair directly facing the drawing room doors.

"Chaperoning, are you?" Stefan mildly inquired, his tone benign, holding Lisaveta in his arms as though he always casually held her while conversing.

"I thought I'd read for a time," Nikki pleasantly replied, his book unopened beside him on the console table.

"And that was the only chair in this block-long palace?"

"The only convenient one," Nikki answered with a grin. "I see all is reconciled." He could see Lisaveta was happy—it was apparent in her beaming face—and Stefan had the look of a triumphant man.

"And if it hadn't been?" Stefan said in a quiet voice.

"I brought my revolver. One never knows when one might need it—reading." He had not, of course, but a measure of coercion existed beneath his amused words.

"Before you two do something adolescent and ruin all this unalloyed bliss," Lisaveta interjected with a smile, "may I point out that all this masculine pride is rather irrelevant since Stefan proposed and I accepted."

"Congratulations." Benevolence and cordiality infused the single word, for beyond the fact that Lisaveta's future was secure, Nikki was genuinely fond of them both. "Should I talk to my priest?" he inquired, rising from his chair.

"So subtle, *mon ami*," Stefan replied with a grin, "but I'll speak to mine instead." And in afterthought for a man used to command, he looked down at Lisaveta. "If that's all right with you, darling," he added with deference.

Lisaveta was currently feeling an over-the-moon happiness and was capable of complacently viewing the yawning jaws of hell with equanimity. "Whatever you think," she said, her voice compliant.

Stefan's eyes widened in mock surprise. "No argument, no contention, no combative response? Had I realized," he went on with teasing brightness, "how simple it was to curtail your temper, I'd have proposed long ago."

"There, you see, the feminine mystique transparent at last," Lisaveta facetiously replied. "I'll teach you everything I know," she promised in a whispered aside.

Her remark immediately refocused Stefan's attention on his original mission. "I'd really like to stay and chat," he said to Nikki, who was beaming visibly at the success of his cousinly pressure, "but I've only a day and half before I have to leave."

"I'll call at your home later, then," Nikki said, "to hear your plans. Do you want me to inform anyone?"

Stefan's answer was staccato swift. "Not just yet," he said, his glance over Lisaveta's head significant with meaning. He had first to face Nadejda and her family. "I'll get back to you."

"Say goodbye," Lisaveta murmured into the sweep of black hair near Stefan's ear, and he promptly did, as anxious as she to be alone, the problem of Nadejda's family instantly discarded in lieu of more gratifying thoughts.

"Have a pleasant day," Nikki volunteered, his doting grin that of an extremely pleased man.

"Thank you," Stefan replied, his face creasing into a broad smile as his eyes met with Lisaveta's. "We will."

The weeks of their separation past, their ruinous jealousy resolved, neither chose to dwell on the unreliable future; they were feeling only intemperate joy. And when Stefan had Lisaveta at last where he'd so often fantasized of late, in his home and bed, softly warm beneath him, he told her how much he loved her with a rare and garlanded poetry she found captivating. She answered him with her own simple words, words she'd contemplated in the long days of their absence and the bitter nights of their separation, words she'd once considered forever denied her. "I love you," she said, "with all my heart."

"I'll never let you go," he quietly replied, the nature of his love less benevolent. It matched the strength he'd fashioned into his destiny, it matched the fear he'd lived with when he thought her indifferent. It spoke, too, of his confidence. The Commander of the Tsar's Cavalry had never suffered defeat. She was his. He was content, and more, he was whole again.

If he'd been asked he wouldn't have been able to answer why he'd abandoned his long-held beliefs so readily. He'd fought against loving her, against acknowledging he cared; he'd told himself his feelings were some aberrant temporary fascination. But he'd discovered his emotions wouldn't so obediently comply to his rationalization or yield to any objectivity.

"I have estimated the influence of Reason upon Love and found that it is like that of a raindrop upon the ocean," Hafiz had written.

And Stefan's own heart understood at last.

They played with teasing silliness that afternoon in his bed made of chased gold. It was large enough—having been cast originally for his Orbeliani great-great-grandfather, who had kept a harem of eight hundred concubines—for facetious games of pursuit. It was soft enough to engulf one in gossamer down and ostentatious enough, Lisaveta bantered, to support Stefan's reputation for exhibitionist play. Rumor had it he'd entertained multiple women in his splendid bed. He didn't deny or confirm the rumor; he only said, "You're my only love…you're my world."

He was gentle when he entered her sweet and heated body after the teasing play and romp; he was so gentle he scarcely breathed for fear of hurting her if she carried his child; he was so gentle she felt as though his body drifted over her, weightless. And the sensations built for both of them with an intensity so extravagant and extreme they were inebriated with combustible vaulting passion. He lay above her afterward and shuddered, eyes shut and breath held; Lisaveta trembled in sweat-sheened excess, every nerve ending wantonly exposed.

Their afternoon was heated and self-indulgent; it was the stuff dreams were made of, it was the enchantment troubadours embroidered in song.

And so unlike, Stefan said with a smile, his previous notions of prenuptial events.

Meanwhile, on the Palace Square where the Taneievs' princely abode faced the vista of Peter the Great's equestrian statue and the gilded domes of the Admiralty, Nadejda was saying, narrow-eyed and livid with anger, "He cannot be allowed to humiliate me here in Saint Petersburg. Don't make any excuses for him, Mama." She swung around in her pacing before the windows to face her mother, the bustle of her pink taffeta gown quivering at her sudden halt. "I won't have it! In Tiflis it didn't matter. Good God, that backwater scarcely has sufficient nobility to play two rubbers of bridge—but here!" Her face was contorted with indignation, her blond curls trembling, her jeweled fingers clenched into unladylike fists. "I will *not* be the laughingstock for his scandalous behavior!"

Her mother, seated calmly behind the tea service, opened her mouth to speak.

"And don't you dare mention his fortune," Nadejda irately exclaimed. "I don't care about his fortune!" One could see how violent were her feelings, for Nadejda had spent the better part of her engagement composing shopping lists against the time she would be Princess Bariatinsky.

While Irina wished her daughter satisfaction or perhaps revenge, she wished her a wealthy husband more...and a little better grasp on her temper. She was a practical woman who was also actively involved in her husband's financial speculations. "I was going to say," she patiently said, "your *father* is interested in his fortune. And also in Bariatinsky's considerable influence in the progress of the war. Papa is directly engaged, as you know, in the cannon contracts."

Irina couldn't go into any detail about those contracts because Nadejda wasn't completely capable of understanding their complexity, the several levels of corruption that had to be coordinated, nor would she have been trustworthy in keeping silent, had she known.

Vladimir Taneiev and Melikoff, along with several officials from the highest levels of government, were involved in the awarding of cannon contracts. Stefan's name as a future son-in-law added credibility to their consortium, as did General Bariatinsky's reputation for honesty.

In addition to the usual bribes required to secure contracts, Vladimir had a personal ancillary scheme to extort further sums of money from the manufacturers. He was soliciting sizable donations for General Bariatinsky's cavalry, as well. Stefan was known for spending his personal funds in outfitting his regiments and no one begrudged the extra sums requested. So Vladimir's very lucrative scheme required General Bariatinsky's presence in his family, at least until the war was over.

"I also don't care about *cannons*," Nadejda petulantly retorted, shredding a potted fern frond between her fingers.

Her mother winced inwardly at her daughter's heresy and at the litter falling on the carpet. The plant stand would have to be turned to hide the mutilation, so she rang for a servant with an unobtrusive tug on the bellpull near her chair. Irina was a compulsively neat person who viewed life with an eye to advantage rather than subscribing to what she considered the fiction of emotion. Emotion was all very well and good for poetry or opera perhaps, but it interfered with sensible plans and practical goals. Nadejda was still very young so she couldn't be expected to understand the realities, and Irina's restraint was gentle. "You *must*, my dear, at least until the war is over."

Nadejda ripped one entire frond from the plant and tossed it to the floor. "Are you telling me," she said, bridling, "I must suffer his indignities?"

"Papa will explain to you, darling." She hoped the servant would come soon.

"I won't marry him unless he is brought to heel. I mean it, Mama! Find me some other rich man to marry." Nadejda's debutante season had been gratifying—ten proposals of marriage and a deluge of suitors. Her pale beauty was all the rage, a superficial although substantial consideration for Stefan along with her other suitors. He'd always favored blond females.

"Certainly, dear, but you must wait until after the war. Now come sit down and calm yourself—Papa will be home directly. I sent Peotr out to fetch him, and when he explains the need to endure Bariatinsky's scandalous behavior for a limited time yet, you'll do your part, I'm sure. And then after we talk to Papa, why don't we go shopping?" Irina's voice was soothing, the tone one would use with a child throwing a tantrum. "Brabant's has a new jeweler who's a magician. Wouldn't you like a necklace like Sophie's with strawberry blossoms, or perhaps some earrings for your new tangerine gown?"

Predictably, the lure of jewels was effective. Nadejda cast a thoughtful glance at her mother, who was patting the sofa cushion beside her, and after a small theatrical sigh crossed the Aubusson carpet.

"What do I get out of this, Mama, besides some new jewelry, since I must put on a good face in the storm of gossip you know will be horrendous?" She obediently seated herself beside her mother, but her expression was stormy.

"Let Papa tell you," her mother said, handing Nadejda a cup of tea with a composed smile. "I believe there's also a rather large sum of money involved should your engagement be broken...."

Her daughter smiled for the first time that day. "How large?"

"I'm not exactly certain."

"Enough for a new sable cape?"

It was her mother's turn to smile. How naive one was at eighteen. "For several dozen I'd say," she replied. "The particulars in the marriage contract are quite specific."

They were more so than he recalled, Stefan discovered late that afternoon when he presented himself at the Taneiev palace; Vladimir had written in addenda to every exigency—all very expensive. And he only had himself to blame, for against his legal counsel he'd waved away every warning for protection.

At the time of his betrothal, intent on the practical issue of marriage, Stefan had been unconcerned with defenses against a change of mind. His purpose, after having finally selected a bride, was to *marry* her…not renege.

Now today, although he hadn't anticipated ready compliance to his request for a dissolution of the engagement, he was appalled at the Byzantine complexities in the contract.

Vladimir's obduracy he'd expected.

And the unsubtle threats.

All of which he'd felt could be suitably managed with offers of money.

But his proposals to negotiate a settlement seemed to fall on deaf ears, and after the tenth refusal, he said in exasperation, "Why don't you tell me what it will take, Vladimir?" He was past diplomacy and restrained courtesy, he was beyond concerns for his poignant past or his uncertain future. He only wanted it finished and concluded at any cost. He was an extremely wealthy man. He wanted it over.

He wanted to marry Lisaveta because she had stolen his heart and he loved her.

Without her, the rose was not fair nor merry the Spring, he thought with rueful regard for the significance of Hafiz's words. At last he had come to understand his heart was in her hands.

And…he wanted his child to have his name. There was no time for a wedding later, not when he was returning to Kars…not when he didn't know—if he'd be coming back.

"What it will take is your honoring your engagement to my daughter," Vladimir flatly declared.

"You'll force me to go to the Tsar," Stefan countered, "if you persist in your obstinacy." Since he'd already tried money, the Tsar was his last threat, and he was not as confident as he sounded. While the Tsar *was* a close personal friend, his father had thought the same thing once. But Stefan knew he wasn't bluffing. He was in truth willing to put his career on the line for Lisaveta, something that even a month ago he would have found unthinkable.

Having had several hours previously to contemplate countermoves to Stefan's expected responses, Vladimir said blandly, his smooth and scented hands steepled near his chin, "If you go to the Tsar, I'll implicate you in the Sesta fodder scandal."

Half a division had been wiped out at Sesta when reinforcements had been unable to come to their aid because of foundering mounts. Five thousand cavalry horses had died from tainted feed that week and the Tsar had vowed to hang the perpetrators regardless of their rank or position. Alexander had taken a personal interest in the case, and three investigating teams had been sent out from Saint Petersburg to unearth the culprits."

"I have reports," Vladimir added, "I can release to the Tsar. Your name could very easily be inserted."

"He won't believe you."

"When I show him the correspondence in your hand, he'll be convinced, I assure you, my dear boy. And I have witnesses. Your disgrace would be complete." Witnesses could be bought, Stefan knew, and documents altered, and Vladimir had the advantage of the Tsar's fervent interest in determining culpability. The newspapers had been following the scandal for weeks; families of the dead soldiers were crying for revenge; the Tsar himself was offering a personal reward for information. It was a cause célèbre without a scapegoat, and Stefan suddenly felt all the nameless fears from the past suffocating him. Disgrace. The word he'd been fighting a lifetime to overcome. Disgrace. He took a steadying breath, grappling with the ungovernable flood of memories. The humiliation of hearing the whispers when one entered a room, and the never-forgotten sidelong glances, assessing and curious. The occasional rudeness and disparagement. The people who always compared him to his father first and seemed surprised when he wasn't an exact duplicate. He'd learned very young to hide any evidence of his feelings, learned to give nothing away in his demeanor or speech or temper.

He felt again at that moment as though those awful years of his father's disgrace were hurtling back, as though all his hard-won triumphs and successes had never occurred or were inconsequential against Vladimir's threat. He felt as if all the doors to the future were closing before him, all means of escape were disappearing from sight.

Vladimir had survived enough years in the bloody battlefield of court intrigue to recognize an expression of discomfiture. His voice was silky with malice when he spoke. "I *thought* you might reconsider, Prince Bariatinsky."

Stefan hesitated, feeling trapped, a rare, almost unprecedented sensation for a man who'd won all his battles because he'd never considered defeat. But the scars were deep when contemplating a repetition of his father's fall from grace. "I'll have to think about what you've said," Stefan carefully replied, wanting an opportunity to regroup and assess his options.

"When are you planning on returning to Kars?"

"Tomorrow."

"In that case you have till noon tomorrow to reach a decision. I'm sure you'll see the practicality of honoring your engagement to my daughter. Once the war is over, well, then—" Vladimir opened his palms expansively "—Nadejda can have her pick of eligible officers."

Stefan controlled his shock. Why hadn't Vladimir mentioned the time element before? Why not indeed? Stefan thought, surveying the corpulent figure opposite him. Because Vladimir preferred flaying a man alive if possible; he had a reputation for taking pleasure in torturing his victims, and had he mentioned the engagement could be regarded as temporary when their conversation began, he would have been deprived of Stefan's torment.

"The engagement could be broken once the war is over," Stefan mildly inquired, "but not now? Why?" Some pertinent reason existed, but in the few hours remaining to him before his return to Kars, there wasn't sufficient time to uncover the truth. One certainty was blatantly obvious, though. Money wasn't going to buy his way out.

"My concern is for my sweet Nadejda, of course," Vladimir replied, blandly. "In the midst of war, there's such a dearth of eligible parties," he said, his smile one of exaggerated sincerity. "She would repine."

"You surprise me, Taneiev," Stefan drawled softly. "I didn't suspect you harbored feelings."

Vladimir looked pained for a theatrical pause. "Nadejda's my dearest treasure," he said with exactitude.

"I'm sure she is," Stefan sardonically replied as he rose to leave, aware now of the enormous settlements exacted in the marriage contracts.

"One thing more, my dear boy, before you go. I'd like you to apologize to Nadejda for the insult you did her at the Gagarins' last evening. She was in attendance at the ball." He spoke with great casualness as though he were asking for the merest favor.

Stefan stood in shocked arrest for a brief moment. Apologize? To the daughter of the man who was threatening him with annihilation? "And if I decline?" he said after a small silence.

"I'd strongly consider," Vladimir said, his gaze devoid of emotion, "dropping a first small hint to the Tsar—a mention that his cavalry commander's name came up during the interrogation of a suspect in the Sesta case this afternoon. An initial slight wedge, as it were." His smile was chill. "I could convey this new detail at a diplomatic soiree tonight where Alexander is scheduled to appear. The rumor could turn out to be a mistake by noon tomorrow should you decide to continue your engagement to my daughter." He looked at Stefan across the expanse of his polished desktop. "Will you," he gently inquired, the way the axman at a beheading might question whether one cared to be blindfolded or not, "be seeing our illustrious Emperor before you return?"

Stefan's flying trip to Saint Petersburg had been purely personal and he'd intended only a brief courtesy call on the Tsar. "I haven't decided," he ambiguously replied, disinclined to supply Vladimir with any information.

"Well," Vladimir briskly said, confident in his victory, "you decide, my boy, although with all your, er, experience with women, surely a simple apology shouldn't be too demanding." When he raised his eyes from contemplation of his manicured nails, his glance was indifferent.

He had little concern for the Tsar or the course of the war, it seemed, if he could so casually contemplate imparting such malevolent lies. Nor did he seem to have any regard for his daughter's sensibilities, either. For she, too, would be touched, however innocently, by Stefan's disgrace. Prince Taneiev's motives were purely selfish, Stefan realized, observing the cool disinterest in Vladimir's eyes. He could consider distressing the Tsar without a qualm.

Checked, Stefan had no recourse, as Vladimir already knew. But his reply came with great difficulty. "Very well," Stefan said.

Vladimir almost looked disappointed, as though the lesser of his humiliations had been chosen, Stefan thought, as though he would have preferred humbling Stefan before the Tsar. A dispassionate impulse surfaced in Stefan's mind, drifting into his consciousness with the placidity of ripples on a pond. How satisfying it would be to put a bullet through Vladimir's chill smile. The cream silk draperies behind his desk would be ruined, Stefan decided with a curious detachment, and on that pleasant thought a small smile curved his mouth upward.

"You find something amusing, Prince Bariatinsky?" Vladimir's voice was smooth as silk.

"Perhaps later I may," Stefan replied.

"Perhaps later we may all find this association amusing."

"I certainly hope so." Stefan glanced at the wall clock. "Now if you'll excuse me. My time is limited."

"Nadejda is expecting you. You'll bring me your decision by noon tomorrow?"

"I'll send a message."

Prince Taneiev didn't reply, but he nodded and the interview was over.

As Stefan followed the footman down the corridor, he debated whether he could call Vladimir's bluff. Should he simply turn around and leave? He could feel the heat of his anger rising, for the thought of the coming act of submission was unnerving and unpalatable.

But he needed time. Time to figure out what to do; time to somehow escape this trap that was closing around him. And for the first time he realized that anything that affected him now would affect Lise, also. His gorge rose at the thought of Taneiev with his talons into Lisaveta. If a few words of pretense to Nadejda would gain him one evening of reprieve, he decided his pride could stand it. Perhaps by tomorrow he would have worked out what to do, although his brain seemed strangely reluctant now.

But it would be the briefest apology in the history of man.

Nadejda was alone in the Grecian drawing room when the servant showed Stefan in. If looks could have killed, her father could have begun counting his settlement money immediately.

She was standing as though she were expecting him, and he decided Vladimir was unquestionably confident. He waited for the servant to close the door before he spoke, and without moving from the vicinity of the entrance, he said, "I've come to apologize. I didn't realize you were at Gagarin's last night." There. It wasn't precisely an apology but a general statement. He took brief pleasure in his evasion.

"Obviously." Her single word was sharp as a knife thrust, her lavender eyes so devoid of warmth his hair rose briefly on the back of his neck. Dressed in a white lace tea gown adorned with red silk roses, she reminded him of blood on a corpse and gave every indication of the same uncompromising coldness. "And in future, I'm sure my father warned you, I will not tolerate such behavior!"

His spine went rigid.

"Nor will I allow that native dress in my presence," she disdainfully added.

Stefan wore the loose trousers and belted shirt of his mother's people, his favored form of dress out of uniform, and far from being the shabby attire Nadejda's tone implied, his garments were luxurious. His black silk blouse was China silk embroidered in gold thread, and his trousers were of wool so fine each yard could be pulled through a woman's ring. The goats that supplied the raw material for the fabric were only found in one small section of the Himalayas and were so fragile they couldn't be sheared; the hair from their coats had to be gathered from the odd residue left on the brambles and bushes of their habitat. And his red kid boots were dyed with precious scarlet madder by his bootmaker in Tabriz.

He could feel the blood begin to throb in his temple; he'd never been spoken to in that tone of voice. He controlled the Tsar's cavalry; he was the wealthiest man in the Trans-Caucasus, perhaps in Russia. "I dress as I please," he said in a low growl. He didn't want to say more; he wished to leave before his temper gave way, and there was no need to speak further with Nadejda.

He'd observed the obligation Vladimir required and he was turning to leave when Nadejda said, "I'm not finished with you yet."

Her father had assured her that afternoon when he'd come home that he would find a means to restrain any further embarrassing incidents by Prince Bariatinsky. He had further assured her that while she must suffer the fiction of their engagement in public, in private she need not. In a vastly simplistic and highly edited fashion he'd explained that Prince Bariatinsky was valuable to their family until the war was over, although, he'd added, he couldn't go into any of the particulars due to the secrecy required in wartime. The visit to Brabant's had further reconciled her to her required role. She was wearing a new and very expensive ruby necklace.

"I expect you to conduct yourself," she said, advancing toward him with revenge in her heart for the scene at the Gagarins', "without any further scandal. Should I hear even the merest breath of misconduct, Papa will have your bars and your command. And I will personally take great pleasure in your disgrace."

Nadejda had been too long assured the world was hers. She had no sense of proportion.

Stefan's uncommon prudence disappeared in an explosive rage. He couldn't go through with this farce if they hanged him tomorrow for high treason. Vladimir be damned! He'd stand up to his threats the way he should have from the beginning. His fleeting display of caution gave way to Stefan's more familiar headstrong boldness. "Consider this engagement over," he tersely said, each word a blunt hammer blow, "as of this moment." And he drew a deep breath to steady a killing instinct.

"You can't," Nadejda raged, her pale skin mottled, her lavender eyes narrowed with spleen.

"I can do anything I please, *mademoiselle*." Stefan was absolutely still, his hands rigid at his sides in an effort to curtail his rash impulse to strike out. "And it pleases me," he softly added, "to terminate this very large mistake."

"Papa will not allow it!" Each of Nadejda's words rang with authority.

Stefan had heard that already in a variety of nuances, but she seemed so very sure he asked, "Why?" in a quiet, menacing voice. She had spoken as though she knew Taneiev's reasons; perhaps she might offer a better reason than the one her father had given.

Nadejda knew immediately she'd misstepped when Stefan's brows came together and his voice softened in query, when his dark eyes seemed to be scrutinizing her with a new attention. "He...Papa wouldn't want me to be embarrassed. Once the war is over, *I'll* break the engagement."

"Yours and your Papa's timetable is intriguing." Stefan's drawl was low and silken, his mind racing, contemplating the circumstances contributing to this obstinate delay.

"There are no men now," she said, the way a child would say, "The candy store is closed."

That remark at least had the ring of sincerity. Stefan wished he had the time to get to the bottom of this matter, but he didn't.

At least he'd had the courage to end this damnable engagement. He felt a great sense of relief, a tidal wave of deliverance.

"You might like to congratulate me," he said with a grin, thinking how simple it had been after all to cut away the impediment of his engagement. "I'm to be married tonight." He was suddenly well-disposed to the world at large, including Nadejda, who was no more than a silly young woman now—detached from his life with a few simple words.

"Papa will kill you," she said in a neutral voice contrasting starkly with her statement, "if you shame our family so."

"He can try," Stefan quietly replied, "but he may not succeed. And you might want to give him that warning." Stefan's eyes narrowed slightly although his smile was still in place. "My bodyguard," he added, his tone soft as velvet, "reverts at time to some of their barbaric Kurdish customs. Tell your father it takes a man eight hours to die—forgive me, *mademoiselle*, for my bluntness—with his entrails on the ground."

Nadejda's face was white as her dress when he left the room. Immune to the perils of his future, as though a decision of the spirit had been made distinct from rational deliberation, he thought only of his freedom, of his escape from Nadejda, and he wondered with a curious speculation whether his father's life would have been different if he'd fought against his disgrace. He had thought at first he could deal with Vladimir's demands, submit enough to buy the time he needed, say yes, when he didn't mean it, apologize to Nadejda for something he didn't feel. But his nature wouldn't allow it, and he was wildly exhilarated now, striding down the hallway, his sensations reminiscent of the excitement he felt in battle.

It was the same—when there was no longer time for apprehension or indecision or any of the debilitating hesitation that marked the cognitive man. The irrepressible energy carried you, drove you, brought victory as if by magic, and Stefan felt at that moment the same triumph. He had succeeded at last in putting the past to rest. What had happened to his father would no longer be his burden. In a way totally unplanned and tumultuous, he'd severed that impediment to his life. As he sailed down the bank of steps to the street in two leaping bounds, the driver glanced at his partner beside him on the carriage seat and said, "Things must have gone well."

"Even better than that from the looks of it."

"Home, Excellency?" the groom holding the door open for Stefan inquired as Stefan reached the blue-lacquered carriage.

"No, to the Winter Palace."

The liveried servant came to attention. "Very good, Excellency.'' His voice was crisp when he repeated the order to the driver.

The Prince was going to see the Tsar.

Fifteen

———◦◦———

The Tsar's equerry had only said, "I'll do what I can."

Stefan paced the small room, knowing he'd faced the entire
Turkish army with less trepidation than he was currently feeling. He'd stop to gaze out the windows on the vista of the
Neva for a moment, or try sitting on the numerous chairs lining
the walls of the chamber, only to find himself pacing again a
few moments later. Alexander could be unpredictable and with
good reason.

He was beset from all sides of the political spectrum and
had survived a dozen assassination attempts in the past three
years. Since he had freed the serfs by manifesto in February
of 1861, Alexander II's reforms had been slowly changing the
character of the Russian Empire. But to many, the wheels of
reform moved too slowly; to others, reform was anathema, and
malcontents of every political persuasion had sought to kill
him. Only last month a bomb had destroyed his dining room.
Had he not arrived late because of his son's illness, he would
have been killed. Alexander had become wary of who was
friend and who was not.

Stefan was relying on his years of devoted service to the
Empire and his friendship with the Tsar as support for his presentation, but he realized his position as cavalry commander
and his popularity were themselves suspect. Most of the palace
coups over the centuries had been initiated in the officer corps

by ambitious men trading on their celebrity and fame and on their control of the elite regiments of the army.

By the time the equerry returned and said, "The Emperor will see you now," Stefan was tense and agitated as well as increasingly gloomy about his prospects of success. Vladimir cultivated his political alliances on a daily basis while Stefan had not.

The Tsar's welcome was cordial, though. Seated at his desk, he gestured Stefan to an adjacent chair and smiled in greeting.

It was at least a friendly beginning. Stefan took a steadying breath as he seated himself. They exchanged social pleasantries first—Alexander asking about Militza and Stefan admiring the new photos of his young family on his desk. The Tsar's desktop was half-covered with framed photos, the ones closest to his work space those of his new children. Framed portraits of his father and mother were prominent on the wall above his desk; even his wife's portrait was in evidence, although it was set back in the second row behind those of his young mistress.

Over tea, brought in on a solid gold tea service, the state of the war was discussed in some detail. Alexander had recently returned from the environs of Pleva, where the Turks still held out, and he was visibly tormented by the thousands of soldiers who'd lost their lives to date. The question of the reinforcements of men and artillery in the Asian campaign was dealt with. Stefan described which divisions were up to strength and which were still waiting for the new troops; he related the progress of the telegraph lines being constructed and described his hopes for victory.

When eventually the reason for his sudden appearance in Saint Petersburg was broached, Stefan answered honestly. "Since the campaign is on hold and I'm totally obsessed with the Countess Lazaroff, I came north to see her."

"When did you arrive?"

"Yesterday."

"And you'll be returning?"

"Tomorrow."

The Tsar smiled. "I see."

Stefan felt the heat rising to his face and he smiled ruefully. "She's most remarkable."

"I agree," Alexander warmly said, "as does the entire male population of the soirees she's attended here in the capital. Did you find the competition formidable?"

"I didn't notice."

"She's amenable then to your interest."

"After," Stefan softly said, "some persuasion."

"She is certainly worth persuading," the Tsar cordially replied. "She's not only beautiful and charming but brilliant, as well. Do you find her education intimidating?" He leaned back in his chair and surveyed Stefan.

"I find everything about her intimidating," Stefan retorted, adding with a smile, "in a most refreshing way. And I'd like to thank you for her sponsorship into society."

"I was more than happy to comply with your request. She's very entertaining."

Stefan's glance went steely for a suspicious moment and they were no longer Tsar and Commander but only two men.

"I meant that in the most benign sense," Alexander II said mildly. He stroked his heavy sideburns for a second or two and then quietly declared, "I'm no longer young, and Catherine and my small family are my comfort."

"Forgive me," Stefan apologized. "As you can see," he said with a sigh, "I'm beyond sanity when it comes to the Countess." Taking a deep breath he plunged on. "Which point, in fact, brings me here today." He went on to describe his current problems with Vladimir and his rather sudden termination of his engagement.

Alexander was quiet throughout Stefan's recital, asking questions only twice, both having to do with the Sesta incident.

"Vladimir threatened to see you tonight," Stefan finished, "and suggest my involvement."

"We'll see that he's detained for a time at the chancellery," Alexander said.

Greatly encouraged by the Tsar's reaction to his story, Stefan dared to add, "But there's something about *him* that doesn't seem quite right. He and his daughter both made remarks along the lines of 'just until the end of the war.' I don't have the time to find out what he's involved in—if it's anything. You know I have to get back to Kars. But perhaps, sir…?'' He hesitated.

Alexander stroked his chin meditatively. "I've never liked Taneiev. Perhaps he should be looked into." He stared at the photo of his two young sons. "Trust is so difficult these days," he said, his voice sad and introspective. He'd become more isolated and suspicious over the past few years, distrustful of friends, appalled by the dissensions and intrigues among his chiefs of staff in the course of the war, aware of the venality of his bureaucracy. He was a man under siege.

"The war's unpopular in some quarters," Stefan said. "Perhaps when it's over things will get better." Stefan might be the Tsar's best field commander, but he had spent years fighting the timid protectionist policies of the general staff, the incompetence of the Grand Dukes who had power in the war councils. He knew indignant voices were often raised in Saint Petersburg against him, against the Tsar and the war.

"I won't give in to the reactionary forces," Alexander declared in his deep, weary voice. "This war must be won or all the lives lost in the Turkish atrocities will be in vain." Russia had been the only country willing to come to the aid of the Christian minority in Turkey.

"We're in a much better position now with reinforcements and supplies almost in place, and the Turks are having problems in Istanbul, too. Various factions are demanding a ceasefire. The war is costly to them, as well. Perhaps if Kars can be breached, it will accelerate their surrender. Bezna-Pasha took his Turkoman troops home last month and vowed not to return. All of the border tribes are restive because they haven't been paid by the Turks. No gold, no Circassians, is a proverb the truth of which can't be denied," Stefan said with a quick grin. His face sobered in the next instant. "The fall campaign could be decisive." Then he smiled again, because he felt on familiar, secure ground. "With the border tribes melting away, the Turks have no cavalry, no scouts, no way of knowing our plans. We can take them this time, Excellency."

"Thank you, Stefan," Alexander gently said, "for your encouraging news, and for all your victories in this war. Your father would have been proud of you." The Emperor still missed his old friend, the Field Marshal; they'd remained in touch until Alex Bariatinsky had died, vacationing together occasionally at Plombières, Ems or Baden-Baden.

"He was Russia's greatest Field Marshal," his son said. Stefan's father's conquests had never been matched before or since, and his sense of honor and duty had been passed on to his son.

"Some say you'll surpass him." The Tsar's smile was benevolent.

"Never, Excellency." Stefan's voice was softly emphatic and he looked away briefly to suppress the wetness welling in his eyes. Whatever soldiering he knew, he'd learned from his father; whatever capabilities he had as a commander, he'd inherited from him. All his skills and talent and aptitude he owed to the man who'd loved him most in the world and had taught him that the measure of one's worth was in one's deeds. And despite the passing years and the sorrow of his disgrace, his father had always been Stefan's only hero.

Alexander II had also had his share of sorrows and he'd always felt a sympathy for Stefan, for the way he'd overcome his father's humiliation and forged a life for himself conspicuous for its success. "I believe I shan't have time to speak with Vladimir tonight," the Tsar said. "My equerries will inform him of my wishes." He smiled then, his thin careworn features brightening. "He should have known better. If I trust anyone, it's you, Stefan. And my congratulations on your marriage plans."

Stefan's dark eyes lighted up first and then his mouth creased into an answering smile. "Thank you. It gives one incentive—" he grinned "—to end the war speedily."

"Excellent idea," the Tsar declared, his weariness less a burden now, his thoughts more buoyant. Stefan was always able to give him hope for victory. "I'll count on you to expedite the Turkish surrender." Reaching over he rang for his aide. "Now, then, we need a special license."

When Stefan left the Winter Palace a half hour later, he held the special license, signed and sealed, in his hand. Vladimir was checkmated, and he had a wedding to organize.

Lisaveta was sleeping when he returned, exhausted from the previous night as well as from their sensual play that afternoon, and Stefan tiptoed into his room in order not to disturb her.

Drawing up a chair, he sat beside the bed, content, happy, pleased and very much in love. He was going to marry her, he thought, with a bubbling jubilation unique to his jaded soul. He was going to marry the silk of her dark curls and the sweetness of her rosy cheeks; he was going to marry her small hand lying on the Venetian lace of the pillow cover and her lush pink mouth and all the multiple and varied wonders of her to the tips of her perfect toes.

He was besotted, he realized, when he reached out to stroke her hair spread out on the pillow, feeling a need to touch her. She delighted him and bewitched him, and very gently in order not to wake her, he stroked the texture of one curl.

Although lightly done, Lisaveta seemed to sense his movement, and her eyes opened. "I missed you," she murmured, her smile drowsy with sleep.

"You had better," he answered, his smile so benevolent the angels could have taken lessons.

Remembering suddenly where he'd gone and why, she sat upright in agitation, the bed linen falling away, her eyelet nightdress pulled askew, the curve of her shoulder bared. The apprehension she'd put aside in sleep came rushing back. "How are you?" she fearfully asked.

Gazing at her, flushed and beautiful, he thought with a stab of terror how close he'd come through pride and arrogance to losing her. Perhaps he could have abducted her again, but he would not have been able to make her stay, for she was too complex or independent or simply not willing to adapt to his wishes. Even if she had stayed he would never have felt completely secure. And he needed her, he realized, the way he needed air to live.

"How am I?" he repeated gently. With exultation and joy

he answered his own question in the utter silence of her apprehension. "I'm free," he said.

She didn't move. He'd expected her to laugh or smile at least, jump with excitement or throw herself into his arms, but she was fearful still, as was her tone of voice. "You can't be. They wouldn't make it that easy. Don't tease me, Stefan, or equivocate if it's not true. It can't be true."

"Have you no faith?" he teased, lounging back in his chair.

"Not in Vladimir Taneiev and his ice-cold daughter." In the course of her stay in Saint Petersburg, the Taneiev family had taken every opportunity to show their malevolence. She was well aware of the full extent of their viciousness.

"Does your faithlessness extend to the Tsar?"

She smiled then, tentatively. "He supports you?"

Stefan drew the special license from his pocket, lifted it so the bold printing was visible and grinned.

She launched herself into his arms like a gamboling puppy and covered his face with wet warm kisses. "I was terrified…I'd never see you…after tomorrow," she whispered between the rhythm of her kisses. "I thought Nadejda would spirit you away—or make you stay away—or somehow barricade you from me." Her murmured voice was an agitated rush of words. "But you're here, you're really here!" Leaning away from him, she gazed at Stefan as if to certify her words. As a blind person might, she ran her hands over his face and down his throat, over the breadth of his shoulders and down his chest, resting them finally, her palms on the embroidered black China silk directly over his heart.

He hadn't touched her except to steady her when she landed in his lap, basking in the glory of her jubilant kisses and joyful hysteria, letting his own sense of unutterable joy inundate his mind.

"I love you," Lisaveta whispered, "so much I thought I'd die if I lost you."

"I love you, *dushka*," he softly said, his dark eyes beneath his heavy brows intense with emotion, "enough to give up my command."

"You didn't!" Her exclamation was an explosive whisper, vibrating with shock.

"I would have."

"No!" Her single word was as firmly declarative as his admission. She'd listened to the sadness in his voice those weeks in the mountains when he'd spoken of his father. She couldn't face him if he'd made that same sacrifice for her.

"If it came to a choice, I would." His statement was without subterfuge or arrogance. No longer the commander of the Tsar's cavalry or his father's son, Stefan was only a man in love, a man who'd discovered happiness after years of dismissing the concept as poetic license. "So…" He covered her small hands with his. "Will you mind a very precipitous wedding tonight?"

"Tonight?" Her squeal was spontaneous feminine surprise, the kind reflecting wholly practical considerations like dresses, flowers, family and guests, all the ritual every young girl dreams of as fairy-tale magic.

"We leave in the morning." Stefan's voice was tolerant male but wholly practical, too. He had a war to fight, and dresses and flowers and family hadn't even remotely crossed his mind.

"In the morning?"

"Am I speaking in some unintelligible language?" he amusedly asked.

"Maybe we shouldn't," Lisaveta abruptly replied.

"Don't even start," Stefan said. "I sold my soul."

"That's what I mean," she protested. "I don't want you to sell your soul." She pulled her hands free. "Maybe you'll be sorry in a week or a year…maybe Vladimir will change the Tsar's mind and then you'll hate me for ruining your life. Maybe—"

"God, Lise, stop being noble."

"I'm not being noble, I just don't want to hurt you. I don't want you to decide later our marriage was too hasty." The petulant moue she made signified her uncertainty and disquietude.

"I could always divorce you—" Stefan's grin was playful

"—if that happened. Boris divorced his wife one weekend when he was out shooting with the Tsar. Alexander signed the special decree and Helene discovered her new status on Monday."

"Well, I could divorce you, too," Lisaveta immediately retorted, her sense of outrage aggravated by his teasing male arrogance and the ease with which he could expedite a divorce if he wished.

"So there. We're perfectly matched. Why not take a chance?" His casual words were disconcerting and reminiscent of the transience of his affairs and, after his last remark about divorce, not precisely the tone conducive to a romantic concept of marriage. She could feel her heart pounding at the nonchalance of his remarks, alarmed he might in truth view this marriage as an indulgent whim. She wanted her deep love returned in kind, and resentment prompted her reply. "I don't wish to marry someone as a speculative venture."

She looked very young in white eyelet and tumbled curls and a petulant scowl, and Stefan thought that although in many ways she was learned beyond her years, she was also ingenuous and unsophisticated in feminine wiles. There wasn't a woman of his acquaintance who would have risked refusing his proposal.

"Look, darling," he said with a winning smile, conscious of her pursed lips and high color as well as the temper in her remark, treading lightly because he was never absolutely sure of her response, "I'm leaving in the morning. I don't want to but I must, and while I prefer not pulling rank on you and I love and adore you in all your moods, you needn't be fearful or noble or testy about our marriage. I'll never divorce you, I swear. I was teasing. So just humor me and say, 'Tonight would be perfect for our wedding,' and I'll have the palace staff do their damnedest to follow every little order you wish to give *and* we'll live happily ever after till the end of time, my word on it, *dushka*." And his smile not only touched her heart with its boyish winsomeness but made her feel guilty for her temper.

"I don't have a wedding dress," she said in a very small voice.

"Oh, Lord," he said softly, "is that what this is all about?"

"No, it isn't," she hotly retorted. Instantly she chastised herself for another overheated response, and with a faint sigh that encompassed the impossibility of putting all the normal wedding preparations into the minutes allotted her, she added, "It's about...everything."

"Everything?" Reaching up to ruffle the curls at her temple, he cordially inquired, "Do I have time for a definition of 'everything'?"

"You're not very romantic." Her expression was that of a pouty small girl and utterly delightful.

He smiled, apologizing, promising to be romantic, this man who had always scoffed at the notion, then pulling her into his arms, he held her tight, thinking himself the luckiest man alive. Not only did he love beyond the mountains of the moon but he'd never be bored.

Her plaintive "ouch" brought him out of his cheerful reverie.

"Your embroidery," she softly reproved, the sheer eyelet of her nightgown no barrier to bristly metallic thread.

Pulling his shirt out of his trousers, Stefan undid the buttons at his neck and tugged his shirt over his head in one swift movement. The dark China silk fell in fluttering folds to the floor. "So fill me in," he said, drawing her back against his chest, "on 'everything,' and we'll have the staff take care of it."

"How much time do I have?" Lisaveta asked, looking up at him. "Does that sound impossibly pragmatic?" she went on in a tentative voice, then answered her own question in the next breath. "Well, maybe it does, but I've always dreamed girlish dreams of frothy gowns and flowers and priestly choirs and candles and music...and true love."

Stefan touched the fullness of her bottom lip lightly with one finger and said with a quiet intensity, "You have true love, *dushka*, and you can also have all your girlish dreams. And there's nothing wrong with being pragmatic...it's your wedding.'' His smile was indulgent. "Is two hours enough?" It was a man's question and he thought a reasonable one.

"Two *hours*?" she wailed.

He could see their concepts of reasonable differed. "Four hours then, how about that?" he generously offered. "But anything after eleven o'clock, I draw the line." He shrugged and gently reminded her, "The Turks won't wait."

"We'll have to tell Nikki and Alisa," she said, capitulating.

"I already told them on the way home."

"Some men are terribly sure of themselves." Her fine brows lifted in teasing rebuke.

He grinned. "Years of practice."

"I can still change my mind," Lisaveta warned, her golden eyes bright with laughter.

"No, you can't."

"Why can't I, pray tell? I'm not *obliged* to marry you." Her glance was mischievous.

Your cousin Nikki may disagree with you there, Stefan thought, but said instead, "All the guests will be disappointed."

"*All* the guests?" she said in a very tiny voice.

"And the Tsar."

"The *Tsar*?" she whispered.

"The chapel candelabra are being polished even as we speak." His expression was amused.

"What if I'd said no?"

"You already said yes."

"I could have changed my mind," she said in a feminine way that over the centuries had been bred into every female on earth—the art of being contrary on principle.

"Well, then I'd have to change it back. I'm good at that." His dark eyes were suddenly as suggestive as his voice, and she was momentarily reminded of his...competence.

"How many guests are invited?" she asked with a studied casualness, aware he was correct in his assurance and wondering in the next beat of her heart how many of his former lovers, how many recipients of his "competence," would be in attendance.

"I think the chapel holds three hundred."

"How many are women?" There. She'd said it. It would have been impossible to be subtle, so her blunt question conveyed the full extent of her concern.

"Just wives of friends," he carefully replied. "I didn't count." Did she really think he was that insensitive?

"I'm jealous," she candidly said.

"So am I. None of your gallants were invited." His voice was gruff.

She smiled at his vigilance. "We agree then."

"I hope so. *I* wasn't dancing with every man in Saint Petersburg."

"I thought you were probably doing something much less innocent wherever you were."

"Well, I wasn't," he huffily said, as if after years of dalliance she should have intuitively realized he was being celibate across two thousand miles of Russia.

"I adore your jealousy." Lisaveta soothed the crease between his black brows.

"Humpf," he muttered, all his territorial feelings too new to fully assimilate.

Reaching up, she kissed him in selfish gratitude and miraculous wonder, her heart so full of love she wanted to laugh and cry and shout her happiness to the world. And when one small tear spilled over her eyelid and trailed down her cheek, Stefan followed it with kisses, his breath warm on her cheek.

"Don't cry," he murmured, "everything will be perfection. I'll be more understanding, promise," he said in blanket pledge to stay her tears, "and I'll never look at another woman and you can have more than four hours if you wish."

He almost said, "I'll hold back the Turks," but the telegram waiting for him when he'd returned from his audience with the Tsar was worrisome. Hussein Pasha was on a forced march from Erzerum. That startling news sharply curtailed Stefan's timetable. Although Hussein's chances of reaching Kars before Stefan were almost impossible, Stefan had learned not to disregard the impossible. At the thought of his return to battle, his arms tightened around Lisaveta.

"Be happy, Lise," he whispered, her warmth vivid antidote to the sudden bleakness of his thoughts, the fragrance of her hair delicate reminder she offered him the ultimate perfumed sweetness of life. "Don't cry...please...I love you so..."

"I'm really happy," Lisaveta incongruously said in a small hiccupy voice. He'd just promised her carte blanche in his masculine attempt at consolation and his extravagant willingness to please her caused even more tears to fall.

"You're making me feel terrible." He cradled her in his arms, distracted by her tears. "Tell me what you want," he said unconditionally. "Anything...just tell me."

"I don't *want* anything," she whispered, gulping to restrain her weeping. "I always cry when I'm truly happy."

"You do?" He lifted her chin with a crooked finger. "Honestly?" He'd never had a woman cry in his arms before. He'd experienced the full gamut of other emotions, but never tears— an indication, perhaps, of his skillful expertise and the casual nature of his relationships.

Lisaveta nodded. "Honestly."

And then, out of desperation and uncertainty, he kissed her, because if he was unsure of tears of happiness, he was secure in the efficacy of kisses.

He was right.

Lisaveta was the one to demur softly some moments later. "Do we have time?" she whispered, holding Stefan close, the intensity of her embrace in contrast to her words.

He lifted his head a scant distance and glanced at the clock on the mantel. "No," he said, lowering his head again to kiss her.

"We should stop," she murmured, "before it's too late."

She could feel his smile on her lips.

"Good idea," he breathed in the minutest exhalation, "if it wasn't too late already."

"We could just have a small wedding." She reached up a caressing hand, her small palm and delicate fingers sliding up the side of his dark-skinned face to glide into the heaviness of his black hair, her words vibrating on his lips. "I don't need a gown or flowers or music." Her mouth curved into a smile. "We'd save a lot of time."

He raised his face a small distance from hers and his tongue traced a wet warm path up the bridge of her nose. "We'll postpone it an hour." His mouth touched her eyebrow in a brushing caress, then her lashes and the high sweep of her cheekbone.

Lisaveta's wedding gown was selected an hour and a half later from an array of fashionable dresses summoned by fiat from every important modiste in Saint Petersburg. It was hand-made lace of enormous value and heavy enough to support the thousands of pearls embellishing its rose-patterned texture. Cut very simply, it was a maiden's gown with a modest décolletage, small bow-trimmed sleeves and a froth of gathers draped into a bustle and lengthy train.

Stefan said, "I like it," when Lisaveta asked; she looked rosy-cheeked and young and so beautiful he felt a small catch in his chest, but then he began breathing again and smiled at his own bewitchment.

He saw that Lisaveta bought all else she needed for her trousseau, as well, and he wasn't without opinions, but they agreed on most styles, as they did later with the tradesmen interviewed for jewelry and flowers and specialty foodstuffs necessary for a wedding on short notice. They argued briefly over the flowers. Lisaveta wanted lilies. Stefan said lilies reminded him of death. Why not orange blossoms or violets or orchids? Orange blossoms were out of season, as were violets, but they took what the florists in Saint Petersburg had in their forcing houses, and they compromised on orchids.

"Small orchids," Lisaveta said, "not the enormous ones."

"*Some* large orchids," Stefan insisted. "They remind me of Grandmama. Her palace was filled with them." And she agreed because she loved him and he had loved his grandmama enough to have her flowers at his wedding.

When she inquired how their guests would know when to arrive, since the time had been changed twice, once to accommodate themselves and once to accommodate Stefan's temperamental chef, Stefan only said, "No problem." His regiment on staff in Saint Petersburg was transporting the messages, and she hadn't realized until then how familiar Stefan was with boundless power, how unhumble his background, how royal his prerogatives, until he'd added, "It's *my* cavalry corps."

She suddenly understood he answered to few men in the world. Considering his unique friendship with the Tsar, perhaps it was safer to say he answered to only one man. His position as cavalry commander didn't fully encompass the additional native tribes pledging allegiance to his family, and on the eastern frontier, the fealty of the nomadic tribes constituted an army in itself. The Chiefs of Staff knew that, the Grand Dukes knew that, and he was treated with careful deference.

The power and authority he wielded was almost unreserved and explained a wedding accomplished with such speed and finesse.

No one refused him.

He had but to indicate his desire and it was accomplished.

He was very different from the man she'd come to know on their journey from Aleksandropol to Tiflis or in the informal surroundings of his mountain lodge. Even his palaces in Tiflis and Saint Petersburg were run without undue pomp. He was human, warm, a natural man without formality. This new image of Stefan as master and commander of all he surveyed made her question for a moment whether she really knew the man she was about to marry.

Sixteen

Five hours later, the chapel was filled with expectant guests, delighted to have been called away from previous engagements to witness the sudden and startling wedding of Stefan Bariatinsky to a beautiful young lady who'd been hidden away from society until short weeks ago. A lady who'd been introduced into society by no less a figure than the Tsar, a lady of the prominent Kuzan family, known over the centuries not only for their wealth but for their unconventionality...a polite word for what the less courteous called excesses. The scandal of his broken engagement to Nadejda, of course, only added piquant expectancy to the festivities.

Those more perceptive of the guests in the chapel noted the absence of all of Stefan's previous paramours.

"It must be love," they whispered to one another.

"But for how long?" the more cynical replied.

"She's a Kuzan," some others murmured, insinuation delicious as sin in their voices. "I'll give it a year."

But Stefan had never been noted for the longevity of his infatuations, and Kuzan or not, no one risked their money on a day more.

Countess Lazaroff's suitors weren't invited, either, they noted. He was jealous. Stefan jealous? The thought was novel. Stefan had always been known for the number and variety of his women. The unspoken comment was in everyone's mind. Would one woman satisfy him?

The site of the wedding was an exuberant baroque chapel dedicated architecturally to an earthly approximation of heaven. Built of white marble, it was accented with tall polished pilasters of lavender amethyst rising to support a cornice leafed in gold under a frescoed ceiling and decorated with a profusion of statuary and gilded motifs. The luxury of material and style combined to give the sanctuary an intensely emotional appeal, like a flamboyant architectural melody. Incorporated into this variation of baroque grandeur was the very Russian addition of thousands of candles, votive and otherwise, in chandeliers and candelabra, in display cabinets of great beauty.

And as if the splendor of marble, amethyst and gold, of frescoes depicting the dazzling light of heaven gleaming on angels and cavorting putti, all illuminated by flickering candlelight, wasn't enough to suggest heaven on earth, orchids, large and small, stark white and delicately hued, were massed in great arrangements throughout the chapel. They tumbled in faultless disorder over the altar, twined up candelabrum stands and torchères, were tied into garlands with angel fern and hung in luxurious swags between pilasters. In contrast to the sumptuous display of flora, each row of gilded chairs in the nave was fronted by a tall basket of stately lilies. "For my wife," Stefan had said to the florist, "but I want colored lilies. The white ones are too funereal."

It was done.

As everything he requested was done.

As was the customary procedure with Stefan Bariatinsky's wishes.

And now in white dress uniform, tall, dark and spectacular, he stood before the gratified eyes of Saint Petersburg's aristocracy, the Savior of Russia, the most decorated soldier in the Empire's history, the man who'd loved hundreds of ladies but never for long, waited to be married.

He seemed remarkably composed, the cynosure for three hundred pairs of eyes, chatting quietly with his priests, smiling occasionally, putting his hand out in casual greeting to a junior prelate who came in late, immune apparently to his guests' curiosity.

A small fanfare of muted horns announced his bride, and when he turned to her, it was plain for all the world to see that he adored her, and she him. The bride and groom smiled at each other, an intimate smile that ignored their guests, the avid curiosity and indeed the world. For that evanescent moment they existed alone, separated by only a white satin carpet strewn with rose petals.

And then in a curious gesture of tender welcome and intrinsic command, he held out his hand to her.

His priests, elaborate in embroidered silver on midnight-blue velvet vestments, flanked him like bearded robed shamans from an ancient time. Scented incense from thousands of flickering candles lent a perfumed ambience to the dazzling white-and-gold interior, muting the soft undertone of fragrant lily.

Lisaveta stood alone in the entrance to the nave, her pearl-encrusted gown and gold-embroidered veil shimmered in the candlelight, the diamonds at her ears and throat—a gift from her bridegroom—catching the light in brilliant display. She raised the small bouquet of white violets she held in one hand toward her bridegroom in silent, minute answer to Stefan—and smiled again, beautiful and assured.

Without a word spoken, every guest understood the nature of their relationship. Prince Bariatinsky and the splendid Countess Lazaroff were not only in love, they were equally matched. In mesmerizing silence the inconceivable concept was absorbed, followed closely by the piquant speculation: how exotic, how accomplished, how brilliant was the Countess to have attained parity with the most lionized man in the Empire.

The organ chords of the processional broke out triumphantly and Lisaveta, arresting the endless possibilities rife in everyone's mind, moved in stately grace toward her bridegroom.

The ceremony was lengthy, protocol carefully observed; Stefan wanted no doubt to the legitimacy of his marriage or his intentions. Before the entire world of Saint Petersburg elite he was marrying Lisaveta, and if there was a child, he was acknowledging it as his. He believed her—and in her—implicitly.

His faith was all the more stunning because he had been a

man so successful with other men's wives and lovers over the years.

He was being offered the glass of wine to drink by the priest, and taking it, he turned to Lise with a smile. Saluting her, he drank and waited while she in turn sipped from her wineglass. They were symbolically toasting to fertility and good fortune—a bit late, he thought, and she seemed to read his mind because she winked at him.

Scandalizing the priests, he responded to her mischievous gesture by pulling her close with his free arm and, bending low, said in a murmur near her ear, the poufed silk tulle of her veil brushing against his cheek, "I love you *dushka*, for a thousand years."

She smiled back her own pledge of love and kissed him gently on the cheek. "Only a thousand years?" she whispered, sweet teasing in her voice.

The buzz of comment rose in the perfumed air at the extraordinary show of affection; Stefan wasn't a demonstrative man.

"Till the mountains crumble into the sea," he whispered, and kissed her very gently. Then straightening, Stefan signaled with a nod of his head and the ceremony continued.

The seated guests looked at one another in silent comment. Now that was like Stefan, they thought, intimidated by neither man nor God nor scowling priests. His brief nod was understated authority from a man intent on his own prerogatives and spontaneity. And his bride hadn't even blushed. Of course, she was a Kuzan. They'd been recognized as beyond blushing several centuries ago.

Lisaveta and Stefan were able to kiss with the priests' blessing after the benediction some time later, and then, beaming with pride, Stefan escorted his bride to the Tsar, seated in the first row. Not only a gesture of courtesy, it was meant as a warning to Vladimir Taneiev; Stefan intended any report going back to Vladimir was perfectly clear on his position with Alexander II.

The reception was glittering and resplendent. Even the Tsar stayed longer than he intended, intrigued by Stefan's Georgian

wines, the charm of his bride, the Gypsy dancers who entertained the guests through dinner and the Cossacks who per-
formed acrobatic feats of great wonder after dessert. Alexander
lingered until the orchestra began playing and he danced twice
with the bride. In leaving he embraced Stefan, a public dem-
onstration of his friendship.

The newlyweds were gracious for an hour more, mingling
with their guests, accepting congratulations and facetious comment with equal good cheer. Stefan had never seemed so relaxed and approachable. The new Princess Bariatinsky, everyone agreed, was a good influence on him.

But Stefan's accommodating nature had its limits, although
his guests were invited to stay and enjoy his wedding ball and
hospitality as long as they wished. His cellars were at their
disposal, he informed them, his chef committed to their gus-
tatory pleasure, the musicians willing to play for a week. He
smiled from the bandstand and waved *au revoir*. He and his
bride, he finished, her hand firmly in his, were off on their
honeymoon. And so saying, he scooped Lisaveta up into his
arms to cheering applause and carried her down the short carpeted range of stairs to the ballroom floor, across its length,
down the corridor to the main staircase and thence down again
and out the opened doors to his waiting carriage.

Acknowledged the good wishes of those of his staff in attendance at the main doors and at his carriage with a ready
smile and cordial thank-yous, he deposited Lisaveta onto the
carriage seat in a tumble of white lace and, climbing in behind
her, signaled for departure.

"How is the time?" Lisaveta asked, since a suppressed agitation was evident beneath Stefan's composed exterior.

"The wedding set me back five hours, but we're still fine."
He hadn't told her of the telegrams—three now since late afternoon—confirming Hussein Pasha's march toward Kars...or
of his decision after the second one to leave as soon as possible
after the wedding and not wait until the next day.

"I'm sorry," Lise teased, "for ruining your schedule." But
under the playfulness of her teasing she was aglow with the
wonder of her love. How impossible she would have thought

the circumstances of her wedding short months ago, how inconceivable to be married to Russia's greatest hero, how strange she'd never dreamed of this eventuality when she'd fallen under Stefan's spell that first night in Aleksandropol. She'd thought herself a civilized female then, capable of participating in an amorous interlude, capable of saying *adieu* when it was over, never knowing intellect was insufficient against overwhelming feelings—against love. Hafiz had known it. Poets and past dwellers on this earth for a millenium had discovered that truth. And now she knew it, too.

His smile flashed white in the lamplit interior of the coach. "I wanted you to ruin my schedule, *dushka*. It was a perfect wedding." She was worth every minute of delay, he thought, taking his wife in his arms, feeling her close, the scent of her hair reminding him of their warm summer nights before Tiflis, when the fragrance of rose was on the air like perfumed seduction. His decision to come north and bring her back was worth every long frustrating hour of his journey. His grip tightening in a spontaneous gesture of assurance, he smiled down at her upturned face. "You belong to me," he said softly, the fullness of his need and love echoing in his voice.

"And you to me," she answered, her voice as quiet. "Do you mind?" she asked then, because Stefan was a man apart, a leader and overlord of vast tribal subjects and troops, and she'd felt his minute reaction to her words.

"I'd never thought of it that way," he honestly replied, possession always having been endowed by strength. This was new, this shared right, and he asked, "Is it in the order of things?"

"It's only fair."

His answer was in the simple kiss he gave her, his lips touching hers lightly, a butterfly kiss of affirmation and love. "Whatever makes you happy," he said, this man who'd stood alone since adolescence, this man who'd felt he never needed anything or anyone. "I'm pleased," he murmured, his mind and heart so filled with love he felt invincible, "to belong to you."

She kissed him then because no matter what his answer she loved him, but his reply had been tempered by her wishes, by his love for her, and she felt overwhelming happiness. "Do we deserve all this good fortune?" she teasingly whispered, her golden eyes like sunshine in the dark.

"I don't know about you, but I certainly do," he emphatically replied, his temperament familiar with life's largess. "I'd been looking for you for years."

"In other women's arms?" Her sarcasm was lighthearted.

"How else do you look?" he casually replied, his tone matching hers.

"Some people might consider 'looking' in another context."

"Really?" His grin was infectious.

"Your looking days are over, you understand."

"Really?" he said again in that same unconvinced tone.

"Really," she said in an inflection bespeaking her own emphatic views on territorial rights.

"Everyone has a mistress tucked away in a little house somewhere."

"*Almost* everyone."

"Think what it will do for my reputation," he said, stroking her hand lightly, "if I change the pattern."

"Think what it will do for the state of your health if you don't." She looked up at him from under her lacy lashes, her glance moderate but firm.

"Are you threatening me with bodily harm?" Teasing insouciance infused his words.

"Absolutely."

"How nice," he said with a smile.

"Don't use that charming smile on me, Stefan, I'm dead serious."

"In that case, *dushka*, I must mend my disreputable ways and start a new trend. We shall make love matches fashionable."

"You don't mind?" Her voice was tentative at the enormity of the change she was demanding, at the realistic application of her emotional requirements.

He thought for a moment of all the years he'd considered a love match the worst possible circumstance, a danger in fact to one's peace of mind. And now, by the grace of God, he was lucky enough to realize how wrong he'd been.

"No," he said very quietly, "I don't mind."

Nikki and Alisa were waiting in Stefan's railcar, having been invited to say their goodbyes in private, and they both rose from the comfortable parlor chairs to greet the newlyweds when they entered the door.

Hugs and kisses were exchanged and pleased wishes accepted for a happy future; the wedding was briefly recapped, they commented on the Tsar's lengthy visit, discussed various guests in passing, and then Alisa went off to the bedroom to help Lisaveta change into a traveling gown.

Nikki and Stefan sat over brandy, their conversation turning to the newest problem in the war. Nikki, a colonel assigned to the Staff College, served as liaison between the Tsar's advisers and the General Staff. "How serious is Hussein Pasha's attempt?" he inquired.

"It's a deadly gamble," Stefan replied. He shrugged then, because both were familiar with the terrain Hussein Pasha was traveling through. "They could die or possibly succeed. But if they make it, will they be in any condition to fight? Even the mountain ponies need *some* water."

"It's a hell of a risk."

"But you can't help admiring him for trying. He's probably gambling his own colonelcy on it."

Nikki smiled. "There's always armchair caution at the top."

"Unfortunately it doesn't win a lot of wars."

"How costly do you anticipate the attack on Kars to be when it comes?"

Stefan had been asked that question too many times to count, the fortified city having withstood two major assaults already. But the words this time seemed to strike more personally, and he experienced a brief sense of vulnerability. "It depends," he replied, repressing his sudden precarious sensation of mortality, "on how much ammunition they've stockpiled inside the fortress." His shoulder lifted in the briefest shrug. "We simply don't know."

"You won't be leading the attack now that—" Nikki paused to select a diplomatic turn of phrase "—you're no longer a bachelor," he finished, deciding against reference to the coming child.

"Of course I will," Stefan replied. "My men expect it." He'd no more think of directing the attack from the safety of the Staff Headquarters behind the lines than he'd consider retreating from battle. His personal leadership was in large part what inspired his troops. He'd always lived with them in the field, undergoing the same hardships, understanding their fears, listening to them talk of their wives and children and lovers. They'd follow him to hell and back.

And in a few days' time, even if Hussein Pasha's reinforcements were added to the defenders of Kars, he'd be leading his men into a kind of hell devised by the Sultan's wish for an invincible fortress. That, too, was an enormous calculated gamble, but if Kars could be taken the Turkish territories in the East would fall and the Sultan's ministers might be forced to the peace table. If Kars fell, the war could be over. If Kars fell, he could be back in Tiflis in less than a month.

"I don't suppose it would do any good to say be careful."

Stefan smiled. "In my own fashion I'm careful." But he understood what Nikki was saying. "And I've reason to be more cautious now," he added. "Will that do?"

Nikki smiled back. "I know how ridiculous words of prudence are in wartime. As if caution ever won a campaign, but..." He sighed. "I know your style of command and it's based more on some goddamned guardian angel watching over you than on any even remote concept of discretion. Take care."

"I intend to."

Both men knew their platitudinous words, no matter how well intended, wouldn't last a second in combat. There one acted on instinct and experience. One did what one did best, and Stefan had always won by risk taking.

"You intend to what?" Lisaveta asked, walking back into the parlor, her traveling dress of forest green bombazine an attractive foil to her golden eyes and peaches-and-cream skin.

"I intend to love you till the end of time," Stefan chivalrously answered. "Are you comfortable now?" he went on, inclined to change the subject to safer ground.

"That wedding gown weighed thirty pounds," Alisa said, "although its dazzling splendor was worth the suffering."

Lisaveta smiled. "One never actually suffers in something that beautiful but, yes, I'm very much more comfortable now." She twirled around, her light silk skirt billowing out in a fluttering bellshape.

Nikki and Stefan had come to their feet when the ladies entered the parlor. Knowing how pressed Stefan was for time, Nikki took his wife's hand and said, "Since they're holding the train for you, we won't stay any longer. *Bon voyage* and all our best wishes."

"You'll let us know how you're feeling," Alisa said, her voice significant in its emphasis.

"You'll be the first to know," Stefan replied with a smile. "We'll telegram."

Hugs and kisses were once more exchanged amid promises to write and visit. No one mentioned the war, but when Nikki and Alisa stepped off onto the platform, the train began moving immediately. Stefan's orders were being obeyed.

"Are you happy?" Stefan asked, his arms around Lise's waist as they stood by the train window, the bustle of the station passing by with increasing speed.

"Words pale," she softly replied, leaning back into the solidness of Stefan's body, all the pain and uncertainty of Nadejda in the past, Stefan's love for her wildly real, like his strength. She couldn't have been happier or more content.

"You must be tired." She seemed small and delicate in his arms and the day had been grueling. They'd worked nonstop arranging the wedding, then entertained their guests for several hours more.

Lisaveta sighed. The evening had been so hectic and chaotic she hadn't had time to think about being tired. Until now. "I am," she said, letting her eyes drift shut for a moment.

"Anyone would be, darling. The schedule's been brutal. Why don't you take a nap?" he suggested. Slipping his arms from around her waist and taking her hands in his, he turned her to face him. "I'll wake you in, say, two hours." The color was gone from her cheeks and fatigue shadowed her eyes.

"You'll wake me?" She didn't resist, Stefan's soft bed temptation in her weariness.

"Promise." His smile was protective. "You and baby need rest."

Her fingers gripped his in a sudden tightening. "Do you...really think so?" She felt so normal; were other women as uncertain as she?

Stefan hadn't had time himself to dwell at any length on that possibility, or perhaps he'd suppressed those thoughts with so much at stake in the attack on Kars. The reality of a child could seriously curtail his style of soldiering, which had, until very recently, been his life. And the thought of having a baby was, in honesty, not completely joyous. It was in too many ways terrifying. It made him vulnerable in a precarious world; it increased the danger of his existence; it opened up long vistas of "tomorrow" when he'd always lived for today. And his responsibilities, which he'd learned to handle with a practiced skill, were now extended to a wife he loved and soon, perhaps, to a child.

Would he think of them as the charge was sounded?

Would his emotional involvement temper his intuitive sense of survival?

Would his risk taking be impeded because he had too much to lose?

He was uncertain of the answers, and that in itself was disconcerting. He wasn't, as a rule, uncertain.

But to his wife, he said, "I *hope* we're having a baby."

Gazing up at him, she tried to gauge his sincerity. "Good," she said after a small pause, "because Alisa's probably right."

Stefan grinned. "Nikki certainly seemed sure. I was almost called out."

Her pale eyes widened. "You weren't *forced* into this marriage?"

"No, darling, I can't be forced into anything."

"You're not just being pleasant?"

He laughed out loud at the notion he'd marry someone "to

be pleasant'' after escaping designing women for years. ''I don't think even my most fervent supporters would see me obliging as a bridegroom out of courtesy alone. You are truly loved, darling, make no mistake.''

Lise smiled a contented Cheshire cat smile. ''You say the nicest things.''

He grinned. ''Years of practice.''

''Which have now come to a screeching halt.''

''Of course.'' But his grin was still in place.

''Are you always this accommodating?''

''Years of practice,'' he repeated, amusement rich in the words, and he kissed her then to erase her small scowl. ''Which,'' he added a moment later, his mouth still close to hers, his voice quiet and grave, ''are now over. Have I told you that I'm looking forward to monogamy?''

His words warmed her heart, his dark eyes so adoring she felt a contented security as bucolic as a Lorrain landscape. ''A novel experience,'' she softly murmured, her mouth lifted in a very small smile, ''for you, I'd guess.''

''But then,'' he replied, his voice a hushed suggestion, ''I'm always open to novel experiences.''

''Libertine.'' It was a whisper only.

''*Former* libertine,'' he quietly corrected her.

''You're a married man now.''

''I like the sound of that with you in my arms, and,'' he went on, no longer jesting, ''I didn't think I'd ever have those feelings.''

''We've the Turks to thank for our meeting,'' she reminded him, touched by the peculiar fate that had taken a hand in their destiny.

''You're right.'' Mention of the Turks, though, effectively altered Stefan's sense of joy. He had enormous work to accomplish mapping his plan of attack before the train reached Vladikavkaz. ''Sleep now,'' he gently said, kissing her tenderly, ''and I'll wake you soon.''

The rhythm of the train and the warmth of Stefan's body, the swaying comfort of being held, were all lulling supplement to her drowsiness. ''You won't forget to wake me?''

The gold flecks shone briefly in his black eyes, brilliant like his smile. "Not a chance, sweetheart. This is my *only* wedding night and I'm not going to miss it."

While Lise slept, Stefan pored over the maps he'd brought with him, coordinating his cavalry with the infantry movements, measuring distances from the artillery positions, trying to estimate the weakest approaches to the city, guessing with calculated experience which defenses would be shored up against attack and which, perhaps, would not. He knew the Turks after all the years of border skirmishing; he knew how Mukhtar Pasha and Mehemet Pasha thought. What he didn't know was the extent of the munitions stored within Kars and, even more daunting, whether the reinforcements coming from the west would reach Kars before him.

He shouldn't have left, of course; he knew that now with a gut-level intensity. But at the time the risk had been minimal or no risk at all. He'd weighed it against his need for Lisaveta and decided he'd have more than a safe margin to accomplish his trip and return. And if Hussein Pasha hadn't decided on this suicide march he'd be well within his schedule. Unfortunately, he was racing against time now. The track to Vladikavkaz had been cleared so his train wouldn't encounter any delays, the engineer had orders to proceed at top speed—Stefan had been assured they could cut ten hours from their normal run—and he was relying on his intrinsic luck after that to carry him through.

Slightly more than two hours later he glanced at the clock on his desk, finished the southwest angle of attack by noting the cavalry regiments to be held in reserve and, setting aside his maps, leaned back in his chair and stretched. The muscles across his shoulders ached and he flexed his arms briefly to relax the tension. So much depended on the attack, so much depended on his assessment of their options. The western campaign in Bulgaria and Romania would be dramatically influenced by the success or failure of the attack on Kars.

And failure was unthinkable.

He'd never failed.

Standing, he pushed his chair back and strode to the windows. Lifting aside the heavy draperies, he stared out into the blackness rushing by, only an occasional twinkle of light in a distant dwelling evidence of another living being. He felt very much alone in the luxurious railway car, as though he stood a solitary figure in a dark void, as though the entire burden of the war's success were on his shoulders. He must be more tired than usual, he thought, to feel the depression so intensely. Much of the burden of the Tsar's wars had been his responsibility for years now and he'd never felt the weight so oppressively.

Perhaps the siege had lasted too long; perhaps they should have attacked sooner; maybe he was experiencing a sense of lost opportunities at not being more insistent in his views in the staff conferences. Shaking away his thoughts of what might have been, he walked to his liquor cabinet and poured himself a small cognac. It was futile to ponder days and weeks that were past, he reminded himself as the first draught of fiery liquor traveled down his throat. He'd never been prone to dwell on unalterable circumstance and he refused to be cast into gloom.

Tomorrow he'd finish the cavalry placements and then begin to deal with Suvarov's artillery sketches. He'd told the old general, who'd come up through the ranks on competence alone, that he could help him pinpoint some of the weaker areas in the Turk's defenses after his months of scouting Kars during the siege. Suvarov's artillery was critical in the period before the attack, and then Stefan's cavalry was the assault arm for the infantry. They had to break through the redoubts, they had to silence the cannon commanding the heights, they had to open the way for the foot soldiers...all possible with the right spirit and elusive, fickle luck. His cavalry had always triumphed in the past, for Russia, for his Tsar...and for his father's memory.

His own future, though, was measured in different proportions from the unstable impetuosity of his past, when time was reckoned by the next battle or the next pretty lady in the next convenient bed. His expanded future included a beautiful woman he loved with a passion that colored his every thought.

And soon he might have a child to carry on the Bariatinsky dynasty, a child he cherished already when he dared to plan beyond Kars.

"For you, Mama and Papa," he softly said, raising his glass to the black night speeding by. "You would have loved them." Taking a deep breath, he added in a husky murmur, "And to luck."

Seventeen

He woke her by lying down beside her on his large bed and pulling her into his arms, where he held her for long minutes, her body warm from sleep. At leisurely intervals he murmured, "I love you," as though the phrase were verbal confirmation of his happiness.

Lisaveta responded with kisses and her own whispered love words, and miles of Russia passed by the darkened bedroom window as they savored their quiet joy. The birch-paneled room was lighted by a single bedside fairy lamp, its pale glow illuminating a limited golden circle hardly reaching the limits of the bed. The dresser, the photos of Stefan's parents on the wall, the black leather campaign chair that had been his father's, were all in shadow. Stefan was still dressed with the exception of his uniform tunic, discarded in the parlor beside his rolls of maps. His long lean body stretched beyond the brilliance of the crystal lamp, the turquoise silk coverlet crushed beneath his boots, his bare torso and arms and slender hands swarthy against Lisaveta's paler flesh and primrose gown. She was tucked close to him, like a small child still half-asleep, her feet covered by the folds of her nightgown. Nestled in the strong curve of his arm, she was thinking she would tell her grandchildren someday how the entire world seemed to be laid at her feet that night in the rushing train traveling south across Russia.

"I've always been lucky," Stefan softly said, touching the delicate sweep of her jaw, trying to put his feelings into words.

"I believe in Gypsy fate and jinns," Lisaveta breathed, her quiet voice imbued with a solemn intensity, understanding what Stefan meant. "I think I always knew you'd appear someday."

His gaze altered minutely and a teasing infused his words. "It took me longer to realize."

"You loved me," she finished with a surety he admired.

"Yes," he agreed. "Although," he went on, irony prominent in his tone, "my timing could have been better."

"We've time now," she said, and reached up to kiss him.

"Three days," he murmured against the softness of her mouth.

"For our honeymoon…"

And for mapping the last details of the attack, he thought. "For our honeymoon," he affirmed, and kissed her very gently.

He undressed her slowly then, untying ribbon bows and undoing small pearl buttons with a delicate slowness. He was in no hurry. In fact, he felt a rare and uncommon drama as if his wedding night should be approached with a kind of leisured sensitivity so it wouldn't end too soon.

Lisaveta sat tranquilly in his lap, absorbing the tactile pleasure of Stefan's touch, the gentleness of his fingers, the brushing sensation of her gown slipping from her body, the strength of Stefan's legs beneath her, the warmth emanating from his powerful frame. Extraordinary feelings of possession overcame her. He was her husband, the word and the sentiment that went with it ones of potent pleasure and startlingly aphrodisiac. It surprised her she would feel that way, that having married him she would want him more, she could love him more, she could feel the heat of his body, his touch, even the sound of his voice, with increased intensity.

But she did, and desiring him beyond the serene lethargy of Stefan's motivations, she began undressing him.

He smiled, a knowing understanding smile because he was familiar with her impatience, could recognize when her breathing altered, could feel the heat of her fingers on his skin.

She unbuckled his belt with mild speed and slid it from its loops. The silver buttons on his breeches came loose next, and he stood then to pull off his boots and strip off the white leather breeches.

"I like the train," she said, kneeling nude and graceful on the bed, her hand on his hip, her smile heated from within. "Don't you?"

It *was* perfection: the isolation, the small and intimate proportions of the room; the starlit night sky visible through the windows; the racing speed, which seemed to place them somehow outside the boundaries of the world.

"We're alone." He said the words so they were special beyond their endearment, as though they meant, as well, that they were forever together.

She threw her arms around him and hugged him close, because she knew their time was precious and their immediate "forever" was only a few days long. His skin felt sleek beneath her hands and cheek, his solid strength her anchor and security, his heart beat steady and strong under her ear. She felt for a moment too fortunate and happy, as if there were an expendable limit to the felicity of her feelings and she were living on borrowed time. "Don't go," she whispered.

He didn't reply and she felt guilty for saying the words, for asking him to do what he couldn't. He stroked her back in a slow soothing rhythm, his palms warm, the pressure of his hands gentle, his heartbeat unaltered. "I won't," he finally said.

She looked up quickly.

"We have today and tomorrow." He was telling her they wouldn't think of menacing prospects now. Tonight she could ask and he would promise that their love and their future would be inviolable for...two days.

It was more than some people ever had. It was more than she'd thought possible even a week ago. She smiled up at him, her golden eyes full of love. "I'm glad you're not going."

"So am I," he said, the fiction theirs, this wedding night a miracle achieved against unprosperous odds, their love a triumph of two spirits validating the power of love.

He needed reminding when the time came later that she wasn't fragile as glass, that she was healthy and young and much too aroused to wish to be treated with such restrained gentleness...although "tame courtesy" were the actual words she used.

"The baby," he said, reminded by Nikki at the station and by his own thoughts, the prospect of fatherhood more and more prominent with his future so insecure. He could no longer disregard or waive the unalterable change in his thinking, no more than he could overlook Lisaveta's pregnancy, and his unease with the precise nuance of making love was natural. He had, to date, not acquired any familiarity with enceinte women.

"I'm fine," Lisaveta softly assured him.

"You're sure."

"I'll be finer soon," she replied in a seductive teasing whisper, "if you remember everything I've taught you in the past."

He laughed. "My apologies, darling, for being too well behaved."

"I think," his newly married wife said, her eyebrows raised in mild reproof, "we've talked enough."

He was braced above her on his elbows, her legs wrapped around his, the heat from her eyes almost tactile, his own glance only fractionally cooler. "That almost sounds like an order," he murmured, his mouth curved in a smile.

"Did I word that improperly?" Lisaveta murmured back. "I meant it to be..." She paused, lifting her hips slightly and rotated them in exquisite slow motion so he felt it in the soles of his feet and the tips of his toes, in his fingers, down his spine and with sensational intoxication in his heated brain. "An unequivocal order," she finished.

He was smiling when he lowered his head to kiss her, and he made certain no one could fault him for excessive deference, although excessiveness in other areas found unqualified favor.

The bed was a shambles soon and the room too hot in short order. Stefan opened the window because the small porcelain stove near the door wouldn't cool down for hours.

It was raining out, a fine misting rain that dampened his hair and made it curl when he stayed in the windswept air for long moments to cool himself. And when he fell back on the bed and pulled Lisaveta in his arms he smelled of pine forests and freshness.

He seemed a young boy suddenly, removed from the pomp of his princely travel and retinue, and she wished with the illogical fantasy of lovers that she'd known him when he was young.

"I love you so much my heart aches," she whispered as he kissed her cheek and nose and chin, small droplets of water falling from his hair.

"No, no, no," he resolutely objected, his voice rich with happiness. "Love me so much your heart spills over with joy…love me, sweetling, with laughter and pleasure…" He cupped her face between his warm palms, his smile infectious, boyish. "Love me with jubilation and rejoicing because that's how I love you and," he added very, very softly, "you're having my *baby*." He said the last word with a hushed reverence, feeling at that moment so deep in love the boundaries of definition would have to be pushed beyond the star line.

His eyes as she gazed up at him were dark passion, his words irresistible, and her answering smile was artless and unreservedly loving. "I'm having your baby." Her quiet declaration had the power to erase long years of sadness and bring full circle a kind of happiness he'd forgotten existed. Her small hands covered his where they lay on her cheeks and she said, as a young schoolgirl might recite a statement of fact, "I love you, Stefan Bariatinsky." And then she grinned like that same young schoolgirl might. "Now what are you going to do about it?"

He laughed, and then his dark glance turned seductive. "I suppose," he murmured, his deep voice husky with suggestion, "I'll have to make you happy."

And he did. Offering her everything, his heart, his soul, his exhilaration, his unconditional love.

She welcomed him on that rain-cooled night with the unrestrained spirit he adored. They made love with extravagant generosity, indulgent to each other first before they were self-indulgent, so in love each melting kiss seemed sweetly new, each peaking splendor and rushing climax rare and precious.

As morning came, they fell asleep in each other's arms, wishing in those illusory, unsubstantial moments before sleep falls that they weren't on a princely railcar speeding south to a killing field.

They slept late into the morning and woke leisurely when the sun was already high in the sky.

Almost half the day gone, Stefan unconsciously thought, as though some internal clock were ticking off the restricted time. And he felt for a short sinking moment as if these few hours were all he was going to be allowed. Determinedly shaking away his brief melancholy, he leaned over and kissed Lisaveta good-morning, and when her eyes slowly opened, he said with a smile and the impatience of a child, or perhaps a prince, "We have to eat."

Familiar with his appetite, Lisaveta said in sleepy, sardonic query, "How did you last so long?"

"Inherent politeness," he teased.

"And you've only been awake thirty seconds."

"That, too." His grin was engaging, although with the dark stubble shading his jaw he had the look of a brigand.

"And I'd better shave," he added, as though he could read her thoughts, his fingers trailing over the contour of his face, "as soon as we eat."

Lisaveta smiled. "You have no patience."

"Should I have?" He asked the question with idle casualness as he reached for the bellpull.

Thinking for a moment of Stefan's particular style of living, Lisaveta said, still smiling, "Perhaps it's too late for you."

"Would you like breakfast or lunch, darling, this time of day?" he inquired, knowing it was years too late for him to learn patience.

Rolling over on her back and stretching, Lisaveta teasingly asked, "Are all you Orbelianis the same?"

"No, of course not," Stefan replied, ignoring the point of

her question. "Some are shorter—the women, you understand—and some are older or younger—"

She smacked him with the flat of her hand on his stomach
and his fingers closed around her wrist before she could strike
him again. "Save that energy for later, darling," he said very
low, his dark eyes amused. "You're going to need it."

Breakfast was sumptuous, served in bed, and as promised,
their renewed energy was put to good use. The afternoon sped
by, as did the evening, in amorous pursuits, their conversation
lighthearted and without substance or topicality.

Neither spoke of the future or the war, although the assault
on Kars loomed specterlike in both their thoughts, the reality
only days away. The terrifying possibility Stefan might die was
too awful for Lisaveta to allow herself to think about, but her
sleep that night was restless. Stefan lay awake after she finally
dozed off, holding her in his arms, his mind on the complexity
of the attack. Not unusual, he reminded himself; he always
detailed the maneuvers of his troops on an internal battlefield,
considering alternative options in endless possibilities. But this
time he experienced an unfamiliar twinge of anxiety, no more
than an infrequent dragging beat of disquietude, but that break
in his concentration kept him awake because it was new.

They reached Vladikavkaz a day and a half later at four in
the morning, ten hours eliminated from the normal run, the
engine firebox red-hot and glowing like a live coal. Even while
the train was still rolling to a stop, a harsh banging erupted on
the railcar door. Stefan, who had been dressed since midnight,
swiftly opened the door, cast one glance over the troop of
horsemen prancing restlessly beyond the station platform and
knew he faced serious problems.

"Hussein Pasha is only three days from Kars!" the young
lieutenant cried. His salute was perfunctory, and forgetting in
his apprehension that he was addressing a corps commander,
he added, "You *must* come immediately!"

Stefan almost smiled at the lieutenant's youthful agitation,
and had his announcement been less ominous, he might have.
How the hell had Hussein Pasha done it? was his next incred-

ulous thought. The land he'd crossed was barren of water or fodder for his horses. A march at that speed and under those conditions must have been lethal to half the Turkish men and mounts. Stefan, as familiar with that country as he was with his own palace grounds, knew just how great that suffering would have been. But regardless of the possible state of Hussein Pasha's army, Stefan's immediate concern was beating him to Kars.

"Give me a minute," he said to the lieutenant, "and bring up my horse."

Standing outside the bedroom door a moment later, he debated whether to wake Lisaveta; she'd slept poorly and had only fallen into a peaceful slumber near morning. He felt guilty waking her, but he found he couldn't leave without holding her one last time, without, he thought, offering what might be a final goodbye to her and his child.

Her cheek was rosy warm to his lips and she only stirred at his caress, but when he sat on the bed, her eyes slowly opened and she smiled before she remembered.

"I have to go," he said softly. "Hussein Pasha is three days from Kars."

"Oh, dear," she whispered, her quiet exclamation full of fear, her gaze quickly taking in his uniform and readiness.

"I've only a minute…they're bringing up my mount. Masha will take care of you. An escort will see you to Tiflis. I love you, *dushka*, with all my heart…and the child, too," he finished in a husky whisper.

She tried to steady her voice before she spoke, knowing he had to leave, knowing the Empire relied on his cavalry corps to help win Kars, knowing her wishes were incidental to the tide of events sweeping over them. "Go with God, Stepka," she said, reaching for him, her voice trembling, her tears spilling over.

He crushed her in his arms, his own eyes wet with unshed tears. "You're my life, *dushka*," he whispered into the softness of her hair. "Take care of our child—" he steadied his voice with effort "—and don't ever forget what we had together…"

His words frightened her, as if he wouldn't be with her to

raise their child, as if he wouldn't be coming back to her. "Be careful," she cried, clinging to him, wanting to hold him forever, wanting to know he was safe in her arms.

"I never take chances," he lied. And when she looked up at his ambiguous phrasing, tears streaming down her face, he added, "I promise, darling, to be careful." His kiss was gentle, honey sweet.

Her mouth tasted of tears and he wished for a moment life weren't so fragile. But the outcome of his race south hung in the balance and with it, perhaps, the future of Kars…and his own future. As a soldier he'd always accepted the uncertainty of life; as a risk taker, he understood it better than most. But as a husband now and a father-to-be, suddenly he felt exposed and unguarded, the delicate balance between victory and death a precarious distinction he'd never considered before. He'd never questioned the duration of his golden halo of protection.

A soft knock at the door interrupted his thoughts.

"I'll be right there," he said. "I have to go," he added in a quiet voice, his simple words intense with feeling. Gently unclasping Lisaveta's arms, he pulled away, gazed at her for a moment more and without speaking stood. The room smelled of her fragrance, and while his men waited he found himself regarding her a few seconds more, as if he were memorizing her image against an uncertain future.

Lisaveta's golden eyes were still soft with sleep, her cheeks flushed a delicate rose, and her lips where he'd just kissed her were still slightly parted, lush like perfect ripe fruit. She was nude beneath the covers, her smooth shoulders and arms and the rise of one breast framed by the blue silk coverlet. She was perfect beauty, she was his adored wife, the mother of his unborn child, and he had to leave her.

How hard it was this time to return to the campaigns that had been until then his entire life. How hard it was to leave her. He shut his eyes briefly and drew in a slow fortifying breath. "I love you," he said in almost a whisper, and then turning, he strode from the room.

Moments later he was mounted, his revolver belted at his waist, his Kurdish knives tucked into the wide leather belt, handy to his reach. He'd checked the ammunition in his rifle in an automatic reflexive action before slinging it across his back. After speaking a few quiet words to Cleo, he took the black burkah offered him and threw it over his shoulders against the predawn chill. Wheeling his horse, he glanced at his mounted escort arrayed in faultless formation behind him.

"Ready, Excellency," the lieutenant replied to Stefan's silent inquiry.

He took one last look back at the lighted window in his railway car, his features expressionless, then bending forward slightly, whispered to Cleo. Her ears twitched as if in answer and she took two prancing steps. The road to Tiflis was familiar to her, and as Stefan straightened in his saddle, she plunged forward.

Lisaveta cried while Stefan's troop galloped down the tree-shaded boulevards of Vladikavkaz and clattered over the Terek bridge; she cried as they rode across the valley plain and began climbing toward the Tomar pass. She cried great gulping sobs as the horses dug in to ascend the sharp incline, their hooves throwing up the rough black gravel of the area. With Stefan riding off to war she might never see him again. He could be dead in a few days, and...if they had a child... Fresh tears of fear and self-pity poured down her cheeks.

But as the sun came up over Guz Damur, falling alike on Stefan's mounted company and his railcar at Vladikavkaz, Lisaveta shakily wiped her tears away, trying at the same time to steady her breathing. Sitting up, she pushed the covers aside. She realized she could cry a thousand years if she wished but it wouldn't bring Stefan back or make him safe. Militza was waiting for her in Tiflis; Stefan wanted her to continue south to his home and stay there with his aunt until the war was over. Although she would have preferred a site closer to Kars, when she'd tried to persuade him the previous night he'd been adamantly opposed. The front could dramatically change, he'd said. Cavalry flanking movements often swung deep and wide, and he didn't want her in jeopardy of capture by the Turks or Bazhis. Aleksandropol was too close to the border, offering little security should the Russians be pushed back. And after her capture last summer, her cavalier attitude about the ease with which one could travel through a war zone had been forever altered. Stefan was right of course, Tiflis was safer, but knowing that didn't make her any less miserable.

First she had to dress. Walking over to the built-in closets opposite the bed, Lisaveta selected a beige serge traveling gown trimmed in black silk braid, one of her numerous trousseau garments. She washed next in the small but luxuriously appointed bathroom adjoining Stefan's bedroom and found herself somewhat cheered by the hand-painted tiles decorating the walls. The glazed tile was a misty blue-green, reminding one of the color of the sea, and at eye level was adorned with a decorative border of frolicking sea creatures. Stefan had names for most of them and she smiled, remembering his facetious introductions of sea life. She felt better when she smiled, and as she dressed her melancholy lifted from the gloominess she'd wallowed in an hour ago. Stefan had always led a charmed life; he was a competent soldier, a brilliant soldier. She'd dwell instead on the positive. So saying, she took one last look in the mirror and opened the door into the small corridor.

When she walked into the parlor a dozen steps later, three officers and Stefan's valet, Ellico, were standing at attention. She instantly received four very correct bows as though she were a person of consequence, a natural result, she realized, of being married to the Tsar's favorite commander, a sudden transformation from her unpretentious past. How long had they been standing there at attention? she wondered with a nervous start. What if she'd decided to wander in in her chemise—or less. Their entire journey had been devoid of servants save for the times food was left on trays, and she hadn't realized the absence of servants was on Stefan's orders. They were present, of course, for Stefan traveled *en prince* as a matter of course; they had simply been out of sight.

"Is Her Excellency ready to travel?" a young subaltern inquired with deference, his white uniform immaculate, his expression studiously reserved.

"Yes, thank you. Do I need a wrap?"

"His Excellency has seen to everything, Your Excellency," he replied, homage and awe in his tone.

Stefan wasn't a mere mortal to this young officer and she, by association, took on a similar distinction. Would she ever learn to be comfortable with such formality and pomp? She was used to building her own camp fire and cooking if necessary when she and Papa traveled with a minimum of guides to some of the more remote areas of the Trans-Caucasus. She certainly was familiar with seeing to her own comfort and care.

"Please call me Lisaveta," she said, in an effort to reduce the rigid deportment, her smile winning.

Her statement apparently stunned the three young officers who'd been entrusted by Stefan with "the most precious woman in the world," to quote their superior, and none of them was sure how to respond to such an irregular suggestion.

"I would prefer it," Lisaveta quietly said, as the surprised silence lengthened.

"Yes, Your Excellency…er…madame…that is…Lisa—veta." The poor man struggled with his sense of protocol and Lisaveta's wishes.

"Stefan would wish me to be comfortable," Lisaveta added, and with her words, the supreme stamp of approval was assured.

All three officers smiled.

Stefan's valet smiled.

"As you wish," their spokesman said, and all four bowed in precision.

Stefan's valet, dressed in blue silk robe and red turban of his Kurdish clan, stepped forward, a small wrapped parcel in his hand. "From His Excellency, Your Excellency," he said, his sense of propriety undiminished. His family had been personal servants to endless generations of Orbelianis and familiarity would be unthinkable, but his smile was genuine and his relayed message touching in its sensitivity. "His Excellency, the Prince, wishes you a safe and happy journey, Your Excellency." The package he placed in her hand was wrapped in blue velvet and tied with gold twine, and Lisaveta fought back her tears at Stefan's thoughtfulness even in the haste of his departure.

"Thank you," she said softly. Then, determined not to embarrass the man they all revered, she added in a voice steadied by sheer force of will, "I'm ready whenever you are."

Stefan's carriage was luxurious, a larger version of the conveyance she'd originally taken from Tiflis months ago. Extra springs had been installed against the primitive quality of the military road, the seats were padded in down and upholstered in silk velvet. Even the walls and floors were covered in thick carpeting to soften the rough jarring of the journey.

When she was alone and the carriage under way, Lisaveta opened Stefan's present. Inside a gold and enamel box, precious in itself, was a small gold locket displaying three oval compartments when opened. A hand-colored photo portrait of Stefan was framed in one compartment and Lisaveta was surprised to see her own image in another. She was wearing her wedding veil in the portrait and she marveled at the speed necessary to develop and tint her picture. And then she recalled Stefan's remark about "his" photographer, whom he'd brought along. She'd assumed the man was needed for the campaign in some way. He was essential instead for this gift.

The third oval was without a picture but its existence was explained in Stefan's familiar hand. "For Baby," he'd written on parchment cut to fit the frame, and a note was tucked into the box.

For a future mama from the proudest papa in the world.

All my love,
Stefan

A baby's picture would be fitted into the small empty frame someday, an astonishing thought in the current turmoil of her emotions. Tentatively placing her hands over her trim stomach, she waited to feel some sign. When would she first know for certain? How soon would she begin to see the changes occur? She wished she had the competence to judge like Alisa or Nikki, who seemed positive. Or even Stefan. But so swiftly had events occurred, she found herself still having to remind herself she was Princess Bariatinsky. She thought about all the new alterations in her life as the carriage rolled through the dark defiles and sunny valleys…about Princess Bariatinsky the wife, and Princess Bariatinsky the mother-to-be. How different they both were from the woman she had been before Stefan, when study and scholarship were her whole life. She had thought herself content then, looking forward to each new day of translation and learning, feeling often an actual friendship with the scholars of Hafiz who had preceded her, recognizing styles and handwriting patterns even in the anonymity of medieval times. But she had come to learn that serenity wasn't equal to passion or contentment commensurate with intoxicating happiness. And this awful and desperate sadness she was feeling now was the price for her loving.

She wished, hoped, yearned to have Stefan's child, a child born of this very special love, a child she hoped would bear a strong resemblance to its father. The next unbidden thought slipped past her defenses. If…if the war didn't go well—a euphemistic phrase for her darkest fears—if…something were to happen to Stefan, he would live on in their baby, he would be with her still.

She needed Masha for support, she thought, frightened and fainthearted; she needed her for reassurance against the nameless terror inundating her soul. Masha would assure her in her blunt straightforward way that Stefan was always victorious; she would reaffirm the fact Stefan was never wounded, he had a guardian angel. Masha would give her courage.

Glancing out the window she saw the snow-covered peaks rimming the distant horizon, noted the numbers on the black-and-white road marker, estimated the number of hours left before they reached Tiflis and prayed in a simple plea, simply put, for strength to withstand all her tormenting anxieties.

Stefan and his men traveled at a full-out gallop, changing mounts regularly from the reserve horses that had been left saddled and ready at all the post stops on the military road. Everyone understood time was precious, any delay could mean the difference between success and defeat. Hussein Pasha might somehow overcome all of nature's obstacles and bring his army to Kars before them, so they rode as if devils from hell were pursuing them. They arrived in Tiflis an astonishing eight hours later, sweat-streaked and dirty, the afternoon sun almost tropical in the sheltered valley.

While his troopers were served a hasty meal, Stefan left to meet with Militza and his solicitor, who were waiting for him in his library. He'd telegraphed from Vladikavkaz before leaving to arrange for Gorkov's presence and sent two additional messages from forts en route so they could estimate his arrival time.

After brief congratulations on his marriage were given and accepted, they immediately concentrated on the business Stefan wanted conducted. Time was at a premium, everyone understood, each minute potentially costly. Gorkov was settled with dispatch at a writing table. Militza had a fresh uniform for Stefan laid out on his desk and without modesty he began stripping off his filthy jacket and issuing instructions. "My will is to be changed in favor of my wife and child," Stefan stated, tossing aside his tunic and bending to pull his boots off.

Gorkov, who hadn't been warned of Stefan's prospective fatherhood, manfully concealed his surprise. "Very good, Your Excellency," he managed to reply in a neutral tone, although his cheeks flushed red at the startling news.

"Do you have time to eat?" his aunt asked as Stefan slid off his breeches. His men were being fed in the morning parlor by a staff on alert since Stefan's last telegram.

"No." He shook his head briefly. "I'll eat on the road. In the event of my death," Stefan briskly went on, stepping into clean leather riding pants, "my wife will inherit everything, my child's portion to be held in trust until its majority." His tanned fingers efficiently buttoned his breeches as he continued. "I think that's fairly simple. In the event the Taneievs attempt to extort more than their settlement share, I'll rely on you and Masha to protect Lise and my child from their depredations." He shrugged into his tunic and swiftly began closing the fastenings. "Fight them in court, but see that Lise and the baby are guarded. I don't trust Vladimir...he's not above the most perverse machinations."

Tugging on his boots, he continued, his voice as crisp as his actions. "Haci will stand as foster father in my place for whatever duties you feel, Masha, are required."

"If he lives," his aunt softly said.

"Yes," Stefan acknowledged, his hands steady, no sign of emotion evident as he strapped on his pistol belt over his immaculate white tunic. Looking up, his voice suddenly husky and an octave lower, he said, "You'll see to things for me, Masha," and opened his arms to her.

She went to him as she had so often in his youth and held him close. He was much larger now than he'd been all those years ago, and poised and assured. She'd seen him overcome much in his young life with equanimity if possible and fighting spirit when necessary. He towered above her, his arms wrapping completely around her now, but he depended on her strength, too, and she'd never fail him. "I'll protect them, Stefan," she said, steadying her voice against her own strong emotions, "as you would yourself."

She seemed so much smaller and more frail each year, he thought, and he wondered when that gradual change had altered their relationship, but he knew she had the courage and the power to protect his family. Swallowing to suppress the lump forming in his throat, he tried to deal with his deep-felt feelings: his childhood memories both happy and sad, never forgotten, only buried for a time; his overwhelming love for Lise, joyous but clouded, too, with loss and all the ominous considerations contingent on the battle for Kars. "Our Kurdish warriors will stand guard, as well," he reminded her. "Rely on them." There wasn't time to deal with emotion.

He moved his aunt away at arm's length and with an attempt at a smile said, "Wish me luck."

"May all the gods watch over you," Militza whispered, gazing at the formidable soldier who had replaced the young boy she'd once consoled. "And don't worry about Lise," she added in a more forceful tone. "I'll see that she and your child are well cared for."

Bending low, he kissed her gently on the cheek and then his hands dropped away from her shoulders. Turning to his counselor, he put out his hand. "Thank you, Gorky, for coming at such short notice." His grip was strong and his natural courtesy brought a smile to Gorkov's face.

"It was my pleasure, Excellency."

Stefan smiled, glanced in swift survey at the papers on his library table that Gorkov had arranged in neat succession and began moving toward them. "I'll sign the papers now and you fill in the particulars. If you have any questions—" he looked over to his aunt "—Masha will make any decisions I may have forgotten."

Militza nodded, unable to speak. His words were too final this time. A new restlessness invested his mood and behavior, although anyone less familiar with Stefan might not have noticed. He was seriously aware for the first time of the impermanence of life. This stop to meet with Gorkov wasn't husbandly efficiency, it was dark premonition.

Stefan reached for the pen Gorkov was holding out for him and a few moments later his task was completed. "Thank you, Masha; thank you, Gorky." He gave a brief flash of his dazzling smile. *"Au revoir."* And he was gone.

Charged with poignant feeling too new and dear to discuss with Militza, Stefan sprinted up the staircase to the bedrooms on the second floor. Entering his room, he walked directly to the small traveling desk that had been his father's. Sitting down, he drew out paper from the gilt-mounted drawer for what might be his last message for his family. Writing to Lise first, he told her how much he loved her, that no superlatives however profound could ever adequately convey his feelings. She was his entire happiness, his world, and he missed her terribly already. His thoughts were brimful with her enchanting image and he'd write every night—if possible. "If I shouldn't return," he wrote at the very last, the words reluctant to be formed by his pen, "I'll always be at your side. From my heart, Stepka."

Folding the page, he slipped it into an envelope with Lisaveta's name boldly scripted on the outside and propped it on his mantel so she'd be sure to see it.

Returning to his desk, he began the most difficult letter he'd ever written, because the simple act of writing meant he was acknowledging his mortality in words, and acknowledging the foreboding shadows of doom that had been plaguing him since Moscow. He wrote slowly, each word melancholy in its implications, for he was addressing his unborn child in a letter the child would only receive if he himself died at Kars.

All his life, Stefan had been conscious of an illusive spirit, a guardian jinn protecting him. Now, in the past few days, he'd experienced curious sensations, elusive shivers of gloom giving warning his charmed life might be over—just as his father's had so suddenly been cast away—and he'd relied on intrinsic luck too long to ignore his feelings.

"Dearest one," he wrote, trying to imagine what his child would look like—chubby and pink and precious as a king's ransom.

> I wish you welcome on your day of birth and kiss your sweet face. If I could have been with your mother holding her hand today, I would have been the happiest of men. I love you, dearest one, with all my heart. Kiss your mama for me and hold her close.
>
> Watching over you,
> Papa

He would have liked to say so much more; he would have liked to tell his son or daughter of the pleasures life held in store, of the joy the birth would bring to the house of Bariatinsky-Orbeliani and to himself; he would have liked to leave a note for every day of his child's life so it might know him, too, and love him. But the desktop clock seemed to be talking to him as its small pendulum swung before his eyes, the soft ticking echoing in the silent room. Hurry, it was admonishing, or all might be lost; hurry, it warned, Hussein Pasha is on the march; hurry…hurry…hurry.

So he addressed an envelope simply "Baby" and slid his note inside. Should he leave it with Georgi to give to Lise later or send it to her in the coming months, or should it go with his will to be read…when necessary? He sighed, debating the options, uncertain, finding it too difficult in the end to reach a decision. Sealing the note, he left it lying on the desk and, standing, took a last look around the room that had been his since adolescence.

Touched by an overwhelming melancholy, he paused at the door for a final glance, then softly closed the door behind him.

Eighteen

~~~~~⟡⟡⟡~~~~~

When Lisaveta's carriage arrived late that evening, her drivers having been under orders from Stefan to travel slowly for the sake of his wife's "delicate health," the entire palace was ablaze with lights, and before Lisaveta could alight, the staff appeared en masse on the drive as if they'd been waiting behind the cypress and rhododendrons lining the raked gravel.

As Lisaveta was handed down from the blue-lacquered carriage, Militza hurried forward to embrace her. "Welcome, Lise, darling, to your home," Stefan's aunt declared warmly, her voice joyful, her smile beaming. "We are all ecstatic with Stefan's choice of bride."

"Thank you, Masha," Lisaveta replied, enchanted with the extent of her reception, wanting very much for Stefan's family and retainers to like her. "I'm happy to be here."

Militza was already leading her over to the line of servants. "You must say hello to everyone. We've all been on pins and needles since word of the wedding reached us. What a clever boy, Stefan is," she added like a doting parent, patting Lisaveta on her arm. "You're perfect."

Lisaveta couldn't have asked for more warmth and affection from Militza and all the staff. As she passed down the line of bobbing and curtsying servants she couldn't have felt more welcome at her own estate. Georgi had a brief speech after which he motioned forward a young child who was carrying a large bouquet of yellow roses. The little girl forgot her lines, but she blushed prettily and thrust the flowers toward Lisaveta with her eyes closed. Stooping down to her level, Lisaveta thanked her and asked her her name.

"Tamar," she whispered so only Lisaveta could hear.

And when Lisaveta hugged her, she immediately became the darling of the staff. Their Prince had done well, they all agreed, exchanging significant smiling glances.

Lisaveta had cautioned herself on her long journey to be realistic about Stefan's participation in the war, to face it stoically as he would wish her to, and she hadn't intended bringing up the subject unless Militza did so first. But as they ascended the stairway into the palace, she found herself asking, "How did Stefan seem when you saw him?" At Militza's hesitation, she quickly added, "He passed through Tiflis, didn't he?" A tiny hope that existed beyond the limits of her logic wished Militza would say he was upstairs sleeping or at the stables organizing his gear or something equally prosaic.

"Stefan stopped briefly this afternoon," Militza said, relegating tiny hopes back to their dreamworld, "to change his uniform and allow his troopers a meal. He stayed no more than twenty minutes with Hussein Pasha on the move." She didn't mention the will, for she knew Lisaveta would find the subject distressing. "How was your journey from Vladikavkaz?" Militza said instead. "Did you find it tiring?"

Lisaveta glanced at the enormous bronze doors opening before them as two liveried footmen put their shoulders to their weight. She thought of Stefan riding somewhere across the high plateau under the same moon that illuminated Tiflis and said with a true weariness, "I *am* fatigued."

"It's the baby and natural. Stefan is vastly pleased," Masha added when Lisaveta's expression indicated her surprise. "He's telling everyone."

"Everyone's so certain," Lisaveta replied in a small voice.

"Stefan says he counts better than you do." Militza was smiling.

Lisaveta blushed.

"You've made him very happy." Her voice was unsteady for only a second before she stabilized it. "And I thank you for that, although,'' she went on, her mouth quirking into a smile, ''I must warn you, the staff is taking this very personally, as well. A new heir to the Bariatinsky-Orbeliani family has been thirty-two years in the waiting.''

Lisaveta laughed with delight, pleased with Stefan's effusiveness and the staff's warmhearted reaction. ''I mustn't disappoint them then.''

''I wouldn't recommend it. I believe they've begun assembling a list of appropriate baby names. Stefan said they can select one of the names.''

''He *is* pleased, isn't he?''

''He's enormously excited, although he's taking pains to appear placid. You've brought him more joy than he'd ever hoped for.''

''I don't know how I lived before I met him. I only hope…I hope it never ends.''

Lisaveta's tone was so melancholy at the last, her thoughts plain. ''Stefan's always been a very lucky man, my dear,'' his aunt assured her, ''and his bodyguard will protect him with their lives. You mustn't worry or fret for his safety. It might harm the baby. Now come,'' she said, taking Lisaveta's hand, ''Chef has insisted on greeting you with a royal repast and if you don't at least taste his numerous dishes, he threatens to cut his wrists.''

''He wouldn't,'' Lisaveta whispered, startled out of her despondency, unfamiliar with the tempestuous personalities of the south, ''would he?''

''We've never dared tempt his stability, my dear.'' Aunt Militza's smile was bland, as though servants threatened suicide every day. ''You needn't eat much,'' she added with a mildness that ignored the drama of the event. ''A taste will do.''

After Lisaveta refreshed herself briefly and changed into a comfortable frock, dinner was served: an incredible spectacle, a sumptuous procession of twenty-two courses, colorful, artistically served delicacies that had obviously been all day in the making. Lisaveta tasted each dish carried in on gold plate while Chef stood beside her, beaming. When the last sweet had been admired and sampled, she said, "Thank you, Josef, I must write my husband and tell him of your genius. Everything was superb."

Josef's smile widened, his red cheeks glowed. "The Princess is most generous."

"Now, Josef," Militza declared, her voice both cordial and firm, "you've intimidated Princess Bariatinsky enough for one night. Kindly have another bottle of Stefan's special golden-white wine brought up and you may all go to sleep."

"Yes, Your Excellency, of course," he replied docilely, as if he hadn't acted the prima donna for the past hour. "As you wish." He bowed himself out with elaborate ritual, followed by the rest of the footmen.

"The staff adore you," Militza said. "You don't know how pleased I am, since Stefan considers them all his family. Thank you, by the way," she added with a smile, "for humoring Josef."

"It wasn't any great sacrifice, Masha, his talents are superb...although at the moment I feel I won't need to eat for a month."

"Some mint tea will help." She raised her hand in an almost imperceptible gesture. Immediately four servants appeared from behind ostensibly closed doors, and Lise marveled both at Masha's casual assumption that someone would come at her small movement and at the servants' hovering presence.

"Mint tea for Princess Bariatinsky. The baby has eaten too much."

Lisaveta colored a soft pink from her throat to her eyebrows.

Masha smiled benignly and four servants beamed down at Lise as if she were the first woman in the universe to have a child.

When the tea and wine were served the ladies retired to a small alcove overlooking the twinkling lights of Tiflis and talked of the war. Militza told Lisaveta the topic was prominent subject matter for the entire population of the city. Word had come yesterday to the general public that Hussein Pasha was advancing toward Kars and the possibility those reinforcements would get through struck terror in the hearts of Tiflis's citizens.

If the Russian army was defeated at Kars, the Turks could march on Tiflis; every coffeehouse and café were undoubtedly crowded with patrons discussing the morbid possibilities, and every private conversation and public debate centered on the need to hold Kars.

"How was Stefan?" Lisaveta asked.

"Rushed and distracted," Militza said. "He didn't even have time to eat."

"Was he worried?" Terrified for his well-being, Lisaveta wanted reassurance.

"No," Militza lied. "Stefan's been fighting the Turks for years."

"Will he get there in time?" It was everyone's fear.

Sitting across from Lisaveta on a white satin loveseat, Militza replied, her dark-eyed gaze direct, "Stefan has never failed."

"I didn't want him to go." Lise's voice was almost a whisper.

There was no adequate or comforting response. Militza wished there were. "He loves you very much; he'll be back." He would try, she knew; he'd fight his way through hell if he had to. She just hoped his strength and courage were enough.

"I'm so afraid." Lisaveta's tea was untouched before her, her face pale with fatigue, her apprehension visible in her golden eyes.

"You'll feel better in the morning. All the black melancholy seems worse somehow when one's tired." Militza wished she could offer some guarantees, something more substantial than platitudes, but it was a deadly game about to be played out at Kars and she couldn't bring herself to lie about that fact. "Drink your tea," she soothingly said, "and then go to sleep. Everything will seem less daunting in the morning."

"I'm sorry to be so fainthearted." Lisaveta's smile over the rim of her teacup was rueful.

"Your concern is natural, my dear. Very soon, though," she added, her smile bolstering, "the Turks will be defeated and we'll *all* breathe easier. You must sleep now." Lisaveta had faint lavender shadows under her eyes. "I'll have you shown up to your room."

"Could I see Stefan's room?" Setting down her teacup, Lisaveta rose. "If you don't mind." She wanted to feel his presence before she slept, wanted to see glimpses of his spirit, wanted to touch his pillow and hairbrush, sit in his chair, smell the scent of him on his clothes.

"Of course." And with the smallest gesture of her hand, a footman appeared. "Are you going to be all right?" There was solicitude in Militza's voice, for Lisaveta's desolation was obvious.

Lisaveta nodded.

"Would you like company?" Militza felt helpless to mitigate her pain. Lise was so new to the warrior's culture, too swiftly separated from her husband, a stranger to so much in Stefan's life.

"No, thank you," she softly replied, "if you don't mind."

They were both being painfully courteous, anxious to please each other.

Militza smiled and then chuckled. "Darling, this is *your* home. Please do exactly as you please."

Lisaveta smiled back. "I see you must have had a hand in Stefan's upbringing."

"One never actually had a hand on Stefan so much as simply being there to pick up the pieces. He was a headstrong boy." Neither her tone nor her expression was disapproving. "He has in fact," she finished, "been the joy of my life."

"He does that, doesn't he?" Lisaveta's features were less grave, her golden eyes taking on a warmth. "Without even trying."

"He does indeed," Militza emphatically replied.

A few moments later, Lisaveta stood on the threshold of Stefan's bedroom suite while the footman lighted several of the wall sconces. The gas flames shimmered and fluttered briefly before the crystal fixtures turned into a brilliant glowing white, and when he left she remained motionless just inside the door, her gaze taking in her husband's bedroom for the first time. One entire wall was curtained in white gauze, luminous now as the moonlight competed with the fitful shadow and light of the enormous interior space, glistening white against the green silk of the side draperies and valances.

Walking slowly over to the windows, Lisaveta remembered a warm summer night scented with lily, and leaning her head against the gossamer curtains, she felt the coolness of the glass beneath her forehead. The warm summer was gone, their time in the mountains long past; she could feel the chill of fall in the air and the bleakness of fear in her heart. So recently married, she might as swiftly be widowed, she morbidly thought. And tonight when she wished Militza to offer her assurances, Stefan's aunt had instead been more subdued than expected. How did soldiers' wives cope? Was there some prayer for consolation, some wish or hope one could petition for, some solace in this awful loneliness?

She moved then as if drawn by invisible hands to Stefan's large bed. The balconies fronted all the bedrooms in this wing and this room was very similar to the one she'd stayed in last time, but Stefan's bed was different, larger, darker, more masculine, a mahogany-and-tulipwood marquetry cut on massive lines. Climbing up onto it, she sat in the middle of the forest green expanse of silk coverlet, looking like a flower blossom in her peach silk gown, her skirt in poufs about her, her glance surveying the immensity of the room.

And that's when she saw it.

A note directly in her line of vision, an envelope with her name on it propped against the mantel. Her heart stood still.

Sliding off the bed, she approached it cautiously, dread and longing both prominent in her mind. Stefan had written it. Short hours ago he'd held that exact envelope in his hand, his words the closest she could come to having him near. She wanted to snatch the letter down and devour the words and feel for a transient moment as though he were here. But apprehension held her hostage against that impulse and she stood beneath the ornate and polished mantel, reluctant to know what her husband might have written her before riding off to war.

She lifted it down finally because her longing was greater than her fear. But the weight of that fear crumbled her to the floor, where she sat before the small fire the footman had set before he left and read Stefan's letter. She cried as his words unfolded across and down the page; she cried for their beauty and tenderness, for his sweetness and devotion. He was more articulate in many ways than she in expressing the imagery of love.

"When the war is over," he'd written, "we'll join the eagles in the mountains and show them our new baby...I can scent the wind and freedom even now."

There was hope in his words and a love so intense she hardly noticed the menace of the closing phrase he had written so reluctantly.

She reread his scrawling script over and over, his strength evident in the rhythm and form of his letters, his spirit alive in his words. In the silence of his room, surrounded by objects familiar to his world, his cologne lingering in the air, photos from childhood displayed on the walls and bureau tops, she could almost hear him speak of his love for her. She could almost hear his deep rich voice echo within the confines of his bedchamber, his love surrounding her, and she prayed to all the benevolent gods to protect him and bring him safely home.

She slept that night in his bed with his note clutched in her hand, as a young child might cling to a cherished toy or a young woman ardently in love to her lover. She dreamed of mountain landscapes and moss-covered mountain pools, of starlit ceilings and a rain-damp bridegroom on a honeymoon night.

It wasn't till morning that she found the second note. She was dressed already and wandering about Stefan's room, thinking as she walked: he sat here and stood here and brushed his long dark hair before this mirror and wore these slippers in his leisure and wrote at this desk—

The small white envelope was addressed with the single word "Baby."

It lay pristine and chaste on the red-embossed leather of the desktop.

He'd left no instructions concerning its unsealing, although addressed as it was to their baby, the implication was perhaps

to wait until its birth. And she intended to, she decided a moment later, as if that punctiliousness would annihilate the panic
beginning to creep into her mind. There was no need to write
to their child now; he'd be home certainly—at some point—in
the months before its birth.

She moved back a step as though she were standing on the
brink of an abyss.

She found herself a moment later seated on a chair on the
far side of the room, clutching the chair arms with undue force,
her eyes trained on the stark white envelope. *Why* had he written?

She poured herself a glass of water from the carafe on the
nearby table and moistened her dry mouth, forcing herself to
look away from the object of her terror. Catherine the Great's
tall cypresses stood majestically against the blue morning sky,
marching down the hill in solemn procession, immune to the
years and her puny fears. She wished she could deal as tena-
ciously with her emotional turmoil and persevere like Catherine's trees.

In the end she rose, walked over to the desk and opened the
envelope as perhaps Stefan had intended.

No! she silently screamed as she read. No! No! *No!* She felt
herself trembling when she'd finished, her heart beating in her
chest as though she'd run ten miles. Stefan had written this
note to his child because he wasn't coming back!

"Masha!" she screamed into the sun-dappled silence of the
room, struck with fright, unable to move. *"Masha!"* she cried.
A bird sang its morning song somewhere beyond the window
as though it were unaware shadows were beginning to cover
the earth. "Masha," she whimpered, helpless against her pain,
a great darkness overtaking her, and she crumpled to the floor.

Lisaveta woke in Stefan's bed, Militza holding her hand, the
room filled with hushed and reverent servants. She remembered
instantly, and her eyes filled with fear.

"You mustn't worry," Militza said, wishing she could
soothe that trepidation. "Stefan wouldn't want you to worry."

"I'm frightened, Masha," Lisaveta breathed, her voice so faint it was barely audible.

"He didn't mean to frighten you, Lise. He only wanted to talk to his child before he left." Militza stroked Lisaveta's hand as one would a distrait child.

"He'll be back?" It was a heartrending plea.

"Of course he will," Aunt Militza firmly declared. "Stefan's invincible." But her own confidence was shaken by Stefan's note. His tone was almost prescient, alarming in a man who'd always felt indomitable. "Would you like to see the vineyards or Stefan's special Barb horses? We could take a small picnic with us and make a day of it." She could have been coaxing a small child.

"When do they plan on attacking?" Lisaveta's voice was strained, her mind immune to the distractions Militza offered.

Militza debated a moment the style of her answer and then decided on the truth. "Tomorrow," she said.

Stefan rode into his cavalry corps headquarters at midnight to find his entire staff had been on the ready since word of Hussein Pasha's march had been received. When he walked into the large tent, a cheer went up and he smiled. "We're slightly pressed for time, I hear," he said, stripping off his gloves, his grin remarkably cheerful. "But we're conveniently *ahead* of Hussein." A collective sigh of relief went round his officers. Prince Bariatinsky was back in time.

A magnum of Cliquot materialized, and while it was being poured, Stefan accepted all the numerous congratulations on his sudden and novel state of matrimony. He took the teasing good-naturedly.

"So you're finally leg-shackled," one of his brigade commanders said, his smile wide. "You're the last one we thought would succumb."

Stefan's brows rose, his eyelids dropped marginally and he observed his grinning officers for a moment with a narrow-eyed smile. "I recommend it," he said.

"In a bit of a hurry, Stash?" Loris Ignatiev sportively inquired, friends with Stefan long enough to press for details.

"I didn't want to give the Countess any opportunity to change her mind." Stefan's reply was mild, amused and unmistakably untrue.

"Was that all?" Loris apparently wasn't going to be satisfied with evasion.

The telegraph line must have been completed, Stefan drolly thought. "You may congratulate me," he pleasantly said. "I'm about to become a father."

"Hip, hip, hooray!" Their cheer brought the dogs in camp into a second-round chorus, and Stefan had to sustain a great number of friendly back-slapping felicitations.

"It'll be the richest brat this side of the Tsar if you're not careful tomorrow," one of the young captains said.

"Don't worry, Karev, I'm going to do my damnedest to make sure my child waits a long time to inherit." Joking about death was common practice, a kind of relief for everyone's tension.

"Speaking of death, how was Michael?" Captain Tamada was a Daghestani Prince and as such found Grand Duke Michael's military incompetence more exasperating than most.

"Polite," Stefan softly said with a quirked smile. He'd stopped first at the tent of the Chiefs of Staff and had been treated with the deference he accepted as his right. Everyone realistically understood that not only was he an extremely competent and successful general for Russia but he also controlled most of the border tribes in the Trans-Caucasus. His name alone could muster a hundred thousand mounted warriors. Not all were presently campaigning for the Tsar, but those not actually committed to Russia at least remained neutral. There wasn't a border tribe that would take arms against their Prince.

"Now, then," Stefan genially said, as though time were not of the essence, "if we've covered all the gossip sufficiently, what say we get down to business?"

Fresh tea was ordered and Stefan unrolled the maps he'd worked on during the train ride to Vladikavkaz. For the next hour he issued orders, explaining in detail what he wanted, what he expected of the cavalry in the attack, what he anticipated as defense from the Turks. His officers took notes, asked questions when they needed clarification, their attention riveted on the tall dark-haired man with the crisp clear voice. Stefan's tanned hands moved gracefully over the maps, detailing the nine forts of Kars, its citadel and numerous batteries and redoubts, pointing out small features of the terrain or indicating areas to approach with caution, stopping occasionally to punctuate his recital with a sharp stabbing finger. He was deferential to his officers, asking for their opinions when he'd fully described the assault plan, listening to those opinions with courtesy and attention. He rubbed his neck from time to time to ease the tension and fatigue from his muscles. Or stood completely still for long periods, concentrating on the details of his officer's recitals, the lantern light modeling his face in dramatic chiaroscuro. When the discussion became repetitive, when mild arguments erupted as to technique, he politely said, "Any more questions, gentlemen?" and after a moment of silence, for they recognized his dismissive tone, he smiled and gently added, "Very good. Wake me in an hour." And lifting the tent flap, he walked out into the cold night air.

In his own tent, his batman had his cot turned down, a new uniform laid out, hot water at the ready and food set out on clean white linen.

"Ivan," Stefan said with grinning affection, "we have the amenities again, I see." Everything was immaculate. "You've been busy during the hiatus. What would I do without you?"

Ivan beamed with pride. "Your father trained me well, Excellency." Fifty years ago Ivan had been a young serf saved from hanging over the theft of a chicken he'd taken to feed his starving family. Stefan's father had interceded, paid the villainous landowner for the chicken *and* Ivan's family and offered Ivan a position. His devotion was unconditional.

"Are we going to win this tomorrow, Ivan?" Stefan asked with a smile as he began washing his hands in the copper basin set on a table near his cot.

"The Bariatinskys are always victorious in battle, Excellency."

Stefan looked at the small elderly man beside him holding a crisp white towel out for him. "I like your confidence," he softly replied, Ivan's peasant certainty in some measure more reassuring than his officers' confidence, as though the very earth and spirit of Mother Russia had affirmed his victory.

Stefan found he couldn't sleep, though. Until tonight he'd always been able to doze off immediately, a habit honed to perfection after years of campaigning, a necessity when sleep was often limited. But now when he should, he couldn't, and he lay on his cot with his eyes closed so Ivan wouldn't fuss.

The battle was going to be desperate, he knew, and its outcome decisive to the war. And, irrelevant to the assault on Kars but oppressively relevant to his sleepless mind, he missed Lisaveta with a wretched miserable despair. There had never been a woman he cared about on the eve of battle so he'd been able to sleep on horseback, on the hard ground, in rainstorms and blinding sun. He'd never loved a woman before and now it colored every thought he entertained as well as those he tried to avoid. It made him hopelessly sad and wildly happy, it caused him to lose much-needed sleep and it impinged dramatically on the assault on Kars.

He might never see Lisaveta again, or ever see his child, he realized. The reflection struck him like a blow and he held his breath for a moment, frantically rationalizing away that possibility. He was never hurt, he reminded himself, never wounded. He was charmed. The familiar phrases should have been more comforting. Two weeks ago they would have been enough, even a week ago they would have been acceptable, but in that time his life had irrevocably changed.

Ivan swiveled around when Stefan abruptly sat up.

"I can't sleep," Stefan brusquely said. "Could I have a glass of tea?"

He dressed while Ivan made fresh tea, putting on his boots and clean tunic, strapping on his revolver belt and his sword scabbard decorated with his Saint George ribbon. At the last he added an extra cartridge bandolier and placed the long-bladed knife within easy reach in his belt.

Standing, he drank his tea and then the small glass of arrack Ivan always handed him before an attack. It warmed his throat and he smiled at Ivan and thanked him. The familiar activities eased the disturbing turmoil in his mind and brought the focus of his thoughts back to the assault.

"We'll dine at Kars tomorrow, Ivan," Stefan said, sliding his hands into his pigskin gloves. "Wish me luck."

"May God ride with you, *batioushka*," Ivan quietly replied, kneeling to kiss Stefan's hand, and as he rose he sketched the sign of the cross in the air between them, the orthodox religion a politic adjunct to his peasant superstition. For added assistance he murmured a cossack maxim having to do with a good horse and strong sword arm, surreptitiously gesturing to ward off the evil eye.

Stefan was smiling broadly when he stepped out into the chill night air. How could he lose, he thought, with God and the peasant spirits on his side?

The troops had been moved into position in the past hour under cover of the moonlit darkness. As was customary for him, Stefan went among his men, talking to them, telling them just what they were to do, offering encouraging words and good-natured chaffing, promising the musicians they would play a waltz in the streets of Kars tomorrow, answering the question asked a hundred times, his smile white against the darkness of his face. Yes, he would be leading the assault in person.

Stefan would be leading the Eleventh Cavalry Division, twelve battalions strong, on the right wing, directing their columns against the Karadagh and Tabias forts, guardians to the citadel. The cavalry had the most serious task to perform—the initial charge, clearing the way for the infantry—and everyone knew, although the orders hadn't yet been given, that they were to carry the forts at any cost. For twenty minutes or more Stefan conversed with his men, taking special care to talk to his noncommissioned officers, who bore the brunt of the decision making once the attack began. When he was satisfied each understood his directives and goals, he stood at the head of his troops for a final prayer. As he always did before battle, he asked for courage and God's grace to see them through. His dark hair whipped by the wind, Stefan stood, head bowed, and spoke the words so they carried across the moonlit army, his men murmuring the prayers with him, row upon shadowed row, calling on God's succor in the coming hours.

This final prayer was a ritual learned at his father's knee, comforting more for the litany than the content. As a cultivated man, Stefan realized Mukhtar Pasha prayed to his God for the same victory. In the end it would be men and not gods who determined the outcome, but the rhythm of the phrases soothed him and the priests' chanting was a calming, familiar musical undertone to the restless agitation gripping him before an attack.

A low hum of conversation broke out afterward as each soldier spoke for a final time to his companions. Haci was trading facetious remarks with one of the Kurdish troopers. The numerous cavalry officers around Stefan were exchanging comments or smoking their last cigarette or checking their weapons. For a small space of time, Stefan stood alone in the midst of his cavalry. Shutting his eyes, he shook his hands briefly at his sides to stimulate the circulation—for his sword grip would be essential in the coming minutes—took a deep breath, opened his eyes and quietly said, "Mount up."

His muted order was immediately obeyed, as though his soft voice had carried to every man in his corps.

Leaning forward in his saddle, he spoke to Cleo, promising her green pastures and respite when Kars was taken, his fingers smoothing the soft velvet of her ears, his voice so low it didn't even carry to Haci at his side. Whether Cleo understood the words or merely responded to his tone and the preparations for battle, she turned her head for a moment and looked at him with her large intelligent eyes. She'd carried Stefan across the plains of Asia on the Kokand campaign and in every battle since with as charmed a life as his own. A bond existed between them that was based not just on sentiment but on mutual need.

With a brushing stroke down her neck, Stefan straightened and turned to survey his officers and men formed in ranks behind him. His cavalry was mounted in tight order, knee to knee. Circassians, Kurds, Daghestanis, cossack lancers and some of the elite Gardes, the grenadiers and infantry arranged behind them by battalion. All eyes were on Stefan, the only general who actually led his men himself, dressed in his white Gardes uniform on his favorite black horse, his tattered banner flaring in the wind, the pennant as medieval in appearance as his Circassian standard bearer dressed in surtout and helmet. The square of silk fastened to a cossack lance had the white cross of Saint George on one side and on the other the letters *S.B.*, for Stefan Bariatinsky, and the date 1872 in yellow on a red ground. It had been carried throughout the Kokand campaign from the taking of Kazan to the subjugation of the Kirghez tribesmen, carried beside him in all the fights that had made him famous as the best young commander in Russia.

The cold was intense and penetrating as they arranged themselves in order of attack in the ravines at the base of the steep ramparts guarding the forts, the wind chilling their blood. A full moon shone from a dark blue sky on the waiting men, on the open plain and valleys of the foothills, on the snow-wrapped mountain ridges glimmering in the distance. A remarkable silence invested the thousands of men, a total silence, for after days of bombardment the guns and cannons had now fallen mute. Even the Turks would now know that an attack was coming after weeks of artillery fire spaced fifteen minutes apart, day and night.

Gazing up at the formidable bulk of Karadagh and Tabias, forts built by Prussian and English engineers to withstand any conceivable attack, Stefan surveyed the ground he knew so well he could see it in his sleep and picked out the routes for each of his battalions in the shadows of the rocky incline.

He was ready, his men were ready, the Turks were holding their breath for the assault.

The time had come.

Wrapping his reins lightly around his left arm, leaving slack for Cleo to maneuver on her own, Stefan raised his right arm and a pulse beat later swept it forward, his signal for the music to play. With banners flying, the Eleventh Cavalry Division disappeared into the cloud of dense white smoke that erupted before them.

The advancing columns were a dark mass in the haze of defensive artillery and rifle fire, moving upward, wavering at times under the intense Turkish volleys, hesitating in instances until supporting regiments carried the mass farther on with their fresh momentum, the army always rolling forward despite the varying terrain or circumstances in an undulating propulsion of human bravery. Stefan rode through the torrent of rifle fire, unmindful of the bullets, his mind once again free of personal concerns, his concentration solely on the progress of the battle, placing himself where he saw encouragement was most needed, moving back and forth across the line of assault urging his men on, rallying them when needed against the withering fire. Men fell around him, his officers and escort were cut down, but he seemed immune to the bullets flying past him, always in the thick of the barrage, impelling his men forward.

Nineteen

~◎~

Behind their redoubts, the Turks were firing with such rapidity a flaming red line of fire tore into the advancing columns. As they drew closer to the entrenchments the second and third attack battalions slowed down and began to falter. In horror, Stefan saw the first break begin, the first men turn in retreat before the annihilating fire storm, and knew not a moment could be lost or his men would lose heart. He had only two battalions of sharpshooters left in reserve, the best in his detachment. Quickly waving them forward, he put himself at the head of these, picking up the stragglers in his rush forward, reaching the troops that were considering retreat and giving them the inspiration of his own courage. He gathered up the whole mass as if with a single sweeping motion of his arm and carried it toward the redoubt with a rush and a cheer.

The entire fortress before them was like a vision of hell, enveloped in flame and smoke, the steady crash of deadly rifle fire a lethal barricade they must cross, but his men pushed on because their general was a dozen yards ahead of them and they wouldn't fail him. Stefan's sword was shot in two twenty yards from the ramparts, tossed aside and replaced in a reflexive blur of motion from his saddle scabbard; his uniform was covered with mud and filth, his cross of Saint George twisted round on his shoulder, his face black with powder and smoke, but he charged forward the last few yards with a savage yell and Cleo soared over the last ditch, the scarp and counterscarp,

over the parapet and swept into the redoubt like a hurricane.
Stefan was smiling, feeling the old frenzied energy and brash-
ness. He heard his own scream with a sense of exhilaration,
heard the answering roar of his troops streaming in behind him
and knew his men would follow him anywhere.

Like a pressured damn breaking, the Turkish defenses crumbled against the onslaught of an army that shouldn't have been
able to reach their entrenchments, that should have retreated
against the superiority of their Peabody-Martini rifles, that was
led by a maniac they all recognized as the phenomenal White
General...Bariatinsky.

And twenty bloody minutes later the Tsar's army had taken
the redoubt.

The question then was how to hold it, dominated as it was
by the Tabias fort, exposed to the fire of sharpshooters concealed behind the next line of trenches and the artillery sights
of the citadel. Stefan knew they would be counterattacked.
Mukhtar Pasha had no other choice but to try to retake Karadagh and hold that and Tabias at any cost. Both armies understood the significance of the forts protecting the entrance to
the citadel.

In less than ten minutes, Stefan's cavalry met the first rush
of the regrouped Turks, giving the grenadiers and infantry time
to scramble over the parapets, giving the last reserves time to
advance up the hill, and ten minutes later what was left of the
cavalry faced the Turkish counterattack pouring down the
earthworks toward them.

The fighting was brutal. Stefan and his Kurdish troopers
were in the thick of the combat, slashing and parrying, slashing
and parrying, the motion of their sword arms dogged and automatic, their bodies numb to any sensation save the drive to
survive. Sweat streamed down their faces despite the frigid
temperatures, their bodies pumping adrenaline in a frantic effort
to thwart death, their minds concentrated with focused intensity
only on stopping the next fatal blow...and the next...and the
next.

They fought mechanically without thought, by instinct alone,
their skill a fusion of courage and tactic so ingrained the ques-

tion of breeding or training was moot. They fought for two hours on the parapets and parade ground and paved squares of a fortress the English and Prussians had guaranteed invincible. They fought while the sky turned a dull gray and the stars lost their brilliance.

Stefan's uniform was no longer distinguishable as white; it was bloodstained and torn from numerous wounds, the worst a saber cut on his right shoulder that had cut clear to the bone. He was fighting now with his left hand. Cleo's reins were wrapped around the saddle pommel, for his right arm was useless even for the light guidance his trained mount might need. Cleo was lathered and foaming, her black coat sleek with moisture. Haci and his men, sword and dagger in hand, marshaled around Stefan, committed to protecting him with their lives. Twice in the past hour Stefan had sent for reinforcements, but in the melee of battle there was no guarantee his dispatches had gotten through and his position was becoming untenable.

With a feeling of unease, Stefan heard the ominous drumbeats of another Turkish attack, the rapid staccato rhythm signaling another sortie. His men heard it too, and knew the sound to be a warning of disaster. Even if Stefan's call for reinforcements had reached their base camp, the ascent up the side of the glacis was so precipitous that troops couldn't be brought up with the same speed as Mukhtar Pasha's attack force, and after hours of fighting, Stefan's remaining men were exhausted, low on ammunition and grimly aware the next Turkish assault could be mortal.

Calling on his last reserves of strength, reaching down beyond his pain and fatigue to an inner strength that had carried him through countless campaigns in the past when the odds were as slim or worse, Stefan shouted to the men, his voice hoarse and raspy, and rode toward the advancing Turks pouring over the entrenchment. They had to stop this attack or all would be lost; he had to rally his men or the hours of fighting would be in vain; he couldn't allow this Turkish counteroffensive to succeed or all the lives lost would have been useless.

Raising his sword high, he spoke to Cleo, nudging her forward with his knees. With her own valiant spirit undiminished, she broke into a trot.

The Turkish rifles ripped into his first line, his bodyguard began to fall, and a moment later Stefan's forward cavalry was fully engaged, the infantry short yards behind. They fought like men with their backs against the wall, knowing there were no options short of death. Soon the ground was slippery with blood, strewn with the dead and dying.

When Haci fell, Stefan saw him go down in the extreme border of his peripheral vision and, shouting for help, jumped from Cleo to go to his aid. The remaining seven of Stefan's guard followed him, and standing back-to-back against the Turks, they protected Haci with their bodies. The waves of Turks seemed unending as Stefan and his bodyguard stood in a circle on the paving stones laid in an intricate variation of a herringbone pattern. They kept coming while daylight rimmed the horizon; they kept coming while Stefan and his Kurds stood unflinching; they kept coming as Turkish bodies piled up in heaps around the phalanx protecting Haci, Stefan's men firing their revolvers in relays like a well-choreographed ballet of death.

But their own casualties mounted, too, against the expensive modern Peabody-Martini rifles the Ottoman Empire had purchased from America, and at last only three of the phalanx remained standing, and then, ten bloody minutes later, none were left....

The battle washed over their bodies in the muted light of dawn, as though their gallant stand had never existed, as though their human lives were no more than a flicker of an eye in the cosmic universe, as though the heir to the Bariatinsky-Orbeliani fortune and honor were a grain of sand on an ocean shore and the battle for Kars a vast tidal wave.

The Tsar's soldiers came up at last as color brightened the sky in numbers sufficient to force a Turkish retreat, but the Turks fought like demons, street to street, house to house, to the very end. Kars was their most important stronghold, the Sultan had poured a fortune into its defenses, and their generals and ruler and religion offered them paradise if they died in its defense. So they died instead of surrendering; they stood and fought at each corner and barricade; the citadel was emptied of defenders, the auxiliary forts and trenches were emptied, and hour after hour the Turks fought until at last it was over.

As the autumn sun shone feebly from its midpoint, a silence began to gather, a silence of dead men and victory, a silence of exhaustion and weary triumph, a silence of Turkish defeat and hesitant Russian hope. The Russian cries began sporadically then, small rejoicing hurrahs from parched throats, exhalations of personal good fortune from men too tired to shout, smiles exchanged with adjacent comrades-in-arms. They had won, they began to realize. The Tsar's army had gained the impregnable, the unconquerable citadel of Islam and its defenders were vanquished. Hurrah! Hurrah! Hurrah!

But only minutes after the roars of victory rose into the chill air, the shouting triumph died away and a still and utter quiet fell over the Russian army. Rumor spread like wildfire through the ranks, the awful news greeted everywhere with breath-stopping despair. The White General, the Field Marshal's admirable son, the Tsar's favorite young general was dead. After the barricades into the city had been breached by his single-handed effort, he'd been slaughtered in an assault of superior numbers, his faithful Kurds fighting with him to the death. Before he could claim victory for having defeated the Sultan's army of the east, he'd fallen.

At first they couldn't believe it. The Prince was never even wounded in battle. It wasn't true, and soon he'd appear to discount the dreadful rumors. But then the fires broke out, set off perhaps by the artillery fire, and when the munitions' dump ignited, half the western escarpment exploded into the sky. The winds picked up the red-hot ashes and the citadel was aflame in less than an hour.

When the blazing inferno was under some control a day later, the awful truth was finally accepted. Prince Bariatinsky must be dead. He might have survived the battle, but no one could have survived the explosion and the apocalyptic fire.

The Empire had paid a grievous price for its victory over the Turks. Many said it was too great; Kars wasn't worth Prince

Bariatinsky's life. The Tsar was said to have cried when news of Stefan's death was telegraphed to Saint Petersburg. He shut himself away for half a day, not allowing even his dearest Catherine to breach his solitude, and when he emerged, his courtiers thought he'd aged ten years.

An hour later the church bells began their sorrowful dirge, from Saint Petersburg to Baku, from Odessa to the emptiness of the Siberian tundra. Throughout the Empire of the Tsar, Stefan Bariatinsky's death was mourned.

Lisaveta went pale when she heard the mourning bells begin to ring, their pealing measured dirge carried on the twilight air up from the valley below, from the thirty-odd churches and bell towers, like a personal message of disaster. Without reason or thought, without need for clarification—for Stefan himself had sensed what lay ahead—she knew...before the Viceroy came. She knew for whom the bells tolled, as though their mournful clamor were directed toward the white marble palace overlooking Tiflis. He's dead...clang, clang, they rang. The Prince is dead...clang, clang. The Prince is dead and dead and dead, clang, clang.

Later in the formal drawing room, Militza sat beside Lisaveta and held her hand as the Viceroy told them what he knew of Stefan's death. The details were still sketchy but Kars had been taken, thanks to Stefan's rallying charge. The citadel was aflame in areas so his body had not yet been recovered, but eyewitnesses had seen him and the last of his Kurdish warriors overrun by a Bazhi attack. Militza asked the necessary questions because Lisaveta found it difficult to respond graciously to a man Stefan had despised.

"Thank you, Prince Melikoff," Militza said at last with a cool dignity that rose to Melikoff's sad and awkward mission, "for bringing us what news you have."

"The archbishop is planning a memorial service tomorrow if you ladies feel able to attend," he mentioned on rising to leave.

"Thank you, we shall," Stefan's aunt replied. "Stefan is a hero to this city."

"To the Empire," the Viceroy added, his manners impeccable.

Lisaveta could no longer conceal her despair. She sobbed openly, fresh tears streaming down her face.

"If you'll excuse us," Militza softly said.

That night Lisaveta slept on Stefan's bed surrounded and atop Stefan's clothes, which she'd carried from his wardrobe. She'd taken scores of his garments and piled them on his bed. His scent lingered in the linen and silk and fine wools, and she'd curled into a pitiable cocoon of misery, snuggling deep into the familiar fragrance of the materials as an injured animal burrows deep into its den to nurse its wounds.

She'd understood on a rational level that men died in battle; she'd even dealt with the fearful possibility of Stefan's death in battle since he'd gone. Or she'd thought she had. She'd known he was celebrated for his daring and bravado, that he wore his white Chevalier Gardes uniform as a taunt to his enemy, as a badge of his own courage…and he'd run the risk for years.

But until this awful moment she hadn't understood the bottomless depths of despair; she hadn't realized it would hurt to breathe, that every second of the day or night she would think, I'll never see him again, never touch him again or laugh when he laughs or know someday he'll come walking through the door again.

And he never would now.

She was so empty inside that she felt as if her own spirit and soul had departed, too. Thoughts of heaven or paradise or God's mercy didn't help or offer any solace because no philosophy, no matter how benevolent, could ever replace Stefan in her life.

Militza did her best to comfort her through the long hours of the night. Her first husband had died in wartime and she understood the desperation of Lisaveta's loss, but she knew too that the time for condolence was later. The grieving came first, the inexorable anguish and pain and tears.

Her own sense of loss was sacrificed for some future time when she could mourn her beloved nephew away from Lise.

Stefan's wife needed her strength and comfort now, not her tears. Thank all the angels in heaven that Lisaveta would have Stefan's child to love, Militza thought, although in her present stricken state of hopelessness she was too distrait to find solace in that fact.

"I want to die, too," Lisaveta murmured, lying in Stefan's bed, too pale and quiet, her voice detached somehow as though she'd partially left the world already.

"No," Militza said simply, offering no argument or banal commonplace. "I won't let you," she finished, her dark Orbeliani eyes fierce with determination. Stefan had left his wife and child in her trust and she wouldn't fail him. "Your baby needs you," she gently added.

"I can't even feel the baby," Lisaveta whispered. She was now certain there would be one, but despair overwhelmed her. "Maybe it died, too."

"Nonsense," Militza replied, her voice soothing despite her emphatic denial. "It's too early to feel the baby...Stefan's baby," she added, taking Lise's ashen face tenderly between her hands. "Stefan's baby," she whispered, willing herself not to cry. "The baby he wanted so much.... Do you know what he ordered before he left for Kars?" Militza began talking then of the plans Stefan had made for the baby. He'd ordered toys in Saint Petersburg, given carte blanche to Madame Drouet for a layette, left instructions for the estate carpenters to add a rocking horse to the nursery like the one he'd had as a child. The Tsar's physician had been retained for the months before Lisaveta's delivery and would be arriving in Tiflis soon after the new year. He'd even said he wanted a grove of cypress planted when the baby was born to commemorate its birth.

Her words seemed to rouse Lisaveta from her lethargy so she continued speaking, telling her of Stefan's childhood, of his first words and toddling steps, of his favorite puppy and pony, how he'd learned to ride almost before he'd learned to walk. She spoke of the way he thrived on competition and soon could outride, outfight, outswim and outrun all the other young warriors. She described Stefan's love for Tiflis and the population's adoration of their Prince. He conversed with everyone when he went down into the city, Militza said, stopping in the cafés or talking to the people in the street. There were times his strolls took on the look of a parade. She depicted Stefan at length in all the varied facets of his life because her conversation kept Lisaveta from drifting away, because each word she uttered seemed to bring her back from the void of her wretchedness, because each memory and reminiscence of Stefan made him more alive and less dead, and the images could be added to Lisaveta's own loving memories of her husband.

"He was a generous warmhearted man," she quietly finished, pleased to see some color back in Lisaveta's cheeks. "And he loved you very much."

"This baby will be part of Stefan, with his beautiful eyes, perhaps, or his smile," Lisaveta murmured, Stefan's presence so real for a moment that she drew in a breath of surprise. "Was he always tall?"

"He was tall in a country of tall men," Militza replied with a smile, rejoicing in Lisaveta's first sign of interest, her first words implying a future.

"We'll teach the baby how to ride young like Stefan." Her golden eyes had taken on life.

"Or her," Militza softly suggested.

"Or her," Lisaveta echoed, her voice warm with feeling. "It's up to us to see to Stefan's wishes, isn't it?" she went on, more animated, some of the old resourcefulness Stefan had admired prominent in her tone. And sitting up slowly, she brushed her heavy chestnut hair away from her face. She smiled, a small rueful upturning of her mouth. "He wouldn't have tolerated all my self-pity, would he?"

Militza smiled back. "Not for long," she quietly replied. "Stefan believed in taking charge of one's life."

"He did, didn't he?" Her pallor had been replaced by a rosy glow of health and her expression was wryly musing.

"Sometimes with a vengeance," Militza said with a wide smile.

"In that case," Lisaveta said, lifting up one of Stefan's shirts and beginning to fold it away, "I mustn't let him down."

How resilient youth is, Militza thought, seeing the ashen

wraith of moments ago restored to a healthy bloom. And how valiant and brave, she mused, gazing at the beautiful young woman who'd brought such happiness to her nephew. "Stefan would be proud of you, my dear," she said softly.

The rumors started almost immediately after his death because the bodies of Stefan and his Kurdish bodyguard had never been found. The logical explanation took into account the fire that swept through the citadel after the battle, a fire that had spread so fast and burnt so high the night sky had been lighted up for a hundred miles. Half the dead bodies and unfortunate wounded were cremated where they lay. The screams of the dying had been more horrible than the bloody hours of battle. The night sky, survivors said, echoed with their shrieking agony, like a scene from hell.

The added and awful tragedy cast a pall over the glorious victory.

But it was the apocalyptic nature of the fire that fueled the first stories of Stefan's rise from the dead.

The mystic tendencies of the peasant mentality and the religious imagery of the common soldier deified in a pagan mythical hopefulness the best and favorite of their leaders. Stefan had always possessed a personal bond with his army; he had fought at their side, ate, slept and suffered with his soldiers, understood their fears, shared their triumphs and the intimacies of their lives. They would not relinquish his memory and refused to concede his death. The White General, the Prince, the Savior of Mirum had never been defeated. Even Kars, the citadel of citadels, had fallen before his courage. He couldn't be dead, no more than he could be defeated.

He'd become a pilgrim, they said, like the pious and gentle Alexander I, wandering the countryside and steppes and forests, searching for peace, seeking solace in the solitude of vast Mother Russia. To touch him was good fortune; to see him even from afar was acknowledgement from God that a better life lay ahead...a life without suffering and pain, a life of serenity and peace.

* * *

Nikki heard the rumors very early, no more than two weeks after the battle. He accepted them as natural for a country unable to come to terms with Stefan's death. The loss of Russia's favorite general had struck the Empire to the core; there was no one to replace Stefan in temperament and charisma, in competence or ability.

Another two weeks passed but the rumors of Stefan's resurrection persisted; they were, in fact, augmented daily by additional reports and new tales. Nikki considered himself a pragmatic man, so he ignored the stories at first when he heard them at the club or in the military offices, and he'd patiently listen to the latest hearsay with a tolerant courtesy. Then one day Haci's name was mentioned in the most current report of Stefan's reappearance. Stefan was in the mountains, rumor had it, nursing his aide back to health. Details were included this time by a villager who had supposedly talked to him.

Nikki went home and set his valet to packing.

And then he went in search of his wife to explain his impractical journey.

Alisa was in the nursery, rocking baby Georgi. When her husband declared his intention in an erratic presentation at the same time hopeful and hopeless, she gazed at him over the head of their youngest child sleeping in her arms and said, "Could it even remotely be true?" Her thoughts were on Lisaveta.

"Realistically, no one could survive the fire," he replied with a small sigh. Nikki had spoken with many of the survivors and he wasn't optimistic about "even remotely." Bodies had been charred to ashes in the flaming inferno. The fact Stefan's body hadn't been recovered wasn't an isolated incident. Thousands of men had disappeared into ashes. "I don't know what to say—" he shrugged, his expression grave "—that won't sound pessimistic…"

"Yet you're going," his wife softly declared. "Why?"

"To set my conscience at ease, I suppose. And for Stefan," Nikki slowly said. "Because I'd want him to look for me, too, even if it was a chance in a million."

* * *

Nikki arrived in Tiflis four days later. He spoke to Militza first for he wasn't certain how Lisaveta was dealing with Stefan's death. If she wasn't emotionally stable, he didn't wish to inform her of his mission. He felt compelled to follow the rumors however unprosperous their substance, however fruitless his search, because his friendship with Stefan demanded it. But something in him did insist on hope. What he hadn't mentioned to Alisa, for it seemed too tenuous even to himself, were his own feelings about Stefan's extraordinary will to survive. In fact, over the years they'd been friends, he'd often wondered if Stefan *recognized* the finality of death or whether he'd do battle with the grim reaper, too, when his time came. And since his body had never been identified—although in the charred remains of so many tragic souls, his could have been as unrecognizable as any other—Nikki retained the minutest, unsubstantial, inexplicable hope Stefan might have lived.

With all his heart and every dim, obscure mystical interpretation of his spirit, he wished the rumors true.

A month had passed since the fall of Kars, slightly longer still since Nikki had seen Lisaveta on her wedding day, and she looked altered walking into the morning room, paler, more delicate, her luminous eyes strangely otherworldly and underscored with dark and melancholy shadows.

"You must eat," he said immediately, rising to greet her.

She smiled. "I am, Nikki, for Stefan's child."

"You're too pale." He took her hands in his and gazed at her in the judgmental familiar way of family. Was she too slender? Her hands perhaps too cool? Did the cranberry shade of her gown accent the whiteness of her skin? She wasn't wearing black, he noted, but knowing her own strength of character and Stefan's superstitious dislike of mourning attire, he wasn't surprised.

"Well, I'll contrive to get out more," she replied politely, aware his concern was motivated by affection and not inclined to argue with him. But in truth, she rarely went out anymore. "You look fit," she declared, intent on transferring the subject away from herself.

Nikki was tanned and lean, dressed in chamois hunting

clothes. "Thank you. Come, sit. Militza must see you go out more," he added with a significant look at Stefan's aunt. "She tells me you're strong enough to hear what I have to say." He was abrupt but pressed by an internal urgency, his thoughts absorbed by his quest. He found he didn't have patience for socializing.

Lisaveta didn't answer immediately, her gaze having swiftly shifted over to Militza, who was seated on an embroidered settee near the sunny windows.

Nikki in turn surveyed Lisaveta for a troubled moment, wondering if he'd be mistaken offering her such slender hope. She was far from robust, her appearance causing him some concern.

Nikki hadn't traveled this distance without some purpose, Lisaveta realized, and for a wishful moment she overlooked the ominous quality of the term "strong enough" and dared to hope. As swiftly, more prudent reflection intervened and she calmed herself, knowing nothing he could say could hurt her beyond the pain she'd already endured. "Don't look so dreadfully worried, Nikki," she declared placidly, "I'm quite healthy."

As she seated herself in a graceful flow of cranberry wool, Nikki pulled up a chair opposite and, sitting down, debated briefly how best to begin. "You've heard the rumors," he decided would be suitable preface. His identical golden eyes held hers in a steady gaze. "About Stefan," he added, because her expression was so emotionless he wasn't sure she understood.

"Only recently," she answered after a short silence.

As Nikki's brows drew together slightly in puzzlement, Militza, seated off to one side, beyond Lisaveta's direct line of vision, indicated to Nikki with a finger to her lips that she'd withheld the information.

"Yesterday, in fact," Lisaveta went on, noting the direction of Nikki's glance, aware suddenly why she hadn't heard sooner. Her face seemed to light with an instant excitement. "Is it possible—"

"The stories are most likely the apocryphal kind that followed the death of Alexander I fifty years ago," Nikki interrupted, not wishing to raise false hopes. "In fact, I'm sure they're equally fanciful, but—"

This time Lisaveta interrupted. "Take me with you." Her statement was unequivocal, touched with an intensity that seemed to vibrate across the small distance separating them. She didn't ask for further clarification or detail. She'd understood immediately why Nikki was in Tiflis and intended including herself in his search.

Nikki shook his head. "It's too dangerous. The fighting is still sporadic around Kars and Erzurum. Although treaty negotiations have begun, no truce has been called yet. I can't expose you to that danger."

Lisaveta looked toward Militza for support. "We could bring some of the grooms...for added safety."

"I'm sorry, my dear, Nikki's right," Militza replied, regret and apology in her tone. "Stefan wouldn't want you to risk your life."

"I'll keep you informed of my progress," Nikki offered, "and send back reports."

"When will you leave?" Lisaveta inquired politely, as though she weren't determined to accompany him, as though her mind weren't already organizing the provisions she'd require for travel in a war zone, as though her bland expression weren't hiding a tumultuous excitement. If there was the slenderest chance Stefan were alive somewhere between here and Istanbul, between here and hell itself, she intended to find him. In fact, when she'd first heard the startling rumor yesterday of the sightings, she'd smiled, as though the words alone had brought him back to life. Once her initial rush of joy had been mitigated by more logical realities and a flurry of questions to Militza, she'd cautioned herself against treacherous dreams, had reminded herself of the magnitude of the fire sweeping Kars. But her spirit had steadfastly ignored practicality and reason; her spirit had begun to hope. And now Nikki was here like a gift from God. Her guide, as it were, in her search.

"I'm leaving in the morning," Nikki replied in answer to Lisaveta's casual inquiry. "Militza's kindly offered the use of Stefan's stables."

"Cleo's back, you know." Her voice was mild but inside she was giddy with elation. Had Cleo's escape been a sign?

"Yes, I'd heard." Militza had taken him to see Stefan's horse directly after he'd arrived at the palace. Eyewitness accounts reported Cleo had been taken as a trophy when the Turks had overrun Stefan's forward position. She'd been hauled rearing and squealing from the scene only to return to camp three days later. And Nikki had thought on hearing the story, had Cleo known Stefan still lived that day? Animals had an affinity, a closeness to their masters beyond the understanding of man. Had she fought to stay with him and returned to his tent to wait for him? Even now she seemed restless and unquiet; she'd tried to break out of her stall twice, Militza had said. It wasn't the normal despondent behavior of a pet mourning its master's death.

"Stefan's been seen with a companion, I understand." Lisaveta's face was no longer pale but infused with vitality and the flush of health. Not only her wishful dreams were involved now. Nikki's presence here indicated a serious plausibility; he wouldn't have taken on this journey without some credible evidence. "Are the same stories circulating in Saint Petersburg?"

"I only heard of a companion once." Nikki didn't mention that the single fact of Haci's name had brought him south for fear of kindling impossible expectations. "The accounts have generally described him alone, in native dress. No mention's been made of wounds or illness, but surely he had to have been seriously hurt. *If*," Nikki carefully added, "the rumors have any substance at all."

"Thank you for taking on this...mission of verification," Lisaveta calmly said, sure her heartbeat could be heard pounding clear across the room. She studied Nikki for a cautious moment, fearful he'd noticed her agitation.

But her cousin seemed to accept her statement at face value. "If nothing else," he said quietly, wanting to make his own expectations clear, "the myth of resurrection will be nullified."

"Yes, of course," Lisaveta agreed, congratulating herself on her novice acting abilities, simultaneously deciding her fur coat was a necessity for the highlands' autumn climate. "Militza,"

she said by way of disassociation, "one of Stefan's coats will
fit Nikki, don't you think? Perhaps the black marten." Did that
sound suitably acceptant and passive?

"Why, yes, I'm sure it will," Militza said, concealing her
relief at Lisaveta's apparent concurrence.

And the day progressed in preparations for Nikki's journey.

Lisaveta and Militza were up early the following morning to
wish Nikki and his escort Godspeed. Provisioned for a month,
they carried additional warm clothing, for snow had been falling sporadically in the mountainous heights near Kars since
September, and November weather could be extremely cold at
those altitudes. Nikki promised to telegraph each day so they
could follow the direction of his search, and with his clearance
from the Tsar, travel in the war zone should not present problems.

Lisaveta pleaded a headache after Nikki's departure, a complaint Militza viewed as reasonable after their busy schedule
yesterday. She then retired to her room and swiftly changed
into a serviceable leather split skirt and matching jacket made
for fall riding. Into a knapsack she'd pulled from Stefan's
closet she crammed an astrakhan jacket, one of Stefan's wool
sweaters, a scarf, riding gloves, a knit cap, a change of under-
clothing and an extra blouse. Snapping the clasps shut, Lisaveta
tossed the bag on her shoulder, and creeping silently down one
of the servants' staircases, she exited the palace through a side
door near the kitchen.

The grooms were startled by her request but obeyed without
question, and in twenty minutes Lisaveta and two of Stefan's
young grooms, hurriedly equipped for travel, were on Nikki's
trail.

Twenty

They overtook his party shortly after midday because Nikki and his men had stopped to lunch and Lisaveta, counting on that eventuality, had pushed on.

"I suppose I'm not surprised," Nikki grumbled, waiting in the middle of the road for her to reach him, his gloved hands braced on his saddle pommel. He'd observed Lisaveta and her escort through his field glasses ten minutes before and, swearing a blue streak, had pulled his horse to a halt.

"I don't imagine I can convince you to turn around and go back to Tiflis," he growled as she cantered up. Each word was a blighting rumble.

"I won't slow you down," Lisaveta declared, full of cheer and unaffected by his annoyance, her cheeks flushed a healthy pink from her ride. "I promise." She was five hours out of Tiflis, perhaps five hours closer to Stefan, or at least, if nothing else, she was accomplishing something other than her aimless walking the past weeks through the great empty corridors of Stefan's palace.

"You might harm the baby," Nikki admonished, his black hair whipped by the wind coming down from the highlands.

"Native women ride until they deliver. I'll be fine."

"If you were a native woman," Nikki sardonically replied, "I wouldn't be concerned."

"I won't go back." Her terse statement was in the style of an imperial edict, and Nikki, married to a woman of singular independence, recognized the tone. Lisaveta's hair was tucked up into a scarlet wool cap and she looked very young in her green leather riding costume despite her air of royal prerogative.

"You *will* slow us down," he asserted, "if I'm allowed the last word." He was smiling now, very faintly, but smiling. He was familiar with assertive women, and he was damned, he thought, with a small resigned sigh, if he didn't admire her pluck.

"If it makes you smile, cousin Nikki," Lisaveta replied with charming acquiescence, "I'll always allow you the last word."

"Or near to it," he teased.

"Yes," she sweetly replied.

They traveled southwest for a week, climbing steadily out of the more temperate climate of Tiflis into the chill mountainous regions approaching Kars. Four days before they'd changed into their fur coats, and they were stopped more often now so Lisaveta could warm up occasionally at a camp fire and walk a bit to maintain the circulation in her feet. But they also halted often to question the native populace about Stefan.

The Kurdish nomads inhabiting the high plateaus around Kars were well acquainted with the Orbelianis, their liege lords until a scant two decades ago when Russia had nominally replaced the old feudal systems of authority. The individual tribes were still faithful to the Orbeliani interests over and above their employment as irregular cavalry to a variety of paymasters. If Stefan had appeared among them, even had their employer been the devil himself, they would have protected him.

But none of the tribes had seen him, neither as pilgrim nor wounded soldier, although all had heard the stories; not a single new scrap of information was gleaned from the natives on their journey upland. Last week the Turkish army had retreated yet again, they were told, and was moving now toward a last stand at the walled and fortified city of Erzurum, for with the fall of Kars the war had turned decidedly in favor of Russia.

They soon overtook Russian troops bound for the offense on Erzurum and often stood aside to let the ambulance trains pass on their trek back to Aleksandropol. Each time, Nikki spoke to the officer in charge: Had they heard any more rumors? Had anyone of Stefan's description been seen? In the case of the ambulance trains, he'd asked to see any unidentified wounded. He wouldn't allow Lisaveta to view those unknown soldiers for most were a heartrending sight.

But the answers were always no. Everyone was aware of the rumors, but not a single person had any more information than the hearsay they already knew. And each day took them deeper into the unpopulated highland, brought them nearer Kars, left them with an intensifying sense of isolation. With winter almost upon them and the snow increasing, the nomadic tribes had disappeared, moving southward to better grazing land. As the miles passed, the movements of troops and wounded became more infrequent, as though the desolate landscape had swallowed up the tiny specks of humanity traveling across its snow-covered vastness.

Their search for Stefan or some trivial clue to his whereabouts that some soldier or officer or local native might recall seemed at times overwhelmingly impossible, a Herculean task sure to defeat their puny human efforts. Even if Stefan had survived the crematorium blazing across the field of Kars, the land was too large, too harsh and inclement to sustain an injured man, too isolated and bereft of habitation.

The morning of their last day of travel before reaching Kars was bitterly cold. Although their tents had been pitched out of the wind in one of the deep ravines slashing through the snow-drifted plateau, and Lisaveta had slept under fur robes, she was freezing when she woke.

"You shouldn't be here, Lise," Nikki said, wrapping his coat around her and helping her settle near the fire. His dark beard, which had grown out during the passage south, was rimmed with frost, his face reddened by the cold.

"I have to, Nikki," she answered, her eyes burning golden bright. "I'm fine." But her face was without color and he could see the effort it took her to keep from shivering.

"Here, this will take off the chill." He handed her a steaming cup of tea from a small trivet placed near the fire. One more day, he decided; they'd talk to the commander left at

Kars, and if he couldn't substantiate the rumors, they'd return to Tiflis. He couldn't further jeopardize Lisaveta's health. "Perhaps today," he said with an encouraging smile, "we may hear something."

Lisaveta smiled over the steaming cup she held to her lips, grateful for Nikki's kindness, forever indebted to him for his determined search for Stefan's remains. She wasn't insensitive to the odds they were facing, and while she dreamed of finding Stefan alive, she knew in her heart the possibility was almost negligible. But this journey was her own private pilgrimage— of hope and need and mourning. Tomorrow she'd grieve her husband's death at the site of his last victory.

The stories of Stefan's rallying charge, the monumental importance of his storming of the western fortifications, his cavalry's heroic stand against the counterattack, which allowed the infantry time to scale the heights, had been related to them every day of their passage south. The recitals had come from officers and enlisted men, from the wounded soldiers returning home and from native warriors who passed them on their travels back to their home villages. All had regarded Lisaveta with the deference due Stefan's widow, calling her "little mother" and kissing her hand, wishing her health and happiness, offering blessings on their child. She'd never realized completely until that journey into the mountains how Stefan had been worshiped and universally loved by all segments of society, by people who had had the good fortune to know him as well as those who only knew of him for his heroic deeds. And each time another person spoke of Stefan with reverence and admiration, she thought how lucky she had been: he had loved her.

Their final day before Kars was silent, conversation difficult when everyone realized their quest had been fruitless, their destination very near and no additional clues unearthed.

"We'll stay the night," Nikki said when the citadel came into sight, an enormous stone fortress spreading across the jagged escarpment, protected on two sides by the hundred-foot drop to the Kars River below. "In the morning we'll talk to the commander, and then if you feel strong enough, we'll start back to Tiflis by midday.''

Lisaveta's first impulse was to refuse, but she was aware that Nikki's tolerance had been pressed beyond his or anyone's limit. His voice, both weary and resolved, indicated that any refusal would be useless. ''I'd like to see…where Stefan…died,'' she softly replied, ''and then I'll be ready to return.'' She understood this was the end of her pilgrimage.

Nikki's sigh condensed in the brittle cold air, only to be swept away in the next moment by the strong northwesterly wind. ''We'll talk to the commander,'' he said, ''but you know the fires destroyed almost everything.''

''I understand.… It would help, though, to see the location. I want to know,'' she said very softly, ''where he was last alive.'' She had come this great distance for confusing and myriad reasons. She longed for hope that Stefan might have survived, but mostly she simply wished to stand in the spot where Stefan last stood and feel him around her; she wanted to breathe the air he last breathed and look out on the scene he saw before he died.

And the next day, after an evening with the commander and a warm bed and the comforts of a well-prepared meal, she and Nikki were taken to the location where Stefan and his bodyguard had stood back-to-back against the Turkish assault. The area had been restored to order, the charred remains removed and buried, the paved square hung with black crepe, a memorial of captured Turkish regimental banners erected in the center of the square. At its base were the farewell offerings of the soldiers Stefan had led to victory. In place of flowers, which were unobtainable in the autumn cold of Kars, his soldiers had left him personal mementos: pictures of their mothers and sweethearts, ribboned medals, small painted icons of patron saints, a favored good-luck charm, a warm jacket or boots, as if Stefan might have need of them, oat straw for Cleo, whom everyone recognized as his favorite charger, jeweled rings of great value. All were offerings from the hearts of the men who would have followed him through the fires of hell itself, and nearly had in the assault on Kars. And nothing had been touched although no guard was posted.

Lisaveta had carried no extraneous baggage with her, so when she wished to leave something for Stefan's memorial, she had nothing of value. Even her wedding ring she'd left behind against the threat of brigands. So her offering was as humble as that of his lowliest soldiers: Slipping off her fur jacket, she pulled Stefan's wool sweater over her head and placed it beneath the Turkish pennants.

"So you'll stay warm," she whispered, kneeling on the frozen ground, tears streaming down her cheeks. "I miss you...so much...." Her breath swirled in wisps on the icy air; her shoulders shook gently with her quiet grief. If only I could hold you and keep you warm, she thought tearfully.

Nikki dared not let her cry, for it was so cold her tears would freeze on her cheeks. Reaching down, he helped Lisaveta up, his gloved hands gentle on her arms. "He'll never be forgotten," he murmured in condolence, slipping her fur jacket back on her shoulders. "The whole nation loved him...." His voice was husky, his own feelings overcome by the poignant evidence of how much Stefan's men adored him.

His death was real, Lisaveta thought sadly, gazing at the benevolent festooned monument of affection. Stefan was truly dead...it was over. Letting Nikki lead her away from the regimental flags and mementos, she faced the stark and merciless truth: the man she loved—the man all Russia idolized and admired—was dead because his courage wasn't shield enough against disastrous odds, and his bravery, ultimately, had only allowed him to die a more gallant death. There was no point in staying any longer, she knew. Nikki was right. Politely declining the commandant's invitation for lunch, she said she wished to return as soon as possible to Tiflis. Stefan's aunt had been left alone and was worried for their safety.

They were back on the road north within the hour, the sun shining brightly as if it approved their decision and were offering the comfort of its warmth for their journey home. But inside Lisaveta felt only a cold emptiness, merciless as the terrain they traveled through. She had wanted so much for the rumors to be true, just as a child wishes for a cherished fantasy to be real, but the harsh reality of Kars had shattered that dream. Tomorrow, perhaps she could begin to think of her future; tomorrow, perhaps she wouldn't feel such wrenching despair. But today she felt drained and heartbroken and so bleak each breath seemed an enormous effort, every mile endless. And as though the universe at last took notice of her sadness, the sun began to dim, the sky turned milky gray and snow began to fall.

In a very short time the wind picked up. Familiar with the storms of that country, Nikki decided they should make for the caravansary at Meskoi. "We should hurry," he said across the small distance between their ponies, the flakes like a fragile veil before their eyes. "We'll wait this out at Meskoi. Are you able—"

"I'm fine," Lisaveta interjected, hiding the misery she was feeling. "Really…" she added in calming response to Nikki's frowning anxiety. "We can pick up the pace."

A moment later the small troop was cantering down the frost-hardened road, evidence of their passage wiped away behind them by the blowing wind and drifting snow, even the sound of tack and bit and bridle muffled by the squall.

A short distance down the road, some miles yet from the shelter they sought, Lisaveta suddenly reined in and said, "Look." She pointed at what looked like two distant figures, small dark shapes across the great expanse of open plain, lost to sight from second to second by the gusting snow.

Nikki had seen the shape or shapes or objects sometime before but hadn't mentioned them, for his primary concern was for Lisaveta. If the storm intensified—a common occurrence in this country—they might not reach the refuge of the caravansary; he couldn't take that chance. "We can't wait for them. We've too far yet to go and visibility is decreasing."

"But they might need help." Even as Lisaveta scanned the area where she'd last seen what might have been two figures, their presence was erased by the blowing snow.

"I'm sure they'll manage. The natives are experienced with

the climate." Every minute counted with the developing storm. Nikki had heard too many stories of lost travelers freezing to death in these blizzards.

"How long will it take to stop and pick them up?" Lisaveta inquired, reluctant to leave another human being out in this storm. "There!" She glimpsed them again, her eyes straining in the diminishing gray light. "It *is* two people, Nikki!" And she pulled her horse to a halt, obliging Nikki to follow suit.

Taking out his binoculars, he focused on the figures. Two native men in black burkahs and fur hats, one apparently helping the other to walk, were making for the military road. Their progress was achingly slow. "They're two native men. They know this terrain. They're dressed for winter. They'll be fine." His voice was dismissive.

"We should help."

Nikki looked at her, his black brows drawn together in a frown. How determined was she?

"The snow's so deep off the road." Lisaveta's statement was in the form of an entreaty, but her voice held an undertone of firmness. "Even if they know the country a storm like this can be dangerous."

Nikki surveyed her for a moment more, saw he wasn't going to win this discussion and sighed. "Are you warm enough? This will take fifteen minutes or so."

Lisaveta was wrapped in Stefan's black marten coat, a white fox hat Nikki had purchased in Kars covering her hair. "After days of being cold, another fifteen minutes can't hurt, and we can all rest in the comfort of the caravansary soon."

Nikki snapped the case shut on his binoculars and then smiled. "A pleasant thought…if we can find the place in this storm." He was doing this against his better judgment, but the time lost arguing with Lisaveta would probably be comparable to that needed to get these man back on the road. Signaling one of his men to follow, he turned his horse, and pulling his wolfskin hat down over his forehead, he plunged off the road.

Even the horses' progress was slow as they struggled through
the drifts, and Lisaveta watched Nikki and his partner labori-

ously close the distance between themselves and the burkah-wrapped figures on foot. Requesting the use of binoculars from one of Nikki's men, she raised them to her eyes and focused on the horsemen, then moving the glasses upward, she caught the native men in the small perimeters of the lenses.

The man helping his companion to walk was unusually tall, she thought, and felt her stomach tighten reflexively...an unconscious reaction she immediately suppressed. The Kurdish tribesmen were often tall, she reminded herself with quelling logic. But still she continued to peer through the binoculars, her heart rate noticeably heightened. The tall man's hands were—

No! She vehemently denied her sentence's conclusion. She wouldn't allow herself to become irrational. The certainty of disappointment would be brutal. Stefan had burned along with thousands of other bodies at Kars. The rumors were simply that—an indication of his soldiers' desperate wish he were still alive. Like hers.

Putting the glasses down, she folded her gloved hands over the leather-covered metal. Cautioning herself to prudent thought, she inhaled slowly to still her agitation and thought with a forced calmness how glad she was Nikki was going to the men's aid. The smaller one appeared seriously incapacitated, the larger man supporting his weight as they struggled through the snow.

No more than a minute passed before prudent caution was cast aside, the glasses were back at her eyes, and she was dreaming impossible dreams even while her rational sensibilities were chastising her insanity. She was hopelessly mad, absurd, unreasonable; she was a dizzy fool. Tears freeze on your face out here, she reminded herself, so be sensible enough not to knowingly seek misery.

But the binoculars were still at her eyes and the tall man's shoulders were a certain span and his dark face even in the shadow of his fur cap and burkah hood was aquiline. Like all the Kurdish natives, she coolly prompted her memory.

But then he brushed one hand over his face in a gesture of fatigue, or perhaps a simple wiping away of the flurry of windswept snow swirling around him, and Lisaveta caught a transient glimpse of luminous green and gold on one finger.

And she knew the Kurds didn't wear jewelry.

And Stefan had always worn a gold-and-emerald signet ring. Which hand, which hand? she wondered frantically, but the gesture was past, the jeweled glimmer disappearing into the burkah folds of his companion's robe. She almost cried then of frustration. She was expecting too much, wanting too much. She was totally irrational for want of Stefan. But irrational or not, she kept the glasses to her eyes, monitoring through a film of unshed tears the two men's progress. Each step was laborious and halting; with sheer physical power the taller man half lifted the smaller man so he could navigate through the deep snow.

Nikki and his trooper were moving toward the men at a pace far exceeding the walking men's advance, the horses plowing through the snow with all the power and strength mountain-bred ponies possessed. They had covered almost two-thirds of the distance to the native men when the tall man lifted his arm, pushed aside his hood and hat and waved his arm in a sweeping arc against the dove-gray sky.

"Stefan!" Lisaveta screamed, and dropped the binoculars. Hauling on her reins, she dug in her heels and whipped her pony off the road, lashing him into a struggling gallop.

Stefan hadn't seen her until then; he'd only just distinguished Nikki, but even faint and faraway and buffeted by the wind, he recognized Lisaveta's voice. Gently lowering the man he'd been helping through the snow, he broke into a stumbling run.

Nikki, too, had forced his mount into a gallop when he saw Stefan, and they reached each other after what seemed endless minutes. Stefan was breathing in great gasping pants but he managed a smile, said, "Get Haci—he has to be carried," and motioned them past with a wave of his arm. Stefan was so winded the last words were too faint to hear, but Nikki understood his message and with a wide smile of acknowledgment swept past him to aid his friend.

Stefan took two steps more and fell to his knees.

No, God, no, Lisaveta pleaded, and she bargained her soul

in the following seconds as she urged her pony to more speed. Don't let him die...I'll do anything. She offered up every sacrifice and overture and resolution for the future if the gods would only heed her cry.

And then Stefan slowly came to his feet.

"Thank you," she whispered, her throat thick with tears.

Stefan stood absolutely still and waited, his breathing ragged, drawing in great gulps of air to his gasping lungs, not capable at the moment of taking another step. His saber wound on his shoulder had opened again with the effort required to transport Haci through the snow, and he could feel the warm blood seeping through his shirt. But he was smiling. He was gaunt and bone-weary and bearded and weak but smiling, because a miracle had occurred and Lisaveta was here.

It took nearly five full minutes for Lisaveta to reach him— five motionless minutes, five windswept, snow-gusting minutes of thankfulness and joy.

She threw herself off her horse at the end as though she had wings, and crashed through the last short distance of drifted snow in great swooping leaps, despite the weight of Stefan's heavy fur coat.

Stefan's arms opened in welcome, his black burkah flaring out in dark winged folds, and she fell into his embrace, her hat toppling into the snow, her tears freezing on her cheeks, laughing and crying and wordless against the splendor of her feelings. They held each other in flushed and trembling silence for long moments, afraid to speak lest they break the spell and the fantasy disappear, wanting only to preserve the spell if it were an illusion.

They were sweetly warm, engulfed in a heated enchantment as if they alone with their utter joy could melt the snows of Kurdistan. But at last, Stefan tentatively touched Lisaveta's face, felt the corporeal reality of its silky texture, brushed his roughened fingertips across the soft curve of her mouth and dared to say, "You're real."

Her face was lifted to his, flushed and rosy-cheeked, snowflakes clinging to her lashes, her golden eyes as sunshine beautiful as he'd remembered, her smile more perfect than memory. "I was afraid, too." And her arms tightened around his waist.

Concealing his wince of pain he smiled back. "I'd dreamed so often the past weeks of precisely this, I thought I'd hallucinated."

"Kiss me, please," Lisaveta whispered, her simple plea underscored with fear and uncertainty. Could she be imagining all this in the desperation of her longing? If he kissed her, if she felt the coolness of his lips on hers, could she in safety know he was real?

"I'll kiss you for a lifetime," Stefan murmured, and touched her lips gently, a sweet aching tenderness filling his heart and soul. The snow blew past them and around them, sparkling crystals falling and melting on their faces, the darkening twilight of the storm surrounding them, and they were complete and whole.

"In all the world…" Lisaveta whispered, the reality of their kiss lingering breath-warm on each other's mouth.

"I was coming home," Stefan answered, his voice husky. He understood her cryptic phrase, knowing that while they both lived, they would have found each other through distance and time and adversity. "But, thank you," he murmured, a small smile creasing his wind-chapped cheek, "for shortening the journey."

"Nikki let me come," Lisaveta replied, her voice still tremulous with emotion.

"Let?" Stefan teased in familiar mocking irony.

And she thought how relentlessly strong he was and seemingly indomitable, holding her against the buffeting wind, chaffing her with his habitual impudence as though they weren't standing knee-deep in the desolate snow-swept landscape of Kurdistan, as if he hadn't been lost to the world for weeks, as though he weren't so debilitated he'd only raised himself from his knees moments ago.

"You're wounded," she exclaimed, guilt-ridden she'd only considered her own happiness.

"Not too badly," he casually replied, the blood from his saber cut running down his chest in a sluggish trickle.

"And I've been thinking only of myself," she apologized. "Let me do something, help you somehow...am I hurting you?" Her arms fell away in self-reproach.

Stefan grinned. "I'm fine, darling, more than fine now. I could recuperate from sheer joy alone. But Haci, though—" His tone abruptly changed, concern drawing his brows together, his voice deepening. "He needs a doctor. I love you," he went on in another mutation of resonance, "you know that, but—" His arms, too, released their hold and he half turned to gauge the progress in bringing Haci forward. Turning back, he softly said, "He's like a brother to me. He's the only one of my bodyguard to survive." His voice broke briefly as he finished. "He saved my life...and now...I must save his."

At the road Haci was transferred from Nikki's arms into Stefan's, and they slowly traveled the last few miles to the caravansary. On the way, Stefan related in a neutral voice how he and his bodyguard had stood together in those last desperate minutes before they'd been overrun and how one by one they'd fallen. He'd been the last standing and his final memory was the rushing charge of Turks coming in for the kill as he screamed his defiance, his sword raised high. He'd been struck from behind a moment later by a saber blow and blackness engulfed him.

"Haci tells me," Stefan quietly said to Nikki and Lisaveta, who flanked his mount as they rode side by side, "he regained consciousness, found I was still breathing and dragged me away into the cellar of a nearby house until the fighting passed us by. We'd been saved, he said, by two Turkish soldiers falling dead on top of us and protecting us from the next counterattack."

Nikki noticed Stefan didn't mention how important that concealment was. It had been a close thing apparently. The Turks routinely bayonetted all enemy wounded. They didn't take prisoners. Their inhumanity extended to their own troops, as well. They brought no ambulances to war, and the handful of surgeons and hospital staff were primarily volunteers from Europe.

"He found horses after the main assault had moved on and

carried me away from what appeared at the time to be a Russian defeat.'' Stefan's smile was gentle. ''Obviously, there was a reversal.''

''Thanks to your charge, the story goes,'' Nikki said.

''Thanks to my soldiers,'' Stefan replied softly.

''He didn't know the ultimate conclusion of the battle when we left, but there were Turks everywhere, Haci said, so he took me into the mountains. He found a shepherd's hut with enough goat cheese and dried millet stored against next season to sustain us. In nursing me back from the grave he endangered his own health. I think he has lung fever…and I didn't know when we started out yesterday whether we were walking into enemy territory or not, but he wouldn't live without medical care so I took the risk. Perhaps we could get to a village at least.… You were a miracle…an answered prayer.'' He looked suddenly defenseless and vulnerable, as he must have felt knowing Haci needed help or he'd die.

''Haci must live,'' he said, exposed and powerless against the angel of death, his voice no more than a whisper. ''I pledged him my word.''

They were traveling down one of the deep-slashed ravines, the red sandstone rising like lofty enclosing walls on either side, the wind silenced, the snow falling gently now in the motionless air.

''We'll be at Meskoi in less than an hour now, Stefan,'' Nikki gently said, ''and Haci will have help.''

Stefan wrapped his burkah more tightly around his friend, oblivious to his own pain and wounds. ''He was raised with me like a brother, we've fought together since we've been sixteen,'' he murmured, ''and I promised him.''

Reaching out, Lisaveta touched Stefan's arm, and when he turned to her, his dark eyes were wet with tears. ''Our sons will be friends,'' he softly whispered. ''I promised him.''

''They will be, Stepka,'' Lisaveta quietly replied, wishing she could bear some of his pain and ease his sorrow. ''We're almost there now. He won't die.''

Twenty-One

❧❦❧

"**Y**ou *are* their darling Prince," Lisaveta said on Christmas morning, her golden eyes warm with happiness as she lay beside Stefan. The heat from the porcelain stove was like summer air, the harmony of church bells mellifluous background to their own blissful pleasure.

The bells had been ringing in triumph for three full days, their resounding melody echoing sweet joy at Stefan's return. All of Tiflis had turned out to welcome him home.

The narrow streets of the old quarter had been decorated with garlands of jasmine and laurel, looped from one overhanging balcony to the next. Every house, rich or poor, had hung out its finest carpets in glowing display. The spacious boulevards had been lined with troops, saluting in the way of the mountain warriors with volleys shot into the air. And over all had sounded the bells, every church pealing its glad tidings that the White General, Prince Bariatinsky, their favorite son, was home. The chimes floated across the misty river, along the steep banks where the bridge built by Alexander the Great still stood, past the Tartar bazaars, where Persian jewelers weighted turquoises by the pound; they reached the dark booths of the Armenian armorers, where the fine gold and silver damascened weapons were fashioned. The bells swept past the fretted balconies, up the steep hills, through the eucalyptus groves to the palace on the heights and then to the mountains beyond.

Stefan lay sprawled at Lisaveta's side, both his arms thrown over his head in peaceful repose, his dark hair and eyes, his entire bronzed body, in stark contrast to the pristine whiteness of the linen sheets. "I know," he said in tranquil surety. "The Orbelianis are well liked." It was a modest statement, considering the ecstasy with which his return was being received. "And Papa was admired for his justice and courage."

Lisaveta marveled briefly at his calm acceptance of the adulation, done without humility or arrogance but rather with a serene grace, both regnant and oddly informal.

"They're devoted to you," she said, as they would be to a divine ruler, she thought.

His slender hand reached out to touch the gentle curve of her shoulder. "As I am to you."

His simple words warmed her. This man whom all of Russia adored and revered loved her. It was heady stuff. But she said softly in the next breath, "I want forever," because she was in her own way imperious. "Am I selfish?" Her question was touched with that dutiful courtesy one learns should supersede egoism.

Stefan smiled. She always was so much more polite than he. "Don't apologize, *dushka*. You must always in this world want only the best…" His fingers drifted up her slender throat and traced the perfection of her graceful jaw, sliding upward to end in a silken caress of her gamine brows. "And in all this world I found you," he tenderly said.

"And I you." He was very beautiful, but more than that, intelligent and kind.

He grinned. "Thanks to the Bazhis and," he added irreverently, "your reckless ignorance."

"It wasn't my fault they attacked so close to Alexsandropol," she protested, cheerful and unintimidated.

"Nothing perhaps was your fault except—"

"Except?" Her pale eyes were amused, although her voice was coolly sardonic.

"Except for your choices of intellectual pursuit. If not for your research on Hafiz, you would have been safely at home doing whatever women are supposed to do."

"Supposed to do?" Her sarcasm was a shade less sportive and her expression now demonstrably attentive.

He enjoyed the small sparks of fire in her eyes, reminded of their first night in Aleksandropol, when they'd amused themselves with various poems of Hafiz...when he'd first realized a woman could inflame his mind and soul as well as his senses. "Well, you know," he deliberately teased, "play the piano, embroider, drink tea and chatter."

"In about one minute, Prince Bariatinsky, you're going to be attacked." Lisaveta's voice was constrained and heated.

"How nice." His drawl was unconstrained and mellow.

"And you'll be forced to retract that damnable drivel."

"And you're going to make me?"

"Yes."

"How nice," he said again, his smile wide.

Her own grin suddenly matched his. "You don't mean it."

He shook his head. "Please don't ever embroider for me."

"I might be able to pick out a tune on the piano," she said playfully.

He groaned theatrically.

"So you don't mind, I gather," she went on in response to his groan, "I haven't any of the feminine repertoire."

"Darling, you're perfect."

"I am, aren't I?"

"And modest."

She grinned. "Like you." Suddenly she thought he might not have a son like him. Would he mind terribly? And how much would she mind if he minded if they had a daughter instead? "What if it's a girl?" she said.

"She'll be Princess Bariatinsky-Orbeliani," he softly replied, "and the church bells will ring for days."

"You wouldn't mind?" Her own voice was equally soft.

"She will be ours, *dushka*, or he will be ours, conceived in love and born in love and raised in love."

"Yes," she said, turning to slide her arms around his neck, wanting to always feel him close beside her. "In all the world..."

"...*our* child," he whispered.

Their kiss was fragrant with hope and happiness and that special delight that comes so rarely in life between two lovers who have found at last the mirror of their souls. And when her mouth lifted from his long moments later, she briefly hugged him tighter as she thought how very close she'd come to losing him.

"You're getting stronger," he teased.

"What if Nikki hadn't heard Haci's name?" she said, ignoring his levity, her thoughts touched with a nightmarish shiver. "He wouldn't have gone looking for you." Her brows were drawn together, her golden eyes pained.

"I would have found my way back anyway," he quietly said, smoothing her creased brows with a gentle finger. He spoke with a quiet clear certitude.

Yes, she thought, you would.

"Although I'm eternally grateful," he said with a grin, "you were difficult enough to invite yourself along, and…grateful as hell—" his smile widened "—you talked me into marrying you."

He rolled away just in time to avoid her swinging fist, and before she could follow to strike him a blow for his impudence, he'd pulled the drawer open on the bedside table and brought out two very small packages. "Peace offerings," he said quickly, sitting up and holding them out to arrest Lisaveta's attack.

She was on her knees beside him, her arm raised, and his smile touched the small golden flecks in his dark eyes. "Clever man," she murmured, her arms slowly lowering to her side. "I adore presents." She smiled. "This may just save your life."

He grinned. "I know."

"If they're sufficiently extravagant," she said facetiously, sitting down beside him.

"It," he corrected. "The other's for baby." And he handed her a small wooden box tied with a red silk ribbon.

Lisaveta slid the ribbon free and lifted the hinged lid on the sandlewood box. Inside, nestled in a bed of crushed green velvet, was a necklace of gold with two jeweled charms attached.

The charms were exquisite miniatures of desert towns, walled and minareted and architecturally detailed. Cloisonné and pounded gold alternated for brickwork on the walls, jewels were windows, the crenellated towers were tipped with precious platinum, the central gates opened on delicate crafted hinges. They were less than an inch in length and on the base of each a small plaque had been set. One read Bokhara—the other Samarkand.

Lisaveta's eyes filled with tears. Like the lover in Hafiz's poem, Stefan was giving her Bokhara and Samarkand.

"For the mole on thy cheek," he whispered, and when she lifted her head and smiled, he saw she was crying. "You don't like it," he teased, uncomfortable with tears.

She shook her head, unable to speak with the lump in her throat.

"You like it?" he said, uncertain of the exact meaning of her head shake.

She nodded.

"Good." He grinned in pleasure and relief. "Now if I kiss away all your tears and you give me a smile, I'll let you have baby's present, too." Bending over he took her hands in his, placed them on his shoulders and proceeded to gently kiss away her tears.

"I love you," Lisaveta murmured as his warm mouth moved over her cheeks, wishing it were possible to define the extent of her happiness, her mind stumbling over all the pleasure words, searching for one adequate to her feelings. "Is it like winning?" she asked obscurely, her voice hushed against Stefan's mouth as he nibbled at her lip.

"Mmm?" he said. She tasted like perfumed nectar or sugared sweets or both together, he thought, wondering if one lost one's mind when passionately in love. He'd never considered himself a fanciful man before.

"Is love like winning a battle for you?" she asked with more clarity, and sat up straighter so Stefan's mouth slid over her chin and into nothingness.

Leaning back on one elbow, he stretched out his lean body before answering. "It's better." His smile was the one his father had seen and his mother and few others—an open, contented, unblemished smile. "Is love like translating the perfect quatrain in Hafiz?" he asked then in analogous query.

"It's better," she said.

And they both smiled.

"You know what I'm feeling," Lisaveta declared.

Stefan nodded. "Exactly. I consider the sensations revolutionary and cataclysmic and also—"

"Balmy."

"How did you know?" He never used the word.

Nor did she. Lisaveta shrugged, then grinned and said, "Perhaps the shaman drums are beating."

"They have," he said with an answering grin, "done a damn good job of looking out for me. And for Haci. We both have futures again." Stefan's friend had recovered in the weeks since the journey to Kars and was back in his village, making plans for an April wedding. "And speaking of futures," he said, holding out the second present, "open this. I want to show you and baby something I hope you'll like."

When she opened the small box wrapped in pale yellow paper, she found a key inside—a door key.

"It's a surprise," Stefan said to her inquiring look. "Now, put this on and I'll show you." Handing her the cherry-red cashmere robe lying on the bed, he rose and, picking up his trousers from where he'd dropped them the previous night, slipped them on.

"I don't like surprises," Lisaveta protested as he pulled her from the bed.

"You'll like this one," he replied, drawing her with him across the room. "It's not for you anyway. It's a surprise for baby, but baby can't see it unless you cooperate." He grinned and put out his hand. "Give me the key."

When she handed it to him they walked the few remaining steps to the door opening into the adjoining room and he slid the key into the lock.

"We've been home only three days," Lisaveta said, bemused and curious, her voice tentative.

"I left instructions with Militza," Stefan said. Pushing the door open, he turned to watch Lisaveta's face.

She stood transfixed on the threshold. A nursery had been installed in the room next door, in the room she'd once occupied, and the previous space was completely transformed.

A lapis lazuli ceiling twinkling with diamond stars shone down on them.

The floor was carpeted in a field of yellow daisies.

The wallpaper was hand-painted with fairy tales.

And in an embrasure near a sunny window stood her cradle—the one that had always graced her old nursery at Rostov.

"My cradle," she exclaimed. The familiar swan shape was swathed in white gauze draperies suspended from a crowned canopy, exactly as she remembered.

"I thought you might like the next generation to sleep where you slept," Stefan said, his smile benevolent. "Come see your silver rattle." And tightening his grip on her hand, he tugged her along.

Her silver rattle, the one given as a gift, her mother had said, by Peter the Great and passed down in her family for more than a century, lay shining on the white silk coverlet.

"Even though you don't like surprises, do you approve of the decor? Feel free to change anything," Stefan quickly added, when Lisaveta didn't answer immediately.

"I like the stars," she said, turning to him with a smile.

"A personal whim. I'm glad you approve."

"And everything else, too," she added, slipping her arms around his waist. "You're incredibly sweet and kind and I love you so much my heart sings."

"We could perform a duet then, *dushka*," Stefan softly whispered, holding her lightly in his arms, "because my heart sings, too…and soon we can harmonize in trio," he added with a grin. Although his voice was buoyant, his words were underlaid with earnestness. "Tell me, Princess Bariatinsky, how you can't live without me."

"I can't," Lisaveta said simply.

"Nor can I without you."

It was a revelation to them both, independent as they were,

that they could so conspicuously and extravagantly savor that constraint.

But in love, of course, it wasn't constraint but fascinating attachment, nor was it binding need so much as affectionate harmony.

And ardent passion, as well.

And fond desire.

"I may not soldier for the Tsar so much," Stefan told her.

"I didn't dare ask."

"I need you more," he quietly said.

"The Bariatinskys have served their share," Lisaveta said, tracing the deep scar running from Stefan's shoulder down his chest. His worst laceration wasn't completely healed yet and his arms were crisscrossed with saber scars. The two bullet wounds in his side would be permanently discolored because they'd been infected so long before adequate treatment. "And the peace treaty will be signed soon. Maybe there won't be any more wars."

He opened his mouth to answer and then decided against his cynical reply. It seemed out of place in the sunny, toy-filled nursery. "I hope not," he said instead. "Haci tells me it's time for us both to sire children and race our ponies." His mouth quirked into a smile. "It's not a bad idea…if you don't mind."

"And if I do?" Lisaveta replied, mischief in her eyes.

His answering grin was wolfish, his dark eyes seductive. He had no intention of devoting himself exclusively to his ponies; the object of his devotion was in his arms.

"We can talk about it," Lisaveta coquettishly said.

"Yes, talk," Stefan agreed in a tone of voice suggestive of several things other than talk. "May I invite you into my bedroom for some preliminary discussion." He loosened her arms from around his waist.

"I might be interested," she replied, affecting demureness.

"Is there something that might further pique your interest, Madame Princess?"

"Yes, as a matter of fact, there is." Her golden eyes were amused.

"Is it something, perhaps, more accessible in a different

venue?'' His body exuded warmth as she stood beside him, his lazy intonation heated in another way.

"In your bed, you mean."

"How astute." His smile was gracious, as if he were familiar with offering paradise to young ladies. "But then your reputation as an intelligent woman is well-known."

"As is yours as a libertine...." There was a rich cordiality beneath her drollery.

"Perhaps we could merge our special..." He paused for a significant moment that seemed to raise the temperature noticeably. "...attributes in a mutually satisfying association," he finished.

"Kiss me and I'll decide," she said with a provocative lift of her shoulder.

He laughed. "You like to give orders," he murmured, one dark brow raised in speculation.

"You should recognize the inclination."

He did, of course, after a decade of command. "We could take turns," he proposed suggestively. "Giving orders, I mean...."

She smiled.

He smiled.

And on that sweet balmy Christmas Day in a shining white palace on the highest hill in Tiflis, they loved each other with exhilaration, joy and passion. Unlike the imperfect world outside their windows, they had found in each other's arms perfect unspoiled love, safe haven and bliss.

Epilogue

Their son, Zekki, was born that spring soon after the peace was signed. And when Stefan resigned his commission shortly after, to the Tsar in person, Alexander II understood.

"Life is too short," Stefan said. "I've tempted fate too long."

"As have we all," Alexander II replied. His words came prophetically to pass when an assassin's bomb claimed his life three years later.

By then Zekki had a sister to share the nursery with, and Stefan and Lisaveta thanked the shamans and benevolent gods for their own good fortune.

Stefan had taken active steps to insure that good fortune, though. Immediately after they'd come back to Tiflis from the Tsar's funeral, he'd begun construction to add more rooms to his mountain lodge.

Alexander III was going to be a reactionary emperor, Stefan said. "We may prefer the mountains more in the years to come," he declared.

Lisaveta understood. "For when the troubles come," she posed, in question and statement both.

"For that," he said.

And in the following years the White General, the Savior of Mirum, the Victor of Kokand and Kars, tended his vineyards and his polo ponies and his growing family.

He may have missed on occasion the inexplicable exhilaration of the charge or the intoxication of victory gained against enormous odds, but he'd seen his father die a useless death after numberless victories for the Empire and Tsar, and life had taught him in the end to hold dear the precious minutes of each day. And he intended now—with that particular strength of purpose that had taken him victorious across the battlefields of Russia—to defend not the borders of the Empire but the sanctity of his content.

* * * * *

Author's Afterword

❧⁓⁓

Two fascinating men inspired *Golden Paradise*. Born a generation apart, they were living legends in their own time, their deeds and accomplishments surpassing those of any fictionalized hero.

Prince Alex Bariatinsky was handsome, wealthy, the privileged scion of the only noble family directly related to the Romanovs, a childhood companion of the Tsarevitch and the object of his sister's, the Grand Duchess Olga's, girlish love. By eighteen he was an established figure among the *jeunesse dorée* of Saint Petersburg, notorious for his good looks and dissipation. Scandal piled upon scandal until the Emperor at last showed his displeasure, banishing him to the Caucasus in disgrace. Alex Bariatinsky soon won military glory, and battle by battle his name became synonymous with victory, culminating at last in Shamyl's final surrender. The subjugation of the Caucasus by Field Marshal Bariatinsky was complete.

Throughout this time, his amorous personal life was legendary, but at thirty-five the Prince's amours were brought to a standstill by the wife of one of his officers. It was a fatal passion leading eventually to his ruin.

Stefan's childhood and family background are based largely on the events surrounding Alex Bariatinsky's liaison with Princess Elizabeth Orbeliani. Damia was substituted as Elizabeth's name in my story to distinguish her more completely as a Georgian princess. And in contrast to the events in *Golden Paradise*, the child born to Alex's and Elizabeth's union was a daughter not a son.

Which brings us to the inspiration for Stefan.

Michael Skobeleff, the son and grandson of a general, himself won his general's epaulets at thirty.

As a youth at university his eccentricities were so expensive and his debts so enormous that his father refused to aid him anymore. He entered the Guards, but again his extravagances exceeded his father's good nature and he was obliged to leave the capital. He entered the Turkistan army, and the Asiatic frontier became for Skobeleff what the frontier of the Caucasus had been for Bariatinsky a generation earlier: a place to either find himself or lose himself.

His expedition to Khiva, however, where with only three Turkoman guides he reconnoitered three hundred and seventy-eight miles of hostile enemy territory in August heats of one hundred and forty-nine degrees, never knowing where they would find water, made him a sensation. Promotions were rapid for him. Asia was the perfect training ground for audacious young officers, and thanks largely to his superlative tactical and strategic abilities, the Khanates of Khiva and Kokand were annexed to the Russian Empire.

He was rewarded with the Governorship of Kokand.

Skobeleff actually did ride into battle on a white horse, dressed in his white dress uniform, covered in perfume and carrying his sword with the diamond hilt, in order, he said, that he might die with his best clothes on. Less facetiously, he wore white in battle so "my fellows can see where I am and know, therefore, whither to follow."

He was called Akh-Pasha by the Turks, meaning the White General, and Osman Pasha, the Turkish commander in the west, predicted that one day Skobeleff would be the Commander-in-Chief of the whole Russian army.

Michael Skobeleff died instead at thirty-seven in a Saint Petersburg brothel under mysterious circumstances.

He had begun to become politically active once the war was successfully concluded, speaking out in Russia and abroad in support of Pan-Slavism. He was perhaps too powerful and too

popular to be allowed such exposure and he'd acquired many
enemies on his rapid rise to fame, influential people who took
issue with his brash style and immense popularity.

I was devastated the first time I read of his death. He was a
man of profound courage and abilities: a poet; a linguist (he
spoke several languages including many Asiatic dialects and
an unaccented English); a scholar of the classics (Horace,
Schiller and Byron were his favorites); a kind commander to
his humblest soldier; a brilliant general who compared in stature to Alexander the Great and Napoleon. What a waste, I
thought.

With literary license I could offer a kinder fate to Stefan.
Michael Skobeleff's spirit lives in him.

New York Times Bestselling Author

REBECCA
BRANDEWYNE

DESTINY'S
DAUGHTER

Determined to track down her father's killers, Bryony St. Blaze
travels to England to find Hamish Neville, the one man who
knows about her father's research of a secret order known as the
Abbey of the Divine.

But after an attempt is made on Bryony's life, the two are
forced to go into hiding, dependent on one another for their
very survival. Piece by piece, they assemble the puzzle to locate
the lost book her father was murdered for. But time is running out.
Can they unlock the secrets of the hidden treasure before the
mysterious and deadly order catches up with them?

"I have been reading and enjoying Rebecca Brandewyne for
years. She is a wonderful writer."
—Jude Deveraux

On sale January 2001 wherever paperbacks are sold!

CARLA NEGGERS

Fun and a little hard work was all Tess Haviland had in mind when she purchased the run-down, nineteenth-century carriage house on Boston's North Shore. She never anticipated getting involved with the local residents, and never imagined what it would be like to own a house rumored to be haunted.

Then Tess discovers a skeleton in the dirt cellar—human remains that suddenly go missing. And she begins to ask questions about the history of her house…and the wealthy, charismatic man who planned to renovate it, until he disappeared a year before. Questions a desperate killer will do anything to silence before the truth exposes that someone got away with murder.

THE CARRIAGE HOUSE

International Bestselling Author

DIANA PALMER

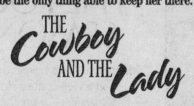

At eighteen, Amanda Carson left
west Texas, family scandal and a man
she was determined to forget. But the Whitehall
empire was vast, and when the powerful family wanted
something, they got it. Now they wanted Amanda—and her
advertising agency. Jace Whitehall, a man Amanda hated and
desired equally, was waiting to finish what began years ago.
Now they must confront searing truths about both their
families. And the very thing that drove Amanda from this
land might be the only thing able to keep her there.

THE Cowboy AND THE Lady

"Nobody tops Diana Palmer."
—Jayne Ann Krentz

Available February 2001 wherever paperbacks are sold!